PALMYRA

Steven Derfler

Library of Congress Control Number:		2018902460
ISBN:	Hardcover	978-1-9845-1126-3
	Softcover	978-1-9845-1125-6
	eBook	978-1-9845-1119-5

Print information available on the last page.

Rev. date: 03/01/2018

To order additional copies of this book, contact:
Xlibris
1-888-795-4274
www.Xlibris.com
Orders@Xlibris.com
773152

TURKEY
Al Qamishli
Al Hasakah
Izaz
Manbij
Aleppo
Idlib
Ar Raqqah
Madinat ath
Thawrah
Al Ladhiqiyah
Dayr az Zawr
MEDI-
TERRA-
NEAN
SEA
Hamah
Tartus
Hims
Abu Kamal
TADMOR / PALMYRA
LEBANON
Beirut
Ad Nabk
Douma
Damascus
IRAQ
Al Qunaytirah
SYRIA
ISRAEL
Dar'a
As Suwayda
JORDAN

CONTENTS

DEDICATION

The history of the human experience is merely "half a history". The world of archaeology puts "flesh onto the bones" of the ancient past, and allows the "what ifs" to often become realities. But all too often, the folly of human nature threatens to impair our efforts to understand our collective history. We should celebrate our humanity with vigor and excitement. Thank you to my friends and colleagues for their support and assistance in this great adventure. CS, ES and DC for editorial advice. Special thanks with love to my wife, daughter and (hopefully, when she's older) my granddaughter for sharing a love of this part of the world and experiencing it with me.

SD

I. To Arad

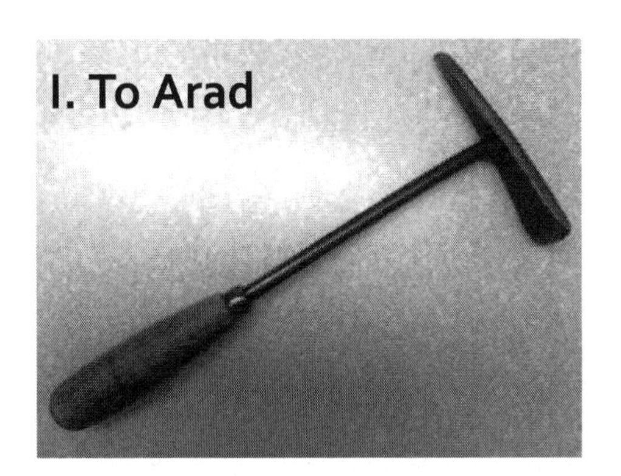

It had been a grueling, yet exhilarating couple of months. My recent trip to Cuba, and the discoveries and revelations regarding Cristoforo Colon's *presumed* final journey had left me more tired than I thought. I returned to Sarasota for a couple of meetings and lectures via Ringling College's Lifelong Learning Program. I had re-charged my teaching batteries after retiring from the university, in part due to 'college student burn'. This was the reverse type of psychological trauma- having to deal with late teen-early twenty-somethings who, in the 21st century, considered it a right to go to school, not a privilege. In other words, they went because it was expected of them by their parents; whether they wanted to be there or not.

These 'brats' were the main reason for retirement. My last semester, I had just about had it, when I was pushed over the edge by one extraordinarily 'entitled' individual. In my syllabi, in bold, italicized instructions, I made it perfectly clear that 'multi-tasking' wasn't all that it was cracked up to be. In my courses, the use of Powerpoint, in conjunction with lecture, meant that you needed to have all of your faculties running on all cylinders in order to stay abreast of the material. So, as a rule, cell phones and laptops were not to be on in class. That is, unless there was a rare occurrence when a cellphone on 'vibrate' was a necessity. Yes, I had a couple of those instances. One student was a paramedic and needed to be on call, for example. As long as I was notified in advance, I had no problem with the exceptions.

However, one kid would have none of that- feeling that he was entitled to use his smartphone, albeit surreptitiously, 'under the table'. In spite of having been warned a number of times, he still insisted on pushing the limit. So one day, as I was lecturing, and using the remote clicker to advance the screens, I slowly walked toward the would-be felon. Everyone else in class saw what was coming and looked on with great expectations. I got to his seat, and suddenly he looked up, shocked. I took his cell phone and removed the battery. I told him that he had two options: he could either take the battery after class and never turn the phone on in the room during lectures, or two, he could take the battery, leave and drop the course.

All the class assumed that he would take the battery after class, having been chastised. But no, he surprised us all and took the battery and stormed out. Later I would find out that he went directly to the Dean's Office and lodged a complaint that his civil rights had been infringed upon and demanded an apology. Well, thank God that the dean had backbone, and from what I was told, laughed in the student's face, told him to get out of his office and drop the class or face an F as a recorded grade. But that did it for me. I remember when I was in university, oh, in the last millennium. We were scared to death of faculty, especially the tenured kind. Their knowledge placed them next to the gods on Olympus; and they earned our respect.

So, the last day of class that semester, I sort of emotionally told my students that it was an honor to work with them, and that they left me with good memories. But I was stepping down to do other things. Those other things, then, involving teaching 'non-traditionally-aged' students who actually wanted to be in the classroom. My father told me, 'when you stop learning, you're dead!' And now, with seniors living longer, more active lives, their inquiring minds want to know... and I love working with them.

After a month's worth of seminars, it was time to return to Israel for a short stay to touch base with friends and colleagues. I planned to head directly to the desert city of Arad.

*****

Arad was my home away from home, and, more often than not, I spent more time there during my tenure as excavator during the four month season in summer. As a result, some of my closest friends live in Arad. In fact, when one of them built a house for his family, there was a room that was added just for my use. So it was no surprise that I would head to the Eastern *Negev* when *my* batteries needed recharging.

I had Skyped with my friends and the director of Masada National Park, Eitan, was lounging against the bumper of his National Parks Authority Jeep, waiting as I exited from the *Ben Gurion* arrivals terminal. I went over, dropped my bag, and embraced the man who I had known for nearly 40 years. He just grinned and slid behind the wheel. I sucked in a deep breath of *Shephelah* air (they should really bottle this stuff) and sat back to enjoy the 90 minute ride south and east.

While we cruised through southern Israel on the relatively new Highway 6, I marveled at the changes in Israel I had seen over the past 45 years. It used to take well over two hours to get from *Ben Gurion* to *Arad*. Today, with the progress of the tollway, Highway 6, you can cruise without interruption all the way to *Kiryat Gat* before taking the *Beersheva/Arad* Road, which itself has been widened to four lanes. For the first part of the journey, we kibbitzed about nothing and everything in general.

As we approached the end of *Kvish Shesh*, the tollway, Eitan asked if we could make a quick stop. I thought, *why not, there's no rush.* So just as we exited, he continued south toward Beersheva. At the *Omer* Junction, he turned east.

"We're headed toward *Tel Sheva*!" I exclaimed. He looked over and grinned that infectious smile of his; the one that still turned the heads of women of all ages.

"*Betach!* Of course! You really have to see the changes over the past year or so. But don't worry, we still don't have to pay to get in!" He knew that was still a touchy situation for me. After all, the last time that I took a group to *Tel Sheva*, I had to pay the entry fee along with everyone else. Our friend, Benaim, had retired from the *Reshut Atiqot*, the Antiquities Authority, and there was a young, wet-behind-the-ears employee who looked like he had just gotten out of the Israel Defense Force (IDF) and active military duty. And, of course, he didn't know me. But Eitan was a *Baal haBayit,* a big-shot legend in the agency. So there was still a bit of *proteksia* there. However it still irked me that I would be treated as a 'commoner' even though I had spent seven seasons of excavation at the tel and was a published member of the staff. Sometimes egos can be a pain.

Once on the Tel, my 'tour guide' instincts kicked in and I walked Eitan around. He invited the junior Israel Parks and Nature (INPA) employee, telling him that whatever he learned about the site paled in comparison to what he would learn with me. I sort of shrugged off the compliment, but the young man was wide-eyed with anticipation. So we ascended the mound and paused just outside the Solomonic Gate. My juices were really flowing now, as I was flooded with thousands of memories that took me back to the formative days of my career.

Under the tutelage of Yohanon Aharoni, perhaps the greatest Israeli archaeologist of his generation, I learned the ropes, how to make all the mistakes, and then correct them. I learned of history and geography, bible and ethnography, archaeology and human nature. This kind, gentle and brilliant man was taken from us too early, in 1975. By then, elevated to senior member of the staff, I was one of those who paid tribute to his memory by being a part of the last season at *Tel Sheva*, a season without his scholarly leadership.

Here, just outside the gate, at the end of that final season in 1976, a tamarisk tree was planted in his memory adjacent to the ancient well that stood as a welcoming presence to all visiting the city. Designed to mirror Abraham's imperative that you offered strangers hospitality in the midst of a harsh desert environment, the well served to quench the thirst of all who sojourned here- without jeopardizing the safety of the city's inhabitants. As I memorialized him, I couldn't help but allow my emotions to get the best of me. Eitan remembered Aharoni as well, but ushered the younger INPA employee a few steps away to let me have a moment of solitary reflection.

I said a silent prayer, wiped my eyes and turned back to the other two, ready to kick into 'guide mode' as we walked past the restored watering hole and through the outer gate of the 2900 year old fortress city.

Eitan was leaning up against the outer gate wall, and I noticed that he was at the same spot that he had leaned against 40 years earlier; a wall that he and I had reconstructed. I mentioned it to him.

"Do you remember..." was all that I got out.

"Of course, *habibi*, this is the spot of the infamous Frenchman, or should I say '*idiote*,' Michel." I was laughing hard now. The young *Reshut* employee hadn't a clue. Eitan went on to explain to the fellow. "It was 1976, after the excavations were over. The municipality of Beersheva, along with the Department of Antiquities and Museums, wanted to showcase the site. Nobody knew at the time, but the government was in the process of applying to The United Nations Educational, Scientific and Cultural Organization (UNESCO), World Heritage Committee, which was in the initial planning stages, to get several archaeological sites in Israel designated as World Heritage sites. Finally, in 1979, the organization took flight. However, it wouldn't be until 2004 that the Israelite *Tels* of *Beersheva*, *Megiddo* and *Hazor* would be nominated and accepted. But in the meantime, the government wanted this site to join the others as part of the Israel Nature and Parks Authority 'Green Card'; designed to give unlimited access to sites under their auspices for a 14-day period."

I turned to the INPA fellow. "However, you probably know them as 'orange cards' for the last decade or so." I laughed. "It must have been a color-blind printer!" He looked clueless.

Eitan continued his tale. "*B'seder*, okay, you and I were contracted with the task of overseeing several volunteers to rebuild the city gate. I remember that the dozen or so were from all over the place- kids who saw the notice at Tel Aviv U. and decided to spend a couple of weeks with us, given room and board for their labor. What a *balagan*, a mess, to teach them the rudiments of architecture and restoration!"

"You had absolutely no patience with them, I remember." I thought back fondly to those days. "You had such an incredible background to begin with. Your father, Jackson, my surrogate Israeli father, was a restorer back in Chad's Ford, PA, before moving you all to Israel, and *Arad*. It was under his tutelage that both of us learned the ropes. It was Jack who was responsible for the *Tel Arad* restoration project, and oversaw us at *Tel Beersheva*. He also was in charge of all the other *Negev* sites like *Masos* and *Malhata*. Give credit where credit is due!" I laughed.

He too laughed about that as he returned to the story. "Anyway, one of the foreigners who joined us was this young Frenchman, Michel. He boasted to us that he was an architecture student at an institute in southern France, *Remulac*. So he said that he was familiar with building techniques. We considered for a moment, thought that it was a plus, and put him in charge of a segment of wall to be rebuilt- giving him three others to assist. I recall that you and I tackled a difficult placement of a couple of large cornerstones, over 300 pounds each, which took us an hour or so. When we were done, we went around the corner to where Michel was. The look on your face when we got to his wall was priceless! A segment of foundation was missing, so Michel grabbed a couple of pick handles and placed them over the gap- spanning the hole. He then proceeded to build a wall *over* the area, creating a *floating wall!* You were ready to go ballistic! I had to restrain you from tearing the Frenchman a new..."

"OK, OK, OK, I remember!" I was laughing hard, joined now by the other two.

"So, *ma koray?* What happened then?" the young man asked.

"As I remember, with one good kick, Eitan knocked the suspended wall over, and was aiming a second kick in the direction of the French fool. He got the message quickly and said that he would be leaving later that afternoon" was my reply.

We all laughed and headed into the gate complex.

The main strata of *Tel Sheva* dated to the United and Divided Monarchies of Ancient Israel; from the 11th- late 8th Centuries BCE. Under Solomon, the city took shape as a royal administrative center, aimed at protecting the country from Egypt to the southwest. It was an oval, roughly 140 x 110 m. in size. A well planned fortress complex, it was protected by an outer and inner stone and brick gate. A circular 'ring road' ran around the city, with interior roads like radii emanating from the center, the acropolis. Three guard rooms flanked the gateway itself. And here the young INPA employee got his first biblical lesson.

"You know, the gate guardroom area was the most important place in the city, because the elders would sit in the city gates and pass judgment. It's mentioned many times in the *Tanaach*; Deuteronomy, Samuel and Joshua to name a few locations."

"But wouldn't they get run over by the chariots?" was the inevitable question.

Ah, the naiveté of youth, I thought. "Precisely! They wouldn't sit *in* the city gates, but in the guardrooms." I smiled, and was rewarded by the young man's smile in return.

We walked through the inner gate, flanked by the guardrooms, and paused for a moment in a small plaza. "This court wasn't here 2800 years ago. It is the location of the last pair of guardrooms.

Solomon remodeled the gate complex, what we called stratum IV, adding a pair to the four created by his father, David. However, much later, during the Persian Period of the late 5th-4th Centuries BCE, an enormous garbage pit was dug here, thus destroying the last two guardrooms. When we excavated it in '71, we moved tons of ashy debris, finally reaching the bottom at about 15 m., around 46 feet. When we finished, it created a real hazard for the excavation and eventual tourist site. The sides were unstable and could collapse. So Yohanon Aharoni called in the IDF. After recording and documenting the area in great detail, the army brought a couple of demolition experts who rigged the area with small explosives in order to collapse the pit. But just before detonation, a couple of pranksters carefully positioned an old pair of tennis shoes, a couple of plastic buckets, a torn t-shirt, a bag of *Bisli*, the most popular Israeli crunch snack for kids of all ages, and a hand-lettered sign that mentioned 'the unknown digger' at the bottom. When the area was cleared, the charges were set off and these tokens were buried for posterity. Should the area ever be dug again, the excavators would be in for a real surprise."

Eitan and I smiled at each other. We knew...

We continued past the restored and reconstructed storehouses adjacent to the city gate to the north. It was here that the nearly century-old debate about Solomon's 'stables' and storehouses would finally be put to rest by Aharoni and his team. Ever since R.A.S. Macalister's excavation of a series of three-unit buildings at *Tel Gezer* in the 1910s, followed by P.L.O. Guy and the University of Pennsylvania at *Tel Megiddo* in the 1920s, and *Tel Hazor* by Yigal Yadin and Hebrew University in the 1950s, archaeologists followed the biblical 'lead' that identified Solomonic 'stables' at these sites as described in 1Kings 9.

'...cities for his chariots, and cities for his horsemen, and that which Solomon desired to build in Jerusalem, and in Lebanon, and in all the land of his dominion.'

However, they would make the cardinal sin of picking and choosing portions of the text to prove or disprove via archaeological evidence. The passage also included,

'And all the cities of store that Solomon had...'

A great mythology arose, and the excavators of *Gezer* and *Megiddo* most notably, would go to great lengths to prove their point- even to the extent of building physical models of chariot and stable complexes complete with projected numbers. For example, at one complex at *Megiddo*, they said that there were 150 chariots and 450 horses, stabled in five buildings. Yadin continued this myth, and once again religiously inclined folks applauded the veracity of the biblical narrative. I was a firsthand eye-witness to the *Tel Sheva* excavations that would debunk this notion. I picked up the narrative.

"Back in 1971, my first season here at *Tel Sheva*, the excavations had begun in earnest in the area here, next to the city gate. Aharoni felt that, being strategically placed, important public buildings could be found here. He was right. Three-unit pillared structures were cleared, abutting the city wall to the west. However, based on the evidence, they were not seen as the 'stables' that everyone thought they were based on *Megiddo*, *Hazor* and *Gezer*.

The overwhelming view; that nearly everyone has come to believe today, is that they are buildings that identify with other structures in the same passage- storehouses."

The young National Parks employee was really intrigued with this. He had been taught, in a rudimentary training, that they were storehouses, but not the in-depth rationale. He begged me to go on.

"I recalled one day in 1973, a couple of years later, when Yadin came to visit our dig and was escorted around by his dear friend, but staunch rival, Aharoni. At the time, Aharoni actually had me explain our interpretation to the great scholar from the Hebrew University. I described our meticulous excavation process, flattering him as I explained that we used the methodology that he and Aharoni developed when they were both in Jerusalem. I glanced at Aharoni and he just smiled. But it was at that point that I had to tread lightly. I patiently outlined all of Yadin's arguments that he made in an article in a magazine called Western Quarterly, for horse lovers. And then I respectfully demolished each and every point made, based on Aharoni's work. This included debunking the notion of Solomon's use of 'pygmy horses' to explain the narrow dimensions of the chambers."

The young man was in awe. "For you to stand up to Yadin! *Chutzpah*, to say the least."

I continued. "Aharoni was smiling all the while, pleased at whatever barb could be launched from 'his side' of the friendly disputation. After all, for decades, whatever Yadin said *must* be God's truth in the world of archaeology."

Eitan broke in, "The story was that, even if the sun was shining, Yadin could spin a tale and make you believe that it was night. He had that kind of charisma, coming out of his landmark *Masada* excavations of 1962-65."

"*Beh ha-yai*, you should know," the younger man interjected. "After all, you are the director of the most famous site in all Israel, if not the world." Eitan smiled at that.

"So, after I explained all this to Yadin, and saw him deep in thought, I knew that my career was over! I glanced over at Aharoni for support, and he merely smiled back at me again. Finally, Yadin said to me, '*Habibi*, my friend, you know that I shtick to my peeshtols.' Now *I* was really confused, until it dawned on me. In Hebrew, 'pistols' and 'guns' are actually the same. So, I apologetically said, 'you mean, 'stick to your guns'.' The friendly response to me was, 'Peeshtols, guns, *lo kidai*, it doesn't make a difference. We can agree to disagree! So you want to come work with me?' He winked. I breathed a sigh of relief that my career was still intact, and Aharoni started to laugh. We all did and proceeded on the Tel tour. And I suggest that we do the same."

After taking a drink from one of the cisterns scattered around the site by the *Reshut* when it took control of the antiquities, we walked over to the recently discovered and opened water system that 'pushed' *Tel Sheva* over the threshold of becoming a World Heritage Site.

Eitan outlined this outstanding discovery, as he happened to be at the site when it was inadvertently discovered a few years back.

"We were on one of the weekly *tiyulim*, tours, sponsored by the *Reshut Atiquot*. As you know, they still like to keep all of us in the loop with new discoveries around the country. Because every day things change in the archaeology world of Israel. That particular trip was designated a Western Negev visit, so we hit sites around *Tel Sheva* as well. During this trip, when we got to the *Tel*, everyone was buzzing with excitement. Just that morning something incredible had occurred. While a bulldozer was clearing a path at the base of the mound between the former excavation camp and the hill, a line of stone was unearthed."

"That's always the way, isn't it?" the young employee laughed. "I always heard that good stuff was found either, one, on the last day of the excavations, or two, by accident!"

We all laughed at this, agreeing, and Eitan continued the tale. "It seemed that the line of stone was actually a row of cover stones that sealed a water channel running west to the *Nahal Beersheva*, one of two riverbeds that protected the site. Once exposed, the salvage archaeology crew discovered that it led to a massive underground, rock-cut series of cisterns that supplied the city from within."

I jumped in at this point. "Back in '71, my first season here, Aharoni's team had discovered the entry to a water supply system on top of the *Tel*. He cleared a major portion of a rather square vertical shaft, with a stone staircase descending around the perimeter.

However, back then, both time and money came into play. Aharoni ascertained that it was identical to the Israelite water systems of *Megiddo*, *Hazor* and *Gezer*, all cleared decades ago. Although he was dying to clear this one as well, his senior staff prevailed and it was left undone. Suddenly, by accident, two decades later, the system would be totally cleared and the results boggled the minds of all."

The work on the water system took several years to explore and stabilize before opening it up to the public. I was fortunate enough to visit the site while this was all in progress. It was mind-boggling, to say the least. When entering the network of passages over a dozen meters below the surface, paths illuminated by flashlights only; the scope of the undertaking 29 centuries earlier was staggering. This vast complex outdid the other Israelite water systems even though they were monuments to human engineering themselves. Tens of thousands of gallons of water could be contained in this labyrinth. They even designed overflow channels and shunts that forced water into other chambers when one became full.

Today, the site is open to all, provided that the visitors wear hardhats. Being that far underground, in spite of all the precautions of the INPA, it was better to be safe than sorry in the event of any stone becoming dislodged. The spiral stone staircase has been strengthened and given handrails. The interior floor has been smoothed and subtle lighting guides the visitors through the passages. It is still an awe-inspiring journey into the past.

We wound our way through the subterranean passages and made our way back to the surface. As we emerged, the first thing that caught our eye was the 'spaceship tower' on the acropolis of the mound.

The face that I made apparently was noticed by the *Reshut* employee. He asked why I seemed to be upset.

"*Habibi*, you've got to be kidding! How could someone *not* be upset! Just look at that monstrosity. It looks like 'Star Wars' met *Tel Sheva*."

"But it's important to have an observation tower to see the panorama of the region and the entire site" was his reply.

"Ah, the naiveté of 'youts' in the world is evident once again." (Okay, so the dialog from the movie *My Cousin Vinny* kicked in here, as Eitan punched me on the shoulder. But he knew...)

"I get it, the view is spectacular, and important. However, wouldn't it have been more appropriate to use a stone-clad tower rather than this circular steel behemoth that is alien to the nature of the site? And it can be seen from the *Beersheva-Omer* Road a few hundred meters away. No, the concept should not trump the esthetic when the two can be married together properly." The young man saw the light, and slowly shook his head in agreement.

We descended the mound then, and rested a bit in the shade by the ticket booth before leaving. A couple of cold Kinley sodas later, we got back in the Jeep and resumed our trip to *Arad.*

*****

As we ascended to the Eastern *Negev* plateau, my journey finally caught up with me and I dozed off. But within 20 minutes, we were racing toward the *Tel Arad* interchange that was just a couple of km from the city limits. The approach to *Arad* was always a delightful experience- a surprise to those who had never been this way before, and a matter of constant amazement at Israeli ingenuity to those who had shared the entry many times. As you drive through a desert wasteland, dotted with Bedouin encampments, you feel as if you have reached the end of civilization. Then suddenly, you pass *Kuseifa*, a Bedouin village, and Highway 80 Junction. From there, rising from the shimmering mirage of desert sandscapes, the outskirts of the development town of *Arad* miraculously come into view. Appearing out of nowhere, the miracle promised by Ben Gurion decades earlier- of making the desert bloom- has come to fruition. The genius of Israeli society is nowhere more evident than here. The approach to the city contains monumental sculptures by both Israeli artists and *Arad* artists.

In November 1960, the *Knesset*, Israel's parliament, examined the possibility of settlement in the northeastern *Negev* desert and the *Arad* area. In January 1961, the final location of the new city was decided 3.5 km southwest of Mount *Kidod*, as well as details about road and water connections. It was to hold 20,000 Israeli pioneers. The foundations of modern *Arad* were laid when the oil company *Nefta* built a work camp in the area in July 1961, consisting of six temporary sheds, after oil was found there in commercial quantities. The town itself, however, was officially founded in 1962 by a group of young Israelis, most of them ex-*kibbutz* and ex-*moshav* members, who were seeking an environment free of the urban ills of overcrowding, traffic, noise, and pollution.

The founding ceremony was held on 21 November, and attended by MK Minister of Trade and Industry Pinchas Sapir.

Until 1964, *Arad* had about 160 families, most of whom were natives. After 1971 *Arad* began absorbing *olim* (Jewish immigrants), mostly from the Soviet Union, but also from English speaking countries and Latin America, and its population increased from 4,000 in 1969 to 10,500 in 1974. Eitan's family was one of the original settlers here, coming from the States with a commitment to helping Israel survive and thrive.

Today *Arad* is located 23 km. west of the southern end of the Dead Sea, and is 45 kms east of *Beersheva*, 111 kms south of Jerusalem, 138 kms southeast of *Tel Aviv*, and 219 kms north of Eilat. The city encompasses 95 sq km.; one of the largest municipal areas in Israel, though it's urban area is smaller. The city's jurisdiction was 44 sq km. The population is a bit more than 24,000 (there are still no traffic lights!)

The themed neighborhoods make up the entire city north of Hwy 31. South of the highway is *Arad's* industrial zone. Major industry includes *Tnuva,* one of Israel's major dairy industry companies, and Motorola. In addition, the Dead Sea Works, *Makteshim*, and *Masada* National Park, are also major employers.

Each neighborhood in Arad contains streets named in a thematic manner; for example, a neighborhood where all streets are named after jewels. The exception to this are the four central quarters which have more conventional street names; and the original two neighborhoods (*Rishonim* = Firsts, and *Ne'urim* = Youth).

The soul of the development city concept was the communal city center, The *Mercaz*.

The life of the town was found here- every *Shabbat* eve everyone would gather for conversation, folk dancing and to enjoy the climate. All of your needs would be met there, as it was the center of economic life for the city as well. Initially, the first neighborhood apartments would be built on the first "ring" of the residential city. However, modern reality soon set in. In 1995 the open-air *Mercaz* would find adjacent to it a competitor, an indoor mall... with airconditioning! The city center area would never be quite the same!

But the central core would remain the cultural center of *Arad*. The *Matnas*, Community Center, completed in 1983, and the *Arad* Visitor Center, would draw people from all over. In 1995, a new hotel, The *Inbar*, would be built on the edge of the *Mercaz*- giving *Arad* its first major hotel in the town center.

During the first half of the 1990s, *Arad* absorbed 6,000 immigrants from the former Soviet Union. The late Prime Minister, Yitzhak Rabin, declared *Arad* a city on 29 June 1995. The city would expand both to the northeast and west. Found in the second tier of neighborhoods is the *Arad* Youth Hostel, major children's garden, and the Orthodox Synagogue. Arad has 22 synagogues; of which 11 are Ashkenazi, 9 are Sephardi, one is Yemenite, and one is Ethiopian. Until fall 2008, the World Union of Jewish Students (WUJS), funded by the Jewish community in the US, had an institute in *Arad* which allowed post-college young Jews from around the world to study Israeli society and the Hebrew language. When WUJS's ownership changed, the institute was moved to Jerusalem. The original building was built in a neighborhood known locally as "The Patios". But they outgrew their 'digs' and built a newer home in 2004 farther to the north near the high school.

Arad has two main tourist attractions—its clean air, which brings asthmatics from all over the world to the city, and its proximity to the Dead Sea, which allows tourists to pay much less for accommodation as well as having municipal services nearby, and still be able to easily reach the sea.

There is a large white monumental sculpture conceived by Yigal Tumarkin in 1968, called *Mitzpe Mo'av* (Mo'av Lookout). It overlooks the view to the Dead Sea. *Arad* has long been considered by many to be a center of cultural and literary arts, evidenced by it many artists in residence- such as Amos Oz, Eddie and Miri Shruster. An Artists Quarter, *Kiryat Omanim*, houses workshops other artists from all over the world.

In 1982, *Arad* made a bold move. It inaugurated a national festival. While music is front and center at the festival, the Municipality has always been keen to use the event as a way of promoting the cultural, hiking and other attractions available in the town and its desert environs with a whole host of activities on offer to visitors over the three days. I remembered those days fondly, when the band would play to sold-out crowds in the football stadium.

*****

We exited and made the turn into town, as the road continued its way down to the Dead Sea Valley. Eitan parked the Jeep in the lot adjacent to the *Mercaz*, and suggested that we stop and get a bite to eat before going to the house. Of course, the only place for us was Don Pedro Pizza. Several years ago, the owner, an Argentinian named David, was taken with the music that the band, Gypsy of Arad, had put together. With Eitan, his brother Ilan, and a couple of other *Aradnikim*, natives from *Arad*, making up a band with a unique blend of rock 'n roll, Sephardic melody, and Hebrew lyrics emerged to form a sound that eventually nearly all of Israel would come to know. David was one of the first to offer a venue, then backing, in this endeavor. As a result, Don Pedro Pizza became an informal 'office' for the band. Others would stop by, and inevitably, food and drink consumed. So, David got a return on his investment in many ways. Business was good. But the years that passed had not been terribly kind to him physically, and he passed away a couple of years earlier. His family kept the restaurant going, and the tradition of Gypsy as well with photos adorning the walls.

David's daughter was delighted to see us as we took seats outside. She stopped by to say hello, and told us of the difficulties endured ever since both the passing of her father and the opening of the mall just a few dozen meters away. The older citizens of *Arad* still patronized the *Mercaz* and all of the establishments there, but the younger generation was hooked on the indoor amenities that the mall had to offer. We commiserated with her a bit, and offered whatever support we could. The one bright spot was that the music of Gypsy still resonated, even with the younger residents of the city. Any concerts given could, with the proper endorsements from the stage, keep the clientele coming to the restaurant.

As we were finishing the meal, I received a text on my cell phone. It was Kati Ben Ya'ir, associate director for the Department of Antiquities and Museums, in Jerusalem. "Call me when you get settled. There's a *balagan* brewing." This message was both cryptic, and entirely out of her comfort zone as far as texting went. So many of us of the 'older' generation preferred real conversation rather than the illiteracies of abbreviated text messages. *Balagan* meant 'mess' in Hebrew- so something was definitely up. As she was a dear friend of both of us, I told Eitanand he stepped on the gas so that we could both speak to her from the comfort, and privacy, of his house on *Hohit* Street.

Within minutes, (remember, *Arad* is still small) we were seated on the sofa in his salon, and I was dialing the number in Jerusalem.

"*Ahlen ya habibti! Ma nishma?* How are you? You're on speaker phone with Eitan as well." After all, it had been a while since I had seen her. All of her assistance regarding the research about Christopher Columbus' final journey had been by Skype, email and telephone. Yet it was essential in helping to offer a plausible solution for where the explorer was put to rest. The mystery and intrigue seemed to finally be laid to rest, so to speak, in Santa Clara, on the island of Cuba.

I smiled as the warm lilt of her voice crossed the telephone line. It was good to hear her.

"So, Bedouin man, now that you've laid Colon to rest, you've decided to grace us with your appearance?" I heard the gaiety in her tone.

"At least I don't have a broken hand and can't call, or write, like other people that we both know!" I grinned at Eitan, seated next to me. His sheepish look said it all. Although we had known each other for nearly 40 years, direct communication when we were continents apart was few and far between. However, it did nothing to weaken our bond of brotherhood- it was just the way it was. And whenever we were together, it was as if no time had passed by at all. That was the true test of real friendship. You didn't have to 'work' at it, it was always there. The sheepish look passed, and he punched me in the bicep.

"Don't worry, I'll get even with you some day. Maybe not today, maybe not tomorrow, but soon...," I whispered in a theatrical-style aside.

"I heard that," Kati said over the phone. "Don't start quoting from *Casablanca* to us..." She laughed.

Real friendship is hard to beat.

She turned serious after the initial banter. "I'm glad that both of you are on the line. I got a call from a colleague in New York, at the UNESCO office. I don't know if you heard, but the horrific situation in Syria just got more, well, 'horrificker'! Is that even a word? I don't know."

"It is now," Eitan responded. "So, *ma koray*? What's up that's even worse than now?"

"A colleague who I've met a couple of times in international conferences has been murdered by the Islamic State in Syria (ISIS) in Palmyra. I met him at a World Heritage Sites Conference a few years ago, and even though he was Syrian, was delighted at the opportunity to work on a committee with me. He was like a father to me- Khaled Asaad."

"I know of him... He's been called the 'Ehud Netzer' of Syria" Eitan broke in. "Netzer's entire life was dedicated to exploring the world of King Herod the Great, and he spent decades at *Herodium*; finally discovering his tomb in 2007. He tragically died on the site three years later, doing what he loved. We should all go that way."

"Asaad spent nearly his entire career at *Palmyra*, didn't he? Close to 50 years? So what happened?" I asked.

"Because he was curator of the Greco-Roman site, deemed to be pagan, and 'out-of-the-realm' of Islam, according to ISIS representatives, he was arrested and 'charged' with 'blasphemous behavior.' He was subsequently beheaded and his corpse hung from one of the columns near the central plaza of the antiquities site- as a warning." Kati was really subdued now. "An 82 year old man! How could he pose a threat to these murderers?" I heard a hitch in her voice, yet she didn't lose control.

"So how do we fit into this picture?" asked Eitan.

"UNESCO is sending someone over here, clandestinely of course, to brainstorm with us regarding the wanton destruction of antiquities in Syria. In addition, hundreds of artifacts that have been stolen from museums or illegally removed from archaeological sites are working their way onto the black market. ISIS is selling them not-so-secretly to unscrupulous individuals, in order to fund their terror and murder. The buyers don't care who knows, or that they can never display their purchases. They simply want the luxury of owning them. We want to find a way to get some of these items back, one way or another- to send a message to both ISIS and illegal buyers that this won't benefit them. It may be a drop in the bucket, but it's a start." Her passion for the subject now could clearly be heard- she was really fired up.

"So we just wait for them to arrive, and they'll outline a plan of attack. But I assume that *Palmyra* will be the focus?" She indicated that it was most likely the starting point. Eitan was really into it now. I assumed that it brought back memories of the *Golani* activity when he was active in the IDF.

*****

Two days later, after some refreshing RnR in the desert city, we got the phone call from Jerusalem that we were expecting. Kati's UNESCO connection had arrived that afternoon and was just settling into his room at the Dan Panorama, on *Keren HaYesod* Street, across the street from the Bloomfield Garden and a short fifteen minute walk from the Jaffa Gate and the Old City. It was the ideal location in the heart of the western portion of the city. In addition, it was only a few minutes from Kati's flat located at *Bnei Batira*.

Eitan quickly cleared his calendar at *Masada* in preparation for the ride up to the capital. I, on the other hand, had no calendar to clear, and was excited at the prospect of another adventure. Since neither of us was sure what would be in store, we each packed a day-bag in case an overnight was required. We knew that there was always space at Kati's place should the need arise. In addition, that afternoon, I also boned up on the World Heritage Site of Palmyra.

This incredible Greco-Roman city was a monument to the ingenuity of the human experience, and its ability to adapt to the harsh desert environment. Palmyra was a part of the Greek Seleucid Empire from the late 4th – 1st Centuries BCE and prospered after it was made part of the Roman Empire in the 1st Century CE. By the late 3rd Century CE, this wealthy city became a 'major player' in the eastern portion of the empire. The city prospered because it straddled a branch of the famed Silk route. The *Palmyrenes* were known for their mercantile abilities and established colonies along the Silk Road. Their operations spread throughout the Roman Empire. The people were a 'Heinz 57 Variety'- primarily a mix of *Amorites, Arameans* and Arabs with a Jewish presence as well. Although a dialect of *Aramean, Palmyrene,* served the everyday community, Greek was the *lingua franca* of the Mediterranean world and thus was also widely spoken in the city.

I also discovered that the 'Jewish connection' was substantial as well. *Tadmor* was the Semitic, and earlier attested original name of the city. It appeared at the beginning of the second millennium BCE. It seemed that the etymology was unclear, perhaps being a derivative of the Semitic word for 'dates'. (*Tamar* probably refers to the groves of date palm trees that surrounded the city)

Palmyra also follows this logic as well. It appears in the writings of the historian Pliny the Elder in the 1st Century CE. If the ancient name of *Tadmor* did refer to dates, then *Palmyra* was a local bastardization of the Greek word for palm- *Palame*.

In 1980, the historic site, including the necropolis outside the walls, was declared a World Heritage Site by UNESCO.

But it was the Jewish connection that was most intriguing to me. *Palmyra* had a Jewish community as early as the *Mishnaic* period; the 1st -3rd centuries CE. The mention of Miriam of *Palmyra* in the Mishnah (vol. Naz. 6:11), meaning 'Study by repetition,' as a contemporary of the 1st Century Rabbi Eliezer seemed to indicate that a Jewish community may have existed there earlier. The rabbis of the Babylonian Talmud resented the city because of its role in helping the Romans and their Empire. But *Palmyra* was also home to the legendary Queen Zenobia, who may have been Jewish.

Archaeologically speaking, in literal obedience to the biblical command referenced in the text, the *Shema* (Dt. 6.4-9) was found carved onto a stone lintel in a building on the site. That passage formed one of the cornerstones of Jewish thought, Jewish prayer, and Jewish life. *"Hear O Israel, the Lord is our God, the Lord is One".* The famed Israeli archaeologist, E.L. Sukenik, of Hebrew University, believed that the building was a synagogue. In addition to that one, other 'house' inscriptions were said to have been found in excavations in the 1930s as well- containing portions of Dt. 7.15 and 25.5. Finally, on another structure, *Shema Yisroel*, *"Hear O Israel"*, was also carved in large letters.

All of them predated the 3rd Century C.E. A number of Jewish funerary inscriptions were also said to have been found. They were dated to the 2nd and 3rd Centuries C.E. Based on these inscriptions, it seemed that the Palmyrene Jewish community was fairly large and conscious of its Judaism, although non-Jewish personal names became increasingly common as the desire to assimilate grew stronger and stronger.

The final bit of evidence, but not at *Palmyra* itself, had to do with burials back in 'the holy land.' Graves of Jews from *Palmyra* were found at the necropolis of *Bet Shearim*, along the slope of *Mt. Carmel*, and also outside of Jerusalem. It was not known whether the bodies were brought to Jerusalem for reburial or whether a community of Palmyrene Jews had settled in the land. What was clear was that *Bet Shearim* had a large number of graves of Syrian Jews, including spacious, richly decorated burial chambers. This cemetery was in use for around 150 years, until its destruction by the Emperor *Constantius Gallus* in 353. *Gallus* showed a preference for the Christian religion, which he favored over all others, including Judaism. Unlike his father *Julius Constantius*, however, *Constantius Gallus* allowed Christians to persecute the pagans and the Jews. Eventually, the Jews reacted, opposing Christian proselytism. *Palmyra's* brief rule over Palestine during that period may have made the transfer of bodies for burial easier. In 352, *Gallus* sent an army to forcefully put down the revolt. *Tiberias* and *Diospolis*, two of the cities conquered by the Jewish rebels, were almost destroyed, while *Diocaesarea* was razed to the ground. Several thousand rebels were killed and a permanent garrison occupied *Galilee*.

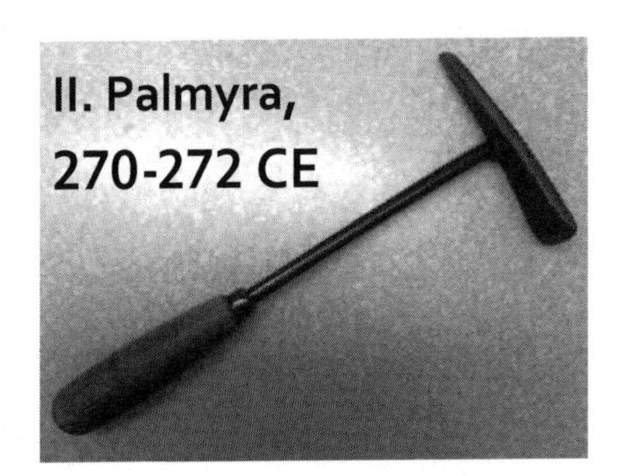

II. Palmyra, 270-272 CE

The city was buzzing with activity. Palmyra, as it was known by some, had become one of the most sought after locations to control in the region, due to the fact that it straddled major crossroads from east to west. Halfway between the Tigris and Euphrates Valleys, and the Orontes River, its oasis had served travelers for millennia. This oasis gave rise to the traditional name of the city, Tadmor, derived from the root 'Tamar,' date palm. However, in recent times, with the incursions of both Greeks and Persians, the translated name of Palmyra had caught on- another sign of the international flavor of the city.

Tadmor had been the genial host of the ancestors of the Jews, the Israelites, as early as the days of fabled King Solomon. In the first book of Kings, it states that 'King Solomon rebuilt Tamar (Tadmor) in the desert in the land and all the store-cities...' At first, this mighty king occupied the region for political gain. It seemed that the rapid rise of the Arameans played a major role in his thinking. But eventually the economic considerations took the upper hand. Solomon needed to maintain his grip on the land bridge that linked Egypt to the southwest with this rich Fertile Crescent of territory to the northeast. Control of Tadmor was essential.

But now, things were different. The spiritual head of the Jews of Palmyra, known as the 'Rav,' mulled things over as he prepared to visit the new building site of the great synagogue; located on the Acropolis of town. Every city in the Greco-Roman world these days had an 'acropolis,' for in Greek it merely meant 'high city.' As a city-state within the greater empire, Palmyra enjoyed a sense of independence for several generations- being granted leeway by the central powers first back in Athens, then Rome itself. Both empires understood the concept of peace and stability in the out provinces, so the granting of a bit of freedom meant security at home. They gladly traded off to ensure their safety, part of which was the gesture of allowing faraway cities to levy local taxes. In Palmyra's case, a tremendous source of income was taxing caravans coming and going from the oasis. These taxes took the form of levies imposed on oasis water use and lodging; two essentials if you were traveling weeks across the desert to your Mediterranean or Arabian Sea destination.

But things had changed, perhaps for the better, the rabbi mused. Palmyra had gotten a sense of its greatness with a degree of arrogance. It kept asking for more and more in this 3rd Century of the Common Era. And when Rome balked at the demanded concessions, Palmyrenes looked to a ruler who would wrest control of the city-state from the authorities back on the Italian Peninsula.

The ruler that would begin this revolution was King Odaenathis. He would sow the seeds of rebellion, but it would be his second wife, Queen Zenobia, who would win the hearts and minds of the people after his assassination in 267. Within two years, she would seize control of Palmyra and create an independent empire.

And who really was this extraordinary woman? Born in their fair city, she was known as 'Bat-Zabbai' in the native Aramaic tongue-meaning the 'daughter of Zabbai.' Athanasius of Alexandria, the Bishop of that city, called her 'a Jewess and follower of Paul of Samosata.' He was the bishop of the city in Asia Minor, who believed that Jesus was a mortal, but imbued with the spirit of God. This put him at odds with the Church in the 3rd Century CE, but was intriguing to elements of the Jewish world; hangers-on who looked with favor upon the 'human' ministry of the Rabbi Jesus, yet chose to disavow the immortality and divinity of the man. If, in fact, she was a member of this small group, it is of no wonder that the rabbis throughout the land denounced her at every turn. The rabbi thought that perhaps he and his ministry would be at risk should he choose to support her as well. It was truly a rock and a hard place that he found himself in. Palmyra was his city, Zenobia his queen, and Judaism his religion. Where would this all lead, he thought to himself.

Already, the tension within the havurah, congregation of Jews, in Palmyra was evident. Rabbinic leadership from as far as Pumbedita and Sura came on 'fact-finding' missions to see exactly what the queen was all about, and what she was up to regarding her city and the Jews there. It became an almost untenable position, as the syncretic nature of the Palmyrene Jews allowed for a great many converts to the faith. The rabbis looked at this as blasphemy. They would say in the

Talmud-"The future destruction of Palmyra will be a day of rejoicing for Israel." In addition, Rabbi Yohanon would also say in one of his tractates, "Blessed be he who will witness the downfall of Tadmor!"

The Rav thought back to those heady, yet violent days. He remembered when the Roman Consul, Tenagino Probus, attempted to regain control of the territory for the glory of Rome, only to be captured and beheaded by Zenobia's army.

All that aside, Palmyra was never as strong and important as it was today in spite of the strained relations with the Jews of the East. The rabbi was astonished that a Jewess could command such respect and authority in this pagan world. Yes, as a religious community the Jews of Palmyra enjoyed spiritual freedom and citizenship, but re-envision a Jewish state after all that had befallen the Jews in the Holy Land at the hands of the Greeks and then Romans? Well, that seemed to certainly solidify the notion of God's benevolence to His people. But did this woman overstep and incur the wrath of Rome? After all, the rabbi knew, she conquered Egypt and declared herself Queen of Egypt as well.

While the Rav was contemplating all of the ramifications of Zenobia's rule, a young lad came running up to him.

"Rav! Rav! Come quickly!" He practically fell at the feet of the community's religious leader, exhausted from his mad dash to find the older man. Astonished, the rabbi lifted the boy to his feet and gently brushed the dust from his tunic. He also took his kerchief from the folds of his gown and wiped the perspiration from the youth's face. He smiled at the boy.

"And what earth-shattering event has made you run like the wind that blows through the central square in order to find me. Are we under the threat of attack by the Persians?" He laughed aloud, trying to make light of the situation.

"Oh no, Rav, it's nothing at all like that. We are under no possibility of ill will being aimed at us... I think." He gave pause to consider. Inadvertently the rabbi had planted a seed of doubt in the boy's mind.

"Of course not! I was only teasing" was the answer designed to set the lad at ease.

"Of course not!" he echoed. "I bring you this from Shimon, the chief architect of the new synagogue." He slipped a wooden cylinder from the folds of his tunic and set it on the ground. He looked around, and picked up four medium sized stones and laid them out in a rectangle. Then he uncapped the lid, and gently slid a scroll fragment out and positioned it so that the four stones could easily be rolled over the edges, to prevent the document from furling up.

"And what do we have here?" asked the Rav as he peered at the writing. He smiled at the lad who stood in awe of the written words before him.

שמעתי ישראל
ה 'אלוהינו, ה' לבד. ואהבת את ה 'אלוהיך בכל לבבך, ובכל נפשך,
ועם כל הכח שלך. שמור את המילים האלה שאני מצווה אתכם היום
בלב שלך. לדקלם אותם לילדים שלך ולדבר עליהם כשאתה בבית
וכאשר אתה רחוק, כשאתה שוכב וכשאתה עולה. לאגד אותם לאות
על ידך, לתקן אותם כסמל על המצח שלך, ולכתוב אותם על מזוזות
ביתך ובשעריך.

"Well Rabbi, it says 'Hear O Israel'..."

"Aha! So what you bring me is the Shema, our holiest prayer!" The rabbi placed his hand on the shoulder of the messenger and very kindly informed him that he did indeed know what it said; thanking him profusely for reminding him of the text in case he should have forgotten it. The lesson was one of support, not denigration, and it was not lost on the young man.

"Of course," he stammered. "I didn't mean anything." At this he blushed as well. "Anyway, Shimon said that this would be the prayer that the stonemason, Yehuda, was carving on the lintel above the main entry of the Bet Knesset."

"Our synagogue will have a wonderful, welcoming inscription atop the central door for all to see." The rabbi was clearly pleased to see this. "But you know, I would love it if you would escort me through town to the construction site. I want to see the work in progress myself."

The boy beamed and took the bearded man's hand and led him to the acropolis of town. "But before we go, stand here by me and close your eyes." The rabbi placed his hands on the head of the boy and whispered another of the age-old prayers of their faith, The Shehechiyeinu. "Baruch ata Adonai... Blessed are you, Eternal God, Sovereign of the universe, who has given us life, sustained us, and helped us to reach this moment."

"Amen" the boy and the rabbi both said in unison. They then walked down the path towards the center of the city. The rabbi looked around as he took the boy's hand. He thought of the beauty of the town, its cosmopolitan nature, its acceptance of its Jewish citizens. He thought about the coming storm, the inevitable clash with the might

of Rome, and what might happen to the city, and to its residents-especially the Jews. A dark cloud passed in the heavens, and a dark cloud of despair blurred his eyes.

"Rav, what's wrong?" the boy asked. He saw the concern on the rabbi's face. The older man shook it off, smiled again, and reassured the boy that he was just looking at the rain cloud above and was hoping that they didn't get wet.

The boy laughed. "Rain is a good thing, isn't it? Doesn't God say, 'If you walk in my statutes, and keep my commandments, and do them; then I will give your rains in their season, and the land will yield its produce, and the trees of the field will yield fruit.'"

The leader of the community smiled at this. Although still young, the boy had learned his lessons well. The rabbi was proud of the education system of the Palmyrene Jews. "Do you remember where that came from?" The boy shook his head.

"Well, don't worry. You remembered it and that's what is important. We need to remember the goodness and grace of Yahweh on high. It came from the book of Leviticus, in chapter 26, verse 3 and 4."

Once again, the boy looked with wonder at the Rav. "How do you remember all this, with everything there is to know in the world?"

The answer was clear to the rabbi. "We remember what Yahweh ordains us to remember, the important things. The rest of life is all commentary." With that, they approached the acropolis and the synagogue building complex.

The chief architect, Shimon, was waiting for them, resting on a recently cut block of black basalt from the Golan Heights, to the south and west. It was a stunning building, standing out in sharp contrast to the rest of its surroundings. When the building committee of the congregation was involved in the stages of planning, the entire congregation with one voice said that the structure should be unique in its vision- a building that all Palmyrenes and visitors to the city would take note of for its beauty.

So the committee was allotted funds to travel to see some synagogues in other communities. They traveled to the Galilee to see some magnificent buildings there. One town in particular stood out to them- Chorazin. Its synagogue was of the new style, the tripartite basilical style. But what really set it apart was the construction material, the black basalt from the Golan. The Chorazin Synagogue stood proudly in the center of town, a deep-gray, almost black; in contrast to some of the beige-yellow limestone of the buildings surrounding it. The pediments and lintels were elegantly carved with floral patterns. It was a sculptural and spiritual masterpiece. And they sought after the master mason, Yehuda bar Nachman. His services were to be contracted upon completion of Chorazin. And now, four years later, this extraordinary artist was applying some of the final touches on his first Syrian synagogue.

Shimon rose and bowed in the presence of the community's spiritual leader. He kissed his hand and the rabbi gently lifted him out of his deep bow. His hand swept across the horizon, encompassing the entirety of the synagogue complex. He was beaming as he spoke to the rabbi.

"She's beautiful, yes?" The pride was evident in his voice. "You know how hard basalt is, so look at the careful precision in cutting the joints. It's all dry-wall masonry. There's not an ounce of mortar between the stones. They are as perfect in fit as is possible by a human hand."

"I agree, the craftsmanship is amazing! But could it be that a divine hand guided the team of stone masons, to achieve such perfection?" Everyone knew the rabbi to be good, very good, with the symbolism that his words painted on a spiritual canvas. But this subtle flattery and holy dimension... Well, it seemed to go above and beyond. Perhaps he was as inspired by the beauty of the structure as well. The rabbi then turned to the stonemason and said,"So tell me, Master Yehuda, where is this final piece of the entry puzzle of which our young friend showed me the drawing?"

The artisan took the rabbi's arm and proudly led him around the corner to the open-air workshop that he had established at the outset. The air was filled with stone dust, and when it settled it coated everything with a fine granulated powder-like covering. The mason quickly apologized for the dust that filled every pore. He grabbed a rag from the workshop table and dipped it in a bucket of water. He

then wringed it out and stepped over to a fairly large slab that rested directly on the ground. Its incredible weight would have collapsed any *type of wooden table. Then the artisan wiped the surface clear of the dust and debris accumulated on it.*

"So what do you think?" his nervousness showed.

The Rav slowly bent over and his finger traced the holy words that were integral to the nature of Judaism. 'Hear, O Israel, the Lord is our God, the Lord is one...'

"Magnificent" he murmured. The project supervisor, Shimon, Yehuda the stonemason, and the boy, barely heard the word escape from the rabbi's mouth. "This will serve as a guiding light for all who enter the synagogue. Words escape me to profess my thanks for all of your efforts." He placed his hands on a shoulder of the foreman and the mason. He asked them to humbly receive his blessing on behalf of the Lord. "Yevhārēkh-khā Adhōnāy veyishmerēkhā... May the LORD bless you and guard you. Yā'ēr Adhōnāy pānāw ēlekhā viḥunnékkā... May the LORD make His face shed light upon you and be gracious unto you. Yissā Adhōnāy pānāw ēlekhā viyāsēm lekhā shālōm... May the LORD lift up His face unto you and give you peace."

They all looked up expectantly at the rabbi, and said in unison, "Amen."

But even as they recited the blessing together, looking forward to the day that the new synagogue could joyously be consecrated, Rome was marshalling her forces for an assault on all that Palmyra controlled.

Within a few months, before the final stone was set in the synagogue, the Emperor Aurelian made every effort to reunify the Roman Empire. This would include the subjugating of Syria. Aurelian would meet Zenobia's army on the Plains of Antioch, just outside the city. The army would be devastated by the Roman assault, survivors fleeing into Antioch proper. Zenobia and the remnants would then flee to Emesa, the modern city of Homs.

Zenobia's army would then find themselves besieged by Aurelian's troops. Leaving her treasury behind, she and her son, Vaballathus, would escape from Emesa, only to be captured by Aurelian's cavalry by the banks of the Euphrates River. With her capture, the rest of the army still in Emesa surrendered. They would be put to death soon after.

As hostages, mother and son were to be taken back to Rome. It seemed that a tragedy occurred on the road to the capital, and Vaballathus died before the end of the journey. Another year passed, before Zenobia finally would be presented to Rome as a 'trophy of war.' During the triumphal parade through the streets of Rome, Zenobia was witnessed as being led through the streets bound in golden chains. She bravely endured the taunts and insults that the gathered crown hurled at her, along with other unmentionable things.

Conflicting reports surround her final days. According to the annals ascribed to the Roman Senator Marcellus Petrus Nutenus, she died soon after her delivery to Rome. However, three rumors of note suggested that she died either by illness, an extended hunger strike, or a beheading.

However, another tale had a happier ending. Apparently Aurelian, stunned by her beauty and dignity in the face of incarceration, granted her freedom. She would go on to live in luxury, and became known for her evolving philosophy on life- something that she learned was a precious commodity in light of her impending death.

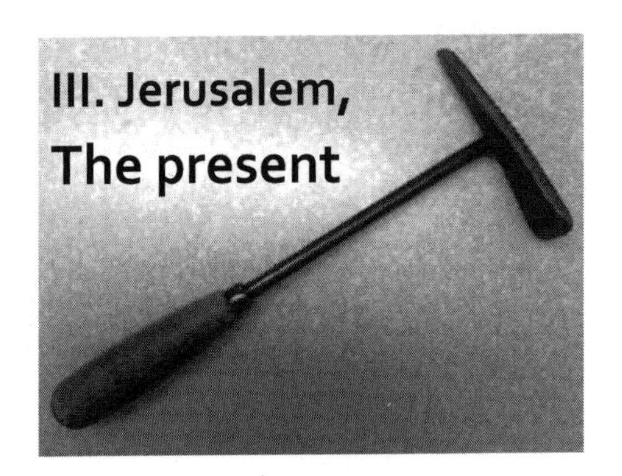

We hopped in the jeep just a little after sunrise. Everything in the Mediterranean Basin, including Israel, always started early. This then meant that there was no 'midday siesta remorse' when most people took a couple of hours off following lunch, then returned to work until 7 or so in the evening. But there was a more practical side to this practice as well. The Mediterranean sun was intense, blinding, during most of the year. And in the old days, 'BAC,' 'Before Air Conditioning,' people needed a way to beat the energy sucking heat of the afternoon. So schedules were created to work around this inopportune time, when everyone's vigor was at an ebb.

I had packed a *cancan*, an insulated water jerrycan, with icewater and a couple of cups. No matter how you traveled, carrying spare water was always a necessity. In addition, I threw in a container of *hummus* and some *pita* for the road. Eitan looked in the back seat and noticed something else.

"*Nu*, so what's the bottle of wine for?" He was laughing.

"It's for our hostess in *Yerushalyim*, it's always protocol to bring something, especially if you may need overnight lodging." I tried to look offended, but clearly couldn't pull it off. Kati Ben Yair was a dear friend of both of us, like a sister to Eitan and well, to me...

We headed off to the west, away from the sunrise, so had no visibility issues. We backtracked down the road toward *Beersheva*, and as we slowed near *Tzomet Shoqet*, Shoket Junction, Eitan enquired as to which way to go.

"What, *you* don't know where you're heading?" Now it was my turn with the 'I gotcha' reply. We both laughed.

"You know, *habibi,* if you weren't like my brother I'd punch you in the shoulder for doubting me. Wait, even if you were like my brother, I should still punch you in the shoulder!" We both laughed at that one. For decades, Clan Campbell in Israel had regarded me as the illegitimate Jewish brother that they never had in Chad's Ford Pennsylvania, before most of the family adopted Judaism after making *Aliyah*, or emigration.

"*Ya hamar*! You donkey's ass! You know full well why I asked. You probably have heard more on the news lately than me. After all, CNN International keeps track of *everything* that might be terror-related here."

"Whether or not it was," I said half under my breath.

"Exactly! That's my point!" He replied. "I just want to make sure that we choose the safest route to the city. So, do we head due north, through *Hevron*, *Halhoul*, *Dhahariya* and *Bet Lechem*? Or do we play it safe for another 20 minutes and hit *Tzomet Malachi* and swing around the West Bank?"

I understood his caution. After all, we were in a government vehicle. Had it been 30 years earlier, as we had done time and time again in the 70s and 80s, there would have been no question. As a matter of fact, I even recalled 'tramping' from *Beersheva* to Jerusalem on the weekend when going to visit Frank Anson in the southern German Quarter of the city near the old train station. But those days were long past after a couple of Palestinian *Intifadas*, a couple of Gulf Wars, and the Gaza incursion of 2013. So it wasn't such a bad thing to ask about all this. I told him that I thought it was a safer bet to swing west, taking Route 40 to *Kiryat Malachi,* known by locals as *Castina*, and then northeast on Hwy 3 into the western side of the city.

"*Tayib*. Okay. But you do know that we're missing one of your favorite linguistic transliteration *Snafus*." He laughed. Eitan was referring to the gas station in the small Arab village of *Dhahariya*, about 15 km north of *Hevron*. Back in the 'good old days' of the British Mandate, between the great world wars, the English built an incredible infrastructure, not so much for the local population to bring it into the 20th century in preparation for future independence, but for just the opposite- with a belief that the sun would *never* set on the British Empire and that she would need to maintain her grip via the latest to keep her military machine well-oiled, and well-petroled. However, she would always employ local manual labor to carry out any menial tasks. So, a sign painter was hired to create the billboard that advertised the petrol station for the village. There was just one small problem, though. He knew absolutely no English, just how to write English letters. As a result, when it was patiently explained to him what letters to paint on the sign, he interpreted the letters based on an Arabic phonetic understanding. In Arabic, there are few distinctions between what linguistics would call a 'plosive'- a sound that is paralleled with a glottal and non-glottal 'stop.' In other words, a 'be' and 'pe' were indistinguishable and therefore not different. So, the creatively enterprising artist took it upon himself to create the sign that then read *"Dhahariya Penzine Station"* for all to see. Of course, for the Palestinian Arabs, they could care less, because they were reading the gas station sign in Arabic. It was the British who would be insulted and offended at what they felt was a blatant slap in the face coming from the '*wogs,*' whom the Brits thought took every opportunity to rebel against their 'benevolent' rule. As a result, the British attempted to re-paint the sign, only to find it re-painted in the same way time and again. After a couple of months of this, the British threw up their hands and gave in. Today, the faded and chipped sign is still there, and a delight to all of us familiar with the linguistic story.

I sighed, as I missed the days when the greatest disturbance on the direct road from *Beersheva* to Jerusalem, Highway 60, was the laughter of vehicle passengers when told the story as the station was passed by.

*****

As we neared *Castina*, traffic slowed considerably. The police had set up a random checkpoint and were asking passengers in all vehicles for *Taodat Za-ut*, Israeli Identity Cards. Even in an INPA Jeep, we were asked to show ID. Eitan handed over his card, and my American passport, and engaged the officer in a bit of idle talk while he scanned the documents in a handheld device.

"I see his partner in the background," I whispered. "You know that they always need to work in pairs because 'one reads and the other writes!'" Eitan burst out laughing.

"*Lama ata tzohek?* Why are you laughing?" the officer demanded. Apparently he took his job quite seriously and was oblivious to the long-standing joke amongst Israelis regarding the capabilities of the National Police. "*Ve ata?* And you, you think that this is funny?" he demanded of me. I put on my 'most confused' look and said "Sorry officer, were you speaking to me? I don't know Hebrew." I also tried to look contrite. He glared and dismissed me.

"These Americans are clowns" he told Eitan in Hebrew. "After all, we're their only ally and look at the mess that they've created with the Iranians."

"I fully agree with you, this idiot is just with me because of orders from the Director of INPA. Something to do with archaeological oversight. Between you and me, he's a *fryer*, a dolt, of the first degree." Eitan winked conspiratorially while I did everything in my power to keep from letting the officer know that I fully understood the conversation, and at the same time keep from punching my friend on the shoulder.

Eitan rolled up the window and turned right, heading towards the capitol. THEN I punched him, hard, on the bicep.

"What do you mean, calling me a dolt?" We were both laughing uncontrollably now, as we headed through the Judean Hills past *Bet Shemesh*. We were nearing one of the natural wonders of the world, the *Soreq* Caves, and I asked my friend if we could stop and stretch our legs. Since we were making good time and didn't have to be at Kati's for another three hours, there was no rush.

Also known as the *Avshalom* Cave, this cave is renowned for its dense concentration of stalactites. The cave is named after Avshalom Shoham, an Israeli soldier killed in the War of Attrition with Egypt that took place between 1968-70, as the two enemies dueled across the Suez Canal. The cave was discovered accidentally in May 1968, while quarrying with explosives. It is nearly 83 m long and at some points over 15 m high. After its discovery, the location of the cave was kept a secret for several years for fear of damage to its natural treasures.

The temperature and the humidity in the cave are constant year round, and it is now open to visitors since 1975. In 2012, a new lighting system was installed to prevent the formation and growth of algae. Some of the stalactites found in the cave are four meters long, and some have been dated as old as 300,000 years. Some meet stalagmites to form stone pillars.

Proteksia is a nice thing, especially given the rising costs of entry into locations under the umbrella of the Nature and Parks Authority. Eitan flashed his ID, and the guard raised the barrier allowing us access to the employee parking lot. It reduced a bit of walking for us, but we still needed to descend down the slope of *Mt. Ye'ela,* a couple of hundred feet before approaching the cave entrance.

Once there, we proceeded through the double 'air-lock' style entry into the cave. If you've never been there, when you enter you have no idea what awaits. It is a dazzling world of natural wonder and beauty. The crystal formations in certain areas create groupings to which the initial explorers gave whimsical names. For example, a cluster of stalagmites rising from the floor consisted of seven short ones and one taller one. The resulting name given to them was Snow White and the Seven Dwarfs. Other formations are called 'The Macaroni Screen' and 'Sombreros.' Perhaps the most enchanting to be named by the explorers was 'Romeo and Juliet'. Here, a stalactite from the ceiling began forming tens of thousands of years ago. Water from the surface seeped down a crack in the bedrock, dripping with wet limestone particles. They then dropped down to into the cavern, creating a stalagmite that rose from the floor. However, at some point in time, the crack in the surface closed- shutting off the water supply. The stalactite and stalagmite had gotten within a few centimeters of each other, only to be denied 'the kiss'. And tragically, they never will.

After wandering through the complex for about half an hour, we returned to the surface. A quick snack of *hummus* and bottled water, and we were back on the road to Jerusalem.

*****

At the same time that we were entering the cave, Kati Ben Ya'ir was waiting outside the *Tahana Mercazit*, the Central Bus Station of Tel Aviv. One of the miracles of the modern state of Israel was its public transportation system. Within a couple of years of creation, the state began to carry out plans to interconnect everyone with everyone else as seamlessly and painlessly as possible. In the early days of statehood, there were very few privately owned cars, so everyone was forced to rely on public transportation. The result was a fairly efficient, and relatively inexpensive, means of getting around the country. All cities and towns had a central bus station, where buses from all over the country would pull in. Then, just outside the station, local bus stops lined the adjacent couple of streets, so that it was easy to get around the city once you had arrived from afar. The planners were smart in that all of the local buslines that snaked around the town eventually returned to the central bus station. So if you were lost in a 'foreign' town, you just simply hopped on a bus and at some point you would be delivered to the central station. It was brilliant, and surprisingly efficient.

But Kati wasn't just waiting for a local Tel Avivi. She was waiting to pick up the UNESCO appointed liaison to deal with the blossoming antiquities destruction in Syria. He would be arriving on the #100 Bus. This bus was a miracle unto itself, for it was the only non-stop bus route from Cairo to Tel Aviv. Until 1978, this was unimaginable to anyone in the world; let alone any Israelis or Egyptians. It was one of those surprising fruits from the tree of peace forged by Menachem Begin and Anwar Sadat.

Apparently UNESCO didn't have it in the budget for this individual to take a flight. But in the agency's defense, time was of the essence. Travel by bus in a military convoy was safer and actually almost as quick now. There no longer were any nonstop flights due to the violence in Sinai. After the recent Metrojet crash that originated out of Sharm, and most likely was brought down by a bomb planted by an al Qaeda operative at the airport, no one was flying over the peninsula any longer. The shortest connection was with Royal Jordanian Airlines through Amman, with an overall duration of well over 8 hours at a cost of over $470 USD. The bus, on the other hand, cost only $90 USD and took around 10 hours. This included the Rafah checkpoint and vehicle change.

As Kati sat in the car just outside the terminal, she idly wondered who the UN would be sending. She was only told to look for someone wearing a blue T-shirt emblazoned with the UNESCO World Heritage Commission logo. She wasn't the most comfortable here, as the decline of the bus station was a well-known fact in Israel. Sprawling over 11 acres in size, with a maze of passages on several floors, only the top three are still in use. On its lowest level, in a tunnel complex long-since abandoned, there are thousands of bats- a veritable 'bat cave' where no one dares to go. In fact, and perhaps only in Israel, this lower level was actually declared *a nature preserve* because of this wildlife! By any stretch of the imagination, it is a terrible, horrible, foul place below ground. But the upper three levels are vibrant and teem with life- albeit the more 'interesting' strata of Israeli society. Small knock-off clothing shops, starving artists, *falafel* entrepreneurs and homeless folks make up this island in the heart of Tel Aviv. And in spite of it all, nearly 100,000 people pass through the terminal's bus loading and unloading docks on a daily basis.

She cracked open a bottle of Kinley Orange, and took a couple of sips when a crowd of people exited the bus station. She saw a man wearing a Minnesota Twins baseball cap pulled over his forehead. He was wearing the telltale blue UNESCO shirt and carried a backpack. Kati couldn't see his face well, but the cap set off an alarm- but not a negative one. *It couldn't be*, she thought. The man paused for a moment and looked around. He took off the cap and wiped his brow.

She jumped out of the car. "Ya Sobhy!" She yelled and ran over to the fellow. He saw her at the same moment and jogged over. He embraced her and, with his traditional bear hug, lifted her several inches off the ground and kissed both cheeks.

"*Ahlen*, ya Kati! How are you my friend? It's been a while now hasn't it?" He was grinning ear to ear, still not putting her down.

"*Bas! Halas*! Enough *habibi*! PUT ME DOWN!" She teasingly pounded him on the back. The Egyptian slowly and gently allowed Kati to land on her feet, then grasped her shoulders and laughed.

"I can't believe that the UN office didn't tell you that it was me coming over. I can't believe that I'm actually here again." Sobhy clearly was delighted to be back in Israel, with the opportunity to work with his friends again. It had been a while since that first time they had met, when he had rediscovered the statue fragment that led to an incredible turn of events- offering substantial archaeological and inscriptional proof that the greatest prophet of ancient Israel, Moses, may have indeed been elevated to the rank of Egyptian pharaoh in the 13th Century BCE. Without the unique collaborative effort of Egyptians, Americans and Israelis, the mystery may never have come to light and subsequently been solved. And after that, the same team collaborated in an international effort to return ancient papyrus scrolls to Egypt after they were stolen by the Germans just prior to World War Two. And a grateful Egyptian government, with Sobhy's help, gave one of the documents that shed light on Egypt's ancient Jewish community and its relationship with Morocco to Israel- offering it 'on permanent loan' to the Israel Museum. These two events forged an eternal bond between those involved. And now a new opportunity presented itself to combat bigotry, racism, and irrationality of the highest degree. Soon the team would all be in place together again in Jerusalem.

Clearly Sobhy was wired. He began to bombard Kati with a thousand questions, but she told him bluntly to 'shut the hell up' until she maneuvered her way out of Tel Aviv and onto the main expressway, Highway 1, that ran from the *Ayalon* Highway 20 east into the *Shephelah* and the *Bab el Wad*, climbing to the Holy City.

"*Tayib*, ok, I get it" he laughed. Looking at the congestion, he remarked that it appeared to be nothing like Cairo's perpetual gridlock. "This is a lull in traffic for us!" He joked.

She punched him in the forearm without taking her eyes off the road, and drove on in silence for another quarter of an hour. It was golden, until Sobhy broke it by commenting on state of Israel's highway system.

"You know, I've always wanted to ride on an express tollway without stopping," he mused, more to himself than Kati.

"Well, you won't get it on this leg of the journey" she answered. "Highway Six runs pretty much northwest/southeast to Dimona in the *Negev*. Since we're heading almost due east, you'll just have to wait. Maybe if we go back to visit in *Arad* after you fill us all in about your new job and what we have to do with it." She smiled that 1000 watt smile and pointed to the road sign that was coming up. "We only have another ten minutes or so 'til the outskirts of the city, *then* the traffic fun begins!"

Sobhy returned the smile and continued gazing out the window, absorbing the sites of this land that he was feeling more and more comfortable with- even though he was Egyptian. *The increasing comfort level may be because I'm a Copt*, he mused, as the holy city came into view the next hill over as they rounded the bend. *We all say 'going up to Jerusalem,' and I can see that it's not just spiritual.* He marveled as the western city came into view.

Kati was spot on regarding her time estimate for the city outskirts. They passed the *Motza* Interchange and headed through the Jerusalem Forest. From there, the true modern entry was under the Bridge of Chords, only completed in 2008. It carries both pedestrians and the Jerusalem Light Rail since 2011. The down side of passing under this incredible piece of functional sculpture is that, just after it, the roads into the heart of the city narrow appreciably and become clogged with traffic that barely crawls along. Fortunately Kati's residence on *Bnai Batira* wasn't too terrible far away.

After an additional 25 minutes or so, she pulled up in front of the apartment building.

"I could have walked here faster from that beautiful bridge," Sobhy quipped.

"Someone bound in a wheel chair could have gotten here faster" she laughed.

"Now *that's* not politically correct!" The Egyptian shot back. He then laughed out loud at his own joke. He looked around and around, swiveling his head like a bobble-head doll. He couldn't put a finger on it. Then smacked the dashboard with his palm.

"I've got it! It's just too quiet here! A residential neighborhood should be loud and raucous in the later afternoon- kids screaming and playing football on the street. Babies should be crying, TVs should be blaring..."

"You want noise- I can always take you back to the bus terminal and return you to Cairo!" Her mock temper only lasted a moment, and she dissolved into tearful laughter. "We like to leave it all at work" she explained. "But on *Shabbat* the sound level must approach that of your city. Everyone's home and family is the most important thing at that time, so... BAAM! Just like Emeril!"

"Who?" Sobhy clearly was lost.

"Ah come on, you know, that Portuguese-French Canadian-American chef who is world famous. When he finishes a dish on his TV show, he hits it with a bit of parsley and says 'BAAM!' when he's done."

"Hmmmm, I must have missed that one on *Al Qahira al Youm* Network." He laughed as well.

They got out and went up the two flights to Kati's home. She pointed the way to one of the guest rooms and reminded Sobhy that it was his 'old' room- used when the group of friends were exploring the Egyptian statue fragment that may have referred to the biblical figure, Moses, as an Egyptian pharaoh. After the long bus ride, he opted to take a short catnap and recharge his batteries before the rest of the team arrived and he explained why he was in Israel on behalf of UNESCO.

*****

Eitan and I were just passing under the Chords Bridge at the same time that Kati and Sobhy were entering her apartment. I suggested that we stop at the *Mahane Yehuda* Market, located just of *Jaffa* Road. The market dates back to the 19th Century during Ottoman Turkish rule. It was developed by local peasants who brought produce to sell in an area somewhat far removed from the Old City. As Jerusalem began to grow outside of the wall of the Old City, residential quarters needed to have their own 'shopping district' close to them. After all, who wanted to walk a couple of miles to buy their basic necessities. This was the key to its success as the market took on its unique, permanent nature during the British Mandate between the world wars.

You know, everyone in the Mideast employs the phrase, "Blame it on the British" for all the woes that have befallen the region. However, in this case, it actually was a good thing that the British did under the authority of the first High Commissioner, Ronald Stores. He quickly understood the importance of the *shuq*, but felt that it was a somewhat depressing, and filthy venue to sell goods. So he set about making it a showplace for both Jerusalemites and visitors- with the hopes of making it a tourist destination.

However, impossibly high taxes, without the benefit of government advance of basic utility infrastructure, prevented the ultimate success of the market as a destination for anyone but a local resident. But over time, after the creation of Israel, the market would expand and the new country's government would remodel, upgrade and expand until it reached the footprint of today. In fact, even a Yeshiva, *Etz Chaim*, would be established and open shops selling to the growing Orthodox Jewish community in the neighborhood.

Today, the *Mahane Yehuda* Management Company blends the traditional with the cutting edge of modern technology to make the market a truly unique place to shop and visit.

Amazingly, we found a parking spot right at the doorstep of the market so to speak. Timing is everything, and we pulled up just as an Israeli *Susita* was pulling out. It was one of the industrial experiments of Israel in the 1960s that was sort of a failure. As we got out of the car, I told Eitan a story about Yohanon Aharoni at Beersheva in 1971, my first year digging with Tel Aviv University's Institute of Archaeology.

As Israel 'grew up' and became an industrialized nation, it desired to become as self-sufficient as possible. In this case, it meant developing its own auto industry. As a result, the *Susita* was born. In a small country, where energy efficiency was important due to the lack of oil, three and four cylinder cars were created. In addition, in order to keep the weight down, these vehicles had fiberglass bodies. This was great, provided that you weren't driving it out in the desert. Aharoni had one of these cars, and brought it down to *Beersheva* during the excavation season. He chose to park it just outside the dig camp compound, under a copse of tamarisk trees. One day, he came down off the site and one of the camp staff came running up to him. He was clearly distraught, and we feared that something disastrous had happened in camp while we were up on the *Tel*. It turned out to be a 'minor' catastrophe. Apparently no one at the *Susita* factory was aware of the 'fiber' in fiberglass... and that camels loved to eat it! The right rear quarter panel was chewed up, fully exposing the wheel. A camel was about a hundred meters away, looking 'full.' Aharoni, after seeing this, took it all in quite calmly for someone who just had his car 'eaten.' The following week, he was dropped off in the excavation camp- opting to have his car return to Tel Aviv. The moral of the story, leave your Susita in a city where camels don't come to visit.

We only had to walk a couple of blocks to get to the heart of the marketplace. I bought a bouquet of flowers for Kati and Eitan a bottle of wine. We then got back to the Jeep, where another vehicle triumphantly waited for us to pull out, praising their good luck.

Another five minutes and we were outside the apartment, waiting to be buzzed into the building. But after several minutes, there still was no answer.

"*Ma koray*? What's happening?" Eitan couldn't figure it out. Neither could I. I rang the bell again, still waiting for a reply. Finally, after another couple of minutes, the buzzer signified the unlocking of the lobby door and we gained admittance. I scratched my head, confused at what was going on, as we made our way up the flights of stairs. When we reached Kati's flat, the door was shut. I looked at Eitan, he at me, and if you looked on Wikipedia under 'confusion' our faces would have been the lead photos.

At last the door opened a crack, and then was thrown wide by... Sobhy!

"*Ahlen, ya majnoon*! Greetings crazy one!" and I was suddenly embraced in the mother of all bearhugs.

*****

After the shock wore off, Eitan and I came back to our senses.

"*YOU* are the UNESCO agent?" Eitan asked. I shook my head as well. How could the recently, newly appointed Director of the

Cairo Museum multi-task in this way, when there were still threats to the museum itself. In spite of the new regime, and the ouster of Mohamed Morsi and his Moslem Brotherhood, the situation in Egypt was still in a state of disarray. After all, the al Qaeda affiliates in Sinai had recently brought down a Russian charter flight, killing all 234 on board. And on the 'mainland,' so to speak, along the Nile Valley, demonstrations and random shootings were still a concern to public safety. So the question begged itself, why?

"*Habibi*, I have just the answer that you are seeking, I think," Sobhy smiled indulgently at all of us. "You see, once I explained my connections with you all, and the great successes that we had regarding the statuette fragment of Israel's pharaoh and the recovery of both Egyptian and Jewish scrolls of significant historical importance, my government, when asked to make a suggestion, made *me* the suggestion!" He laughed boisterously at this.

"I'm not sure that I follow this logic" Kati said. "It seems somewhat convoluted and obtuse."

"There you go with the 100 *shekel* words again," Eitan shook his head with a smile.

Sobhy went on, "It appears that ISIS is flooding the black market with illicit small-scale antiquities; making outrageous sums of money from selling them through an underground network to collectors with real money and no real concern for *any* country's antiquities protection. They just want to own ancient artifacts at any cost. Both UNESCO and Interpol feel that our network, meaning us here in this room and our other friends and contacts, can make a difference."

"But why us? How can Israelis and an American Jew 'fly under the radar' when Syria is the main 'playground' here?" Eitan asked the question that was on all our minds.

"We have a conference call with one of your professional colleagues tomorrow morning, and she will explain everything in great detail and how we all fit in. I just want to sweeten the pot and tell you this- the potential sale of Jewish artifacts from Palmyra, during the reign of the Queen Zenobia, are the 'in' to try to stop the pipeline. Is that intrigue enough for you?" Sobhy gave us all that sly look of his that got him through many tight squeezes during his quest to do away with the corruption that was rampant in the Supreme Council of Antiquities and the Cairo Museum before he took over.

We all agreed to withhold our final decisions until the conference call first thing the next morning. It was all so cryptic, but again, that's just the teaser that we were all used to. We all turned in relatively early in expectation of the call at first light.

*****

I awoke to the glorious smell of freshly brewed coffee. There is nothing like Israel's Elite brand of the dark, rich brew designed to rouse the dead. I had used it for the many years' worth of students on the various excavations that I had been a part of. After all, for some, five am comes awfully soon for some if they chose to party the previous evening. And I needed them to at least be alert enough not to put a pickax through their foot on the dig. I rolled out of bed, splashed some cold water on my face and shook out the cobwebs. I heard a bit of banging around in the kitchen and peeked my head in to see what was going on.

Kati was slicing and dicing tomatoes, cucumbers, onions and olives as part of the traditional Israeli salad. Meanwhile, eggs were busily bouncing around in boiling water, nearing their hardboiled state. Sobhy was slicing thick slabs of a wonderful, crusty loaf. I grabbed some dishes and started setting the table.

"So where's Sleeping Beauty?" he asked.

"If you mean Eitan, he's still gently snoring his way through a dream I suppose." I knew that Eitan was notorious for being able to sleep through anything, anywhere, at any time. He had learned that from his army days. The others were aware as well, based on our previous exploits. They laughed and told me that I needed to light a fire under him.

"But not a real one, after all, it is my apartment" Kati added with a wink. Table set, the task was now before me to rouse the dead, or nearly dead, from their sleep. On the way to the living room and sleeper sofa, I grabbed the bottle of Kati's fragrance from the bathroom and headed down the hall. I passed the uncorked bottle under his nose and tickled his ear.

"*Ya'allah, Adi, ma at osa habibti*? Oh, my sweet *Adi*, what are you doing to me?" He gently moaned in his sleep.

Kati had just come in and overheard this. She punched him playfully on the arm.

"Who the hell is *Adi*?" She laughed. Eitan rolled off the sleeper and fell onto the floor. For a moment he clearly had no idea where he was. Then it hit him, or rather, Kati hit him-again! Sobhy threw a towel at Eitan, and we were all out of control by now.

"*Aruhat boker, kulam*! Breakfast is ready! We have a call to receive very soon." Kati herded us all into the small dinette and we feasted, Israeli style. As Sobhy dug in with a vengeance, he told us between mouthfuls that this was what he missed the most about his past visits to Israel- the breakfasts.

"Obviously!" Eitan rolled his eyes at this. We all laughed and finished eating just before the computer trilled the 'Skype calling' tune.

"*Bonjour*! *Saba el Kheir*!" As the Skype image came into view. A diminutive brunette with pixie-cut hair appeared on the computer screen. Joanne Farchakh, university professor and director of the non-profit '*Biladi*' or 'homeland' Agency, smiled at us. Immediately I recognized her, but the name hadn't rung any bells until I saw her. I suddenly put everything together. I had heard the professor speak at the Archaeological Institute of America annual meetings a few years ago. She spoke passionately about the destruction of antiquities in Iraq at that time, warning about the spread of this cultural disaster throughout the region if left unchecked. With Peter G. Stone, she had co-authored *The Destruction of Cultural Heritage in Iraq*, and as a result, had won the 2011 James R. Wiseman Book Award from the AIA.

"Professor Farchakh, it's an honor to speak, er Skype, with you today. We are all delighted to have the opportunity to work with you, in spite of the horrific series of events that has tragically brought us together. You have had the opportunity to view the email that I sent out earlier outlining the two main 'adventures' that we have all shared together- actions that seem to be in the same, er, arena." Sobhy, ever the diplomat, clearly was trying to instill in her confidence that we were the right group with whom to collaborate. He was searching for the right words to use. I was impressed with the skills that he had developed since becoming Director of the Cairo Museum.

"*Ahlen ya* Sobhy. Could you mean maybe 'in the same ballpark?" Professor Farchakh laughed. "I am familiar with American idioms."

"Of course, you have worked closely with academics from all over," Sobhy replied. "Collaboration is essential in our business, and now even more essential in trying to recover lost antiquities from these barbarians. As we say in Egypt, *Eid wahda matsa'afsh!*" Before I could say anything, because none of the rest of us knew that phrase, Dr. Farchakh broke in.

"Ah, I see what you mean- 'One hand doesn't clap.' Yes, I know that Egyptian saying. I agree, teamwork is essential to get something done."

Eitan, Kati and I looked at each other and Kati winked at us. Sobhy and Farchakh had quickly 'connected,' which bode well for future collaboration.

"*Ahlen ya* professor." Kati introduced herself, but was cut short.

"Please, all of you, call me Joanne, and I will call you by your names as well. How do you Americans put it, 'standing on ceremony?' Well, we won't do that, based on what we all know of each other, it feels like we have shared similar stories and events. I for one feel very comfortable with this endeavor and hope that you all feel the same."

"Yes, I think that I speak for the three of us here and are in full agreement- Joanne." The two women smiled at each other. Kati went on, "So what can you tell us, and how can we help in the repatriation of artifacts?"

"As you are aware, I started to work with scholars when this problem first arose in Iraq during the Second Gulf War of 2003. Now it has spread to ISIL, or ISIS for Syria, and is even more widespread and insidious because the funds raised go to aid and abet violence and terror to the ultimate degree. This illicit means of financing ISIS' operation is almost impossible to detect, let alone prosecute. The terrorists take the money to fund their horrible agenda. In the process, to cover their tracks, they destroy the evidence by blowing up buildings, shrines, temples that then conceals their assault against humanity."

She then cited scores of Syrian artifacts already circulating on the black market in Western Europe. The 'm.o.' was a perfect one. Scholars and Interpol would have no idea what was robbed, or subsequently destroyed, in the razing of an archaeological site. This then meant that no one ultimately knew what artifacts in fact had been illegally sold. Prof. Farchakh based her theory on over a decade of work. At first, she discovered, ISIL went at it on archaeological sites that they occupied. They would attack with a vengeance, gleefully videotaping the wanton destruction of the ancient past with jackhammers, sledgehammers, chisels- then artfully posting it online for the world to see. They would take pleasure in the collective international community mourning the loss of these treasures.

Sobhy then added what he knew, "And now, inadvertently, both the UN and international human rights agencies fall into the ISIS trap and in essence 'work' for it. Now, ISIS no longer has to put out its own video propaganda. They destroy ancient sites piecemeal, leaking short footage one incident at a time. The international world picks up on this and rebroadcasts the 'atrocities' time and again- a much more effective way for ISIS to get its imagery out."

"Precisely." Farchakh was in full agreement with his assessment. "You fit in with your connections from New York to *Nineveh*, so to speak." At this she looked in the direction of Sobhy. "But to be even more precise, your intimate knowledge of ancient Jewish culture and archaeology can perhaps save some Hebrew inscriptions that are in extreme jeopardy, according to my sources." She pointed at both Kati and me on the screen.

We knew that we had our work cut out for us, but were excited about the possibilities of rescuing artifacts, especially ones associated with the biblical connection. Joanne agreed to Skype us in a couple of days with more information, and we broke the connection.

"*Tayib*, okay, the situation is spread out on the table before us," said the Egyptian. "And it's clear that something needs to be done to rescue these artifacts- and done well in advance of any military success that may come. So how do we do it?"

An uncomfortable silence descended on the four friends. It only lasted for a few minutes though. Kati's eyes lit up, and I knew that the wheels were turning faster and faster in that brain of hers. "The war can be to our benefit!" The room was brilliantly lit by her smile, although the three of us looked perplexed. She went on to explain her idea.

The human tragedy that was Syria was more devastating to her civilian population that anything else, including the three-way military struggle between the government (or what was left of it), the rebels and ISIS. The locals dodged bullets and IEDs coming at them from the three factions. No one knew who to trust. And scores of dead and wounded littered streets in nearly every village on a daily basis. A few dozen kilometers to the west, across the UN monitored DMZ, Israeli civilians and soldiers could hear, and almost see, the intense suffering of Syria's villagers. As word got back to Israelis, they knew that they needed to do something outside of any military option. In spite of much of the world's skewed opinion of Israel as a militaristic conqueror and subjugator of the

Palestinian community- bent on an 'imperialistic obliteration of this downtrodden people' that was the message screamed from the rooftops by the Boycott, Divestment, Sanctions (BDS) Movement supporters and anti-semites around the planet- Israel actually was one of the most compassionate democracies worldwide; not just in the Mideast.

Yes, we are all aware of exceptions to the rule- after all, Israelis are mere humans. And yes, violence has been visited illegally, unjustly. But overall, Israel's track record was head and shoulders about the rest of the nations. Her citizens demonstrated uncounted times in the last 70 years their work on behalf of all people, Jew or Arab, when it came to everyone's overall welfare. It was this premise that Kati felt would be the key to our mission.

For almost two decades, Israeli medical staff in the north of the country surreptitiously worked with counterparts in both Lebanon and Syria to aid civilians in need of medical assistance. One of the leaders in this push was Dr. Shaul Shasha. For nearly 50 years, the Galilee Medical Center (GMC) in Nahariyya served northern Israel proudly. Starting as a series of small Scandinavian-style huts, it has since grown to a facility with over 450 doctors, 1200 nurses and scores of paramedics. In addition, due to its place in Israel, a vast underground facility was constructed- designed to protect everyone facing the onslaught of random missile attacks. This facility would include triage areas, operating theatres and intensive care recovery wards as well.

After his 'retirement' (in Israel, that's an oxymoron!) his legacy was continued by Dr. Masoud Barhoum. When conferred with a number of honors by the UN's Director for UNESCO, Irina Bokova, Dr. Barhoum would say, *"As the first Arab Christian director of any major government organization of its size, I am a representative of the true diversity of Israel and the Israeli people. The Galilee Medical Center, which I am proud to call my home institution, has had the unique privilege to care for not just young Israeli citizens. There are some people who believe that Arabs and Jews can never coexist. There are people who believe that Arabs and Jews should be segregated – and others who believe that Israel already actively segregates. This initiative shows us that people of all races, backgrounds and religions can and do coexist in Israel. That integration of this sort, in hospitals and in schools, is the cornerstone for healthy coexistence."*

He was referring to a somewhat clandestine program operated by the Israeli government since 2013. With the war in Syrian beginning to reach atrocious levels of violence visited on her civilians, Israel decided to quietly put the word out that wounded Syrian civilians, should they be able to make their way to the frontier in the Golan, would be taken in and given medical treatment by Israel. This would all be done in secret, with identities hidden, to protect these Syrians from reprisal by relatives or others when they returned to their country. Since 2013, over 3000 Syrians would be treated at the GMC. They come in the middle of the night across the no-person's-land in the Golan, greeted by the IDF, who whisks them away in silent ambulances into Israel's northern heartland formedical aid.

Treating horrific wounds most Israelis medicos had never seen before, the hospital staff humanitarian mission would be severely tested. The type of wounds coming from Syrian sniper rifles is devastating to the body. It's not the bullet, but the shock wave as the large caliber bullet passes through the body from long-range. Enormous portions of the body's soft tissue are literally 'blown away' by the concussion- leaving war-criminal like wounds that need repair. But in addition are the victims of Assad's gas attacks as well; something the Israelis have been preparing for in the last few decades- never imagining that they would use these trained skills on foreign civilians.

When Kati finished her explanation, Sobhy sat back, stunned. He clearly had never heard of the level of horror playing out in Syria. Like a majority of countries in the Arab world, the censorship of media imagery by a government was more the rule rather than the exception. Although Egypt was somewhat more liberal in its approach, and slightly more democratic than most other Arab states, the Supreme Council of Armed Forces under the continued leadership of General al Sisi still tended to shield its civilians from Syria's atrocities and the wanton destruction of the state's infrastructure. For the most part, this was not necessarily the desire to protect its citizens from the horror of war, but to try, in secret, to prevent her own from rebelling in a more violent fashion. After the first couple of months of the Egyptian Spring of 2011, the violent aspects of the popular overthrow of the Mubarak Regime subsided. Yes, demonstrations still abounded, and yes, random acts of terror occurred. But for the most part, Egyptians hoped that the system could reset itself and the country get back on stable footing in a peaceful way.

Sobhy's substantial respect for Israel was taken to a new level. He was profoundly moved by what Kati told everyone.

"*Ya'Allah!*" He proclaimed. "Why doesn't the world know about all this? Why is Israel keeping silent about the good that it's doing? I don't get it."

Everyone looked at him with that 'patronizing grandpa you should have known better' look. Suddenly, the light-bulb 'aha' moment clicked on in his head. He ruefully smiled.

"I get it now. It's that age-old fine line between public relations and secrecy. Of course Israel wants to shout to the world about the good it is trying to do. Of course Israel wants to prove that it deserves a place in the region, and be a positive contributing presence. But at what cost? The Syrian refugees, upon returning home, could find themselves in the headlights of horrific retribution even by relatives should they know that they were treated in Israel."

Kati smiled at him. "You're 120% right, *habibi.* But Israel has taken small steps lately in announcing these humanitarian gestures. Our President, Reuven Rivlin, has publicly visited the Galilee Med Center now, alluding to their work without going into great detail. And in addition, a documentary was created, called "The Syrian Patient." It was to be broadcast on our *Arutz Ehad,* Channel One. However, it was postponed by the army censor for a couple of months. Portions that were felt to compromise the safety of some of the Syrian patients were edited out in order to protect their identity."

"So what do we do?" The Egyptian asked.

"How would like to have Syrian citizenship?" Eitan winked and smiled at him.

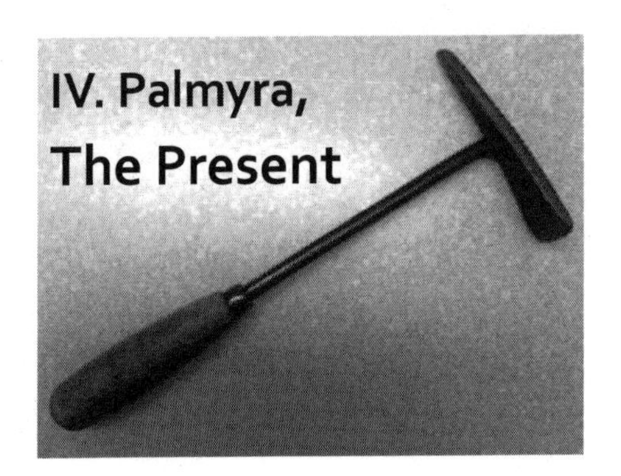

IV. Palmyra, The Present

Although it was already mid-morning, the sky still hadn't lightened. This was due to the heavy smoke that hung over the city- the lingering cloud that was the result of the dawn air strike by a squadron of Belgian fighters. Their task was to soften up or destroy ISIS positions on the outskirts of the city, before Syrian rebels launched a ground assault. However, the Syrian civilians would bear the brunt of the missile strikes. ISIS fighters were too deeply dug in to suffer much. Only a direct hit would wipe out their positions and, so far, the Belgians had only succeeded in taking out one anti-aircraft gun position and a secondary headquarters building. The terrorists were embedded in their shelters; while Palmyra's civilian population scrambled for a safety that simply didn't exist above grade. A dozen innocent civilians were killed by the explosions, and dozens more were murdered by ISIS as they tried to storm the dug-in ISIS positions, seeking a respite from the air attack.

Immediately after the jets flew back to their base in Turkey, while the pall blanketed the town, ISIS media crews began to video the civilian carnage. The voiceovers were strident in their condemnation of the allied air campaign. In addition, the language used was quite clear- *all* of the dead Syrians had been martyred at the hands of the infidels of the west, none by ISIS. What the ISIS commanders didn't know was that a brave Syrian boy shot footage with his cellphone of the ISIS massacre and quickly uploaded it before his battery died. The five minute clip went viral, and was picked up by media networks all over the world. The sad part about it was that the video was 'preaching to the choir,' there weren't enough Syrians with operating cell phones or computers to see the lie unfold against their brethren. The jammed radio airwaves for a 12-mile radius around Palmyra were ISIS controlled, and their message was loud and clear. No westerners were going to help; rather, they were going to destroy indiscriminately. It was their way of ridding the world of the *WOG*, 'the Wiley Oriental Gentleman,' a term of disdain that had been around since the British and French Mandates following World War One.

The reality was that ISIS now embarked on a campaign of terror designed to destroy Palmyra and its pagan heritage. What had been the jewel of Syria 2300 years ago was in the crosshairs of eradication at the hands of the barbarian.

Palmyra was sacked after a second revolt. Aurelian lamented in a letter to one of his lieutenants, "We have not spared the women, we have slain the children, we have butchered the old men." Today, that dire role is being enacted by the ISIS invaders. They have killed scores of civilians near Palmyra and executed soldiers in its ancient amphitheater, in order to make yet another grotesque video documenting a new age of barbarism. In a region once ruled by a strong-willed queen, women who don't bend to ISIS' narrow beliefs may be sold into sex slavery. Perhaps Zenobia's ambition outstripped her resources, but the ideal of an Arab empire equal to that of Rome still animates the dreams of many. The great Arab civilization of modern time still awaits its champion; but it is the values embodied by Zenobia and her city that will be the hallmarks of its success, and not ISIS' rejection of modernity, its persecution of believers in other faiths, its subjugation of women, and its abolition of history.

*****

Abu Bakr al-Baghdadi, whose real name was Ibrahim al-Badri, was had been a lecturer of Islamic studies and an *Imam* at mosques in Baghdad and Falluja. He had also served as an officer in the army of Saddam Hussein. After being interred as a prisoner of war by the US for several years following the Second Gulf War, he was released. However, during his time in prison, he became a radical Moslem, intent on the destruction of his corner of the world in order to re-envision it in the name of *Allah*. However, the methodology he would choose to employ would be one of violent terror. Once he moved to Syria, he would go on to become the leader of ISIL.

ISIS believed Palmyra to be somehow a distinctively Arab place, where Zenobia stood up to the Roman emperor. "Concerning the historical city, we will preserve it," an ISIS commander, Abu Laith al-Saudi, told a Syrian radio station. "What we will do is pulverize the statues the miscreants used to pray to." However, ISIS' rationale would actually run counter to what al- Saudi claimed, and for a very practical reason- income. Anything 'not bolted down' would be pillaged by ISIS. But it wouldn't be destroyed. The few You Tube videos and pictures that were distributed by the PR people of the Islamic State were all a smokescreen. The portable art, no matter how offensive to their religious philosophy, would be hoarded and auctioned off on the black market to international antiquities dealers and shady private owners. It is almost incredible to believe that there were wealthy people who would pay a small fortune to procure some of the world's most wonderful pieces of art- illegally. These folks would then put it on private display in an unbelievably secure basement vault- for their eyes only (without 007 in sight!). It gave them pleasure to sit in front of this magnificent testimony to the artistic talents of the human experience, without another soul having knowledge of it. And the worst part of it, they probably don't even care, their egos are so immense. These high end theft recipients actually would feel that they were the rightful owners.

Khaled al-Asaad was known as 'Mr. Palmyra.' He had a lifelong connection to the town, having been born into a prominent family in the area in 1934. In fact, he even named one of his daughters 'Zenobia,' after the famed Palmyrene Queen.

Although he had a degree in history from Damascus University he had no formal training in archaeology - all his knowledge in this field was self-taught. He had spent 40 years of his life involved in the ancient city and its preservation. Eventually, curating the ruins at the UNESCO World Heritage site would become his life's work.

As ISIS moved closer and closer to the city, surrounding and besieging it, al-Asaad and his son-in-law Khalil actively participated in the rescue of 400 antiquities even as the town was being taken over by the terrorists. As he was finally making plans for his family's escape, he was captured by enemy.

Their anger was palpable. The local warlord, *Abu Nidal*, 'Father of the Struggle,' in charge of the siege of Palmyra was livid. Hundreds of antiquities appeared to have been spirited off, and Abu Bakr al-Bagdadi would be furious. There were no fewer than seven 'investors,' ready to spend upwards of $11 million dollars for the most prized of antiquities that were to be removed from the ancient city once the siege was successful. But now, with the local museum and the site relatively stripped of portable art, the loss of this income would mean the very real possibility that Abu Nidal would lose his life as al-Bagdadi vented his wrath at the one he deemed to be responsible for this loss.

As a result, *Abu Nidal* would stall for time, and ruthlessly torture al-Asaad, by then anold man well into his 80s. *'He should break soon, and I will recover the lost items, and all will be well with Abu Bakr,'* he confidently thought.

Meanwhile, one of his lieutenants, Mohamed el Moussa, an erstwhile, yet entirely unworldly *Jihadi*, had befriended one of the former guards of the archaeological site. He had struck up a conversation with the man and learned of a number of inscribed stones that still littered the site. Apparently they had not yet been removed for safekeeping by the 'western pawn,' al-Asaad. "They are sure to fetch a very good price on the black market," said the local Syrian. Of course, he was fervently hoping that the ISIS fighter would not kill him after getting the information from him. He asked for assurances for his life, and that of his family as well. After all, the artifacts were deemed to be priceless- but he was sure that they could command a 'down-to-earth' mini-fortune to unscrupulous collectors. ISIS certainly wasn't going to stand on ceremony if they could make money off western greed.

El Moussa was not the brightest oil lamp in the desert. He actually did promise the man safety and security for his entire family- if they would flee from Palmyra after having been given a letter of safe transit and vowed that they would never return or speak of the man's perfidy. Now el Moussa needed to secure a letter of transit. He smiled briefly as he remembered an old movie he once saw about Morocco in World War II.

'Rick, you've got to get me the letters of transit!' said Signor Ugarte. El Moussa remembered the actor, a fellow who looked like a ferret, thought the fighter. Peter Lorre's acting skills could have that effect on even the most uneducated person, decades later. As he laughed out loud, the former guard suddenly feared for his life- misinterpreting the outbreak as one of ruthless cold-heartedness. His eyes flitted from el Moussa to the doorway and back. As the ISIS underling pulled his *keffiyeh* edge away from his face and began to wipe his tearing eyes, the Syrian jumped up and kicked dirt into the fighter's eyes. Blinded for a moment, he fell off his stool. The Palmyrene guard burst out the door of the small hut and started to run away from the excavation site's office area and storage facility. Roaring in anger and embarrassed that he was bested by this 'nobody,' he quickly wiped his face and exploded out the door

in a rage. Brandishing his AK-74, he spun around twice before seeing the fleeing man- already 50 meters away. The only thought was one of revenge, and he raised the weapon before even thinking. He had the gun set on three-round bursts, as ordained by his commanding officer, *Abu Nidal*. But his blind rage made him sight and then hold the trigger down, emptying the entire 30-round magazine. Only a few bullets found their mark, but that was all that was needed. The guard was down.

El Moussa lowered his weapon and walked slowly to the fallen Syrian. A nudge with the toe of his sandal was all it took. The man was dead. And now he had no clue as to the whereabouts of the inscribed stones, nor how to further get into the good graces of his commanding officer. He simply had to scour the site and see if he could find them. He absently wondered if he would be able to identify an inscribed stone. He hadn't told a soul, but el Moussa was illiterate. His faith, learned by rote, had gotten him this far in the *Jihad*, but he was worried that his dreams could be dashed now.

Should he confide in a comrade, or keep this all to himself? The man's body would soon enough be ravaged by the wild dogs that foraged the citadel area after dark- the area long abandoned by the local civilian population. And in these days of 'The Wild West' as his commanding officer called it, fond of US western movies in spite of his blind hatred for all western ideology, no one bothered counting rounds of ammunition. He could always request more and not even worry about giving an account of the expended rounds.

After shaking free an *Al Rashid 100s* cigarette from a slightly crumpled pack and lighting it, el Moussa took a deep drag and felt the raw burn travel down his throat. Ever since the Americans had pulled out of Iraq, the 'good stuff,' American-made smokes, was either no longer available or completely affordable. In the past, his friends had lavishly bestowed on all the ISIS fighters these spoils of war. Now, they were all scrounging for anything that was within their meager price range. 'These must be made of camel dung,' he thought.

But as he finished and threw the butt in the dust, he realized that he needed to act on his own. He couldn't trust anyone. One thing that he had learned at the expense of others, was that *jihadis* would just as readily turn in fellow *jihadis* in order to get ahead, as kill an infidel. So now, he needed to find those inscriptions, and fast. His life may be at risk if he didn't come through.

His plan was simple. He would seek out one of the older fighters who had been at Palmyra from the outset and ask for a 'tour' of the remains that were going to be destroyed by the ISIS operatives. He would call it 'getting to be familiar' with the ensuing task. Certainly no one could fault him for this zealousness. After all, weren't all good Moslems supposed to be zealous in their defense of the faith and the teachings of the Prophet Mohamed? This good plan would be put into action the next morning, he vowed.

El Moussa smiled as he went off to the storage tent to replenish his ammunition, and surreptitiously survey the company of troops to find a suitable 'guide.'

As he walked through the makeshift encampment, he was dismayed to find many 'old' men. By that, he meant those who had survived numerous encounters with both Syrian soldiers and rebels. It seemed that the triangular war that had been raging in Syria for decades had taken its toll on the population. From the Assad family's assault on civilians beginning in the early 1980s to the present, to ISIS' blitz into the countryside from neighboring Iraq, to Russian airstrikes in support of a tottering governmental regime, hundreds of thousands were killed, injured or displaced. The land was nearly devoid of population, with a mass exodus flooding Jordan to the southeast, Turkey to the northwest and the Lebanon to the west. And with more and more crossing borders every day, these neighboring states were reaching a breaking point as well. The frustration of this tragic group became more and more evident, as they lashed out at their benefactors, rioting and wreaking havoc on an already taxed infrastructure. As a result, the Arab states were taking a hard look at humanitarian policies in order to protect themselves from the potential of their own civil wars- fueled by the inordinate amount of support initially offered to refugees in comparison to what they historically had offered their own civilian populations.

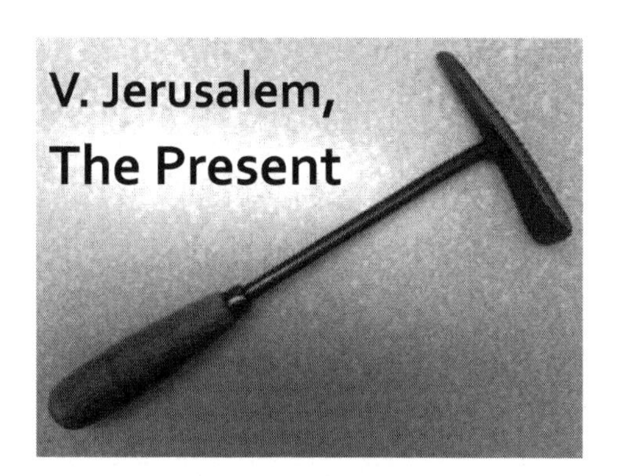

The plan was audacious, but extremely reasonable. And Kati was not kidding when she said that we had to make Sobhy a Syrian refugee. It really wouldn't be that difficult. After all, Eli Cohen was able to fool the Syrians almost two generations ago. I mentioned that to the group, and the Egyptian sat up with a start.

"But if memory serves me correctly, it didn't end well for him!" He grimaced.

"Yeah, he eventually was caught out as an Israeli spy, but the good that he did in passing along vital information that saved the lives of hundreds of members of Israel's famed Golani Brigade, well, as the American commercial on TV says, 'Priceless!'" I didn't reiterate the final ending. Cohen's remains are still somewhere in Syria, most likely in an unmarked grave. I recalled a symposium that was organized in 2016 in Tiberias that remembered his exploits as an Israeli hero, and that the Israelis don't take their history, their existence, lightly. Everyone is remembered in one way or another.

"Remind me of the good parts," Sobhy said. I went on to recount his tale.

The Mossad recruited Eli Cohen after Director-General Meir Amit, looking for a special agent to infiltrate the Syrian government, found his file. He was then given a false identity as a Syrian businessman who was returning to the country after living in Argentina for several years. To establish his cover, Cohen moved to Argentina in 1961. Cohen moved to Damascus in February 1962 under the alias Kamel Amin Thaabet. Cohen continued his social life as he had done in Argentina. He spent considerable time in cafes listening to political gossip. He also held parties at his home, which turned into orgies for high-placed Syrian ministers, businessmen, and others. The other Syrians found him lavish in his expenditures on their behalf. Eventually, these contacts were extended to Syrian officers and high-ranking officials in Damascus. During a period of four years, through the end of 1964, he sent an extraordinary amount of intelligence to the Israeli Army radio and secret letters. His most famous achievement was during a couple of tours of the Golan Heights with staff officers that he had befriended in the Syrian army. Cohen made repeated visits to the southern frontier zone, providing photographs and sketches of Syrian positions. He collected intelligence on the Syrian fortifications there. Feigning sympathy for the soldiers exposed to the sun, Cohen had Eucalyptus trees planted at every bunker. The trees were used as targeting markers by the Israeli military during the Six-Day War and enabled Israel to capture the Golan Heights with incredible in two days.

Cohen learned of a secret plan by Syria to create three successive defensive lines of bunkers and mortars; the IDF had expected to encounter only a single line. They attacked armed with this information.

A new Syrian Intelligence Colonel, Ahmed Su'edani, trusted no one. He became aware of the fact that there was a spy in Syria's midst- but he didn't know who it was, or for whom they worked. Syria's new global BFF, the Soviet Union, made a gift of a great deal of espionage equipment to aid their allies. Using Soviet-made radio-frequency tracking equipment, aided by hired Soviet experts, a period of radio silence was observed. With everyone off the air, it was hoped that any illegal transmissions could be identified. Large numbers of questionable radio transmissions were detected and traced to their source. On 24 January 1965, Syrian security officers broke into Cohen's apartment where he was caught in the middle of a transmission to Israel. On 18 May 1965, Cohen was publicly hanged in Marjeh Square in Damascus. For decades, repeated requests for his body were made via the UN and Red Cross, to no avail. In a bizarre, cruel and painful twist, on 20 September 2016, a video of Cohen's body after his execution was posted on Facebook by an unknown Syrian group called "Syrian art treasures." This was fifty years later. No video of the execution was previously known to exist.

The mood turned somber, and the silence was broken by our Egyptian friend, Sobhy.

"To peace, brotherhood and sisterhood, and to all of us. *L'chaim!*". We raised our glasses and, with resolve, began to put together the details of our archaeological rescue mission of Syrian Jewish antiquities. I smiled at our modern day 'Egyptian Eli Cohen' and fervently prayed for a safer outcome for him.

We all vowed to visit his memorial plaque on Mt. Herzl, Israeli's main military cemetery in Jerusalem. It was located in the Garden of the Missing Soldiers- dedicated to Eliahu (Eli) Cohen.

*****

In order to carry out this seemingly impossible task, many others needed to be recruited on a 'need to know' basis. After all, plausible deniability was the rule rather than the exception these days. A friend of Eitan's, Asa Ben Dov, formerly in the IDF intelligence corps, was enlisted to give us some ideas. After Eitan outlined the plan, Ben Dov went one step further, so enthusiastic was he for the project. In the Mideast there is a version of the 'six degrees of Kevin Bacon.' But in this case, it was 'the friend of a cousin of a friend who knew someone who was connected...' Ben Dov had that kind of connection who got official 'unofficial' help to create this legend for Sobhy.

So who was this 'mystery man?The legend that was painstakingly being created was that of an Egyptian family that came to southern Syria generations earlier. In this earlier age, before Israel, during the chaos of the late 30s/early 40s, travel was no less a harrowing experience, but a simpler one without the presence of the Jewish state yet. Originally from Alexandria, they emigrated across northern Sinai, through El Arish and Gaza. From there, they skirted the coast and the Jewish presence in and around Tel Aviv, through the hill country and on into the Galilee. At that point, they navigated the northern shore of the Sea, and the southern edge of the Golan. The rolling hills around the small village of As Suwayda eventually became home.

The 'legend maker' in Jerusalem chose this town because it was a Druze village in the midst of a prominent Greek Orthodox Christian community. This was ideal, because Sobhy's family were Coptic Christians. We were told by Ben Dov that a high percentage of any created identity should have a significant portion of truth and familiarity in it. This would keep the operative in a familiar zone, and less liable to make slip-ups if and when he was under pressure.

The name Druze is derived from the name of Muhammad bin Ismail Nashtakin ad-Darazī (from Persian *darzi*, "seamster") who was an early preacher. The faith was preached by Hamza ibn 'Alī ibn Ahmad, an Ismaili mystic and scholar. He came to Egypt in 1014 and gathered leaders from across the known world to establish the movement. Because of this connection with Egypt, Sobhy, too, knew a great deal about them. In Lebanon, Syria, Israel and Jordan, the Druze have official recognition as a separate religious community with their own religious court system.

There were other reasons as well to 'locate' Sobhy's family in this town. He was 'created' as a history teacher, and his familiarity with ancient history was an ideal background. The city was founded by the Nabataeans as *Suada*. It became known as *Dionysias* in the Hellenistic period and later during the Roman Empire, for the god Dionysus, patron of wine - the city is situated in a famous ancient wine-producing region. The name *Dionysias* replaced the former Nabataean name of *Suada* in 149 CE after the Nabataean assimilation by the conquering Romans.

Dionysias was a part of the Roman province of Arabia Petraea, and received the rights of *Civitas*, citizenry, under the reign of Commodus between 180–185 CE. This name remained in use during the Byzantine Empire. *Dionysias* then was a diocese under the auspices of a bishop from *Bosra* to the southeast.

Yaqut al-Hamawi noted in the 1220s that *As Suwaida* was "a village of the Hauran Province." He was an Arab biographer and geographer of Greek origin, renowned for his encyclopedic writings on the Moslem world. Born in Constantinople, Yāqūt became a slave of a trader named Askar ibn Abi Nasr al-Hamawi who lived in Baghdad, Iraq.

As Sobhy would call it, this portion of the background of his fictional identity was a 'no-brainer' (he had picked up waaay too many English 'idiots' as he said!) because of his true field of study. This gave his 'creators' a tremendous sense of optimism that he would be successful. However, there were a myriad of rough edges to work out. He would work with a linguist on Syrian Arabic nuances vs Egyptian ones. This wasn't too much of a difficulty because, if questioned, he could merely pass it off as coming from speaking with grandparents who spoke with an Egyptian dialect when a young boy.

The most difficult task was that of appearance. Not so much his image, as someone of Arab ancestry, but as a wounded individual. Once again, Eitan's numerous and varied contacts were of great value. Back at the beginning of the 1980s, Hollywood decided that the story of Masada and its mountain-top fortress, was an impelling one. As a result, ABC created a mini-series that later was condensed into a two hour and forty minute movie. Truth be told, the mini-series, although lengthy, was the much better docu-drama as it told the story in-depth. (I would have said 'fleshed out' but that was reserved for the fictional portion surrounding the role of actress Barbara Carrera).

This incredible cinematic event that recalled the siege, conquest and occupation of Masada at the end of the Jewish Revolt against Rome in 73 CE was primarily filmed at the mountain. At least, all of the exterior scenes were filmed there. Interior shots were all done on a soundstage in London. As a result, no one working on the set from Arad got a chance to see the actress in person. Because of the desire to be as historically accurate (outside of the love-story that was deemed essential by Hollywood). Hundreds of *Aradnikim* were employed during the several months that the filming entailed. A mini-Masada was constructed to the west of the actual Judean Desert site, compressed in size to only a few dozen meters north/south rather than the real 600 x 300 meter mountaintop. Everything was made of timber and Styrofoam, but looked quite authentic. Gaffers, 'shleppers,' construction workers, cooks, cleaners and extras were all given a decent wage during the production. In addition, a handful of archaeologists based in the Negev were given the task of 'vetting' the architecture, the costumes, the daily utensils and weaponry, etc. to ensure authenticity. In this vein, both Eitan and I were cast in this role. Even to this day, adjacent to the Roman ramp on the west side of the mountain, the base of the movie set battering ram and several small ballistas adorn the landscape; as kind of a reproduction archaeological park.

So what was our reward? To serve as extras in the film itself! However, Hollywood would succumb to stereotyping in its approach. If you watch the film closely, you'll see what is meant. All of those cast as Judean men, opposed to the Romans, had a pre-requisite beard! Not so with the 'Roman centurions and decurions.' As a result, I was 'cast' as a Roman soldier since I was beardless! (The moustache was hidden by my helmet!)

But the limited on-screen violence and bloodshed was accurate through the miracle of big-screen illusion. A couple of Israeli make-up artists, considered to be the best in the country at that time, were enlisted for the filming. Their talent was remarkable. The blood and gore were 'real' to the vast majority of people witnessing it. Both of them had long-since retired from work full time, but Eitan was able to track one of them, Lior Bat Rimon, and placed a phone call, thus securing her talents. She told him that she could be in Jerusalem in a couple of days, and that something like an appendix scar was *shum davar,* nothing, for her to create. This was pivotal, as it could mean the difference of life or death for Sobhy, should Syrian authorities discover who he was.

*****

Across town, Asa Ben Dov was putting the final touches on the background legend that Sobhy would take into Syria. The intelligence office had worked with him nonstop to provide an almost impenetrable deep cover. He would turn up facts that were airtight, given the situation in Syria.

We decided to meet at the Aroma Café on El Rov Street, in the Mamilla District. It was an ideal spot, just outside the Jaffa Gate of the Old City, and a stone's throw (is that a terrible way to put it?) from *Mishkenot Sha'ananim*, the Jerusalem Artist's Quarter. It was created in the early 1970s by then Mayor Teddy Kollek, an extraordinary visionary and man of peace and reconciliation. In 1973, *Mishkenot Sha'ananim* became a destination for internationally acclaimed authors, artists and musicians visiting Israel- as scholar-in-residence.

But this wasn't always the case for this area. Following the War of Independence, and after the cease-fire which stretched into a 19-year armistice, the Hinnom Valley separating the Old City from western Jerusalem became a no-person's land. It lay devastated, under the watchful eyes of the Jordanians to the east, Israelis to the west and the UN to the south. Uncleared, active minefields, barbed wire and ruined buildings were the rule, rather than exception. I remember the story of a good friend of mine, Hesh Rabin, who recounted the tragic losses incurred by his grandparents, who had made *Aliya*, emigration, to Palestine in the 1920s and made a second-floor walk-up apartment their home for over two decades. With the UN partition vote in November of 1947, violence began to escalate to unimaginable heights aimed at civilians in the holy city. This wasn't limited to Jews, but all Jerusalemites suffered.

At the behest of other family members, the elders 'temporarily' relocated to Paris until the situation settled down. They never returned. Both ended up dying in Paris, heartbroken at their inability to go back to their apartment. But the younger members of the family never told them the reality of the situation. Grandma Rabinovitch (the younger generations had changed their name to Rabin) had a silver framed picture of the Hinnom Valley apartment building on a side table in her XIVth Arrondisement flat. No one told her that the only thing left of her former home was one wall with a bathtub precariously hanging in space, over the rubble of the original building. Nothing else remained.

The district remained in that tragic state until two years after the June 1967 War, when, after the dust settled, Israel began to clear the area, paving the way for the Mamilla District and mall. It was a far cry from the glamorous memories of the past.

Retired colonel Ben Dov sauntered into the coffee shop, not at all looking like a 'retired' military intelligence officer. But of course, regrettably, in Israel, one is never fully 'retired' from a military obligation due to the precarious political and military situation that Israel found itself constantly a part of- in spite of peace with two of her neighbors, Jordan and Egypt. Slung over his shoulder was the ubiquitous backpack that every Israeli seemed to be stapled to from youth.

Eitan greeted him warmly, with a hug, grabbed his arm and brought him over to the table tucked into the far corner of the coffee bar. We got him 'the best cup of coffee in Israel' according to the ads, while we all introduced ourselves. The café wasn't too noisy, but with a loud enough 'hum' to keep any but someone specifically trained in the craft from really overhearing and getting the gist of conversations. As befitting an Israeli officer, he informally dove right in to the research that he had done to create the new Syrian persona.

"Here's what I've come up with, and it's really amazing, even if I do say so myself" he declared.

"It better be, my life's in the balance," Sobhy muttered under his breath. I nudged him in the ribs, but just gently. I fully appreciated his concern.

"I think that I've found just the right balance, and it was an accident, really, that I stumbled upon this stuff. When you came to me, Eitan, with the proposal, and the blessings of both our government and the UN's UNESCO, I thought back to a few years ago just when things were heating up in the Syrian civil war. We were trying to find a way to exploit the growing rift between the Syrian government and her minorities, to give yet another added dimension to Assad's instability. I remembered an article I read in the Lebanon Daily Star. That got me to thinking... You know, that *Bourek* looks really good!" He eyed Eitan's plate enviously.

"*B'seder!* Okay! I'll get you one... potato and onion filled I assume!" Eitan laughed and went to the counter. Upon his return, after a bite, wiping the sesame seeds from his chin, Ben Dov continued to relate his idea to us.

"I found this article about one of Assad's trusted officers, Issam Zahreddine. In 2013 he was promoted from Brigadier General to Major General in the southern district."

"How does this help us?" I asked.

"Well, Zahreddine was originally from the village of Tarba, in the As-Suwaida Governate. His family are Druze, and he was considered to be the most prominent and high-ranking member of the Druze community to work for the Assad regime. " We started to see where this might be going.

Ben Dov continued. "When he was promoted, he was designated to lead the army against the rebels in the southern area where he and his family came from. The hope was that 'a local boy' could sway the community to support the state. However, in 2013, a group of Druze religious figures in Suwaida took the unprecedented step of challenging the regime by urging members of the sect to desert the military, while giving their blessing to the killing of notorious "murderers." Zahreddine was also singled out for assassination. As a result, he was forced to flee the area and was relocated to the area around Raqqa- where he continued his murderous assault on the civilian population. Some said that the extreme violence was personal. So here's my thought, that our friend Sobhy's new identity would be that of a distant relative of the Zahreddine clan. He source of his 'wounding' would not have been a concern to the Israelis, as they were offering humanitarian and medical aid to all Syrian civilians. Then, after being repatriated into the Syrian Golan, he would be 'welcomed back' on the governmental side of things. This would then ideally position him to carry out his task in Palmyra. Because of the widespread damage to infrastructure in Syria, and the fact that smaller governates in the countryside still used paper, it would be almost impossible to verify any of these small details that were only relayed by Sobhy, orally, or with whatever documentation we provided him with on the ground." Ben Dov smiled, sipped his coffee, and swept up the final crumbs of his *Bourek*. "Anybody care for another, my turn to buy" as he got up and headed for the bar.

While we took in everything that he told us, Eitan's phone chirped. He listened for a few moments and disconnected. Lior Bat-Rimon was now consulting with FIRMA Production House, located in Tel Aviv. It was a testament to the direction that Israeli film was headed. After all, over the past decade, four Israeli movies had gotten Oscar nominations for Best Foreign Film. The industry had come light years from its roots with the Geva Film Labs in 1949. She was on the way from Tel Aviv. It wouldn't take long, as the newly constructed light-rail from Tel Aviv to Jerusalem had cut travel time between the two cities to half an hour. Unbelievable! Her stop was only a few minute walk from where we sat, so the smell of fresh-baked *bourekas* was just too overwhelming...

As we finished our second, and Sobhy's third, round of *bourekas* and coffee, a diminutive, salt-n-pepper haired woman 'blew in' to the Aroma Café. I meant it, literally. This dynamo-like powerhouse of a woman almost overwhelmed anyone and anything in her path. Although barely topping five feet in stature, her presence indicated a personality that stood head and shoulders above those in her presence. In many regards, she reminded me of a dear friend, Orit Adato, former Brigadier General in the IDF who commanded the woman's corps and then, upon 'retiring,' became the Commandant of the Israeli Prison System. Remember what I said about 'retiring'? It was that same psyche that transcended everything in the face of extreme confidence (and competence).

But even before she sat down and greeted us, she hit the coffee bar with a vengeance, ordering an *ahwa masbout*, the thick, dark, sweet Turkish coffee that most in Israel referred to as 'mud.' After that, she came over to the table, plopped down in a chair, draping her leg over the armrest, looking like an eternal college student, and took a sip.

"Aahhhhh, heaven," was her initial response. "I've been up for hours completing the make-up portion of a scene from a film that I was commandeered to work on by the company. It's a war film based on our Lebanese debacle a bit over a decade ago." She quickly downed the thick brew, looked at Eitan, and requested another cup. He smiled, got up, and headed to the bar. "I'm Lior, just in case you hadn't figured it," she laughed. If there was any tension, it was immediately dissipated.

"So," Kati said, "let's get to it! I understand that there's no one better in the industry than you."

With a bit of false modesty, Lior simply said, "Israeli film has made unbelievable strides in the 21st century. The miracle of Israeli cinema in the last 10 years isn't measured just by the number of films or their public reception, but by what has been a revolution in production quality. With it comes the extraordinarily real imagery projected on the screen. This has in part been due to technology. But more to the point, it has also been due to the strides made in costume and make-up. Remember the old days of and gelatinous blood, like what we used on *Masada*? That's over and done with. Heavy foundation make-up that was essential with distance shots is no longer necessary because of the sophisticated camera equipment. Now, due to low-level light video cameras such as the JVC GY-HM600 ProHD Camera, we don't have to rely on the 'clown-cheeks in gaslit footlights syndrome' employing early 20th century technology. As a matter of fact, there are actually some *metumtamim,* assholes, in the production side, who honestly feel that make-up artists are no longer needed because of this new equipment!" She was starting to get really hot under her collar. This was very dangerous, because she *wasn't* wearing a collar, just a tee-shirt.

Eitan, got up, put a hand on her shoulder, and told her that he was getting her something to eat; too much caffeine on an empty stomach was making her irritable. We all laughed at this and Lior 'chilled out' a bit.

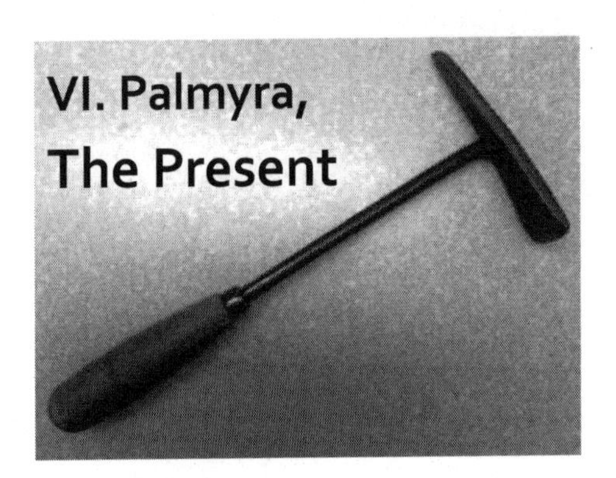

Mohamed el Moussa hadn't slept well in what seemed like a decade. If it wasn't the deplorable conditions he found himself in as the noose tightened around Palmyra, it was the recurring series of nightmares that scared him so much that he feared his heart might stop. The horrific scenes that kept replaying in his head, of violence, bloodlust and terror, were enough to give him a heart attack, or so he thought. He and those in his cadre alternately were the target of attacks by the Syrian government troops, rebels, and Russian and Allied plane bombing runs. When he awoke drenched in sweat, he came around to the sound of the very bombardments that were the focus of his dreams. So, he thought, were they really dreams, or just the background noise of the surrounding reality that was now his life. From one moment to the next he could never be sure; just yesterday he rose to the sound of artillery, the stench of cordite and the visionless eyes of one of the ISIS faithful who apparently had ventured too close to a window ledge during the night and suffered the consequences. If anything, el Moussa had learned to heed the advice of the group commanders. They repeatedly warned of the technology employed by the Syrian army. Night vision glasses were distributed to the army snipers, so that they could ply their lethal trade around the clock. Every evening, the Syrian bedded down in the interior corner of a room, far from an area where the sniper could zero in on him. So far, this had served him well. But who knew how much longer his luck would hold. Seventy-two virgins be damned, he wanted death to come as a result of old age, not a Soviet-era Dragunov rifle.

The milky light of dawn filtered through a hazy concoction of windborne dust and ash. The combat of the past few days had all but obliterated any notion of a clean, fresh daybreak. Added to this toxic mix was the wispy smoke of a few small campfires. Handfuls of men surrounded each, nursing a watered-down cup of coffee and scrap of stale *pita* bread. Although their officers admonished them against setting fires, lest the enemy zero-in on them, no one paid heed any more. The constant, lingering pall that hung over the city meant that no one could ascertain where the smoke came from. El Moussa dusted off the best that he could, grabbed his battered Kalachnikov which had been with him since the beginning, over a century ago, or so he thought, and picked his way to a fire where he recognized a couple of the men. Well, not men any longer- his eyes told him. These were just teens. *Shouldn't they be in school, studying, chasing girls, promenading down their village streets with an arrogant swagger,* he thought. He started to smile, but then shook his head violently. *This is what we're fighting against, or at least what they told us in Friday sermons.* The image of normalcy quickly left him. But it was replaced with doubt that had been nagging him for the past year or so. Was that life before the war so bad? He no longer knew, or for that matter, really cared. He just wanted to live out the day.

In order to do that, he surmised, he would have to get out of this militant mindset, melt into the countryside, and live his life quietly until things sorted themselves out. But how to do that? There were no jobs to speak of out there. People farmed their own small plots, in isolated villages, away from major fighting. If they needed something like cooking gas, they could save up a bit of extra produce and barter it to someone who had a bit of extra benzene. El Moussa had neither land, money nor barter-able goods. He only knew how to fight.

He lit an *al Rashid 100* cigarette, sat back, and pondered his situation. He remembered the artifacts that he saw and had briefly mentioned to Abu Bakr al Baghdadi,, his commander, with whom he had hoped to ingratiate himself regarding the antiquities business. Al Bagdadi had initially brushed him off, and in the intervening week or so seemed to have entirely forgotten the episode in light of the recent aerial bombardment and struggle to survive. But el Moussa hadn't forgotten. He made the decision that he would have to try to sell these antiquities on his own, pocket the money, escape the ragtag terror army, and then blend into the countryside far from Palmyra. His plan then evolved- with the necessity of finding an abandoned plot of land essential so that he could settle down in anonymity. He wouldn't need to know a single thing about farming, as the money that he got for selling an antiquity or two could quietly make small purchases in order to survive. But first, he needed to find another 'old-timer' who might secretly point him in the right direction.

Slowly, the Syrian wandered between campfires. It was harder and harder to find anyone of his age. Finally, as the mist, fog and smoke began to dissipate in mid-morning, he came upon a battered group squatting around a smoldering barrel that had served the night before for warmth, and now to warm water for weak tea. One of the men glanced up, with a look of vague recognition, and beckoned him over.

"El Moussa, right?" The man asked. Mohamed nodded warily. "It's me, Ahmed Taybieh. If I remember, we trained together in the *Beka'a* over a century ago! And even though we didn't really know each other back then, we are from the same village I think." He heartily laughed at his own small joke. El Moussa gave a half-hearted smile and pulled up a flat paving stone that had been liberated from a ruined house nearby. He gratefully accepted the cup of watery tea and took a deep draught. He closed his eyes, allowing the warmth to penetrate his body. *Perhaps this man might have some answers that I'm looking for about the ruins, and just maybe he'd want to become a partner of sorts in order to get out of here. I'd gladly give him a portion,* he thought.

"*Yallah*, come on with me. I have to make a round of the camp" Taybieh said after allowing time to finish the tea and catch up a bit on what they had been doing since being separated after their training. Reluctantly, el Moussa got up and followed the war-weary combatant. He saw himself in the way that his comrade slowly rose on stiff joints, rolled his neck to loosen days of kinks and knots that had formed, and give a faint sigh of resignation. *Yes, this could probably be the man also looking for a way out.* A glimmer of hope might be seen now.

The two men worked their way around the encampment in a methodical fashion. Going counter-clockwise, el Moussa realized that their last inspection station took them immediately adjacent to the once-magnificent ruins of Palmyra, reduced in most places to rubble. He thought that now might be the time to broach the subject.

"So, *habibi*, what do you think of the blasphemous site of Palmyra now? There's nothing remaining of the sacrilegious temples of the ancestors. After all, *Allah*, praised be His Name, was the creator, the shaper, the maker of the Day of Doom, and eternal guardian of the believers." El Moussa had recited some of the 99 Most Beautiful Names of Allah in order to test the waters of belief of his re-acquaintance.

"You know, I think that I am a good Moslem, but when I look at Syria and the devastation, much killing was done in the name of *Allah*, the compassionate and merciful, I wonder where the compassion and mercy has gone. If He is testing us, how long does this interminable test continue, and does it continue if, in His eyes, we are failures?"

El Moussa smiled, and he was certain that this was the man to help him find a way out.

As they skirted the perimeter, they approached the once-impressive Tetrapylon, a square structure of four plinths that held four columns, the wrath of ISIS fundamentalists became evident. Two of the four columns and their bases had been reduced to piles of rubble. The official news agency of the Syrian regime, SANA, had reported that the monumental gate had been "intentionally destroyed using explosives." UNESCO branded the actions as 'cultural cleansing' of the past in order to conform to ISIS' strict interpretation of Islam. Irina Bokova, the head of UNESCO, further condemned the group, saying that it "shows how extremists are terrified by history and culture."

"I recalled all of that," Taybieh confided. "I was there when it happened. We had taken the site, and we engaged in an intense fire-fight with Syrian soldiers. According to my commander, many of them fled into the antiquities park. We were ordered in and killed a couple of dozen of them. When things quieted down, I was assigned the task of gathering the Syrian soldiers' weapons and ammunition. It wasn't so pleasant, but since we all were using Kalachnikovs, the 7.62mm bullets were interchangeable. Also some of us were able to replace our own, battle-worn guns. Yes, I know the hype, that the AK47 had been around since, well, 1947 (hence its name) and were almost indestructible, but there is a shelf life. Plus, the Syrian soldiers wouldn't be needing them anymore. *Allah* be praised." He laughed uneasily, know full well that the situation could just as easily been reversed.

"So what do you make of all that?" el Moussa continued to probe in what he took to be a round-about fashion. His comrade stated that, in essence, he felt that ISIS philosophy had gone a bit far. After all, the past was long before the Prophet, praised be His name, and that the world had evolved spiritually to Islam. Now the religious beliefs of Jews and Christians, he mused, was an altogether different story. Yes, they were People of the Book, and deserved credit for such. However, they willfully ignored the newest teachings of the Prophet and God. They had been given ample time to adapt to the Seal of Prophecy, yet continued to choose not to do so. As a result, *their* society and faith could be destroyed in order to rebuild under the umbrella of Islam. It was, in the ISIS spiritual leadership's eyes, a deliberate transgression and therefore was punishable by all means in God's eyes. The physical destruction of synagogues, churches, community centers and entire communities was seen as a necessary evil.

"And what of the artifacts of antiquity, like at Palmyra? Do we grind them totally into the dust? Or is there a way to gain benefit for our cause in the meantime?" Now he got to the nub of his line of inquiry.

"The infidels seem to have an extraordinary passion for ancient things, even if they are not part of their direct culture. Look at the way that members of the *Dar al Harb*, the world of unbelievers, continually flocked to all the ancient cities of the Mideast in their relentless search for the foundations of humankind. All they need to do is read the *Koran*." Taybieh was passionate in his belief, whether it was true or not. He went on to say that he felt that the tables should be turned on the infidels. If they persisted on trying to save these idolatrous bits of history, ISIS should reap the rewards of this misguided approach. In other words, it was in the best interest of the cause that these foreigners pay to preserve the pagan past, and that ISIS should be the recipient of the money. After all, the *Koran* makes it perfectly clear that anything we think that we own in this world is only a trust from *Allah*. And only after we tithe freely and generously are we able to be compensated in our lifetimes. But how would that compensation occur, and would it be sufficient to lead them out of this nightmare and into a somewhat decent world?

As they walked through the archaeological debris, el Moussa kicked at some of the rubble with the toe of his combat boot.

"*Stana Schwayeh*! Stop! Wait a minute! What are you doing?" Taybieh grabbed his arm and pulled him back from the ruins. "This is, was, an archaeological site! Have you no respect for our Syrian history, even though it's not Islamic? It is still under our control, and unless we hear otherwise from our officers, we should protect it. Only when they give us an order do we act. LEAVE IT ALL ALONE!" Now this gave el Moussa a glimmer of hope. If Taybieh truly felt this way, then perhaps, to a small degree, he had enough respect for antiquities to prevent them from being blown up or sold by ISIS commanders. Yet on the other hand, maybe he could, with subtlety, convince him that some artifacts could be sold on the side for *their* just rewards after all that they'd been through.

"So, let me understand this. You're saying that it was wrong to destroy these ancient places, since they are still a part of our heritage? But now that some of them are destroyed, it would be wrong to crush them into dust, that we should allow the 'ruined ruins' to remain?"

"*Aywa*, yes. They shouldn't be further damaged" Taybieh confirmed.

"But, when the war is over, and we triumph in the name of Islam, what will become of these places? Won't the imams order them totally destroyed and remove all memory of the pagan past, *Allah* be praised" El Moussa probed further.

Taybieh hesitated, faltered in his reply. "I suppose that's right. But I'm not sure that I agree to that idea of complete destruction. Maybe it would be best to make the ruins unrecognizable and then leave the rubble as a reminder..."

"Meanhwhile..." el Moussa pressed him, "the world still places a value on these bits and pieces of history- just look at all the museums that contain parts of our heritage. And I understand that they paid more money for them than you and I have ever seen in our lives. Do you think that it's fair to us, risking our lives, the lives of our families, for *Allah*, praised be His name, for Islam, for the purity of faith and people?"

The other Syrian stopped walking and sat down on a wall fragment. He drew his pack of smokes, lit one, and offered it to el Moussa. Then he took one for himself and took a deep breath, sucking in the foul smoke of the local brand. Clearly he was intrigued. They looked each other in the eye, unsure as to what was next. The tension was palpable, but then el Moussa 'dove' into the deep end.

"If the foreigners are so interested, couldn't we help them a bit in their quest to preserve the ancient past, but then get rewarded in a small way? Shouldn't we get rewarded in a small way? After all, our loyalty to *Da'esh*, and don't get me wrong, I care deeply for the cause and love *Allah* with all my heart, but our loyaltyhasn't given us a good life so far. Yes, we've had our needs taken care of- food, uniforms, weapons, etc. But what of our families? All I've seen is bloodshed, violence, the deaths of my friends, and not a *Lira* to my name. What harm would it do, *could* it do, if we were to 'liberate' just a couple of pieces and get them to someone who would take care of them, and give us a bit of change to send to our loved ones? I really see no harm. I already have an inscribed piece of stone hidden away if I could just get up enough courage. I have a cousin, who knows a friend, whose nephew goes back and forth between lines" he held out his hands, palm's up- making his point clear.

Taybieh looked away, his eyes taking a far-off view as he considered the proposal. "What you say has some merit. Your words mostly seem to fit what I think. But give me a bit of time to let you know. Maybe by the end of today..." Both men sat back, finished their cigarettes, and resumed their patrol. But their minds were on the conversation.

*****

That evening, around their 'designated fire barrel' the two were unusually quiet. Their companions took note, saw that they were preoccupied with something, and let them be. After their dinner of pita, rice and scrawny boiled chicken, they got up to take a walk around. However, they would only go to the perimeter, as it could be too dangerous to venture any farther. They had learned their lessons well now that ISIS was on the defensive- the territory under their control shrinking on a daily basis.

When they were between sentries, Taybieh broke the silence quietly. "I think that I agree, we should go for it." El Moussa stopped abruptly, looked hard and deep into his friend's soul, and smiled.

"*Ya'Allah*!" He clasped the other's shoulder. "Tomorrow I'll show you the piece, and we can put the plan into action." He then took the other man's arm, and linked together, they slowly returned to camp.

*****

Dawn filtered through the haze, as it had done for weeks now- smoky and polluted with the residue of war. The same old-same old routine of weak tea, stale flatbread and, if lucky, a bit of goat cheese would make up breakfast. Then it would be topped off by a smoke, before getting the commander's orders. Al-Bagdadi himself had come to this group of fighters to inspire them with a pep talk. But it was lukewarm at best. It seemed that even the great Ibrihim al Badriwas was losing the will to carry on in the face of defeat. But the men gave the appearance of enthusiastic support.

After the cheering subsided, and the troop dispersed to carry out their assigned tasks, the two Syrians discovered that their orders would separate them for the next day or so. Parting words of encouragement promised that the aim of their conversation would continue eventually. It was sealed with a hug and kisses on both cheeks. Their mood was elated, but in a subdued way. After el Moussa was out of sight, Taybieh sat down and took stock of the situation.

Little did el Moussa know, but Taybieh actually had a change of heart after he slept on the offer. After all, he wasn't a clan member with el Moussa, didn't have any village or family loyalty to him. Why should he split any kind of payment with the man for selling antiquities in secret? Okay, it was his idea, but still... he needed to look out for the Taybieh family's needs and perhaps then slip off to rejoin them in his birth village. But he had to be the 'sole survivor' of all this, leaving no evidence of any sort behind. Realizing what he had to do, he stood a bit straighter as he headed over to the commander's tent. Thirty yards out, he approached the first line of guards. They were stationed at the distance deemed to be outside a blast zone from an IED, should a disillusioned ISIS fighter wish to make a point. He smiled, stopped, and held out his arms and spread his legs for the inevitable 'pat-down.' Once done, the guard even smiled and waved him on to the next line, another 10 yards on. The same procedure, but this time the guard asked his business and told him to wait. He disappeared in the tent beyond, and Taybieh lit up and bided his time.

"So I hear that you have some news for me that might bolster morale" Abu Bakr al-Baghdadi beckoned Taybieh into the tent after the vetting process. "If this is so, *Allah* be praised, we certainly could use some good news. Please, sit." Ahmed glanced about nervously and sat opposite the commander on a worn carpet, on the other side of the fire pit. The troop leader poured a glass of tea and offered it to his fighter. "Drink, then we'll talk." His smile seemed to be genuine, but in this day and age, who knew...

After a few minutes of idle talk, the typical desert way of a polite entry into an intense conversation, the gist of the matter was now at hand. Al Baghdadi listened intently to the tale told by his Syrian commando. He paid attention to the undercurrent of complaint about conditions and pay for his fighters. But these were nothing compared to his interpretation of treasonous activity by one of his own. This insubordination and lack of discipline dismayed him far more than the issue of intolerable conditions, poor pay, lack of reliable weapons and ammunition. He demanded absolute loyalty regardless of the situation, and for a breach in loyalty, a trial was essential. He saw it as an attempt to undermine his authority and, ultimately, undermine the cause. However, the case would be taken to a makeshift Islamic court. The local imam would oversee the case, someone whose loyalty was to Abu Bakr al-Baghdadi first, *Allah* second.

In the meantime, Mohamed el Moussa wandered around the perimeter of Palmyra. To the casual observer, it was a meander around the site with no clear-cut goal. However, he knew just where he was going. Around 400 meters from the main camp's headquarters, not far from the theatre that was recently blown up, the Syrian abruptly turned into the heart of the ancient city. Another 30 meters in, and he stopped by a pile of rubble. As nondescript as it seemed, he found the precise spot that he had hidden a stone lintel fragment. This was inscribed in an indecipherable script that clearly wasn't Arabic. For that matter, he barely could read Arabic. He just knew it had to be important. He brushed it off, looked at it and traced the outline of the letters once more, and returned it to its spot in the pile. He then threw a few handfuls of debris on it, strategically placed a couple of plain stones over it and walked back to camp. He would seek out Taybieh later in the day now that he was sure that he could trust him, show him the stone and proceed from there.

As the sun began to set over the camp, el Moussa sought out the same barrel fire that he had left at the start of day. He found Taybieh there, looking restless and antsy. He walked up slightly behind him and put his hand on his shoulder. The Syrian jumped up and turned around. The apprehensive look in his eyes alarmed Mohamed. *What in God's name spooked my friend,* he thought. *Why is he so nervous, twitchy?* When asked, Ahmed took a couple of deep breaths and forced his heart to slow down. "It's nothing *habibi*, I just got back from a patrol and saw several of our wounded companions. It was shocking. A couple of them reached out for us in the patrol, begging for help. We sidestepped them. When I got back to camp, I was thinking of them, then you touched me from behind, and I thought, well, I thought that one of the wounded had actually followed me back here!"

"*Yaweli, yaweli*! What a horrible story, I feel for you brother."

"And how was your day?" He clearly had calmed down now that his story was accepted.

El Moussa lowered his voice. "I found the inscription again. It was right where I first discovered it. I wanted to show it to you, but our assignments separated us. I am certain, praise *Allah*, it will be worth a lot to us once we make the proper connection. But I'm not quite sure..."

"Don't worry, I can take care of that. I have a contact. We can arrange it tomorrow."

The younger Syrian smiled at his friend. He was sure that he had made the right decision in trusting him and showing him the strange inscription. At first, apprehensive about sharing the envisioned wealth for the antiquity sale, he knew that he hadn't the proper acquaintances to make it happen. After all, fifty percent of something was a whole lot better that one hundred of nothing, and maybe even your life. In addition, now he had someone to watch his back and vice versa. That meant doubly wary and watchful for others. But then, on the other hand, what about betrayal? *No, Taybieh would never do that to me. He's just as desperate to get out of this hell-hole and back to the village. The only reason he's still here is because he scrapes together a few Pounds here and there and gets them back to his family.* El Moussa sat back and seemed more at peace than he had been for a long time.

Taybieh noted this and asked, "You look like the cat that caught the canary."

The reply caught had Taybieh a bit off guard. "It's better to be a free dog than a caged lion". He suddenly realized that el Moussa was sharper than he gave him credit for. Although he didn't know what he discovered, he realized, finally, that the lofty, idealistic goals of the Islamic revolutionaries were as corrupt, unjust and violent as anyone else's goals. *Allah* was not the driving force, but the convenient rationale. And for this, el Moussa was ready to escape the organization. Selling the antiquity was his way out. This could cause a problem for Taybieh, as he was seen as the other man's closest friend in the encampment. And as for friendship- did el Moussa really know who his companion in combat was. Taybieh's family was in more extreme straights than anyone knew. He saw the inscription's sale as the only way to rectify this. He recalled the Arab proverb- *"A little debt makes a debtor, a great one an enemy".* This led to another remembrance. "*Your tongue is your horse? if you take care of it, it takes care of you; if you betray it, betrays it will."* He had to betray el Moussa, even though they were brothers in arms. Family was of the most importance, and all else paled.

Asa Ben Dov had put the final touches on the background legend that Sobhy would take into Syria. The intelligence officer was pleased with the outcome. It seemed to be airtight, especially since the chaotic situation in Syria had made governmental oversight nearly non-existent. Apparently 'the cloud' was little used, if at all, by an antiquated Syrian computer network. Whatever wifi infrastructure had been nominally created almost a decade ago had received no maintenance or upgrade for years. And paper outside of Damascus was blowing in the wind. In addition, local authorities may or may not continue to serve the central government, depending on location and indigenous population. This made Ben Dov's task relatively easy.

The 'coffee shop *kvutza*', the coffee shop group as they jokingly referred to themselves now, looked expectantly at the retired intelligence colonel. He grabbed his army backpack from under the table and drew out a fistful of documents. Tumbled on the table were a variety of dog-eared, worn and, in one instance, almost illegible papers necessary to wend your way through life in the Syrian war zone. Ben Dov held them up one by one.

"First, we have the essential Syrian identity card. This one is the most important, and has been the most difficult, to copy. Apparently the Assad regime, for fear that it is entirely losing its grip on the civilian population, even in government-held territory, is forcing its citizens to 'buy' at extorted rates, official identification papers. These exorbitant fees are going to help finance the war effort. In fact, those seeking papers, although Syrian citizens, were on 'the other side' of the civil war in most cases. It's extortion. The usual price for obtaining a passport, for example, was around 4800 Syrian Pounds, about $9 USD. My contacts told me that it is now $300, or 160,000 Pounds; entirely out of the reach of an average Syrian. Given that the average wage now is just under $40 a month, well, you can do the math. And that's for professionals, like doctors, lawyers, educators. This is one example- remember that you also needed insurance, driving license, voter registration, etc. The price really adds up."

"So who am I?" Sobhy asked.

"You're still Sobhy, but with an entirely different identity. I have found that it's much easier, more secure, and for you my friend, personally safer, if the basics remain the same. There's less a chance of, how do you say *l'fashayl*?"

"To screw up!" All of us answered in unison with a good deal of laughter.

The battered booklet looked as old as its decade-dated validation date. Sobhy had provided a copy of his Egyptian Supreme Council of Antiquities ID photograph that was a handful of years old, and it fit the age frame in a suitable fashion. I said something to the effect that he had never looked better, and Sobhy punched me in the arm. The others laughed, I rubbed the 'sore spot' and Ben Dov continued to explain the intricacies of the booklet's features. It still had almost 5 years remaining before renewal. Egyptian stamps relating to 2 previous 'visits' were faded and one even had a coffee cup ring stain overlaying it. The intelligence guru related that Syrian officials had been so lackadaisical in their approach for years, that their lack of respect of official civilian documentation was well known and that disdain for their constituents led to a disrespect for the system-as opposed to most countries where ID papers or passports were seen as the epitome of citizenship and treaty with dignity, if not reverence.

Other papers that rounded out the 'identity kit' included an equally aged and battered driver's license, medical card, and a couple of old receipts from local venues.

Sobhy swept up the pile and examined them with a critical eye. After all, it was his life that was at risk should any of these documents be questioned. He poured over them diligently, and at one point took the medical ID and crumpled it in his fist. Then he creased it a couple of times, as if it sat in his wallet for weeks. Then the pile was slid back across the table to Ben Dov.

"Now I approve!" Sobhy exclaimed with a triumphant smile that might have belied his nervousness.

Once the discussions of identity and history were done, the more difficult part of getting Sobhy to look the part of a Syrian refugee who got medical treatment from the Israelis in the north needed to be addressed. For that, we decided to go over to Kati's flat on *Bnei Batira*, just a few minutes' walk to the west. There, whatever would be done, would happen in private. Lior would ply her trade.

*****

Sobhy and I remained at Aroma for a few minutes, while the others slowly made their way slightly across town. We didn't want anyone to remember a 'tour group'-like promenade of people to any location. It's those kind of little details that can run a train off its tracks so to speak. And yes, there were a handful of Arab Israelis and Palestinians who came and went in Jerusalem that might want to enhance their pocket change by telling others what they might have seen on any given day in Jerusalem.

So after another coffee, and *bourekas* for Sobhy (of course) we headed out and window-shopped a bit. We crossed over *Yitzhak Kariv* Street to the corner of King David Street. We slowly walked past the King David Hotel from the other side. The sidewalk in front of the iconic (and expensive) hotel had a recently installed police booth that straddled the path. Apparently, another international 'fact-finding' delegation was slated to arrive in a day or so; hence, the added precautions. This took us in front of one of the more upscale modern art galleries in the city, Yosi Mattityahu Contemporary Judaica Gallery. It was here, several years ago, that I had purchased a numbered Chagall lithograph for my folks. We paused in front of the storefront. I remarked that business must have been quite good, as we noted the prices on the works that were displayed. Of course, the price tags were nothing compared to those across the street, in the lobby gallery of the King David, Judaica of Avi Luvaton. I told my Egyptian friend that someone he had met in Arad, Eddi Shruster, one of Arad's preeminent artists, had a couple of pieces of his on consignment there. Since Eddi was a multi-media artist, one of his bronze sculptures, that of a rooster, standing 2 meters high, had been for sale there. I noted that Eddi was doing quite well, thank you, since the piece had sold for about 30,000 New Israeli Shekels, or $7,100 dollars.

Sobhy let out a low whistle, duly impressed with Eddi's art. "I remember meeting him and his wife, Miri. Didn't she make all sorts of stuffed dolls?"

I teased and admonished him. "Don't *ever* call them dolls to her face! To Miri, a 'doll' was a child's toy. These were 'replica human miniatures,' as she put it."

He joked back. "But if I recall, they were 'pudgeballs, like, oh, what were those stuffed dolls called a few years ago, Cabbage

Patch Dolls!" We both laughed. But in the end agreed that they were dolls, regardless of Miri's thinking.

We continued west to *HaPalmach* Street, which turned into *Sderot Shai Agnon*. From there, another few minutes and we intersected with *Bnei Batira*. The tree-lined street was much cooler than the broader, sun-baked avenues we walked on to this point. It was a welcome relief. Up a couple of flights, a knock on the door, and we were welcomed in by the rest of the group.

The first thing that Sobhy noticed was the aroma of cooking. He crinkled up his nose, took a deep breath, and smiled.

"*Shakshuka! Ya weli, Ya weli*! Just like my mother used to make!" You could almost see him salivating, drooling, like a St. Bernard.

"I don't think that this was exactly your mother's recipe" Kati said. "Unless she was a Bedouin woman of the *Abu Reqaiq* Tribe near *Tel Sheva*. I learned this one from Wadfa, your buddy's 'bedouin mama' But you know, *shakshuka* is *shakshuka* is *shakshuka*. After all, how many ways can you really create it?"

"Or ruin it," I said under my breath. Sobhy glanced my way. He glared a bit.

"I heard that!" Kati had ears like a bat. No, I didn't mean like a bat! She had an extraordinary sense of hearing... I felt that my thoughts were being read by her ESP, and I was in really deep...

"Heard what? All I said was 'or RUN with it!'"

A bit of quick thinking would get me out of this one, or so I fervently hoped. After all, we had a job to do. "Let's eat something first, then get to it," I finished. Kati smiled a 1000 watt smile, but I saw something in the glint of her eye that hinted that she *may* have heard what she thought she heard, but really wasn't sure she heard it so she would pretend that what she heard I had reiterated when she heard it a second time... got it?

*****

In the meantime, while we were straightening out the *shakshuka balagan*, the meal mess, and Sobhy was digging in with a gusto, Lior set up shop on the dining room table. All sorts of containers came out of her shoulder bag; liquids and powders, and what seemed like silly putty and glue. I felt like I was 10 years old again and this was playtime. But it was deadly serious, and I knew it.

She clearly knew what she was doing. She stared at Sobhy for a long while. When he 'came up for air' after devouring his plate of food, he glanced over and saw her appraising him.

"What? Do I have sauce on my chin, the plate wasn't *all* that full you know, it was a regular helping. And I didn't even take any pitabread to sop up the tomato sauce." He looked and sounded like a petulant child with his hand caught in the cookie jar and trying to make amends for it. Eitan and Kati laughed, and Ben Dov simply shook his head. He wasn't quite used to the insider stuff that we had become used to over the past few years of working together.

Lior shook her head in mock dismay, and said, "Don't get a big head about you, *el Masri*, Egyptian. You're not *that* great to look at. Not bad, not bad at all, but nothing for me to write home to my *safta*, grandma, about!" We all got a good laugh out of that one, and Sobhy, well, Sobhy was a tad crestfallen.

"However, I *am* interested in your body!" His eyes really lit up now. She went on, "But only in regard to creating your personal injuries!" Sobhy went immediately from eyes lit up to round disks of shock and perhaps a bit of horror as well.

"Don't worry, we'll fake the injuries, and create equally fake scars that I guarantee will last about a month just in case things take a little longer than we planned. Just don't take long, hot baths for any extended periods of time. The 'scar tissue' might dissolve and that could cause a problem.

Sobhy looked relieved. "Don't worry, where I'm going there probably isn't enough clean drinking water, let alone some for bathing. I think that I'll be just fine. How do we start?"

"Take off your shirt please." Sobhy smiled and pulled his 'T' over his head. Lior examined his torso, pleased that there wasn't a lot of body hair that could cause a problem. She commented on this and he asked about the significance.

"Well, it's clear that, just in case if I had to shave a bit of your chest hair away from the location that I would put a fake scar, it wouldn't grow back to a sufficient level that would correspond to the age of the wound. Should anyone look closely, this could be a telltale giveaway and put you at risk."

Ben Dov smiled knowingly. Although she was 'just' a make-up artist, she really understood the logistics of the discipline and all of the parameters that needed to be addressed. Lior rose dozens of points in everyone's estimation. Eitan actually applauded this explanation. Lior blushed a bit and continued with her exam. "I thought about the kind of wounds that Sobhy 'should suffer'. To me, a bullet that grazed the arm wouldn't be quite enough. That kind of flesh wound could be patched up, bandaged, and the person given a dose of antibiotic. I realize that there isn't a lot of that stuff in Syria these days, but it's my understanding that there is enough to give out one dose per patient- but no more. Then I thought about IEDs and the havoc that they wreak on the body. In my opinion, a lower leg wound and torso puncture would be indicative of such a small scale explosion. So, those 2 wounds are my recommendation."

"Will it hurt?" Sobhy asked, ever the child.

"Not at all," was her reply. "It will be applied with a sort of rubber cement adhesive that is not water soluble, bonds to the skin nicely, won't come off with rubbing... But of course if you get caught and they slice it off your flesh..." She offered up the hint of a smile. You never saw eyes grow so large in alarm, as the Egyptian's. You've heard of saucer-shaped eyes. Well, his were *dinner plate-sized eyes* at this joking pronouncement. Everyone in the room tried to hold back their laughter, but that lasted only a minute or so. The tension was broken- something that we all needed.

Just then there was a knock on the door. Kati looked through the peephole and saw a young man holding yet another backpack. "*Mi zeh*? Who's there?" she asked from behind the door.

"*Yesh li kufsa bishfil Ben Dov*, I have a box for Ben Dov" was the reply.

"*Rok rega*, what a minute." Ben Dov was beckoned to the peephole. He took one look and smiled. He opened the door, took the box with thanks, and kicked it shut with his foot.

"I have presents for Sobhy!" He sat down at the coffee table and emptied the contents of the box onto it. "Now that the package is here, let's go over it before Lior 'butchers' our friend. So what do we have? Hmmm, let's start with the basics. A tee shirt is no big deal, especially if 90% of them have labels torn out due to use and age. So that we can get anywhere here. But other clothing can be specific and can aid in the cover story. For example, here are a pair of well-worn Cheap Monday Jeans direct, in a roundabout way, from the Alghoussoun Men's Store on *Dwelaa* Street in Damascus. The used underwear, don't worry, it may be used but is well-laundered, is generic but may have come from there as well. The battered tennis shoes are BATA, purchased in Jordan." He pulled yet another item out. "The army jacket is pure Syrian military, but with a well-used air to it."

Sobhy sniffed and wrinked his nose. "Yes, I can smell what you mean!" The faint aroma of cordite seemed to be a part of the jacket's memory. Ben Dov went on.

"Now that you're fitted out with apparel, we need to fill your pockets and your wallet.

"What's in your wallet?" I laughed and asked. Everyone else in the room stared at me at though I was from another planet. I grinned back a bit sheepishly. "Well, er, that's from an American television commercial... sorry." No matter, they still looked at me as if I was the long lost intellectually challenged cousin who sat in the corner; misunderstood by all the relatives.

"Okay, enough of the *idiot,*" and Ben Dov continued. He pulled out a couple of dated and creased receipts. One was from the Warm Apple Pie Restaurant, located one block from Sun Hotel, in old Palmyra. Another was from Sobhy's supposed home town of *As Suwayda*. It was from the Museum. "Just remember," he admonished the Egyptian, the museum has a rich collection of mosaics but no pictures are allowed. This could be a 'tripping up point' that you may be asked to show them a photo or two. Don't! Finally, a second validation of your interest in archaeology is an admission stub to the 1st century Temple of the Sun God, off Hwy 110; near Old *Suwayda*. Of course, don't forget the thousands of Syrian Pounds. All of these are dated to a couple of months ago. This would have been just prior to your 'wounding and treatment over there.'"

Sobhy looked at the pile of wadded up bills and let out a low whistle. "I didn't realize that I was a rich Syrian peasant!" He said.

"Don't get a big head!" Eitan laughed. "58 Syrian Pounds = $1." Sobhy was positively deflated, like the currency.

On the corner of the table lay a battered cell phone. It was a BLU 4.0 Android phone, a slightly older L3 model with a cracked screen. "You have a prepaid account with Syriatel, one that, on the books, has been active for 2 years, but not used for 2 months or so. Your account for this is that you have been 'on the dark side' being taken care of for wounds suffered. Oh, by the way, should you have trouble with the phone, the assistance number is 111 over there".

We all were impressed with the detail. A lack of detail could be the difference between life and death for our friend. "Finally," Ben Dov said, "the phone is a very small, very old school, flip phone."

"What's that for, a call to Gibbs?" I laughed at my own joke. The others simply stared again at the 'idiot cousin' in the room. After a moment, I was vindicated by Lior, of all people.

"Wow! NCIS! That's so way cool. I watch it whenever I can on Cable USA channel! He's so retro cool I can't possibly imagine." She grinned and high-fived me, then slapped me on the back of my head. "Take that, Probie!" The others, well, they glanced at each other and confirmed that there were now *two* idiot cousins in the room who nobody would pay attention to.

"So what's the purpose if I might ask?" Sobhy was also trying to pay as great attention to detail as possible.

Ben Dov replied, "It's a dedicated burner phone, untraceable, without the ability to call any numbers except one. And there's no voice call capability. That number is a silent call to a hot line within the *Agaf Modi'in*, the intelligence section of the IDF. It will be monitored 24/7 once you get sent over. Should you need immediate, and I mean immediate, extrication, push #1 on the phone and send. Then hang up. A chopper will be dispatched to get you faster than you can say "Golda Meir.' You'll need to get somewhere out in the open where it could land. It's a stealth helo, and will come in quieter than a church mouse."

Now it was Sobhy's turn to get a bit nervous. "But if they do ask me stuff, and empty my pockets, and find the phone, what then. They'll go to caller ID and see the number etc. Then I'm toast." He suddenly looked dismayed.

"Not to worry *habibi*; everything will be disabled on the phone after the single call, so don't order take away pizza! This includes the GPS chip. So if any bad guys do question you, you will simply say that your original phone was 'fried' by the Israelis or some such statement, and that a friend gave you his old BLU to borrow until you could get a new one. Play sort of naïve, say something like you thought that, even if it was no good, you could get a little bit of something for it in trade when you go to get your new one." Ben Dov smiled reassuringly and it seemed to assuage the Egyptian's fears- for the time being.

The make-up artist gave a sharp rap on the dining room table. "Hello! Is anybody out there? I *do* need to make some changes to our friend here, so he won't get killed in Syria."

"You mean some plastic surgery improvements?" Eitan threw his 2 shekels' worth into the mix. Sobhy shot him a look that was a combination of annoyance and envy. After all, Eitan's past reputation with the ladies was rather well known, and Sobhy had quickly learned it as well.

"Enough boys! Let's get to it." The materials were all ready to go. First, Lior inspected his torso one more time to ascertain the abdominal 'scar.' Once located, she quickly swabbed the area with alcohol. When Sobhy saw this, a look of concern flitted across his face. He knew that a prep like this was always a prelude to cutting. She saw this and assured him that it was simply remove any body oil on the surface so that the adhesive would stick tightly to the skin. He sighed with relief. Then, the artist's talents took over on autopilot. She quickly mixed the 'scar tissue' rubber cement-like paste, adding in a trifle of tint that came close to, but not exactly like, Sobhy's skin color. After all, scars don't fully match skin tone, if at all, for many years. This hue was designed to look recent, not too old and not too immediate. I remarked that it was like the 3 bears syndrome. Once again, I got the look of pity reserved for the idiot cousin.

"*B'seder*, okay. Now lie down for about an hour and try not to move around so much. This has to really set up. By then, you should be able to move about, bend, twist, and the scar should easily move with you just like for real." Sobhy lay down on the sofa and grabbed the TV remote.

"Maybe I can find that NCIS show you're always talking about. Gotta learn how to use a flip phone." He grinned and put his feet up. A couple of the group got up and went out for a coffee.

*****

An hour later, when everyone had recongregated, Lior got Sobhy up and walking around, *sans* shirt. She ran him through some small callisthenic-like drills and pronounced everything good to go. The 'scar' moved with the same fluidity of motion as Sobhy did and showed no signs of degradation or peeling. Happy with the result, she turned her attention to his calf. The same prep work was done, with no 'Sobhy apprehension' and a short linear 'scar' was traced nearly to his ankle. The same admonition not to move around for an hour was announced. This time, the Egyptian opted for a nap rather than TV. I grabbed my Amazon Fire to read, and the others went off to the coffee shop again.

Once again, after the prerequisite time, everything was given the green light. Now, all that was left was to get Sobhy to the north of Israel, then onto the Israeli controlled portion of the Golan, and mixed in with a group of Syrian civilians returning to what was left of their homes after obtaining medical treatment.

Mohamed el Moussa felt good about the coming couple of days. Taybieh assured him of securing a buyer for the carved stone, and then splitting the bounty. He also assured him of figuring a way to escape the camp quietly, quickly, and making the proverbial 'bee-line' back to their small village, back to family, back to obscurity. He had gone to sleep complacent with his thoughts.

When he awoke, he noted that the camp cot in the tent next to him was vacant. *Where was Taybieh?* he wondered. He got up and out of the tent and walked 15 meters to the spigot that supplied water to this part of the encampment. Although not the ideal situation, he completed the act of *Wudu*, the partial ritual ablution needed for purity in order to pray. He washed his hands up to the wrist three times, he rinsed his mouth three times, and cleansed his nostrils by sniffing air and blowing it out three times.

Then, he washed his face three times, followed by his right arm to the elbow, and then the left- again, three times. He began to relax and feel at ease in a way that he hadn't felt in weeks. He was at peace. He concluded the ritual purification by water by wiping his ears, neck and finally his feet up to the ankles- again, three times each.

He then headed back to his tent, and retrieved his prayer rug, his *sajjada*. Measuring only about 60 x 90 cm, it was his private mosque, his spiritual sanctuary. In Islam, it's not required that one goes to a 'brick and adobe' mosque to pray. Because you never know when you'll be near to one, especially since the obligation to pray is five times a day, there is the ability to pray individually. This is in addition to the fact that 85% of all Moslem prayer can be done by the individual. Actually, the notion of attending a service at the Friday Mosque is a derivative of that idea. El Moussa began the ritual.

"Allah-hoo Akbar," Allah is Great.

"Subhaan-Allaah wal-hamdu Lillaah wa laa ilaaha ill-Allaah wa Allaah-hoo akbar wa laa hawla wa la quwwata illa Billaah," Glory be to *Allah*, praise be to *Allah*, there is no God except *Allah*, *Allah* is Most great and there is no power and no strength except with *Allah*...

He concluded the morning prayers, different from others only with the recitation of the passage, "prayer is better than sleep," and got up to fold and put away his rug. Stretching, he turned and opened the tent flap. He couldn't believe his eyes, because outside, waiting for him, were three guards armed with their AK47s, standing next to Ahmed Taybieh, his friend- all with harsh looks in their eyes.

"In the name of the military governing body of *Daesh*, the Caliphate of Syria and the Levant, we are placing you under arrest for treason, for theft of property belonging to the Islamic State, and for apostasy." A stunned look crossed his face, and he thought that he detected a flicker of guilt pass beyond Taybieh's eyes, as two of the guards roughly grabbed his arms and walked him through the compound to one of the few permanent buildings that housed a makeshift jail.

Inside, he saw the regional commander, Abu Bakr al-Baghdadi, whose real name was Ibrahim al-Badriwas. He was told that the troop leader had the right to assume the role of *Qadi*, the Islamic judge, in this instance. The nature of ISIS' legal system was a bizarre extension of Islamic law, *Sharia*. To them, anyone who claimed knowledge of the *Koran* and the laws found within could call himself a judge. The notion was 'doubled down' because al-Baghdadi declared the area a war zone and therefore declared his decisions to be valid given the situation. This did not bode well for the younger man.

He was propelled further into the room with a shove that nearly drove him to his knees, it was so forceful. As he staggered to a stop just a couple of feet from the table that the commander sat at, he was confronted by the cruelest of smiles. Al-Baghdadi's scar that traced his jawline puckered so that it almost looked like a double death's head grin. Now el Moussa began to shake a bit. He turned and looked around the room at the other guards, at Taybieh, and a couple of other 'officers' lounging on pillows against the wall. When they noticed his look, they turned away from him; a move that was designed to deliberately isolate him.

The *Qadi* addressed him somewhat informally, as part of the opening round of inquiry. It was supposed to put the room at ease. Rather, the tension was ratcheted up a couple of notches. The usual formality of identification of the accused, family patrilineage, recruitment date with ISIS, rank were all asked and answered in a monotone. The next round of questions raised created a heightened awareness in the room by all.

"And who do you have to represent you in this holy court?" Was the question asked of el Moussa. He looked like a Thompson's Gazelle caught in the headlights; stunned at what he was going through.

"I request that Ahmed Taybieh represent me." His fervent response caught all off guard, notably his former friend. Before anyone else could respond, Taybieh strode forward and placed his hands on the table in front of the commander.

"In the name of *Allah*, praised be His name, I am neither a friend or supporter of this traitor." And now the truth came out. "After all, *I* was the one who overheard a conversation and chose to turn in this snake who sought to use our cause for his own reward. Not just his own reward, but also to do acts counter to our belief in destroying objects of blasphemy!" Ahmed spat on the dirt floor of the room at the feet of el Moussa and returned to his place along the wall.

No one in his right ISIS mind would ever serve as a defense representative. The inferred acceptance of philosophy and subsequent collusion in trying to justify el Moussa's actions would mean certain death for the advocate as well as the defendant should the assumed verdict of guilty be conferred. As a result, he found that he would have to be his own lawyer- with little or no hope of success. But he did have a bit of an advantage. He was more aware of *Sharia* than the majority of ISIS followers, which may include the commander al Baghdadi, and perhaps even the self-proclaimed Imam of the district, Sheikh Hassan. For the ISIS recruits, a weak knowledge of Islamic law could mean many things. It could, and often did, mean a genuine ignorance of even basic religious precepts. Although this wasn't always the case. People often join radical militant movements for a wide variety of intersecting reasons, including religious beliefs, politics, economics and more.

Article 3 of the 1973 Syrian Constitution declared Islamic jurisprudence as one of Syria's main sources of legislation. The Personal Status Law 59 of 1953 (amended by Law 34 of 1975) was essentially a codified version of Islamic law. The Code of Personal Status was applied to Moslems by separate *Sharia* courts. But since ISIS didn't recognize the legitimacy of the Syrian regime, it simply tossed out all of the Syrian legal system, even though it was in sync with many of ISIS' aims. The so-called 'courts' that were set up in all encampments were showcase venues. In essence, with judge and jury already in the pocket of strict Islamic law, they were designed to scare the wits out of the ignorant recruits and ensure their loyalty and unwavering support. Don't give them an option to think, *tell* them what to think, and you have them.

"Given the nature of think blasphemous crime, we will wait til the morrow, when Imam Sheikh Hassan will arrive" Al Baghadi handed down his decision. "This will then allow for there to be two *Qadis* to hear the defense and pass judgement. This should not be in the hands of a single judge." The crowd that had gathered murmured its consent as el Moussa was led back to the single room block structure that would serve as his jail.

*****

The night seemed to last a month or more. The straw pallet was bug-infested, the windowless, airless chamber a sweltering box of stagnant air. El Moussa had to pound on the door for half an hour, screaming for someone to bring him some water. Finally, at some time in the dead of night, a guard brought a small jug of dirty water to the prisoner. Thirst overcame his fear of some water-borne disease, and he downed the roughly two liters of liquid in just a couple of gulps. He wiped his mouth with the back of his hand and fell back down onto the mattress, shivering with dread- it certainly wasn't from the cold.

Apparently he fell into a semi-conscious state for a couple of hours, because he heard the sounds of a slowly wakening camp outside the room. Shortly thereafter, a new guard, apparently there had been a shift change, opened the door and handed el Moussa a crust of old *pita* and a hunk of moldy cheese. He then set down another jug of water.

"Eat, you dog! You need your strength for your *Muhakama*, your 'trial.' He laughed derisively.

"What's so funny?"

"*Everyone* in camp already knows the verdict! This is just for the rest of Syria to see. If you ask me, it's a waste of a bullet- we're running a bit low! And you don't suffer. If it were up to me, and most of the rest of us, we'd prefer you died slowly, painfully. There's nothing like a good stoning! After all, remember the Prophet Ibrihim, blessings be upon him."

Oh no, thought el Moussa. *As they say, a little bit of knowledge is a dangerous thing. I am going to get the whole PR children's story view of religion from him; which is the appropriate level of understanding for this idiot.*

"So I don't need to tell you about the potential sacrifice of Ishmael by his father, as a test from *Allah*. On his way to sacrifice his son, the Devil appeared three times to Abraham to dissuade him from fulfilling his duty. Abraham stoned the Devil with seven stones each time he appeared to him" stated the guard.

He went on to describe how this came to be translated into one of the major acts involved in the *Hajj*, the pilgrimage to *Makka*. During Mohamed's last visit to the holy city following his triumphant return in 632 CE, he re-enacted a series of events that surrounded not only the story of Ibrihim, but the subsequent story of Hagar and Ishmael wandering in the desert before being rescued by *Allah.*

After standing on the plain of A*rafat*, pilgrims spend the night on a plain called *Muzdalifah*. There, they gather 70 stones with which to pelt three stone pillars representing the Devil. The next day, the day of *Eid-ul-Adha*, the Feast of the Sacrifice, pilgrims stone the largest of the three pillars with seven stones. Then, for the next three days, pilgrims pelt each of the three stone pillars with seven stones. *Ramī al-jamarāt,* The Stoning of the Devil ritual, is considered the most dangerous part of the pilgrimage, as enormous crowds of pilgrims on or near the *Jamarat* Bridge can cause people to be crushed. On several occasions, thousands of participants have suffocated or been trampled to death in stampedes. The latest of these ritual crushes occurred on September 24, 2015 in *Mina* when at least 2,411 pilgrims were killed. Today the Saudi government has built three walls (formerly the pillars) that pilgrims throw stones at now. The stones fall harmlessly into a dry moat surrounding these walls.

Mohamed couldn't help himself, and verbally attacked the guard. "The stoning of the three *jamarāt* is, in essence, the trampling upon the despots and waging war against all of them. By stoning the pillars, pilgrims openly declare their enmity to the Devil. This has NOTHING to do with the history of our people before the advent of the Prophet, peace be upon Him."

As he turned away, a hand grabbed him by the shoulder and spun him around. The impact of the butt of an AK-47 launched 1000 stars in his eyes, before blackness engulfed him. Apparently the scheduled trial was forced into a brief recess, until el Moussa came back into the world of consciousness.

*****

Just after noon that day, when el Moussa regained his senses, another guard detail waiting outside his door heard him stir. The door slowly swung open, and two other foot soldiers roughly grabbed him and dragged him to the *Majlis*, the meeting tent, where his trial was set to begin.

"I welcome Sheikh Hassan to our camp," intoned Commander al Baghdadi. "It is an honor and a privilege for me to join with him in adjudicating this case of treason and blasphemy. It is of great importance to the cause to make an example for all both in the camp and on the outside- that disrespect, blasphemy and theft be prosecuted to the full extent of *Sharia*. And if the outcome of this trial dissuades even one of our followers from thinking about material gain that is counter to all we believe in... then we will have succeeded in our goal of maintaining the spiritual purity of all within our honorable troop of fighters in the name of Allah!"

With this, a loud murmur ran through the dozen or so witnesses inside and was then picked up by the hundreds standing just outside the entry, awaiting the decision. "*Allahu Akhbar! Allahu Akhbar!* God is Great!" A few shots rang out, as exuberant fighters raised their weapons and loosed a few rounds into the sky. As el Moussa heard this coming from outside, he idly wondered whether the spent bullets that would inevitably fall to the ground might strike him dead- or whether by chance kill his 'legal' persecutors sitting opposite him at the table.

The butt of a nine-millimeter pistol banged down on the tabletop. "I call this *majlis*, this council, to session! Mohamed el Moussa has been accused of blasphemy, thievery, attempting to consort with the enemy, defrauding the Caliphate of potential income and apostasy. Any or all of them hold the death penalty if found guilty."

Why not add to the list a broken tail-light on my camel! El Moussa thought. He had resigned himself to the fact that he would die an agonizing death at the hands of these rabid idiots, with no thought of a fair trial in the cards. And to think that he had considered himself to be one of those most fervent of followers of ISIS in the early days. Did he lose his way, or did ISIS and its leaders? Was the pure goal of an Islamic state, following Islamic Law, tainted and corrupted to such a degree that it could be influenced by the basest aspects of human nature? These were the things that made up the picture show of life in his mind's eye. As the war went on, and it became more and more difficult to support his family, the notion of protection of your homestead and all those within, an integral part of Islam, became of the essence. The family is considered to be of utmost importance, so Islam gives priority to its safety. He recalled one of the passages drilled into him by his father, before his marriage. "*O you who believe! Protect yourselves and your families against a Fire (Hell) whose fuel is men and stones, over which are (appointed) angels stern (and) severe, who disobey not the commands they receive from Allah, but do that which they are commanded." (Surah Tahrim:6) When coupled with his newfound respect for antiquity, and its preservation (never mind that he could have financially benefitted for his family's sake), el Moussa felt that he had attempted the right thing, and that it was ISIS that had lost its way. Just as Allah certainly didn't believe in the total destruction of humankind, He certainly didn't feel that the destruction of the record of humankind would in any way serve the Master of the World. In his current state, el Moussa struggled to remember the 99 Most Beautiful Names of Allah. But he did say a silent prayer to Him, addressing some of those names that he felt were the most relevant.*

"The Most Compassionate, The Beneficent, The Gracious, the Grantor of security, the Protector, the Forgiver, the Grantor and Acceptor of repentance, the Just, the Equitable, and finally, the Patient one..."

Suddenly, an open hand slapped him hard across the face, and he was jolted out of his reverie.

"I was addressing you, *kha'en*, you *kalb*! You traitorous dog!" Imam Hassan raged at him.

"*Na'am*? What? I was praying!" Came the response.

"How do you plead, and on what basis? We need to know before we continue the trial," Al Baghdadi was a bit more civil; cold, but civil.

"I know what I have been accused of, and the circumstances that have been described by Ahmed Taybieh, my accuser, are in error. He certainly didn't know the whole story, *because I never* got around to telling him the whole story and my intent. You must hear me out on this, and then you will have no option but to find me innocent."

Although the look in Sheikh Hassan's eye was one of religious zeal, and perhaps anger, he nodded his assent to the plea. Abu Bakr al Baghdadi also nodded his assent. El Moussa found that he had been holding his breath, and then let it out with an audible *whoosh*. One of the fighters in the room murmured something and those immediately around him started to laugh. The pistol came down again with a hard crack!

"What's so funny that you disrupt this court of law!" Both of the judges stood up and scanned the room, looking for the transgressor. "If no one comes forward, I will clear this *majlis* and everything will be behind the closed door! So who is it?"

A grizzled, scarred veteran took a step forward. By his looks, and smell, he hadn't taken care of his personal hygiene for a week or more, and in this desert heat, well...

"It was me, *Qadi*, I was the one." He shuffled his feet and his toe outlined a small circle in the dirt floor. "I simply whispered that the sound was like a pig farting! My apologies." Now everyone else in the room started to snicker. Sheikh Hassan allowed the fleetest small smile pass his face before resuming his stern countenance.

"I demand silence!" And the room suddenly hushed. "Although what you said may have been somewhat close to the truth, the gravity of this trial demands respect for S*haria* and the court. There will be no more outbursts, no matter how appropriate they may seem! My final words on this. The accused will continue his defense."

The silence inside made it clear that all within had taken the chastisement to heart and that there would not be another infantile outbreak again. The assumption was that the next demonstration would be one of jubilation at the 'guilty' verdict. The trial proceeded.

The prosecution was straightforward, condemning el Moussa for a number of transgressions. The first was willfully ignoring a direct military order from his commander, Abu Bakr al Baghdadi (who just happened to be one of the judges). That order was to aid in the destruction of the idolatrous statuary and archaeological record of the pagan society of Palmyra before the advent of Islam and the injection of *Allah's* latest and final message to the world through the Prophet Mohamed, peace be upon Him. This then led to the recounting of another set of transgressions; those revolving around the potential stealing and subsequent selling of antiquities for personal, willful gain. Should ISIS have wished to profit from the sale of artifacts on a wholesale level, it would have done so at the highest level, the prosecution stated. In other words, this action would not have been the purview of the local militia leadership, but from the highest levels of the Caliphate in the so-called capitol, *Raqqa*. However, any selling of antiquities would have been done with the utmost secrecy in order to generate revenue for the cash-poor rebellion. Doing this on a small, local scale was tantamount to treasonous profiteering.

Al Baghdadi sat back in his chair, pleased with the way that he delivered the prosecutorial line of attack against the fighter. He glanced at Imam Sheikh Hassan and caught him nodding in agreement to the way that all of the evidence had been delivered.

El Moussa was clearly agitated. His eyes darted about the stuffy room, looking in vain for someone to give an indication that there was support for him among the troops. But there was none; only a few hard stares, or eyes that sought out any sign of ants crawling across the floor, or counting the cracks in the block walls, or looking *anywhere* other than at the prisoner. He saw that his only hope was to mount a passionate, emotional defense that, while he might be found guilty, could find him looking at prison time and yet save his life. He took a deep breath and faced the panel of two judges in front of him.

"I have been accused of several offenses, and in truth, am guilty of one of them, but not for the reasons given by Commandant al Baghdadi. Yes, I discovered a stone that was engraved with some sort of inscription. It was in a language other than Arabic, for that I am sure. What the language was I can't say. However, it was old, very old. What I am about to say will shock some of you that I dare speak it aloud, and it will come as a surprise to a few of you, but I must address it as it is the reason for all that I did." He then outlined his plan to sell the object in order to preserve his family, since no salary had been dispersed to the fighters for several months. But he also added the fact that he intended to turn over half the money to the district commander for the cause. He went on.

"The man sitting in front of you, Abu Bakr al Baghdadi, is remiss in his duties as local commander of our ISIS unit. He has been negligent, indifferent to the idea of raising funds locally to support his militia, notably in this day when there is a severe lack of funds due to external pressure on preventing us from getting the oil revenue from the fields that we control. He should be the one on trial, for his dereliction of duty, not a poor man like me only trying to protect my family."

This led to an uproar in the camp and the court of Qadi Sheikh Hassan. First, the room erupted, then as word got out, a tremendous din arose among the surrounding fighters who caught wind of the inflammatory accusations. Those inside were forced to bar the door to prevent an onrush from the outside crowd. Al Baghdadi got on his phone and called in reinforcements from the edge of camp to come and enact crowd control over the ever increasingly violent commotion only steps away. As men rushed to cordon off the building, the rage that was seething in the commander came to the surface.

"You dog, how dare you insult me and my goals for our glorious cause! How dare you malign my integrity as a pious leader of Islam! How dare you slander my intentions!" He fumed and spluttered, the spittle flying from his mouth, nearly reaching across the room to where el Moussa was standing, held by the soldiers flanking him. Had they not supported him, he would have fallen back and away from the one judge's outburst. Sheikh Hassan stood up quickly and forcefully placed his hands on the commander, preventing him from rising. He whispered that it would not be in the best interests of the trial, of Islam, of ISIS, should al Baghdadi extract his own personal vengeance on the prisoner. He told al Baghdadi to take a deep breath, quietly recite a prayer of thanksgiving to *Allah,* praised be His name, and reassert control over the proceedings. The other man looked up at him, slowly nodded his assent, and allowed the fire in his eyes to die down; smoldering still, but not as inflamed as just moments ago. He still was able to maintain control over his emotions, albeit in the face of the implied order of the *Qadi* towering next to him.

"We will resume this trial as soon as the situation outside calms down and order is re-instated in the camp. We certainly don't want to let any procedural issues taint the verdict to be reached soon."

*****

The door to the makeshift 'cell' slammed shut and el Moussa took a deep breath. He leaned back against a wall and slid down until he sat with his back to it. He took his face in his hands and rubbed it vigorously, as if attempting to wipe away the ever darkening nightmare of his imprisonment, trial, and assuming the worst, imminent execution. With the increasing evidence of the disintegration of the discipline of ISIS, and the subsequent corruption that ran rampant within, el Moussa kept questioning why he was handpicked for a show trial. The only thing that he could think of was the defense that he dared to speak in public- that Al Baghdadi and the higher-ups were all directly involved in the selling out of ISIS for their own personal wealth in order to fade into the hills once ISIS was defeated. As a scapegoat, his trial deflected all issues of illegal activity away from the leadership.

The prisoner didn't care any more about his life, but was worried about his family. If this indeed was a show trial, would the publicity put everyone dear to him in harm's way? Would they be persecuted, or killed by outraged followers? Or in the least bad case, would they be shunned, yet left alone? All of these thoughts raced through his mind as he drifted off into an uneasy, fitful, sleep.

In what seemed like just a few moments of restless slumber, the door to his room banged open and a different set of guards roughly manhandled him into wakefulness. Disoriented, as his hands were ziplocked behind his back and he was forced out the door, the blazing sun made him realize that an entire night had passed. Because of his loosely bound feet, he was frog-walked to the building where the trial was held.

The entire compound was devoid of soldiers. Apparently, an order had gone out to clear the courtyard prior to the reconvening of the trial, in order to prevent another potential outburst and riot like yesterday. To el Moussa, it was an eerie premonition that he wouldn't live to see anyone else.

Upon entering the room, he noticed that it too was empty, except for the guards, Ahmed Taybieh, his accuser and the judges before him. *Apparently the fewer involved the better it was for this farce to play out*, he thought.

His legs were unbound, but his hands remained cuffed in front of him. The Qadi, Sheikh Hassan addressed him in a civil fashion.

"Mohamed el Moussa, you made serious accusations against not only my colleague, Abu Bakr Al Baghdadi, but the entire basis of the Caliphate of *Allah*, praised be His name. Your charges are both serious and threatening to the cause. For that reason, we recessed for a day to investigate the claims, after all, this *is* a court in accordance to *Sharia.* All claims are taken into account and looked into, because we are reasonable men in the work of God and accommodate all reports of malfeasance in our cause."

El Moussa listened carefully and allowed himself the merest glimmer of hope. But that hope would soon be dashed unmercifully. It would be the other judge, Al Baghdadi, who, with a triumphant glint in his eye, would make the pronouncement.

"Since your accusation against me, we have interviewed dozens of fighters in this camp, and gone through the inventory of blasphemous items that were to be disposed of and have found no discrepancies. *All* items to be destroyed have been eradicated, as testified to by our valiant soldiers. *All* items inventoried to be demolished have been seen at Palmyra, including the one you were going to sell for illicit profit, and await their fate. Therefore, we, the judges of this trial, have come to the conclusion that your claims of corruption and improper conduct were merely a ruse to deflect from your own guilt. As a result, we have no other recourse than to convict you on the most serious charges of usurper of the cause, and traitor to your military unit."

El Moussa heard this rendering with disbelief, and visibly sagged. He was prevented from falling to the ground by the two guards who propped him up between them.

"You are convicted of *irtidād*, apostasy, which is the equivalent of treason. For this, even though the death penalty is allowed in Islam, forgiveness is preferable. Forgiveness, together with peace, is a predominant *Qur'anic* theme."

Another glimmer of hope flitted across his face. When Al Baghdadi saw this, he fumed. He leaned over to Sheikh Hassan and vehemently whispered to him. The two engaged in an extraordinarily heated exchange. However, no one else in the room could make out what they were arguing about. The commander slammed his fist onto the tabletop, and the coffee mug and pens danced about. After several back-and-forths between him and the *imam*, a smug, satisfied look crossed his face. He sat back and folded his arms across his chest and waited for the sheikh to address the prisoner.

"Mohamed el Moussa, we have reached a verdict in your trial. However, due to the significant gravity of the charges, we will reconvene in the courtyard outside in front of the congregation of believers immediately following noon prayers. You are to be remanded until then. It's only a couple of hours away." With that, the two judges got up and left the room. The guards followed a few moments later with el Moussa between them.

*****

"Allah Akbar! Allah Akbar!" The call of the *muezzin*, the chanter of the call to prayer, echoed throughout the encampment. As men slowly shuffled their way to line up for the midday prayers, el Moussa joined them spiritually, but from his locked cell. He reflected on life, family, and his actions. He begged forgiveness

for the distinct possibility that he would be killed and therefore abandon his family. However, he *did not* seek forgiveness and repentance for what he was accused of doing. He repeated a *Dua*, an invocation, that, according to Mohamed (peace be upon Him) was at the essence of worship.

O Allah, I ask for your health in this world and in the Hereafter. O Allah, I ask You for your forgiveness, for soundness of faith and for security in this world and the safety of my family...

A short time later, the door creaked open and the guards, along with a somber Ahmed Taybieh, entered and rebound the prisoner.

"I just want to say that I didn't mean..." began Taybieh.

"Just shut up! I thought that you were my friend? I thought that we trusted each other and wanted to protect our families and allow them to survive!" Spat el Moussa.

Taken a bit aback by the vehemence of the verbal attack, Taybieh continued. "I was going to say that I never meant for it to turn out this way. For you to be arrested. I never thought that the imam would go so far in the trial. That you'd be reprimanded, given some shit-work to do in camp as punishment. I *never* even considered the charges of blasphemy or apostasy. Please believe me!" He almost begged el Moussa. But the prisoner was turned away in order to be ziplocked again and didn't respond. They all then walked out into the harsh desert sunlight.

By this time, dozens of fighters had been summoned back to the open courtyard. They milled about, smoking and chatting amongst themselves. When the door opened, they all turned in unison toward the entourage coming forth. First, the two judges came out, acknowledging the crowd like they were pop stars. This led to a raucous cheering and several rounds of applause. A few of the soldiers pointed their AK47s to the sky and loosed several celebratory rounds. But things quieted down quickly when the prisoner, el Moussa, and his guards entered the courtyard. An undercurrent of murmuring was the background noise. When Taybieh emerged, several pointed at him as the hero who turned in the one they supposed was the true traitor.

Sheikh Hassan waved him arms in a downward motion, indicating that the crowd should hush itself in preparation for the handing down of the verdict. Several also stamped out their cigarettes, in deference to the holy man's presence. He gently coughed into his hand, clearing his throat.

"In the name of *Allah*, the Beneficent, the Merciful. May *Allah* send His blessings upon Mohamed and his progeny." A murmur of agreement spread throughout those in attendance. "We have deliberated long and hard concerning the charges leveled at the defendant, Mohamed el Moussa. As the trial progressed, other charges were added as the evidence came in slowly and with great care for detail. Apostasy, *irtidād,* blasphemy, thievery, were all examined with a meticulousness not seen in this camp before. Mohamed El Moussa has been found guilty of all of these charges."

A shout arose as the masses cheered as one voice.

The sheikh held up his hand to quiet them. "However, in his compassion and mercy, *Allah* gave the option for leniency regarding these charges. So the guilty verdict for these offenses does not involve the death penalty."

Looks of confusion, a groundswell of disagreement, began to arise from the crowd. It seemed hostile enough to el Moussa that he felt they would charge the group in front of them, including him, and take matters into their own hands. Al Baghdadi saw this as well. He ran to the front of the entourage and held up both hands.

"*Bas! Halas!* Enough! Stop this!" It was a combination plea and order to his men. They listened to him and piped down. "You have not heard the entire verdict, so be patient for one more moment. There were additional charges, as my esteemed colleague, Sheikh Hassan, made clear to you. They were of greater importance, and bore considerably more weight, than these others that did not involve capital punishment. Here is the major charge that will take care of everything that you demand. Mohamed el Moussa is found guilty of *Fasad fil-ardh*, 'spreading mischief in the land.' Islam permits the death penalty, by stoning, for anyone who threatens to undermine the authority or destabilise the state. In this instance, it relates to the Caliphate. Therefore, this trial is over, and the sentence of death is conveyed to Mohamed el Moussa, to be carried out tomorrow. *Allah* be praised!"

Taybieh smiled inwardly. He could now carry out his own plan designed to sell the same antiquity that his former friend was found guilty of trying to do. Now he could finance an escape from this cause that had gone so terribly wrong, and was certain to self-destruct within weeks. He could melt into the countryside and rejoin his family. He could resume being a small farmer, content with a quiet life far from the turmoil that he endured for the last few years.

With that, the two judges walked through the adoring crowd, nearly rabid with joy. Many grabbed their hands and kissed them as they left the area. With all eyes on the judges, no one noticed that el Moussa had collapsed into the arms of his guards, who then dragged him back to his cell to await the sentence.

*****

Overnight, heavy artillery shelling from the Syrian army left a pall over the ISIS encampment. There was no wind, so the cloud of dust and debris slowly, slowly settled over the ever-shrinking ISIS stronghold. Although it had not sustained any major strikes, the choking air had its effect on the center of the Caliphate's operations here. Everyone woke to the sound of coughing, hacking, spitting out gobs of pollutants. Nearly everyone now walked around with *keffiyehs* wrapped around faces rather than their heads.

Taybieh was at the edge of the camp, walking rapidly to the south, toward the loyalist controlled territory. He was on the Palmyra/Damascus Road, with his goal the small village of Seba Biyar. It was midway to the capital city. There he hoped to make contact with one of the scores of 'entrepreneurs' who were taking advantage of the chaos that was Syria- for their own personal gain. He hoped to join their ranks. He patted the flap on the pocket of his filthy tunic. In it was a sketch of the inscribed stone that started all this *Khara*, this shit, at the beginning. Even though he was not close, he thought of the other man he called 'friend.'

In the distance behind him, Taybieh could have sworn he heard a couple of 'thuds' of rocks finding their targets, amidst the swelling roar of a crowd engaged in carrying out one of the worst death penalties one could imagine...

Everyone piled into a couple of SUVs for the journey to the north. One of them was a nondescript Kia Picanto that belonged to the IDF. But you could never tell as it was 'plainclothes.' The other was Eitan's Suzuki Crossover, owned by the *Reshut Atiqot*, the INPA. However, everyone understood that it was Eitan's simply by default. He had use of a 'company car' from the Reshut for well over 30 years and had never had to buy one on his own. The plan was to take everyone to the frontier, and then only the civilian looking Picanto, with Sobhy, Eitan and Ben Dov, would continue into the Golan. The rest of us would 'stage' in Hammat Gader and serve as support for them.

It was agreed that the route should be one that was out of the prying eyes of anyone in the Palestinian Authority (PA) territory, lest any of them get unduly suspicious and begin nosing around. In addition, it was much safer to travel through Israel than occupied regions or the PA. We headed west, through Romema and under the Harp Bridge, the western entry into the city. From there we hit highway 1, the six-lane road that linked Jerusalem with Tel Aviv. Descending through the Judean Hills to the S*hephelah*, the transition to the coast, it pretty much followed the route that so many War of Independence stories were based on- the *Bab el Wad*. The roadbed is littered with the skeletal remains of dozens of World War II era half-tracks, transports and jeeps that all played an integral role in trying to keep the road to Jerusalem open in the tumultuous period between March and the end of May 1948.

The Palestinian Arab irregulars, backed up by the Jordanian Arab Legion, had situated themselves on the high ground in hilltop villages, designed to dominate and close the Tel Aviv – Jerusalem corridor.

As we drove through the area, Eitan pointed out the location of what had been the Palestinian village of *Deir Yassin*. Although quite small, it was in a position of strategic importance. Palestinian irregulars had taken over the village, and consistently were at an advantage when it came to blocking convoys on their way to relieve the besieged city of Jerusalem. Heavy fighting led to civilian casualties. 9 April 1948 saw the destruction of *Deir Yasin.* Nearly 260 would be killed according to all Arab current news releases at that time. It was a rallying cry for the Arab world in its fight against the eventual Jewish state. Remember, this is prior to the creation of the State of Israel and its Palestinian counterpart. So we are talking about civil war- not a war between two nations. Fearing the eventual loss of nearly one-third of his kingdom when the Palestinian state would be created, King Abdullah of Jordan would call it a turning point- making an invasion "impossible" to stop. Should he and the other Arab states succeed in destroying the Jewish presence, the notion of an independent Palestinian entity would become a moot point.

Hazam Nusseibeh, the news editor of the Palestine Broadcasting Service at the time, gave an interview to the BBC in 1998. *"I asked Dr. Khalidi in 1948 how we should cover the story. He said, 'We must make the most of this.' A press release, stated that children were murdered, pregnant women were raped, all sorts of atrocities."* New reports, released fifty years later in 1998, made by Arab survivors, have indicated that there was no massacre of civilians. The stories of rape angered the villagers, who complained to the Arab emergency committee that their wives and daughters were being exploited in the service of propaganda. Abu Mahmud, who lived in *Deir Yassin* in 1948, was one of those who complained. He told the BBC *"We said, 'There was no rape.'"* A study by Bir Zeit University, a Palestinian university incorporated in 1975, was based on discussions with each family from the village. They arrived at a figure of 107 Arabs dead. In fact, the attackers left open an escape corridor from the village and more than 200 residents left unharmed. The episode also sparked a controversy within the Arab world, because of its PR intent. Dr. Khalidi said, *"We have to say this, so the Arab armies will come to liberate Palestine from the Jews."* Nusseibeh told the BBC 50 years later, *"This was our biggest mistake. We did not realize how our people would react. As soon as they heard that women had been raped at Deir Yassin, Palestinians fled in terror."* In other words, the trumped up story sowed panic among the Palestinian civilian population and they fled from their homes in scores of villages, to eventually become embittered refugees living in camps in Jordan.

In addition, during the pullout of British troops who had been commanded by General Sir Gordon Macmillan, the British had turned over to the Arab side several of the Taggart-style forts that they had constructed designed to protect the area during the Mandate. These decade-old forts were constructed on a design that originated when Tegart was seconded to India earlier in the 20th Century. They were highly successful in controlling the Indian insurgency. Although they were named for their designer, Sir Charles Tegart, as they say, something gets lost in translation. In transliterating from English to Hebrew, 'Tegart' became known as 'Taggert'.

The most famous of these forts was the Latrun Police Station, which was of key strategic value in controlling the Tel Aviv road. About 25 km from Jerusalem, it was at the base of the climb through the *Bab el Wad*. On 24 May 1948, with the Jordanian Legion firmly ensconced in the fort, it was attacked by Israel's newly created 7th Armored Brigade. Arik Sharon, then a platoon commander, was wounded at Latrun along with many of his soldiers. The attack was repulsed, with the Israelis suffering heavy losses. The station would remain in Jordanian hands after the cease-fire and remain so until captured by Israel in the 1967 war. Today it is a memorial and museum dedicated to Israel's armored corps.

As a result of this failed attack, a plan had to be devised that could ensure communications and resupply of Jerusalem from Tel Aviv. The plan to create a 'by-pass' road that would skirt the major defensive positions of the Arabs that dominated the road through the Judean Hills. The Israelis would call it *Operation Nachshon*. But colloquially it was called the 'The Burma Road', named after the infamous road built by the Allies in Indochina in World War II. Over 2800 tons of food made it to Jerusalem during the siege of the city. Running from the *Shephelah* into the Jerusalem Mountains near *Sha'ar Hagai* and *Mizpe Nachshon*, it was an engineering marvel due to the fact that a majority of it was built by hand, since it was near impossible to get heavy equipment there.

From the Latrun Fort, the road headed a bit northwest, past Ben Gurion Airport and the town of Lod. Ben Gurion was situated about 55 km from Jerusalem and 18 or so from Tel Aviv. Just past the original Green Line that served as the armistice between Israel and Jordan following the 1949 cease fire, the airport served both communities, the heart of the population corridor, equally well due to the highway system.

We hit *Tzomet Galuyot*, the major junction that linked Highway 1 and Highway 20, which ran north/south through Tel Aviv, and raced through the *Ayalon* on the way to the renumbered Highway 2 (which in essence was the same as 20. As Jack Webb used to say, 'Only the names have been changed to protect the innocent!'). But in Israel, there are NO innocent drivers. They ALL have the right of way, know where they're going, and race along with impunity. The standing joke about Jewish males goes as far back as Moses. After wandering in the desert, the children of Israel became exasperated, and said, 'look, there's an oasis up ahead! Let's ask directions!' To which Moses replied, 'Its ok, I know where I'm going!' Forty years later... 😊

But on a more modern note, I commented to Sobhy about the National Police System in Israel. "You know, they always travel in pairs in their squad cars here. Do you have any idea as to why?" I asked him.

He pondered for a moment, knowing that if I asked the question, there had to be some sort of catch, some sort of smart-ass answer that he didn't want to fall prey to. "Okay, I give up *habibi*. Tell me, friend, why do Israeli police always work in pairs?"

Eitan jumped in gleefully, "*Ehad kotav, ehad koray*! One reads and one writes!" Sobhy roared with laughter at that, commenting that it was basically the same thing in Egypt. The difference being the level of reading ability over there.

By that time, we had passed the natural boundary of the *Yarkon* River between Tel Aviv proper and *Ramat HaSharon*, a northern suburb; this also was the northern limit of the Land of the Philistines in antiquity. Here, their last outpost could be seen off to the right of us not far from the Tel Aviv University campus-Tel Qasile. Excavated in the 1970s, it was home to one of the best preserved Philistine temple complexes ever unearthed.

Traffic thinned out a bit, and we flew past *Herzliyya*, a bedroom community that many consider to be one of the more affluent areas in Israel, on the way to *Netanya*. Once passed, as the day began to wane, we zoomed past Mt. Carmel and Haifa on the way to an overnite at the Palm Beach in Acco.

It was one of those places that had its glory days in the 1990s, had fallen on somewhat hard times by the early 2000s, and now was in the slow process of remodeling and re-marketing itself; with a fair amount of success. Located a couple of kms south of the Old City of Acco proper, its sunset views of the Mediterranean and the Crusader harbor were stunning. In addition, its private beach, tennis and pool facilities, made it a natural 'go to' place. The new ownership was working very hard on bringing it back. But the prices remained low for the time being and it still maintained a fairly good level of comfort. It was much better than staying in town for the same price.

*****

The next morning, after the typical Israeli breakfast feast, we continued our journey north past Acco proper to Nahariyya, just south of the Lebanese border. This stop was crucial to our mission, because it would be here that all the 'medical' pieces of Sobhy's cover would fall into place. We pulled into the parking lot of the Golan Medical Center, where we were to meet with Dr. Leonid Kohan, the chief of cosmetic surgery and burns. He had been apprised of our visit, and to an extent, the aim of our activity. However, once again following the Jack Webb motto of changing names to protect the innocent, he had been given sufficiently vague information that would prevent any tongue slippage. Since we had called the evening before from Acco to reconfirm, he was waiting for us in the lobby of the 21st century facility.

A short, rotund man, he reminded me of a Santa Claus sans beard. This even went down to the small details, like wire-rim glasses. However, the exterior image belied the interior man. He was a tough, no-nonsense individual with as much warmth as a January day in Minnesota. We all had been warned of this by our IDF contact, but were still somewhat put off by his matter-of-fact brusqueness. Yet, in spite of it all, we had been reassured time and again that, if there ever was a need in that field of burn medicine, no one in the world could match his talents. As the introductions were being completed, I whispered to Eitan that it was a good thing that the majority of his patients were unconscious and could care less about bedside manner. He tried to refrain from laughing, but it didn't work. Everyone, including Dr. Kohan, looked his way. The group peered quizzically at him, while Kohan glared with a knife-like stare.

"*Slicha*, excuse me. *Ani mitzta'ere*. I'm sorry. I drifted away for a moment, thinking about the last time I was in Nahariyya with this girl I was seeing..."

"Do tell!!" Spat out Dr. Kohan. His disdain was palpable, "I *do* have important work to do with my real patients!" He turned and walked down the hall a couple of steps. After half a dozen, and not hearing any footsteps behind, he stopped, turned and gestured impatiently.

"*Yallah*! Come you all. You need my help and I'm willing to lend a hand, but certainly not in the public spaces of this great facility. To my offices... *mahair*! hurry up."

We looked at each other, Eitan started to laugh again. The others looked at him like he was the *kibbutz idiote,* and me? Well, I just smiled and followed down the hall after the entourage.

It was here that all of our opinions of the esteemed, although arrogant, Dr. Leonid Kohan changed. When we got to the burn wing of the facility, he slowed down to a stroll. This state-of-the-art unit consisted of entirely glass-walled sterile rooms that allowed for medical staff viewing directly from the nurses' station- in addition to the electronic monitoring that went on round the clock. If, and when, family were allowed brief visits, power curtains gave privacy. However, these were few and far between. It only happened when the patient was released to more traditional care after the initial critical check-in to the burn unit and the situation considered to be stable enough for visits. Although this was pure hell for the family, it was essential because of the risk of infection.

Dr. Kohan paused for a moment at each of the occupied glass rooms. He glanced at the digitally projected charts on the front wall before him, gazed at the patient with a warmth and concern that suddenly summoned back the kindly Santa Claus imagery first noted, and then would say something to the nursing staff if he deemed it necessary. Once, he left us and entered the room. We couldn't hear anything, so thick was the class wall; but we could see the genuine smile, gentle touch, and grateful response of the person in the bed. Was the gruff demeanor a façade? Sobhy was bold enough to approach the doctor as we moved between windows.

"That's all a game that you play isn't it?" he remarked quietly so the others couldn't hear.

At first, the medical genius glared and harrumphed a bit, then sort of visibly softened. "*B'seder*, okay, you've seen it," he replied. "I can't imagine the pain and agony, and yes, eventually in some cases, the sorrow of the family when nothing else could be done. It grieves me dearly, and I throw everything that I have into trying to save these good souls and restore their lives as best as I can, if I can. But it is overwhelming. So I create a hard-shell about me. It protects me a bit, allows for a small modicum of sanity. But certainly not much."

Led by Eitan, each of us came over to the medical man and grasped his hand in thanks. Kati and Lior gave 'Santa' a group hug. And, true to the Santa image, his cheeks reddened, beneath a couple of tear-swelled eyes. A bit embarrassed, he broke off the hug and proceeded down the hall. We followed a moment later, to give him some time to recompose himself and his 'hardened' image.

It took us nearly half an hour to get to his suite of offices. We all sat down in the conference room just outside his private lab. Coffee was waiting. With the door shut, Dr. Kohan dropped all the pretenses and was as genuine as you could imagine. He discussed with us just a bit of his work, an indication of his true modesty. He then moved on to what he referred to as 'Operation Hollywood.'

"So you're all about rescuing some of our ancient Jewish history before it gets destroyed by ISIS? And you think that by doing it surreptitiously, under the covers, it will work better than anything else?"

Asa Ben Dov, the military man, answered this question. He made it clear that official Israeli involvement would be used as an excuse for ISIS, *Hezbollah*, and perhaps even the Syrian military to widen its relatively quiet war on the Jewish state. "We certainly don't need a greater *balagan*, a problem, for us."

"But what of the work I'm doing here? Doesn't it fall under the category of widening the potential of the conflict?" Dr. Kohan was confused.

"I think that the tremendous good that you're doing here for the civilian victims of the war over there is not only the right thing to do but is also a great PR incentive for us as well. Please don't misunderstand me, it's not that aspect that is the leading issue here. It is not just *hasbara*, pro-Israel posturing, but the showing of the world the true nature of Israel with regard to *tikkun olam*, repairing the world." Ben Dov was on a roll and once you get an Israeli soldier moving forward, well, watch out. He went on. "Think back to all the natural and human-made disasters in the world over the past several decades. I remember when the organization, *Hatzalah*, or *Chevra Hatzalah*, which loosely translates as 'Company of Rescuers' was first founded. The IDF's Home Front Command Rescue Unit was formed thirty years ago after two major

By מייח 7 (Own work) [Public domain], Under Creative Commons (CC BY-SA 4.0)
https://creativecommons.org/licenses/by-sa/4.0/deed.en

attacks by Hezbollah against IDF staff units in Tyre, during the First Lebanon War in 1982-1983."

Ben Dov continued on, listing the major actions taken by this extraordinary group of Israelis, around the world. They aided the victims of the earthquake in Turkey in 1999, and *Hatzalah* members were among the first responders to the World Trade Center on September 11, 2001. They rushed to the scene of the earthquake in Haiti in 2010, the Fukushima disaster in Japan in 2011, and the devastating tsunami in Thailand in 2012. In the past few years, a team from the Israeli Home Front Command's Rescue Unit left for the Philippines less than 24 hours after the scope of the disaster there from Typhoon Haiyan in 2013 became known.

Finally, the trio of disasters in North America showed the agencies at their finest. In 2017, IsrAID and iAid, Israel's chief humanitarian aid groups, sent relief teams and crucial supplies to help during Tropical Storm Harvey. Turning to Florida, a team from Israel Rescue Coalition and *United Hatzalah* arrived in Miami after Hurricane Irma.

The third disaster struck Mexico. The Israeli military sent a contingent of 70 specialists to Mexico to help in the rescue effort in the wake of the deadly earthquake. The team included 25 engineers who inspected buildings for stability, and medical, logistics and technical workers. In accordance to Jewish Law, the IDF chief rabbi granted the team special dispensation for the mission, since they operated during the *Rosh Hashanah* holiday, the Jewish New Year.

Eitan was heavily involved in the development of one unit in Arad. "We Israelis appreciated the chance to show the world another side of the IDF, and the country on the whole, that was totally different from those images on the news that constantly reviewed the Israeli occupation of the West Bank; such as soldiers at checkpoints or using tear gas, rubber bullets, batons to disperse Palestinian demonstrators. We were all so pissed off and frustrated about our negative image around the world, which today is only getting worse, particularly in Europe. In many cases, legitimate critics of Israel are joined by anti-Israel and anti-Zionist groups like the BDS motivated by their own interests or by blind hatred."

"It seems that nearly every Israeli, at one time or another, has worked with one of the agencies involved," Lior Bat Rimon added her story as well. "I even had a close friend, an Orthodox Jew, work with the most horrible, yet necessary, organizations you can imagine. It was ZAKA, *Zihuy Korbanot Ason,* 'disaster victim identification.' I can't possibly envision how those people could do that job without losing a bit of their humanity."

Dr. Kohan nodded and quietly said, "I was one of those." It explained much. "Perhaps we could use something a bit more fortifying when we now can get down to business."

In a small cupboard tucked away in a corner of his spacious office, Kohan pulled out a bottle of Stock 84. Sobhy's eyes lit up like *Tahrir* Square in Cairo. An extraordinary brandy produced in the beautiful town of Trieste in northeast Italy, it was noted for being mellow and smooth. Its name came from the year it was created, 1884.

"Not many people outside of Israel and southern Europe are familiar with this. Personally, I love a drop every now and then." And there it was, the proverbial twinkle in Santa's eyes! Dr. Kohan *did* have that other side after all. Our coffees duly laced, we sat down and told him exactly why the documents were required and forced Sobhy to lose all sense of modesty as he partially stripped down to allow for a 'medical examination' of his healing wounds.

Dr. Kohan's eyes widened a bit when he saw 'the wounds.' He quickly assumed the role of the world-class burn and cosmetic surgery doctor that had earned him numerous international accolades. He put on his reading glasses to get a better look, the scars were so real. His first cursory inspection was a visual one, peering intensely at the 'scar tissue' from all angles. His initial response was very compelling, and heartening, to us all.

"My first response in seeing Sobhy's torso was one of relief. Let me explain. If I were to see this man's body wound, I would be concerned at the scope of the primary intrusion into his body. But the good news is that I would be relieved at the lack of redness and irritation that would have indicated inflammation and perhaps infection. In other words, I am tremendously impressed with your colleague, Lior, and her skills. This is, for all intents and purposes, keloidal scar tissue sustained from a major wound. Now, I'll perform the next level of exam."

Dr. Kohan now turned his attentions to the physical side of the exam. He put on latex gloves, as he would in any medical exam, and gently ran his fingers over the raised tissue. He lightly probed and pushed a bit. Asked if there was any pain and palpitated the surrounding area. After 5 minutes of this he sat back and snapped off the gloves.

"You're healing well my friend," he joked to Sobhy, who theatrically wiped his brow and let out a whoosh of relief. This broke the tension, and everyone laughed a bit at this comedic routine.

"You should take this on the road to the Camel Comedy Club in Tel Aviv" exclaimed Kati as she wiped tears from her eyes. "They are sorely lacking in good routines. *Wallah*, really, we all needed this!"

A new set of gloves were donned, and the doctor turned to the leg wound. He followed the same technique here as well. After a few minutes his pronouncement was the same- that Sobhy was healing nicely. His only suggestion was that, at the end of a long day, Sobhy feign a tiredness and soreness, and favor that leg just a bit. He said that would be typical of a leg wound of that nature a few months old. The abdominal wound would not be as stressed in normal day-to-day physical activity by someone not involved in manual labor. These insights were precisely the kind of further background information that our Egyptian friend would need on the ground in Syria.

"Now for the easy part," Ben Dov spoke up. "We need to create the type of vague, yet medically detailed, records that match the kind that you create for all the refugees from Syria that you treat and subsequently release to go back home. This is in case some overachieving low-level, or is it low-life, official in ISIS feels the need to have something to do and tries to electronically discover something. After all, they are very good at their version of electronic warfare. Just look at the ads they place on Facebook, and the scores of YouTube videos extolling their virtues."

Led by Dr. Kohan, we descended one flight to the records department of the medical facility. There, we got what was determined to be a complete set of documents that would reference all of the care that Sobhy 'received' a few months ago in the hospital. The doctor even appropriated a duplicate copy of some x-rays from other patients that approximated the same two wounds the he had 'suffered.' However, the second set had the name changed to match the newly created file. A couple of benign doctor's exam letters were also run off to give to our colleague.

Sobhy took them and immediately crumpled and creased them. He then stepped on them and rubbed them across the floor. Then, to the surprise of the doctor and the records facility secretary, he asked for her cup of coffee sitting on her desk. He then took the cup and drizzled some drops down the side of the cup. After that, he took the cup and set it on one of the documents, pushed a bit and took it away. Left on the crumpled form was a beautiful coffee cup ring!

"Now it truly looks aged!" Sobhy was delighted with the antiquity of the papers that would then go into his wallet. We were now set to go on to the Golan.

*****

That afternoon, we set across the *Galil*, heading east and the Golan Heights. We took the smaller, less traveled roads so that we would not run into too many folks. It was scenic, and extraordinarily relaxing. On Highway 89 we drove past *Tel Kabri* and *Tell el-Qahweh*, 'the mound of coffee.' It was one of the largest Middle Bronze Age Canaanite palaces in ancient Israel, over 3700 years old. I remarked at the discovery there of frescoes on the walls that were Minoan in origin. To date, they are still the only frescoes of that Aegean culture ever discovered in Israel.

Still on the 89, a mid-afternoon snack would be eaten at Meron, along the slopes of Mt. Meron. Rising over 1200 m above sea level, it was the highest peak within Israel. In 1965, a 20,000 acre nature reserve was declared. An additional 350 acres were declared part of the reserve in 2005. It was along the slopes of Mt. Meron that the ancient 4th and 5th century community and synagogue of Khirbet Shema was excavated in the early 1980s under the direction of Eric Myers of Duke University and Tom Kraabel of the University of Minnesota. It was a joint project that met with a great deal of success. We ate at Hummous Eliyahu and thoroughly enjoyed the Israeli fast food.

From there, we would continue to Highway 91 at *Tzomet HaGalilit*, near Rosh Pinna and Safed. As we laid out our route over coffee, Kati noted that we were now in the land of the *Kabbalists*. We had entered into the region that was home to some of the most famous mystic rabbis of Judaism, such as Rav Isaac Luria, considered by most people to be the founder of contemporary *Kabbalah*. Luria was born in 1534 in Jerusalem in the area of the city that is now the Old *Yishuv* Court Museum. He was born to an Ashkenazic father and a Sephardic mother. He died in 1572 and is buried just outside of Safed.

Sobhy was vaguely familiar with the term, but asked for a clearer meaning. Surprisingly, it was our make-up artist who took us all unawares, as she announced that she was a modern practitioner of *Kabbalah*, and would be happy to explain it. Who better to describe the *Kabbalah* than an adherent, so Lior was more than happy to give the '5 *shekel*' overview.

"Our Lior is full of surprises for us," was Kati's response. "*B'vakasha*, please, go on." I felt our timetable slipping just a bit, but ordered us all another round of coffee. While I was getting the tray loaded, Sobhy shouted at me not to forget one of the dessert cheese *bourekas* that he saw in a glass case on the counter.

Kabbalah, means a "received tradition." It is a discipline and school of thought that originates in Judaism. Some say that it is the 'soul' of our *Torah*. According to *Kabbalah*, the true essence of God is so transcendent that it cannot be described, except with reference to what it is not.

Kabbalah is meant to explain the relationship between an unchanging, eternal and mysterious *Ein Sof* (infinity) and the mortal and finite universe (God's creation). Teachings defined the inner meaning of both the Hebrew Bible and traditional Rabbinic literature and their hidden aspects. Kabbalah emerged in the 12th century in Southern France and Spain with the mysterious appearance of the key text, the *Zohar*, meaning 'splendor,' and later was a key component in the Jewish mystical renaissance of 16th century Ottoman Turkish Palestine.

One prominent Orthodox Jew said basically, "It's nonsense, but it's Jewish nonsense, and the study of anything Jewish, even nonsense, is worthwhile."

Like most subjects of Jewish belief, the area of mysticism is wide open to personal interpretation. These misunderstandings stem largely from the fact that the teachings of *Kabbalah* have been so badly distorted by mystics and occultists.

Kati jumped in to explain about the tomb of one its more famous rabbis. "One of the town's most well-known landmarks is the tomb of Honi the *Ha Magel*, 'the circler.' The presence of this shrine here attracted a large Gerrer Hassid population in the early 1800s. They were Hassidic Jews from *Góra Kalwaria*, a small town in Poland."

"Okay, I'm lost," Sobhy said as he brushed his *bourekas* crumbs from his shirtfront. "But I'm going to need another one of these if the explanation gets too deep." He winked, got up and headed back to the counter.

Upon his return, with a napkin wrapped 'carb' bomb, Kati told the story of this mystic rabbi. "Honi the Rabbi, known as 'the circler,' lived in the 1st century BCE here in the *Galil.* According to the tradition, there was little or no rainfall one winter, and there was a drought."

"So the crops were thirsty and the people were dying! Or was it the people were thirsty and the crops were dying?" Sobhy smiled between bites. Kati laughed and went on.

"I guess you could say that both ways! But as the story went, Honi drew a circle in the dust and boldly proclaimed to God, in front of his constituents in the village, that he would not move from this circle until God brought abundant rain to save the community. Well, as we say in Yiddish, it started to 'pish' a little. This wasn't enough for the rabbi. He stayed in the circle and continued to pray until, finally, a downpour occurred and the drought was broken."

"I think that he watched the 5-day extended forecast on the Weather Channel," was Eitan's response. We all laughed at that as we began to pack up in order to continue our journey to the eastern side of the Galilee, en route to our final destination, the Golan.

As we were leaving the fast food restaurant, a young IDF soldier was standing outside on the sidewalk, passing out leaflets to everyone. I grabbed one, quickly scanned it, and passed it around to the others. It was a government travel advisory brochure for the Occupied Territories, designed to prevent as best as possible any terror attacks on travelers. It was a reality check on the sometimes precarious world of Israel and her immediate Arab neighbors.

We proceeded along Highway 91 on the way to our armistice line crossing at the *Gesher Banot Yakkov*, The Daughters of Jacob Bridge. The name ascribed to it only dated to the age of the Crusades, but remained intact to this day. It was just opposite a small *wadi* from *Tzomet Gadot,* the *Gadot* interchange. This site served as a fortified Syrian military outpost complete with communication trenches and concrete bunkers, surrounded by barbed wire and minefields. From this base, the Syrians were able to fire down at *Kibbutz Gadot* and to command the *Banot Yaakov* Bridge. At the end of the Six Day War, the Syrians fled from the incredibly heroic attack of the IDF's *Golani* Brigade and the site now serves as a memorial for the soldiers who fell conquering the Golan Heights.

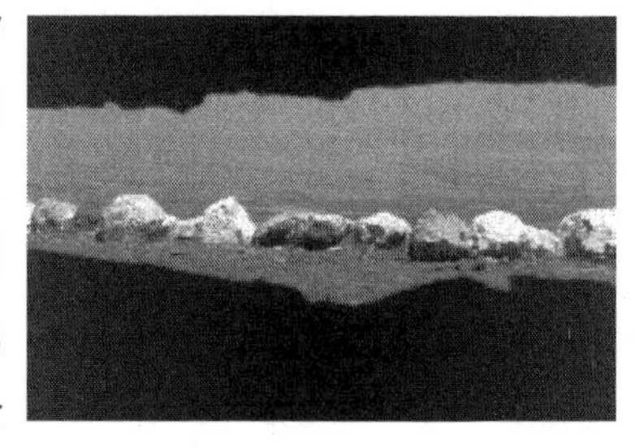

It was a sobering experience for Sobhy. We were all aware of his stories regarding the wars in Sinai, and his participation. Every time that I glanced at him, and his scarred wrist, I was reminded of the violence and tragedy on both sides of the equation. His 'permanent watch' as he called it, was the result of an Israeli bullet that shattered both the ulna and radius in the 1973 Yom Kippur War. Ever since we had hashed it out over a few Stella beers in Cairo, we were even more closely binded together in our resolve to try to prevent any more bloodshed. As Abbie Natan said in his tagline from his pirate radio station that broadcast off the coast of Israel in the Mediterranean (borrowed from Menachem Begin), "No more war, no more bloodshed... peace. Coming to you live from somewhere in the Mediterranean, this is *Ram Kol HaShalom*, the Voice of Peace. 1500 Khz on your radio dial." *Zichronot*... memories.

We now headed southeast on Highway 9088 past Qatzrin, an Israeli settlement organized as a local council in the Golan

Heights that was known as the 'capital of the Golan'. The Golan Heights Winery is located nearby, to the east. We decided that we would spend one last night together at Qatzrin as a final jumping off point for Sobhy. The Villa Golan, a small BnB, rent out all four rooms to us. Eitan and I were delighted when we discovered that it had a bbq grill. There were very fond memories of dozens of barbecues *al ha aish*, on the grill, in Arad during many years of excavations in the south. A quick trip to the grocery got us all the stuff that we needed, and a wonderful, quiet evening was spent on the Golan.

The next morning dawned bright and clear. A perfect day for touring the Golan, but regrettably that was not the final intention. However, we did take a bit of an advantage as we were not in any sort of immediate rush. Before leaving Jerusalem, our last intelligence report stated that the ISIS contingent was too preoccupied with the Syrian army onslaught to worry about blowing up any Palmyra antiquities- for the moment. Turning south on the 808 road, we stopped at Gamla Falls, the highest waterfall in the Golan at 51m. Because of its close proximity to the falls, the road was also called *HaMapalim* Road, 'waterfalls road.' Sobhy made a request that we simply couldn't turn down. He said that he had no idea when he might bathe again before getting out of Syria, so he asked if we might all take a dip in the cool, fresh water. It was unanimous- all felt that it was a great idea, so like little kids, we stripped down to shorts and took the plunge. For almost an hour we frolicked like teenagers in the crisp waters at the base of the falls. We laid out in the sun, warming and drying ourselves before heading to our final stop, when we would say *l'hitraot*, see you soon, to our Egyptian friend.

Only a short drive farther on, and we went past the little town of *Gamla*. The name of *Gamla* comes from the Arabic word for camel, *gamal*, because of its curious location on a narrow ridge 10 km north of the Sea of Galilee. After an intense fight with the Romans during the First Revolt that broke out in 66 CE, all its 9000 citizens were killed. Because of this horrific event, *Gamla* sometimes was called 'the Masada of the North.' *Gamla* was first discovered after 1967 when Israel occupied and later annexed this part of the Golan. The archaeologist Shmaryahu Gutmann would make it his life's work. *Gamla* has a 1st Century CE synagogue in the eastern part of the city that today has been restored. Many Israeli youth will come here with their families to celebrate Bar and Bat Mitzvot.

Our final leg took us to *Salukiya*, the Eden Spring and past *Ramat Magshamim*, 'the heights of the dream fulfillers. Here was the point of entry that was chosen for Sobhy.

*****

We all disembarked from the vehicle at the edge of a wheat field. The afternoon was warm but not overly so. Up in the Golan, the humidity of the Sea of Galilee was a memory, and it was actually quite pleasant- except for the task at hand. One by one, we bade 'til laters' with Sobhy, warm hugs and kisses on the cheeks. During the final leg of the drive, Ben Dov went over Sobhy from head to toes, making sure that his clothing was proper, going through his wallet with all its dog-eared documents. After ascertaining that there was absolutely nothing that could tie him with anyone in Israel, except for the Golan Medical Center stuff, it was time to separate. From there, Sobhy would be faced with a 2 km walk to the Golan armistice line. The IDF had a special checkpoint designed for the Syrian civilian medical cases. This is where Sobhy was headed.

Due to the extreme secrecy of the mission, no one outside of our small group was aware of Sobhy, or was alerted to his identity. He was entirely on his own now. At the checkpoint, and IDF soldier took his papers politely, but silently. Sobhy made a single effort at engaging him in a bit of mindless banter, but a quick wave of the hand silenced him.

"*Taodat za'hut*, your identity card, please." Although Sobhy by now was very familiar with Hebrew, he feigned ignorance, much as a Syrian refugee would.

"*Na'am*? What did you say?" Was his response in Arabic. The soldier, as was the case with most Israelis, switched languages with relative facility. In Arabic, he repeated the question. "Can I please have your identity papers?"

"Aah" Sobhy smiled. He reached slowly into his back pocket and with two fingers pulled out his wallet. In addition, everything else was put into a small plastic tray on the table next to the line that he had stood in.

The soldier smiled back at him and started to go through the papers. "It says here, Mr. Sobhy..."

"Just Sobhy please. 'Mr.' was my father," once again, the Sobhy charm disarmed the young warrior and the border tension eased just a bit.

"*Tayib*, ok. So Sobhy, you worked for the Supreme Council of Antiquities in Egypt for quite some time. Then, what, you went back home, *to a war zone*? I find that hard to imagine, when you had such a good life in Egypt." A harder stare was conjured up.

"It was my family. As you say, I did have a very good life in Egypt. But what would that say about my role as a son and brother to those I love if I couldn't get them out or care for them. If the only option left to me was to return to try to help them as best as I could. And as it turned out, I was the one who was wounded by God knows who. You have family, don't you Mr. IDF, and I don't mean that as an insult. I just don't know your name."

"Asaf."

"Excuse me?"

The soldier looked at Sobhy directly in the eyes. "My name is Asaf. I'm from Degania, not too far from here." He held out his hand, and the Egyptian shook it with warmth and vigor.

"So I have one final question for you Sobhy. Why are there no numbers called or received on your mobile BLU cellphone. That seems just a bit suspicious."

Sobhy replied with a direct, reasonable answer. He told the Israeli that all the cell towers in southwest Syria were either down or not functioning. But, unfortunately, he felt that there wasn't anyone he could call due to the chaotic state of affairs. On top of all that, he wasn't even sure where any family were scattered by now.

After all, it had been a couple of months since he crossed over to obtain medical attention here in Israel.

The young soldier left him for a moment and went to the checkpoint hut to speak with his commanding officer. Sobhy could see a somewhat forceful discussion, with a great deal of gesturing involved. He smiled inwardly as he remembered something that he had been told a long time ago. *How do you prevent anyone from the Mediterranean region from talking? The answer, tie their hands behind their backs!* When the IDF guard returned moments later, he handed Sobhy all of his personal belongings, including the cell phone. A genuinely warm smile creased his face and he wished the 'Syrian refugee' all the luck in the world in finding his home and his family safe.

"Be careful over there," he admonished. "In today's world, the Syrians hate each other almost more than they hate us here in Israel. As your saying goes, *Yom Asal, Yom Basal.* One day's honey, another is onions. I hope that today is filled with honey."

With that, Sobhy passed through a 25 m strip of 'no person's land' and suddenly found himself in the Syrian Arab Republic, or what was left of it. At first blush, it seemed no different from the Israeli side of the Golan. And then it struck him- the silence. He heard no signs of human activity whatsoever. There were no vehicles, no people in the fields, no one at all. And on top of all that, there were no birds; no chirping, flying around overhead... no lively nature. This more than anything scared him.

From the road map that he had memorized in Jerusalem, he quickly identified the small road that ran east. A quick glance upward at the blazing sun, and he started to walk toward his first 'checkpoint'- the small village of *Tasil*. It was about 5 km away. From there, he hoped to catch a bus to his 'hometown' of *As Suwayda*.

Since we wouldn't hear anything for a while, the rest of us slowly made our way south, just to the east of the *Kinneret*, the Sea of Galilee. We stopped at a wonderful, small accommodation on the edge of the Golan Heights, spending the night at the delightful *Kfar Haruv* (carob) Peace Village Lodge overlooking the simmering water reflected in the rapidly setting sun. The village with its wooden cabins and luxurious suites made for a unique experience. Twenty seven wooden cabins were situated in the midst of a beautiful garden, spacious lawns and herb gardens. An organic cafeteria rounded out this wonderful, relaxing overnight stay. But in the backs of our minds, Sobhy and his welfare loomed large.

As we headed back down the Golan the next morning, Lior noted that we were driving close to the *Hammath Gader* springs.

"I've never been, although I've driven through the area with my family before. We always stopped at *En Gev* for St. Peter's fish and a swim, but never in the sulphur springs."

"That settles it," as Eitan pulled the wheel onto the access road of the INPA site. "My *proteksia* will get us all in with no problem." That's what happens when you're with the director of a National Park when he visits another park location.

So, upon entering, our first stop was the farthest away- the Roman bathhouse complex, dated to the late first and early second centuries. It fell upon me to give the '5 shekel' tour of the locale. As we walked through, I explained the penchant of the Romans for bathing; wherever they were in their empire. Apparently the Emperor Hadrian had the greatest obsession, as his bathhouses were found scattered all over his lands, from Bath, England, to Tivoli, to *Hammath Gader*. Roman engineering was at its finest in these endeavors. In addition, it appeared that there was a universal 'architectural firm' that carried out all of the planning, since all of the complexes were of the same design and scale. However, this particular facility would be constructed by the Xth Legion of his army.

The concept was simple. Create a resort-style facility with different levels of relaxation based on various degrees of hot spring water temperatures, top it all off with a final cool dip and rinse in fresh water, and your guests would love you for it. But be sure to include a bit of spirituality as well. The Roman god of healing and medicine, Asclepius, was well received here to be sure. A series of pools of various sizes and degrees of Sulphur percentage could be found here. The water was ingeniously transported in via a hydraulic system that, through the use of water pressure in stepped down ceramic pipes, increased pressure so that the water flowed uphill from the initial spring. There were 'gargoyle' fountainheads that filled the main rectangular pool. Although the water flowed constantly through these 'spigots' when the sluice gate at the spring was open, the rate of water flow could be adjusted by popping a stone plug into the mouth of each figurehead. At that spring, at the edge of the complex, the water temperature was a 'mild' 42 degrees

Celsius, or about 108 Fahrenheit. But in addition, it contained a concentration of 4.7% Sulphur. Needless to say, the aroma of rotten eggs could be noticed dozens of meters away.

As we continued the mini-tour, I also noted that the Romans were one of the first societies to address their constituents' illnesses as well. Leprosy was a well-documented illness. It also was known that, although there was no cure at that time, the hot sulfurous waters relieved symptoms. However, since no one at that time knew about the bacteria that caused the disease, the effects of the illness could be lessened in these hot baths. But no Roman in his or her right mind would bath in the same pool for fear of contracting the disease. As a result, a small 'leper's pool' just outside of the bathhouse complex was created for those afflicted.

From the archaeological site, we went to the modern spring facility, changed, and took the plunge. Once past the aroma, the relief that surged through our bodies at the gentle pressure of the hot sulfurous water melted us all in more ways than one. But 10 minutes was really the maximum recommended. From there, a quick freshwater shower rinse and we headed back to the vehicle to continue our journey. On the way to the parking lot we passed the modern crocodile farm that was residence for over 200 critters.

After a snack we were well fortified for the ride back to Jerusalem. Once there, we would just have to cool our jets until we heard anything.

He never thought that isolation in the midst of desolation could be so painful. Almost as soon as Sobhy crossed the line into Syria, he noticed a distinct return to the '19th century.' He tried to convince himself that much of it was simply due to a different culture and lifestyle, but quickly disabused himself of that notion. Yes, the fields, and those left to work them, seemed to be reliant on a different technology (or lack of). But he wasn't sure if it was due to the decade-old civil war that ravaged the countryside, or if it was simply the Arab cultural mindset maintaining a field operations technique that was centuries old, yet proven to nominally work with little or no distractions. Or, for him, was it a case of 'Israeli technology envy' that focused things in black and white.

The archaeologist in Sobhy noted that the agriculture being practiced here on the fringe of the Syrian desert was a reversion back to the dry farming subsistence level that had been used in this part of the world for thousands of years. It would truly only be during the height of the Nabatean Empire about 2000 years ago that spring water irrigation, using terraces and dams, would come into play. The Israeli archaeologist Avram Negev really pointed this out in his seminal work concerning the Nabateans in the 1960s-80s. As a matter of fact, he even reconstructed a farm adjacent to the ancient Nabatean city of Shivta, reconstructing the water supply system. Today, carob, fig, almond, pistachio and peach trees thrive, based on ancient technology. In addition, grapevines also supply the community needs.

But something got lost at the end of antiquity. The Persian conquests of the region in the 6th century CE brought an end to these innovations. Today's modern Bedouin have reverted to the dry farming techniques that pre-dated Nabatean advances, and the Syrian villagers simply continued these age-old traditions.

Sobhy sat down under one of the scrawny Acacia trees, suited for this environment, and drank deeply from the water bottle that he had purchased at a roadside stand right after his crossing. He closed his eyes and remembered the discussions with Eitan and Kati about the great strides made by citizens of what would become Israel during its formative years; designed to find a way for the new immigrants of the late 19th and early 20th century to survive in the backward province of the Ottoman Empire.

The region's first true agronomy experiment, the *Mikveh Israel* agricultural school, was established in 1870. This was followed by the Agricultural Experiment Station, funded by the Jewish

Agency and established in 1921- under the auspices of the British Mandate. Their mission was to conduct research for the creation of small farms with intensive agriculture; specializing in mixed farming of fruit trees, cattle, chicken, vegetables and cereals. It would be the precursor of the Israeli *kibbutz*. The research station, headed by Itzhak Elazari-Volcani and located in Rehovot, was the first scientific institute in Palestine. Its stepchild, the Agricultural Research Organization, was established in 1971, incorporating all agricultural research within the Ministry of Agriculture of the Israeli Government. From that point on, *everything* seemed to be within reach of discovery and implementation.

It was no surprise that just about that time as well *Kibbutz Netafim* was founded in 1965. Netafim pioneered the revolutionary concept of drip revolution, creating a paradigm shift toward low-flow agricultural irrigation. Today it is a worldwide pioneer in smart drip and micro-irrigation, starting from the idea of Israeli engineer Simcha Blass calling for the release of water in controlled, slow drips for precise crop irrigation. Water conservation decreased the use of pesticides and herbicides and would be something that the entire world could get behind. Now the kibbutz-owned company operates in 112 countries with 13 factories throughout the world.

He must have dozed a bit, as the sun was now beginning to set over the mountains of the Galilee to his west. He best get going, *Tasil* was still a way off on foot. With virtually no civilian automotive traffic in this part of Syria, it would be a dusty, hot trek for him. As he continued, he passed a couple of abandoned concrete bus shelters. Bullet-pocked, rusting bus route signs bolted to the shelters were no longer relevant. Every so often, he turned to look back down the road that he had just walked, searching in vain for a dust cloud that might indicate a coming vehicle of any sort.

Finally, with daylight nearly gone, Sobhy reached the small town of *Tasil*. But it reminded him of a ghost town, the kind that you saw on American TV westerns. Here, though, rather than tumbleweed, it was the ubiquitous desert 'broombush' that bounced along the dust-laden streets. Only a handful of people could be seen in a community that had numbered around 15,000 after the 2004 governmental census. Many of the buildings bore the signs of the never-ending civil war, some damaged beyond repair. Initially, it had fallen under the control of the Free Syrian Army (FSA). But ISIS and its terrorists captured the town in a pre-dawn attack in late February 2017. The military unit responsible for this was the Khalid Ibn Al Walid Army. Located very close to the juncture of the Israeli-Syrian armistice line, and the Jordanian-Israeli and Jordanian-Syrian borders, both Israel and Jordan increased their military preparedness in case ISIS decided to try something to broaden the conflict. But soon after, a Syrian rebel military group that was an ally of the FSA re-took *Tasil*, although the neighboring villes of Sahem al-Golan and Adwan remained firmly within the ISIS grip. As a result, Tasil's population had shrunk to a couple of thousand as most fled farther to the north to escape the violence and bloodshed.

The Egyptian stumbled upon the small building on the main street that had served as the bus terminal. However, it looked as if it were abandoned. He pushed open the door, forcing it inward past piles of litter and debris, calling out for someone, anyone. There was no immediate answer, so he started to explore just a bit, knowing that he had only about 45 minutes until darkness enveloped the community. He would need to find a place to stay.

"*Amkin ana asa'idk*? How can I help you?" Sobhy nearly jumped out of his boots. He turned to see a wizened old man, or one who 'looked' old, enter from a back room. He was filthy, his clothes badly shredded and ill-fitting. Yet he carried himself with a dignity that defied the situation. "I am, er, *was*, the station master here before everything entered the realm of *Shaitan*, the Devil."

"My name is Sobhy, originally from *As Suwayda*, having worked in archaeology in Egypt for many years. I came back to find my family, was wounded, was treated by the Israelis, and now have returned to try to get back to the town and find them. I am wondering about any buses or other way to get there."

The other man, shook his hand, and gave him a rueful smile. "I am most honored to meet you, but have bad news for you. We had a thriving community, and yes, a bus that linked us with *As Suwayda* once every day. You said that you were wounded, was it combat? Were you just caught up in things? Are you on any particular side in this horror? What was it like in Israel?" The questions poured out of his mouth in rapid fire, as if he hadn't spoken to anyone in a long time.

Sobhy recalled his cover and recounted it in a vague fashion. It would have been something a Syrian refugee would have said, and not expanded on, lest he find himself among people of 'the wrong side.' His answers seemed to satisfy the former terminal manager, almost as if he was used to caution and a lack of depth in anyone's responses anymore. He nodded to 'his guest,' as he thought of him now.

"There are no longer any buses to anywhere now. There is no petrol, there are no visitors or travelers. There is no town. No one from the government dares to come here, not even the military. And with ISIS and the rebels bouncing back and forth, with us caught in the middle, who can blame them?" His sadness broke Sobhy's heart. But he still felt a sense of optimism in the man. "Someday, *inshallah,* it will all be over. Someday *Tasil* will become *Tasil* again." The man gazed out the broken window toward the main street and gestured with his arm. "We've been around for five hundred years, we will survive and recover from this as well."

Sobhy grasped his hands, and gave the man a reassuring shake. He admired the man's resolve but wasn't sure if it would be fulfilled.

"Are there any places to stay the night tonight, as I certainly don't want to be caught out in the open with no shelter. And given the war, well..."

The other man shook his head emphatically. He indicated that the only two hotels in town were no longer functioning. One had been blown up, the other abandoned. Everything in that one had been stripped by surviving villagers for their personal use.

"However, I can help, if you can help me. In the back room here, which had been my well-appointed office, I have been living quietly and out of sight. The water still runs, the bathroom is in decent shape. I have a small refrigerator and hotplate. I make out, out of sight. I stay hidden for much of the day. No one really knows I'm here. I can allow you to stay, but you need to help me too. If you have any supplies with you, I would appreciate them. If you have a mobile phone, maybe I can make a call if it works. So, what do you say?"

Sobhy didn't even need to think about, and immediately agreed to everything. He figured that he could restock on his meager food supply when he got to a working community. If the cell towers were intact, he could allow the man to use his BLU phone. But he did ask two things on his side of the equation. Life had been made more difficult due to the Syrian military jacket that he had been supplied with. The assumption made in Israel was that this was still Syrian army territory. This clearly was not now the case. It was something that Asa Ben Dov didn't quite envision when he outfitted the Egyptian. Whether it was an indication of where his 'loyalty' was would not even be asked before a sniper might single him out. The station manager was wearing a *galabiya* with a worn suit coat over it. This type of garb was typical for older Arab men. Sobhy asked if he was cold at night. The old man said the older you get, the colder you get, whether it was cold or not. As a result, he offered to exchange coats. The older man gratefully accepted it in exchange for the suit coat. Sobhy now didn't call undue attention to himself in this area of contention between the Syrian military, the rebels and ISIS. But the second request might prove to be more difficult. He needed the local man to help him find a way to *As Suwayda* as soon as the sun came up. However, a handshake and smile of gratitude sealed the deal.

*****

The futon wasn't the most comfortable, or the cleanest, but nevertheless Sobhy slept restlessly for several hours. With the sun coming up, the smell of coffee forced him upright. He rinsed his face and hands, and 'scrubbed' his teeth with an index finger to at least get some of the grit out. Then, he followed his nose into the small, walled courtyard behind the derelict station. He saw his military jacket bent low over a small propane burner, and the one-handled pot of Turkish coffee simmering.

"*Saba al kheir*, good morning *effendi*!" The man didn't even bother turning around.

"*Ahlen rais*. How did you know I was here?" was Sobhy's reply.

"And how do you think that I have survived this *hara*, this shit, of a life for all these months?" Now he turned around with 2 cups of steaming 'mud' in his hands. "Call it a sixth sense if you want, but there you have it. Now, over on that small table is some pita bread and a bowl of *hummous*. It's not much, but at least it'll help jumpstart the day."

The Egyptian came over and plopped down on an upended wooden crate. He gratefully took the cup of coffee and drank deeply. With a contented sigh, he tore off a piece of bread and dipped it in the paste. The kindness of strangers in a strange land still amazed him. He made a mental note that, when this was all over, to try to get some money to this caring individual to help tide him over until Syria resolved itself.

"I hope that you slept well, I did thanks to your generous field jacket that kept me warm all night." The man was still wrapped in it. Sobhy waved off the thanks, stating that both mutually benefitted from the exchange. Over breakfast, they continued to trade their stories. It was a good way for Sobhy to practice his cover and get used to it. Apparently, Ben Dov had really done his homework, as the former station manager nodded in agreement several times and not a single eyebrow was raised. Apparently, his story was one typical to southwest Syrian villagers. When asked a bit about life in *Tasil*, the man spoke of the beauty of the village, warmth of the people, and pride in their country. He shook his head at all this and kept mumbling that it was no more. But the real shock came when he disclosed his age- only 32. To Sobhy, he looked twice that, if not more. When pressed, all he could do was shrug at the Egyptian and say something about war doing this to people unaccustomed to violence and depravation. At that, both men gave a silent thanks to *Allah* for allowing them to survive another day out in the Syrian desert.

Over another pot of coffee, the former station manager wracked his brain for ways to get Sobhy to *As Suwayda*. There were few options since no public transportation had existed for months. But he did have one idea- the typical Arabic way of doing things. He asked to make a second call on Sobhy's cell phone. Even though it wasn't a 'Kevin Bacon' moment (that wouldn't have been *Halal* according to Moslem dietary laws!) he began a contact chain. You know the drill, that a cousin had a friend who had a cousin who had another cousin who knew someone that could borrow a vehicle... and all through one phone call.

Well, as it would turn out, that person about a million times removed from the bus manager was actually going in the direction of *As Suwayda* to *Sab' Abar*. In fact, it was the road which was half-way to *Tadmur/Palmyra* itself. This had some interesting ramifications should his original plans run amiss. But Sobhy would cross that *wadi* when he reached it. The connection would arrive at the ruined terminal in early afternoon. Then, if all went well, it was only an hour to his 'hometown,' they just had to be patient and wait. It was a trait that Sobhy had developed well from the world of field archaeology. Patience led to results, no matter how infuriatingly slow it might be.

While they waited, another pot of coffee came and went. It was a good thing, since Sobhy was beginning to nod off due to his lack of a solidly good night's rest. In the interim, he practiced his 'legend' in even greater depth now that he trusted the station manager. This gave Sobhy the confidence that he wasn't completely sure of before.

The ride eventually got to the station. Introductions were made all around. But, as usual, the departure was delayed over another cup of coffee and small talk. In the Arab world, business was *never* gotten down to until all queries about the family, cousins, distantly removed cousins, even out of favor cousins, were exhausted. Then, and only then, would serious discussions start. This was the way of the desert, and then would become the way of the village. There was no need to rush things. After all, a good cup of coffee was a good cup of coffee.

Thankfully, the driver was a man of few words. This meant that Sobhy wouldn't be unduly grilled during the hour long drive to his 'hometown.'

*****

As promised, the timetable was kept. There were no intermediate roadblocks by either Syrian forces or rebels. It seemed that everyone took the late afternoon off for siesta. Although *As Suwayda* was a larger community, the civil war had a habit of reducing burbs of all sizes into ghost towns. In many ways, it resembled *Tasil*, exuding a dreary sense of forlornness and abandonment. The Egyptian graciously thanked his ride, slipped a couple of hundred Pounds to the man in a warm handshake, for petrol, he explained, and grabbed his pack from the rear. His driver/ companion was staying with friends in *As Suwayda* for a day or so. Since Sobhy planned to stay a couple of days there also, in order to give some time to make his connections, he gave out his mobile number, just in case he needed to revise his plans and make his way to Palmyra without anyone to help.

As the vehicle drove away, Sobhy surveyed the area to determine where to head. As always, the answer was the local coffee house. It was inevitably the hub of both news and gossip- but male dominated. Even in the 21st century, far from metropolitan Damascus, the liberation of Syrian women was still a dream for the majority. Sobhy went in and sat down heavily, with a fairly audible sigh that drew the attention of a couple of other patrons. The *barrista*, if you could call him that, walked over to the table, wiping his hands on a grimy apron. Sobhy glanced at him, and idly wondered if the man's hands actually got dirtier by using the apron tied around his waist.

"*Ahlen, saba el khier rais.* Good day sir. What can I offer you as a means of refreshment?" The waiter/beverage maker/proprietor/busboy (there simply was no one else working, or so it seemed) was pleasant enough. But was it enough to induce the stranger in town to buy something to drink and, *Allah* be praised, even want something to eat! Apparently so, as Sobhy ordered a Turkish coffee and small piece of baklava. As the proprietor headed back to the kitchen area, Sobhy addressed him from the now distant table.

"Might you have a newspaper that I could catch up on? I've been away for quite some time and need to reconnect." This was the kind of opening that Sobhy hoped would begin a conversation that might open some doors and get him the contacts that he needed. The proprietor continued walking away, but waved his hand in recognition of the request.

A few minutes later, the coffee and sweet arrived at his table. The aproned man lingered for just a moment. At first, Sobhy thought that it was to see if everything delivered was okay. But after nodding his approval of both the snack and beverage, the man still stood near his table.

"Can I help you with something, friend? Did I not make it clear that everything is as fine as I could expect in this establishment?"

He had to get a small 'dig' in, but he said it with a smile- diffusing the situation.

"It's not that, *rais*. We don't get many strangers here in *As Suwayda*, ever since the escalation of the war here in the south. I merely wondered what circumstances brought you here?" The man fidgeted a little, seeminglysurprised at his somewhat bold challenge.

"Well, truth be told, I am estranged yet not 'a stranger' as you put it."

A look of confusion flashed across the waiter's face and settled there. He clearly was not expecting that kind of reply. Sobhy was on the offensive, and as he liked to put it whenever talking about his favorite futbol team, 'Ali, back in Cairo- take it all the way down the pitch to score the winning goal.

"My family is originally from this town, but I left to go to the University of Aleppo to study archaeology back in 1972. I became hooked on Egyptology and..."

He was interrupted, "Wait, our own glorious heritage wasn't good enough for you?" The man roared with laughter. Sobhy joined in.

"No, it was, as you say, 'glorious,' but the mystique of the pyramids called to me. I soon discovered it to be much, much more- and even more fascinating than those triangular things in the sky that rose above the desert sands." Both men began to enjoy the conversation, and Sobhy ever-so-slightly began to maneuver it in the direction that he wanted. The waiter pulled out a chair and sat down after returning quickly with another cup of coffee for Sobhy and one for himself.

"So what happened then?" He was clearly intrigued.

"I finished my studies and got, can you believe it, a *paid* internship with Egypt's Supreme Council of Antiquities. From little more than a glorified paid laborer, I slowly moved my way up until I began to direct projects for the government. Can you imagine..."

Now the man was impressed beyond imagination. Sobhy 'wowed' him with tales of discovery for about half an hour. He even pulled out his battered SCA identity card. He then glanced at his watch and remarked that he needed to find a place to stay, as he had been led to believe by others that there was no one left of his family in the community. The coffee house owner inquired as to the family name; and when Sobhy mentioned it, he sadly put his hand on the Egyptian's shoulder and gently corroborated this. Things were falling into place. Sobhy looked accordingly sad, but not too much, as he already had 'the inkling' as he put it. But confirmation was confirmation. There was a spare room above the coffee house, and the owner graciously offered it for a couple of nights. Sobhy clasped the other's hands firmly and accepted the offer. Silently he hoped it was in better shape than the establishment below it. He was pleasantly surprised, as the room was sparse, yet spotless. The washroom down the hall was in the same condition, and for this he was eternally grateful. Now he could begin to kick the plan of attack into high gear.

*****

The following morning, a refreshed man walked down the stairs and into the coffee house. The fantastic aroma had woken him from a dead sleep, but in a good way. How could anyone stay in bed with that rich, nutty smell rising through the floor? Sobhy greeted the owner/waiter/chef/dishwasher/accountant with a warm smile and handshake. It appeared that the other man was equally pleased to see the Egyptian as well. Apparently the wartime situation meant that business was slow, and companionship in a mostly abandoned town even slower. A cup of coffee magically appeared in his hand that was stretched out to Sobhy, who took it and inhaled deeply before sipping. His eyes shone with pleasure.

"Aah," was all that he could say for a moment or two. Then, "I haven't slept this well in quite a while, even while I was in the Israeli hospital." When asked, he added further detail about how he had been 'wounded' just after returning to Syria from Egypt to begin his quest for his family. He vividly described his sojourn in the north of Israel. The details were easy since he had been well schooled in his cover. But in addition, due to his ongoing relationship with Eitan, Kati and the other Israelis, an added warmth of authenticity was mixed in to the cover. The end result was a 'real' presentation. The shop owner was moved by this, and frankly admitted that he had developed a greater respect for someone seen as the enemy- the Israelis. In fact, he was so impressed with these impressions, that he fervently hoped that, when all was over in this damned civil war, Israel and Syria might open doors of diplomacy the way that Egypt and Jordan had done decades earlier.

Sobhy concurred but needed to more firmly establish his *bona fides* with the ISIS encampment on the outskirts of town in order to move forward in his plan. In a circumspect way, he asked the 'coffee king' about travel risks in the vicinity, ISIS, the rebels and anyone else that he might need to be concerned with as he would attempt to head a bit farther north to find out any more information about his 'family.'

"You know, *habibi*, I still think that many of the young men who claim to be with ISIS, or those fighting alongside the rebels against the government, are so screwed up due to the war that they don't know what to believe. I think that they are just looking for a place to belong, to have 'friendships.'" He did the international sign for 'air quotes' with his fingers. "I put that in quotes because I still feel that they suffer spiritually and emotionally from this war, and losing family and friends, and are truly lost. They need to come back to being a part of village communal life the way that it was a decade ago. Then they'll heal and come to their senses. We still have many of them who, on occasion, come back into town and frequent this place, looking for neighbors, friends... anyone who represented normalcy."

"So how can you be so sure of this?" Sobhy was wary.

The man ruefully smiled, "I can't be certain, but I will tell you that when they come, it's without their weapons, without their bluster, without the arrogance that they exhibit when they come with their military 'buddies.' That's what I feel, and that's what gives me hope."

"I have the name of a man whose family were close friends of my relatives, and perhaps I can find him and speak with him as well. You know, any lead no matter how small can be helpful. Actually, it's that community connection that is prevalent throughout our culture. He is a friend of a friend's cousin who was at times a business associate of one of my family members- in other words, a reliably 'close' companion!" Sobhy began to laugh at this, and the coffee house entrepreneur heartily joined in. After a couple of minutes, with tears streaming down his cheeks, he composed himself.

"So who is this 20 times removed 'relative'?" He started laughing again. "We're all relatives, eh?"

Sobhy looked at him in a funny way. "You don't have any Canadian blood in you, do you?" He had a sly look, while the other man had a totally confused appearance, as if the Egyptian had taken leave of his senses. When confronted with this perplexed man, he realized that his linguistic joke about Canadians had fallen flatter than 90% of the car tires in the abandoned town. "Forget it, but you know, I have something here." He pulled out one of the badly creased and dirtied documents from his wallet. He thought about it for a moment, then promptly forgot about the American TV commercial that was transplanted to Israel about stuff and credit cards and 'what's in your wallet' as it most likely would have gone *whoosh* over his companion's head. Instead, he showed him a forged handwritten note that vouched for Sobhy, from a village relative, dated nearly a year ago. It might serve as an 'in.'

Still laughing, when the man read the note he immediately sobered up. Wiping his eyes, he placed a hand on Sobhy's arm. "I can't tell you how sorry I am, but your relative is dead and his friend, the one you talked about, hasn't been seen in months." The sorrow in his voice was evident.

"But I was supposed to talk with this guy, Mohamed el Moussa, because, as you see in the letter, he had an interest, at least back then, in our ancient past. And with everyone now dead or missing..." His voice trailed off. One last squeeze of his arm, and the shopkeeper left him alone in his thoughts for a while.

I guess that now I'll have to make my way to Palmyra and work all this out on my own. This damn country is so screwed up, everyone is dying left and right!

He slammed a fist down on the table and the coffee cups did a little dance. Good thing that they were empty. The proprietor quickly turned around and glanced at Sobhy, concern etched on his face. The other two patrons merely glanced up, saw nothing really out of the ordinary, and returned to staring into their cups vacantly. Sobhy got up, waved to the owner, and told him that he was 'going for a walk' and would return shortly.

*****

Thanks to Allah that there were clouds. He couldn't imagine living in this environment without air conditioning. He smiled at that. Was he getting soft, did the better than average life of an Egyptologist put cracks in his hardened 'excavation life' shell of years ago? He idly thought that when this was all over he had to get back in the field. He fondly remembered his days working with the

German and Swiss archaeologists on Elephantine Island opposite Aswan. As a young archaeologist, he was delighted to be sent down to Aswan. He would work with an agency that had been digging for over 140 years in Egypt- the German Archaeological Institute, *Deutsches Archäologisches Institut*. Sometimes their arrogance riled him, but he would learn that it was a *German* trait, not a German archaeologist's trait. In fact, he was actually surprised that their work, in the middle part of the 20th century, was designed to rectify errors of their predecessors, the French. This area was part of the French concession that worked there between 1902 and 1908. In order to find papyri, the former 'excavators,' Sobhy preferred 'pot hunters and grave robbers,' dug deep holes into the ancient settlement on the island. His work with the Germans centered on the area of the Temple of Khnum. He was involved with the re-excavation of a 4-room house ascribed to the ancient Israelites in Egypt. The French had butchered that area as well. The Germans that he worked with were always blaming the French excavators for shoddy fieldwork and recording and documenting. (And Sobhy had always thought it was 'blame it on British' according to his archaeological friends.) He was very proud of that work, as the ongoing excavations by the *DAI* in the ancient town uncovered scores of artifacts, now on display in the Aswan Museum.

He was shaken from his reverie because the clouds had broken, and the street he was walking on had turned into steam bath-like passage. He quickly determined the shady side of the nearly deserted street and headed toward it. Once in shadow, yet still in the high 90 degree range, he checked his bearings and found his way back to the coffee house. He knew what he had to do. He needed to head north and east to Palmyra, with or without help, and retrieve the archaeological piece or pieces that were threatened with annihilation. Even though the couple of Syrians he had met and trusted completely were on his side, he was in a precarious spot. He was coming from a governmental position; and, even though it was an Egyptian governmental position, it was still the opposition. He needed to try to ingratiate himself with anti-government people on the fringe of Syrian society here.

He felt that it would not be too great a problem, because everything and everyone were part of lines that were so blurred not even the 2001 movie computer, Hal, could sort it out. When he got back, he had to make a series of subtle inquiries. But first things first. He found another small building that was abandoned and simply walked in the battered door. No one approached him or questioned him. He found a few more pieces of clothing, and changed his civilian clothes again, piling the old set into a small rucksack he found discarded in a corner. He now had a couple of sets of clothing, originally Syrian, to complement the set given in Israel. A perfect way to blend in was in hand.

Once back at the shop, another cup of coffee was offered, with relief evident on the proprietor's face. He really had worried about his new friend, and Sobhy would not soon forget it. The two sat at the same table over fresh cups of coffee. Sobhy inquired about the driver who had brought him from *Tasil.* He recalled that the man indicated that he would be in *As Suwayda* a couple of days, and then was going to *Sab' Abar.*

'Mr. Coffee,' as Sobhy now referred to the shopkeeper in his own mind, lit up when he mentioned the other town.

He snapped his fingers. "*Yaweli, yaweli*! I've just remembered! Your cousin, *Alayhi salaam*, peace be upon him, and his soul, was last stationed in *Sab' Abar*. Maybe el Moussa is there. You know, with communications so bad..."

Sobhy now was beaming like a party on *Eid al Adha*, one of the major Islamic festivals and celebrations that commemorated Ibrahim's willingness to sacrifice Ishmael in total devotion to *Allah*. "That's it, I'll look for him in that town, and then take things from there." He high-fived 'Mr. Coffee,' who by now was smiling as well. "We just need to find that driver."

One of the coffee-shop regulars was called over. A small confab was held, and he went off- dispatched to find the truck driver and bring him to the coffee house.

The driver was more than happy to take Sobhy with him, provided he could afford to pay. With a shrug that said 'business is business,' Sobhy agreed. The Egyptian still had a thick wad of Syrian Pounds. With his back turned, he peeled off several hundred (remember 58 Syrian Pounds=$1 USD) and turned back, wondering if it was enough. The man whistled under his breath. He hadn't seen that much in quite a while. It was accepted with a nod of agreement. With that accomplished in less than an hour, plans were set in concrete for departure the next morning to *Sab' Abar*, and the journey now would be placed back on track.

*****

The next day dawned bright, clear, and, surprise, hot. Once again the smell of fresh roasted and brewed coffee was his alarm clock. He quickly cleaned up, not wanting to miss the truck driver and ride. Downstairs, everyone was waiting, coffee and *bourekas* in hand. The coffeehouse owner had a nylon grocery bag filled with snacks for the road. He gave it to Sobhy in the midst of an enormous bear hug.

Slowly the men made their way to *Sab' Abar.* All along the road, signs of a war-torn nation littered the shoulder. Burned out vehicles, shell-pocked and in ruins, left a grievous impression on the men. Not a single storefront or vegetable stand remained open between the two communities. However, roughly constructed roadblocks and checkpoints bristling with radio antennas could be found every couple of miles. Why? Because they belonged to different militias, or ISIS groups with each running its own security operation. This led to confusion and, many times, unnecessarily violent confrontation between rival units for control of this small, yet important road. It reminded Sobhy of street gang warfare that he saw on TV movies or cop shows emanating from the US In spite of the hassle, Sobhy was secretly pleased. His identification papers passed muster at every stop even though they were scrutinized carefully. Because of the constant need for vigilance, both Sobhy and the driver were exhausted by the time they rolled into *Sab' Abar* by mid-afternoon.

As a final courtesy, and sign of thanks, Sobhy offered to buy the truck driver a meal before they parted company. On the outskirts of town, due to the back and forth ravages of the war, a 'restaurant' was a tent sheltering a couple of tables that held a fryer and rough food prep area, with a refrigerator powered by an extension cord that ran into the house located to the rear. A handful of tables and wooden chairs sat precariously on the sidewalk. The only food available was falafel, chips and beverages. Simple, but filling fare for a society constantly on the go. The two ordered and looked for a place. No tables were empty, but a few had open places. They walked over to a partly occupied table and asked if they could sit. The weary man waved his hand, indicating a 'whatever' attitude and the men sat. They struck up a conversation.

The man said that he was Ahmed Taybieh, originally from *As Suwayda*, but involved in the civil war for more months than he could remember. *Kismet, what luck*, was Sobhy's first thought. And in a vague, roundabout way, inquired about people from that town. Taybieh had no knowledge of Sobhy's 'family,' since he had been a farmer outside the village, leaving when he was in his late teens. But when Sobhy mentioned Mohamed el Moussa, a flash of something passed behind the eye of the fighter.

"*Wallah,* he and I left town together and were in the same unit for months. He was perhaps my closest friend." A look of pain now settled in.

"What do you mean 'was,'" demanded Sobhy, perhaps a bit too strongly.

"He... he was... he was killed in an action just days ago," was all that Taybieh could get out. He took a sip of water and composed himself. Not a word was said about the real way that el Moussa had died, or his role in getting his friend executed. "He was my best friend, but you know, in a war you don't want to have 'best friends.' The pain is just too great if there is loss. So I distanced myself from everyone... except him. Because we were from the same town. Something ran deeper than just brothers in arms, in combat. Yeah, there is a level of trust in battle with fighters to watch your blind side, and hope that they do the same. But on a personal level you really need to disconnect emotionally. So that'swhat I did with all but him."

Sobhy looked hard at him, and 95% believed him. But something nagged him- he just couldn't pinpoint it. But was the 95% enough to trust the other man. He weighed the pros and cons silently and then decided that he had no choice.

At that point, the truck driver wiped his chin with his napkin and rose from the table. He thanked Sobhy for the companionship, which tacitly included the fee that the Egyptian paid. He knew well enough, in this civil war environment, not to speak about money in front of unknown individuals, lest they be tempted to take advantage. It could easily end up with someone robbed and left for dead. The other two men rose and shook hands all around. Sobhy hugged the driver, and whispered a quiet *shukran*, thank you, for the discretion. He then walked over to his Peugeot tender and fired it up. With a belch of black smoke, the man waved out the side window and slowly made his way out of town to finish whatever business he had originally come to complete. Since Sobhy had nowhere to go, he sat back down and gestured to the chair opposite. Although it was a calculated risk, he felt that his best option was to open up just a bit to the Syrian fighter. Over another cup Taybieh went on with his story.

"You know, that part about closeness with Mohamed- it even went beyond just village friendship. In these horrible times, with no money around, and needing a way to help our families out as best as we could..."

"*Aywa*, yes, I understand the need for family support. I was faced with that decades ago in the '73 War with the Zionists," Sobhy knew how to make a connection. "I fought in the Valley of Tears. We called it that because of the massive number of destroyed tanks that were burning. I was with the 7th Division when we broke through near *Ahmadiyeh* in the north. There were nearly 1300 tanks available to back us up. But things went terribly wrong. By the third day of the battle, after all our initial successes, our fucking general staff screwed

us all. They didn't plan for anything more than a lightning attack. There were not enough reservists, reserve tanks, or ammunition available. Even though we surrounded an Israeli tank brigade, our Syrian supply trains were turning around and withdrawing because our Syrian General Staff had decided to retreat!" Sobhy supplied just the right amount of anger and sorrow in his tone. The other man nodded in agreement. "But I must say, now, I have grudging respect for our 'original' enemy. Their resolve, their tactics, their ability to fight, are something to be envious of- if only we had the same leadership in our army we might not be in this current situation. And another thing I have learned just now- the Israelis have the finest medical care in this entire part of the world. Just look at me." Sobhy pulled up his shirt and rolled up his pants leg. He indicated the two 'scars' that he said were 'courtesy of the Israelis.' But he hastened to add that they were a result of his trauma treatment after being caught in a firefight in the Syrian civil war- not battle with the Israeli forces.

Taybieh gave out a low whistle. "From the looks of these, if you hadn't made it to the Israeli side of the Golan, you'd probably be dead."

"There's no disagreement there, *Allah* works in mysterious ways," was Sobhy's reply.

The hook was now in place and Sobhy felt that Taybieh could be reeled in. He didn't know that the Syrian was already halfway on his side. Taybieh went deeper into his story as well, now both men shared combat stories. He said that, just before the last skirmish his unit was involved in, and just before el Moussa had been 'killed' they had discussed their respective family situations. Both men were tired of war after so long, and both were very worried about their families and how to get money to them, because excuses had worn thin. Their officers told them that, due to the military gains made by the enemies, the oil revenue and illicit archaeological artifact sale revenue had plummeted. So no one in their region had gotten any payments for months. The food supply had dwindled as well. Ammunition was becoming harder to come by. And now, with the US and its other allies using bombing raids on convoys and troop movements, not even nighttime transfers were getting through. Modern technology, like the infrared night vision cameras, made sure of that.

"We were tired of war. El Moussa and I made a decision. If the money from antiquities was going back to command centers like in Raqqa, and we, the ones getting killed, weren't getting paid to take care of our families, we considered getting the money ourselves. We thought hard about what was fair and decided that if we could find some small stuff and sell on whatever black market we could find, then we could take care of our loved ones. Just when we were set to move on this, he lost his life. I took a short leave from the battlefields around Palmyra and was heading back down to *As Suwayda* when I ran into you. I hoped to figure something out, because el Moussa was the one with all the connections in this regard. I'm at a loss now."

It took everything in his power to keep from smiling. Sobhy had stumbled upon a potentially new partner to help rescue Palmyrene artifacts. He decided to play his wild card from his real life, the work with the Supreme Council of Antiquities back in Egypt. He explained to the Syrian about his stint with the SCA, and his work in the field of archaeology and Egyptology. Although not directly involved in Near East archaeology, the interconnections and cultural mixing of the entire eastern Mediterranean region gave him a keen eye that definitely would be of help however they decided to proceed. He went on to describe in detail his ongoing relationship with the Egyptians, and that his contacts were still solidly in place. He hinted at the abilities of these contacts to serve as conduits for the illicit world of black market artifact trading. In fact, he even intimated that some of these people might be interested in helping to finance operations, on a trial basis. Should things pan out, well, the sky was indeed the limit. If the two should team up, then they could actually conduct a bidding war to see who might offer the largest percentage. However, and this was an enormous 'however,' they had to prove themselves, and establish a track record before anyone would work with them. At this, Sobhy sat back and sipped more coffee while he waited for Taybieh to let it all sink in.

They both became lost in thought. Each man wanted to find a way to gain the upper hand, even though both were fairly sure that this would be a winning proposition. Taybieh needed an outlet with connections. Sobhy needed to recover artifacts before they were wantonly destroyed. 'Win-win' was the codeword. Finally, Taybieh broke the easy, but charged, silence. He reached deep into a pocket and pulled out a crumpled piece of paper. He placed it on the table between them and smoothed out the creases. He then leaned forward and whispered to Sobhy.

"This was given to me by my friend. He said that he sketched it after seeing this stone in the ruins of what he took to be an ancient temple in the heart of Palmyra. I can vouch that he was a very good artist, from way before the war. He had a way with a pencil; seeing something and making that 'eye-to-brain-to-hand' connection that most of us don't know."

Sobhy jumped in, hoping that it wasn't too intellectual an approach to this Syrian peasant-turned-fighter. "You know, I get what you're saying. Here's why I agree. With modern stuff making our lives easier, like electronics and cell phones and digital cameras and the like, we have become dumber, not more advanced."

He was met with a blank look, "I don't get it."

"*Tayib*, okay, try this. You say that you don't have that talent to put things on paper that you see in detail. But imagine this, as little as 50 years ago, before all this electronic stuff, both you and I needed to find a way to remember things, and we all could sketch what we saw *because we had to!*"

Taybieh got it. He understood this comparison now. "So we have made ourselves less able because we have technology to use." He slammed his open palm on the table in triumph.

Sobhy let the man have his 'aha' moment, and while he basked in his newfound knowledge, Sobhy examined the sketch in detail. It was very crude, very rough in execution. However, he saw the inscription almost as if it were a rubbing. He had to ask. "How did our friend do this?"

"I think that he took the paper and rubbed it on the stone. Then he outlined the bumps with his pencil. At least, that's what I think."

That would explain part of the crudeness, and faintness, of what was now presumed to be a rubbing. Clearly el Moussa was unfamiliar with any written language other than Arabic. But Sobhy recognized it for what it was- an Aramaic inscription. A cousin to Hebrew, it meant that this was one of the artifacts that the UNESCO archaeologist, Professor Joanne Farchakh, had referenced, and that Sobhy, as the UNESCO representative, was to try to retrieve. He tried to hide his excitement, and in doing so, downplayed the value.

"You know how we Arabs are with regard to what we say, what we mean, what we ultimately do. We are always 'ramping things up' as the Americans say. We tend to exaggerate things in order to open the lines of negotiation until we actually get what we were initially hoping for in many instances. This is most clear in the *shuq*, the market. Have you ever noticed what prices are for us, against what the shopkeeper tries to get from an outsider, or worse, a tourist?"

He went on to describe the typical interchange with a tourist. The whole notion was that 'eye contact was the kiss of death,' If you even glanced at a shop display, or the shopkeeper himself, then you were hooked. If the price seemed too outrageous, it most likely was. If the tourist said 'no,' the shop owner was still certain he had a sale. If the guest said 'no, no,' the proprietor thought the 'prey' was playing hard-to-get. If the visitor said 'no, no, no' and began to walk away, the big guns were employed. A gentle arm tug, and the promise of a free glass of mint tea to further discuss the 'sale' would be laid on the table. Finally, when the by now exasperated foreigner shrugged off the tea and arm grab, and practically ran out of the shop, did the owner at last come to the realization that 'it would be a hard sale'!

Taybieh burst out laughing at this, and when he caught his breath, said, "I see where you're coming from. Perhaps we should not make too much of this drawing until we get to Palmyra and examine it for ourselves. Maybe el Moussa was trying to get someone's foot in the door of the shop." Sobhy smiled. The other man had played right into his hand. Now, they just needed to get to Palmyra some way.

*****

Once again, 'Arab networking' kicked into high gear, even in a small town like *Sab' Abar.* Ahmed Taybieh got out his cell phone and made a call or two. He was able to connect with a friend of a friend, who had a friend, who had a cousin who owned a 30 plus year Toyota Hilux Tender. It was the vehicle of choice for nearly all fighters in Syria, no matter what side of the militant coin they were on. Taybieh was all smiles when he announced to Sobhy that the two of them were going to take a walk *only* a couple blocks over to see the truck and negotiate payment. Although extremely leery, Sobhy downed the remainder of his coffee, grabbed the final bite of his croissant, and headed down the street. True to his word, *only a little under a mile later,* (remember, it's all relative, it's all 'creative measuring') the two men came to a small repair garage. In this wartime environment, auto and truck repair was one of the few industries that still thrived.

The friend of a friend's friend's cousin, who owned the shop, shook hands with them, offered them tea, which Taybieh graciously turned down, to Sobhy's relief, then took them around back. There they saw the pickup with more rust than metal, and 250 km on the odometer. (Don't worry, the engine was rebuilt only 140 km ago, was the grinned answer to the unspoken question.) Mechanics aside, duct tape and bondo kept it on the road.

After the traditional handshake rather than contract, the Syrians sealed the 'rental' deal with shots of *Arak* that they threw back with a shudder and a gasp. It wouldn't have been so bad if it were a legitimate alcoholic brew, rather than the 'bootleg' stuff that it seemed everyone in rural Syria was making- a supposed antidote to the consciousness of war.

Taybieh motioned to Sobhy to step forward. The Egyptian was reluctant to do so, afraid that he might have to indulge in the drink-fest. But instead, Taybieh whispered about paying half up front and half upon return. With a silent sigh of relief, Sobhy took out his Syrian wad of bills and quickly counted off the required sum. The other man saw his dreams coming true, as he hastily grabbed the stack and stuffed it in his pocket, lest it fly away from him. On that parting note, the two set out to further inspect the vehicle and prepare to depart for Palmyra to the northeast. Sobhy wanted to find a roll of duct tape just in case, but the town was without a single hardware store that was still stocked.

XI. Jerusalem

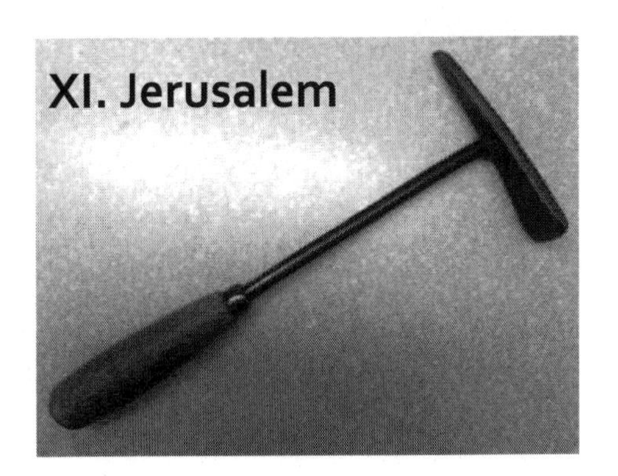

The drive back to the Ben Ya'ir flat was a quiet, uneventful one. Apparently everyone was lost in their own thoughts- with Sobhy and his perilous mission at the forefront. No one expected to hear from him soon, yet all were anxious to know that things were going in the right direction, and that the Egyptian was safe.

The trip back was a quick one. We opted to use the Jordan Valley road, Highway 90, past Bet Shean. There we stopped for refreshment and the "*sherutim*," a bathroom break. We would need to drive rapidly along the Valley, because of travel restrictions since the area was still disputed and under military control. A few minutes south of Bet Shean was the *Sde Trumot* junction. Here was the northernmost military checkpoint. From there we flew down the Valley. This part of the road was dedicated to the late Minister of Tourism, Rehavim Ze'evi, who was assassinated by Hamdi Quran of the Popular Front for the Liberation of Palestine in 2001. He was an Israeli general and politician who founded the right-wing nationalist *Moledet* party, mainly advocating population transfer. It was renamed *Derekh Gandi* (Gandhi's Road) because Ze'evi was nicknamed after Mahatma Gandhi.

"But why was he nicknamed 'Gandhi,' if his views were so right-wing and counter to what I thought Mahatma stood for?" It was a good question from Lior, the make-up artist.

"You're young, and probably don't even remember those days," was Eitan's reply. He was met by a loud 'Harrumph.' "It goes back to his high school days. During his youth, Ze'evi went to school in *Givat HaShlosha*, a kibbutz just east of the Tel Aviv area. One night, according to the story, he shaved his head, wrapped a towel round his waist and entered the kibbutz dining room. The shaved head and towel around his waist was similar to the way that Gandhi looked and dressed. Remember, Ze'evi was born in 1926 and Gandhi was a notable newsmaker when the Israeli was in high school. This radical act earned him *Gandhi* as his nickname; and it stuck with him for the rest of his life. However, there is also an alternative tradition. The nickname is also attributed to the long Arab dress, the *galabiya*, worn as a disguise during his underground days in the Palmach, before the IDF."

"That's something even I didn't know," I stated. With the history lesson done, we all stared out the windows as the Jordan Valley passed by on the way to the Jericho by-pass.

Just south of No'omi, Highway 90 swung a bit east around the Palestinian city of Jericho. Once past, it continued south until we reached the *Beit HaArava* junction. There we connected with Highway 1 and the road to Jerusalem. Just before reaching *Mitzpe Jericho,* we finally rose out of the Dead Sea Valley and reached sea level. The entire day had been spent descending

from 65m below sea level at the Sea of Galilee, to 415 m below at the Dead Sea. The air inversion, and extraordinary low pressure of life below sea level, was oppressive- as was the temperature. But, within a couple of hundred feet of the 'sea level' sign, the weighty atmosphere lessened appreciatively. The air felt lighter, cooler, and more refreshing. It also lightened the mood considerably. It was now only another hour and change ride to the holy city.

As we drove along the *Wadi Qelt*, the only major west/east passage from the coast, through Jerusalem, to the Dead Sea, Eitan and I recalled one of our early treks through the desert. We walked from Jerusalem to the area of Herodian Jericho, through the wadi. It was a 'lovely' 8 hour journey, covering around 30 km or so... *but downhill!* In the process, we had stopped at St. George's Monastery. I always maintain that you run the risk of 'meeting God' in the desert, and apparently the Greek Orthodox monks in antiquity felt the same. John of Thebes first constructed the self-sustaining community along the northern cliff face of the wadi, coming from Egypt in 480 CE. He was a religious hermit in every sense.

"So why wasn't it named St. John's?" The ever-inquisitive Lior asked.

"Apparently he wasn't the most famous personality there, just the founder. The most famous was Gorgias of Coziba, from Cyprus." Eitan continued, "The monastery had a really rocky existence..."

Everybody groaned at that. "What? Oh wait, I get it now! That was pretty good even though I didn't realize it." Eitan smiled a bit sheepishly and went on. "It was destroyed a few times, and then rebuilt; first by the Persians in 614, rebuilt by the Crusaders. Once the Crusaders were expelled, it fell into disrepair. It wouldn't be until 1878, that the monastery would be restored when a Greek Orthodox monk, Kalinikos, came to the desert. It took nearly 25 years."

"And how do you know all this?" Kati playfully punched his bicep.

"Sometimes I do listen to our resident archaeologist!" He shot back, then roared with laughter. We all joined in and gazed at the monastery, clinging like a Thompson's Gazelle, as we sped past it on the way west. There were only 20 km to go.

*****

The road approaching the eastern side of the city was somewhat bleak as well. It climbed steadily from the Judean Desert past the relatively recent Israeli town of *Ma'ale Adumim*, then past the small Palestinian village of *Abu Dis* just off to the left. *Abu Dis* was one of the villages that had networked together on the eastern side of the city; the others being *E- Zakariya* and *Silwan.* They were the nucleus of one of Israel's proposals on the table regarding the status of Jerusalem for both Palestinians and Israelis. The Palestinian Authority, along with most of the Arab world, insisted on 'East Jerusalem' being their capital. This rankled a significant portion of the world in general, because it meant a reversion back to the partition of the city- similar to that of the time between 1949 and 1967. For all of its glorious 3000- year history, the city was only divided for 19 years. It was only during that time that the inaccurate terminology of 'East' and 'West' Jerusalem arose in the media. Yes, there is an eastern, predominantly Arab, district of the city. And yes, there is a western, predominantly Israeli, district. But there has never been an East Jerusalem or West Jerusalem per se.

I recalled to the group that in the state of Minnesota, in U.S., there are distinct cities like North St. Paul, West St. Paul and South St. Paul. They all have their own city halls, police, water, sewage, etc. In other words, they are their own entities. That was never the case for Jerusalem. It should never be a divided city. In fact, during the tenure of one of the most sensitive individuals regarding the Israeli/Palestinian issue, Mayor Teddy Kollek, the reunited city worked beautifully for a couple of decades.

However, another aspect of the role of Jerusalem was its perception of a place of extraordinary holiness for Islam. Yes, *El Quds*, The Holy, was integral to the faith. But the fact is that it was a very distant third in the hierarchy of cities for its holiness- far behind Mecca and Medina. Although it is assumed that the Prophet

Mohamed visited the city, there is no hard and fast evidence other than the dream that is related; stating that Mohamed made a nocturnal journey to visit Allah on his horse, *Buraq*. This event transpired from the Noble Sanctuary, the sacred *Haram esh- Sharif*, The Temple Mount to the Jewish and Christian world.

This notion seemed to be supported by the Arab world itself with regard to the sacred precinct. The argument put forth was as follows. After the 1948 War, when the city was partitioned by the UN, with the Old City and the eastern side given over to Jordanian occupation, the entire Arab world had access to its third holiest location. But not a single Arab leader, except King Abdullah I of Jordan, went to pay their respects to this Islamic site. He did it only once, in 1951. It was only after the city was reunited in 1967 that the hue and cry arose from the Arab world to reconquer and reclaim their holy shrine; and remove it from control by the Israelis- a distinct 'otherness'.

Lior chimed in, "The Christians have Jerusalem, Rome, and Constantinople. The Moslems have Mecca, Medina and Jerusalem. But we only have Jerusalem, Jerusalem and Jerusalem." None of us could have said it better.

The proposal that had some traction on and off was that the three small villages be united in a federation of sorts, to form the Palestinian side of the city. This would leave the city itself intact, and readily accessible to members of all faiths, without dividing it up again- which would be a true tragedy.

We slowly made the climb toward Augusta Victoria Hospital located near the saddle between the Mt. of Olives and Mt. Scopas. The combination of hospital and church complex was built just prior to World War I in honor of the Empress Augusta Victoria, the wife of German Kaiser Wilhelm II, who visited Jerusalem in 1898. It served the Axis powers as a military hospital during the war, and doubled as the command center for both the Germans and Ottoman Turks. And as Jerusalem would change hands, so too would the wounded military taken care of in the facility- from the British during the Mandate and World War II, to the Jordanian Arab Legion during Jordan's occupation. During the 1967 Six Day War with Israel, the compound suffered a great deal of damage, with the upper floor severely compromised. It would take over 20 years to be refurbished and reconstructed. Today, it has a preeminent oncology facility, paired with the Peres Center for Peace in offering cancer treatments for Palestinian children.

We decided to take a breather not far from the complex, on the summit of the Mt. of Olives, to catch the view of the spectacular sunset over the Old City and Temple Mt. just to the west. This was located by *A-Tur*, the highest point of the mountain, just above the massive Jewish cemetery located down the western slope. This is unquestionably the most significant Jewish cemetery in the world. It was first created 3000 years ago, when Jerusalem became the capital of ancient Israel under Solomon. Some say that there were well over 200,000 burials along the slopes of this holy mountain. Since the beginning of Judaism, Jews have wanted to be buried on the Mount of Olives, based on the Jewish tradition that, when a messianic personality comes, the resurrection of the dead will begin there.

And his feet shall stand in that day upon the Mount of Olives, which is before Jerusalem on the east, and the Mount of Olives shall cleave in the midst thereof toward the east and toward the west, and there shall be a very great valley; and half of the mountain shall remove toward the north, and half of it toward the south. (Zech 14:4)

By the end of 1949, and throughout the Jordanian occupation and rule of the site, some Arab residents uprooted tombstones and thousands of other tombstones were desecrated. Although in later years King Hussein of Jordan played a major role in the pursuit of peace with Israel, and in attempting to resolve many issues surrounding the Palestinians, he made a couple of grievous errors in the late 60s and 70s. He permitted the construction of the Intercontinental Hotel on the summit of the Mount of Olives. His engineers used tombstones and crushed them in order to make concrete to build the hotel. Graves were also demolished for parking lots. As a result, after the reunification of the city, the hotel was blacklisted by great numbers of tourist agencies because of its horrific history. Between 1949 and 1967, stones from the cemetery were even used in latrine construction at a Jordanian Army barracks. Following the 1967 Six-Day War and the Israeli reunification, the government began restoration work and re-opened the cemetery for burials once again.

Another questionable decision, this time by the Israelis, also focused on building activity on the Mt. of Olives. The construction of the Brigham Young University Jerusalem Center for Near Eastern Studies, better known locally as the Mormon University, was extraordinarily controversial due to concerns that the Mormons would engage in missionary activities; a hallmark of their religious activity around the world. After the Mormons pledged not to proselytize in Israel, work on the building was approved. By 1984, the church began construction. The center opened in 1988. However, because of political events, years at a time would pass without new students matriculating at the center.

"This reminds me of a Mormon story or two," I quipped as we stood overlooking the valley, watching the setting sun. Everyone looked at me and groaned. Everyone, that is, except Lior. She still was unfamiliar with my story-telling and told all gathered that she loved stories. After a bit of ribbing, I told the excavation story of Dawn, 'the early Mormon.'

The excavations at Tel Sheva, from 1969-1976, under Tel Aviv University's Institute of Archaeology, was one of the first major student/volunteer field schools ever created. It was a consortium of schools- including Brigham Young University, which we nicknamed 'Breed 'em Young,' because of their penchant for large families. This was way before the school complex was even thought of on Mt. of Olives; yet it indicated the Mormon community's great support for the State of Israel. Each year on the excavation, they contributed not only financially, but with students. They averaged in the neighborhood of 30 student volunteers per excavation session; about a third of our collective workforce. One season, a member of their group caught the eye of one of the staff, a fellow named Hesh. (short for Heschel, which he truly hated). The young lady in question was named 'Dawn', and Hesh promptly nicknamed her 'the early Mormon'! But 'early'? She never was on time. Why? Because she actually got up 20 minutes before necessary (meaning at 4.10 am) *so that she could put on make-up!*

It was surreal to say the least. After a short period of trying to woo her, and getting nowhere, Hesh eventually turned his sights elsewhere. Her rebuff stung him just a bit, as he considered himself to be quite the ladies' man. At the end of the season, he let his frustration get the better of him. We were all on the top of the Tel, watching the BYU tour bus load up and leave the excavation camp. Hesh picked up a good sized stone and hurled it at the bus as it began to leave the parking lot. It was a good hundred meters away. We heard a thunk! It was a miracle, apparently he had hit the bus with his toss.

Our friend Legrande, a Mormon staff member of the excavation, was with us. He promptly declared the act to be a 'miracle,' and proclaimed Hesh to be a Mormon 'saint'! Following the event, Hesh ripped off his shirt and threw it into a Persian Period ash pit, about 2400 years old, and buried it. All except a torn fragment, which he held out. It was declared 'a religious relic' and became part of the folklore of the Tel Sheva excavation memories.

That led to other short anecdotes about Hesh, including the one regarding alcohol in the camp at Tel Sheva. We were located about 9 km outside of town, with little means of getting there easily. Beer was somewhat available at a kiosk that was set up by a local Beershevite to supply us with necessities- toothpaste, soap, shampoo, razors... Beer (at a cost). But one week, that of July 4, an impromptu celebration had drained the camp. Hesh's brother, Lenny, an architect in Haifa, had come to visit. He lived just outside the city in Kibbutz *Ein Hamifratz*. Apparently the kibbutz exposed and captured someone that they dubbed a 'KGB spy.' Remember, this was in the early 70s, and the USSR was still a major player in the Mideast, notably Syria and Egypt. So once this individual was turned over to the Mossad for interrogation, his private belongings were divided up amongst kibbutz members. Lenny opted for the man's bottle of witch hazel. When Lenny came down to visit, he had it with him. He of all people had an answer for our lack of alcoholic beverages. He told us to get a laundry list of items, including a large pot. These items included olives, oranges and lemon-lime soda. We were ordered to pour them into the pot. Then Lenny pulled out his bottle of tannic-acid based liquid and ceremoniously dumped it into the vessel- then he stirred, and stirred, and stirred. Although witch hazel itself is based on tannic-acid content, and usually used externally, a short internal shot is not fatal. Once the potion was fully cooked, Lenny then spooned a small amount into a glass with a ladle and drank. The look on his face said it all. One hit, and you were good for the rest of the week! You couldn't take any more. But it solved our problem until the next day's shipment of 'legitimate' beverages arrived.

The group laughed, some with tears forming in their eyes, as they were familiar with many of my dig tales, but Lior remained wide-eyed and in awe. Until, that is, Eitan took her aside and whispered a few things in her ear. Immediately, a 'sunburn' color began to rise from her neck and cover her face. Kati made a reference to Wikipedia and seeing Lior's face on the page titled 'embarrassment.' Now everyone, including the young artist, laughed in unison as we returned to our vehicle and entered Jerusalem. It was a short drive down into and back out of the *Wadi Joz* as we ascended to the west. A sharp left took us onto the Paratrooper's Road that ran parallel to the Old City walls and fronted the Damascus Gate. A minute or two waiting for the light rail to proceed in across the road, and we rolled by the previous partition line, opposite Notre Dame Cathedral and international pilgrim guest house, between the eastern and western city that existed for 19 years; until the reunification in 1967. From there, only a few blocks remained until *Bnei Batira* Street and Kati's flat.

■■

Throughout 1981 and 1982, the Israeli government reported to the international community that over 270 terrorist attacks against Israel had the fingerprint of the PLO on them. Israel, the Occupied Territories, the perimeter armistice lines with Jordan and Lebanon, were all targets of terror and violence. Perhaps Israel was looking for an excuse to deal with an organization that many third world nations 'looked up to', and voted consistently against any sanctions or military operation whenever Israel and her allies proposed such actions. But with her civilian population constantly under the cloud of terror, she felt that she had no alternative.

On 6 June 1982, the 1982 Lebanon War, *Milhemet Levanon Harishona*, 'the first Lebanon war,' was launched. Colloquially it was called Operation Peace for Galilee, *Mivtsa Shlom HaGalil*. It consisted of a three-pronged attack into Lebanon and its border with Syria.

The main thrust crossed the armistice at *Rosh Haniqra* along the Mediterranean coast. Also known as the Ladder of Tyre, this natural wonder of the geological world was also a symbol of the failed policies of the British Mandate half a century earlier. When this land was 'deeded' to the British as a spoil of World War I, the original Turkish Railroad line from Beirut and Damascus through Haifa, Tel Aviv, and North Sinai to Alexandria Egypt was a communication and transportation marvel. Touted as a link between Europe, the Mideast and Africa, the British brought their timetable and mechanical efficiency to the line and expanded on its success. However, with the civil violence that rocked the region following the end of World War II, and the subsequent UN creation of several nation-states that were directly linked to British withdrawal, the rail line between Israel and Lebanon that had gone through the mountain at *Rosh HaNiqra* was sealed and the route discontinued.

Eventually using over 60,000 troops and 800 tanks, Israel would cross into her northern neighbor, breaching what had been known for a couple of decades as 'the Good Fence'. There had been a tacit understanding regarding the 80-mile border between Israel and Lebanon since after the 1973 Yom Kippur War,

as neither wanted to enter into a military confrontation. This was notable because, when the two nation states were created, families and friends were often caught on opposite sides of the line. This created an extraordinary hardship that neither state wanted. As a result, the armistice line was 'porous.' The main border crossing through which goods and workers crossed becoming the Fatima Gate crossing near Metula.

At the time, southern Lebanon was controlled by the Maronite Christians and the South Lebanese Army, as a breakaway Free Lebanon State between 1978 and 1984. It was during the civil war in Lebanon in 1976 that Israel supported the Maronite militias in their battle with the PLO. The Good Fence ceased to exist with Israel's withdrawal from southern Lebanon in 2000.

Back in 1982, when the Israelis entered into Lebanon to try to bring PLO terror attacks to an end, the army requested a small team to follow, when the various areas were stabilized, to conduct archaeological surveys. Archaeology of the ancient world knows no modern boundaries or borders. Ancient civilizations crisscrossed all of the region with their militaries and played a major role in shaping the history and culture of the area. I had learned very early on in my studies that archaeology of the biblical world meant that you had to study the art, archaeology, culture and politics that also affected the area- meaning such relatively far-flung societies as those of Egypt, Asia Minor, Persia, Babylon, Greece and Rome- with the list going on and on. So it was not out of the academic realm for Israel to take advantage of this moment in time. Only no one could ever have imagined it lasting until 2000.

So, following in the army's 'tank treads,' I was invited to be a part of one of the survey teams to take a look at ancient sites not yet excavated by the Lebanese and their academic colleagues. We drove north from the frontier, past *Naqourah* and *Ras el Bayyada* to *Tyre*, ancient *Tsur*. Because of the nature of the international archaeological community, we reached out to a Lebanese excavator, Hamzeh Arsuf, who escorted us part of the way. He pointed out numerous small sites near *Ash Shawmara* and *Al Mansuri*. These were dutifully plotted in our notebooks, along with the map coordinates as supplied to us by the IDF officer escorting us. Based on what we saw on the surface, these sites ranged in age from prehistory through the Crusader Era. In other words, archaeologically speaking, the Armistice Line between Israel and Lebanon was merely a 'line in the sand'. The ancient history of the region was seamless.

In addition, Arsuf showed us another site near *Dayr Qarun*. This one was extremely painful to him, as it was reported to him as a site exposed during road construction but left out in the open. After the violence broke out, the site was systematically looted and robbed. Nothing remained but holes in the ground. He said that he now knew what other archaeologists in Syria and Iraq, Iran and Afghanistan, were feeling regarding the wanton destruction by fundamentalists regardless of religious belief.

After spending 2 days with Arsuf and gleaning a treasure trove of data for the future- should peace ever really break out, we thanked him as we continued north. We passed Sidon en route to Beirut. We got to an overlook of the airport near the suburb of *Hadet,* but were prevented from continuing on due to the military operations in the city proper. As a result, like Moses on Mt. Nebo, we looked down on Beirut, but wouldn't be allowed to enter. We were then told that our mission was completed as best as could be expected, and escorted back to the Good Fence and Israel. It was quite the experience.

The Siege of Beirut began on 14 June. The Israelis chose to keep the city under siege rather than forcibly capturing it, as they were unwilling to accept the heavy casualties that the intense street fighting would have required to capture the city. Israeli forces bombarded targets within Beirut from land, sea, and air, and attempted to assassinate Palestinian leaders through airstrikes. The siege lasted until August, when an agreement was reached. More than 14,000 PLO combatants evacuated the country later that month.

There were quite a number of revelations as a result of the outcome of the war. Israel uncovered a trove of documentation outlining the true nature of the PLO- not as a mere terror unit but on the par with a standing army. There were between 15,000 and 18,000 fighters used by the PLO. Many of their officers were trained in the Soviet Union, attested to by certificates and other documentation in Russian. Heavy weapons consisted of about 60 T-34, T-54 and T-55 tanks and up to 250 130mm and 155 mm artillery pieces, many BM21 Katyusha multiple-rocket launchers and heavy mortars. As a comparison, the Syrian Army deployed over 30,000 troops in Lebanon.

The tragedy of the *Sabra* and *Shatila* Refugee camp slaughter of between 762 and 3,500 civilians, mostly Palestinians and Lebanese Shiites, was conducted in the two neighborhoods on the 16 September. It was carried out by the Phalange, a predominantly Christian Lebanese right-wing party. The massacre took place under the pretext of retaliating for the assassination of the recently elected Lebanese president, Bachir Gemayel, the leader of the Lebanese *Kataeb* Party. The initial finger-pointing was aimed directly at Israel because the Phalange were considered to be allies and it was assumed that they could not pull this off without direct Israeli aid. In 1983, the Israeli Kahan Commission, appointed to investigate the incident, found that Israeli military personnel, aware that a massacre was in progress, had failed to take serious steps to stop it. However, the commission also pointedly made the case that there was no evidence linking any direct Israeli action.

By late September 1982, the PLO had withdrawn most of its forces from Lebanon and relocated to Tunisia. The Syrian government declared Arafat a *persona non-grata* in 1984. While this may have looked good in the eyes of the world it would have disastrous repercussions down the road. With Arafat and the PLO out of Lebanon, Syria in fact paved the way for the rise of other militant groups, particularly Hezbollah.

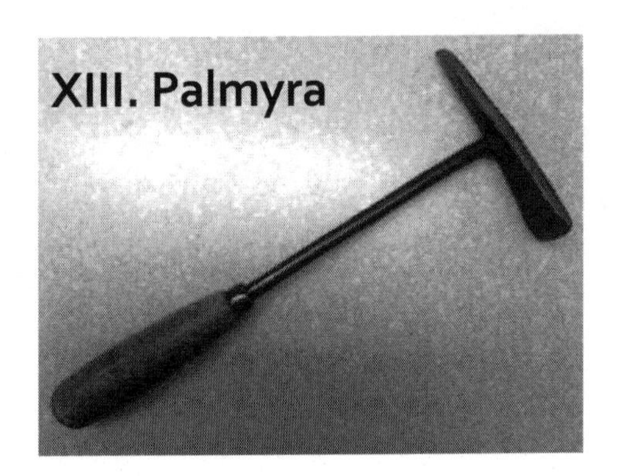

Sobhy and Taybieh spoke little on the drive north and east to Palmyra. They both assumed the trip would take them into the second, or even third, day of travel given the civil war environment. It was a depressing journey. To Sobhy, it was a replay of his crossing into Syria just a couple of days ago and it reminded him of his Sinai experience of 1973. Burnt out hulks of vehicles lined the two lane road. Artillery shells had cratered both sides of the asphalt strip and in some places the pock-marked road was narrowed down to a single lane of traffic. As a result, Taybieh, the driver, had to be extremely cautious since, oftentimes without warning, he would find an approaching vehicle bearing down at him at an alarming pace. And if it was a truck of any size and weight, the notion of survival of the fittest found the Syrian slowing dramatically and putting his two right tires on the shoulder- rather than play chicken with an oncoming mechanical beast.

They traveled on paved Highway 110 until the village of *Shaqqa*. In order to save time, Taybieh turned right onto a well-used dirt path. He declared it to be a shortcut. He clearly didn't want to go anywhere near Damascus. But even better, he went on, it was 'off the radar' of militant groups because it was unsuitable for large vehicle traffic. This meant that no troops or weapons could be transported on the road, so it was not deemed of high military value or a threat to anyone. This shortcut took them past the hamlet of *Az Zalaf*. As the sun began to set, they were faced with the dilemma of finding a place to spend the night. Both men were resigned to sleeping in the car when they noticed a handwritten sign taped to the window of a nondescript home. It stated that there was a 'room to rent- with running water in the bathroom.' Sobhy chuckled at this and thought about 'luxuries' in a war zone. Both men looked at each other and, with a nod, pulled off the path. Sobhy peeled off a couple of hundred worth of bills and gave them to the ecstatic homeowner. A windfall like this was apparently like winning the 'lotto' in Syria. The man even offered coffee, pita and a bit of goat cheese the next morning before they left. Sobhy was going to say something about the 'continental breakfast' but thought better of it.

The next morning they reconnected with Highway 53, a paved road a little over 50 km east northeast of Damascus. It would eventually become Highway 90 to Palmyra.

The checkpoints became much more numerous as they got onto 90 to the city. The two opted to take a short break before entering the town proper. On the outskirts they came across a small *mahana ahwa*, coffee shop, the *Al-Nawfara* Coffee Shop. Here, over coffee and a pastry, they worked on their plan. To stay in Taybieh's good graces, Sobhy offered to buy- the Syrian certainly didn't refuse.

The rough outline that they came up with called for Taybieh to re-enter the militant compound and re-establish himself. Because he was only away a few days, it wouldn't be a problem. He insisted that it wasn't like he had deserted, or fled his post or anything like that. He would stress that it was a quick trip home to visit sick parents. In the current environment of Syria, that was not something out of the ordinary and it was a common enough occurrence. In addition, since he had been instrumental in 'outing the traitor' el Moussa (not to be mentioned to Sobhy, obviously) he would readily be welcomed back. Once in the good graces of his commander, he could bring Sobhy into camp as a potential recruit to the cause. Sobhy's back story would be sufficient enough to pass muster. Taybieh would stress that Sobhy was only exploring possibilities and his only two choices were joining them or recusing himself entirely from the conflict. Although the second option was not as palatable to the militants, his oath that, should he choose not to join, he would not enlist in any other military activities against them, would be good enough. Taybieh's endorsement would see to that.

Depending on the length of time that this might take, Sobhy scouted out a small hostel that was adjacent to the coffee house, and prepared to get a room for the night should it come to that. The Al Faris Hotel was by the entrance to the town, on the left. It was a very nice and clean place with big rooms and a nice owner. A single room was only 300 SYP. Sobhy was amazed at his luck, and equally amazed to discover this oasis of civility in the midst of a war-torn tragedy. He silently filed it away as a definite place to come to see ancient Palmyra if and when the civil war abated.

*****

Taybieh drove the truck several more km over the cratered road, until he got to one of his unit's checkpoints. He slowed to a crawl. According to the protocols that he learned when on 'the other side' of the checkpoint, he kept his right hand on the steering wheel, while his left he dangled out the driver-side window. This indicated that he didn't have a weapon in one hand with the other on the wheel. Of course this didn't preclude any kind of IED in the truck. This he knew from experience. Just a few months ago, the checkpoint that he was manning with a couple of other comrades was approached by a nearly identical vehicle to the one that he was driving. No one recognized it, or the driver, and they waved their arms with palms facing down, in a downward motion, indicating that the driver should slow and stop a few dozen meters from the barrier. The driver slowed, but failed to stop. One of Taybieh's comrades got a bit antsy and fired a few shots into the air. The spooked driver began to speed up. At once, the entire checkpoint opened fire. The pickup went up in a ball of smoke and flame. Whether it was the gas tank, or a load of explosives didn't make a difference to the guards. They all just breathed a sigh of relief that no one on their side of the barrier was hurt.

As Taybieh slowly approached the point where he was to halt, he saw a couple of faces that he recognized. They weren't close friends, but familiar enough that, when he shouted and waved his hand, they acknowledged that they knew him and waved him on to them.

He stopped at the raised barrier and got out and shook the hands of each of the men. A few pleasantries were exchanged, the prerequisite inquiries as to family welfare, and they beckoned him to the small tin-roofed hut. He came in and sat down, and magically a small demi-tasse of Turkish coffee appeared on the scarred wooden table. Each took a sip of their coffees, and the informal interrogation began. It was the usual 'how are you? Where have you been? What have you been doing?'

Then, after a few moments, the real question came out, 'Why did you disappear from us and explain yourself.' But there was a 'please' attached to the end of it, indicating that, provided the right answers were given, it was merely a formality.

Taybieh began to relax. His well-rehearsed response came out in a heartfelt story of sorrow and fear. He just couldn't believe that his close friend from his village was a traitor to the cause. And he certainly couldn't imagine anyone as pious as el Moussa would try to sell antiquities for his own benefit. Even though times were tough economically for all of their families back home, sacrifices needed to be made. The idols of infidels needed to be destroyed in the name of *Allah*, the Merciful, the Compassionate... and family should never get in the way of the 'now,' because Paradise awaited all in the service of God.

He saw in the eyes of his interrogators that his answers were deemed suitable, and as a result, was told to go visit the regional commander, Abu Bakr al-Baghdadi, and give his report. With a haphazard salute to those manning the checkpoint, he turned to get into the truck. But then he rapidly did an 'about face' and marched back to the militant in charge. He took him aside and, with a hand on his shoulder, told him about Sobhy. He made it clear that this 'Syrian' who had returned from Egypt could be invaluable when it came to getting the greatest fees for the archaeological objects that were to be sold to help in the group's finances. Taybieh made it clear that someone with an archaeology background could see the artifacts for what they really were, and what their real value was. This would ensure the greatest cash flow possible. The checkpoint chief got on his radio and informed the headquarters back near the ancient site of Palmyra. Apparently al Baghdadi himself got on the horn, as the man in front of Taybieh immediately became more deferential to the person on the other end. Peppered with a series of 'yessirs' and 'of courses,' the man practically saluted the radio when he signed off. The end result was that, with Taybieh vouching for him, Sobhy could also proceed to Palmyra. Taybieh breathed a sigh of relief and smiled. However, he told the fighters that he would make his way to Palmyra the next morning, as he and his companion had journeyed for nearly 3 days. He returned to the al Faris Hotel and explained everything to Sobhy. But by this time, it was early evening. The room had already been paid for, and a lukewarm shower sounded absolutely delightful at this point in time.

*****

A desert *hamsin*, or sandstorm, had blown in from the southeast during the night. As a result, the sunrise was blocked by a thick haze. When you think of a sandstorm, rule out the 'French

Foreign Legion' movie view of not being able to see your hand in front of your face, and gale-like winds blowing relentlessly, stinging you with a million needle-like projectiles. Sandstorms here are more like a thick fog of suspended grains of sand, moved ever-so-gently along at only a couple of miles an hour. The sand simply hangs in the air, clogging everything, but softly. It was a common enough experience for Sobhy, who had seen many of them blowing in from the Western Sahara into Egypt. They could last for days on end. But Taybieh, on the other hand, was scared to death of this phenomenon. He knew it was trouble when he got up in the morning and walked across the room to the bathroom on a layer of sandy grit. He pulled back the curtain and saw nothing but a yellowish mass outside. With a look of fright on his face, the young Syrian grabbed his prayer rug and began the morning ritual; with an earnestness he had not spiritually felt in months. On the other hand, Sobhy merely went out to perform his morning ablutions as if it were normal.

The last time he had seen this had been in Aswan. He was staying at the Cataract Hotel- the Old Cataract to be precise. Completed in 1899 by Thomas Cook for European travelers, it was *the* place to stay in Aswan. The view from the terrace was stunning, overlooking Elephantine Island in the middle of the Nile. For years, other visitors to Aswan would make their way to the southern end of the city, where the hotel sat, to have a Turkish coffee or mint tea on the veranda. This became so popular that actual hotel-staying guests were squeezed out of the terrace. The hotel staff was forced to erect a guard booth at the beginning of the kilometer long road from the corniche- designed to turn away anyone without a room key.

In 1961, a new 10 story wing of the hotel was built adjacent to the original hotel, complete with Olympic sized pool. With all the modern amenities, it became the go-to part of the complex and the original structure deteriorated. It wouldn't be until an international film crew came to the Old Cataract Hotel with its goal to film Agatha Christie's Hercule Poirot masterpiece of sleuthing, Death on the Nile, in 1978, that portions of the old dowager were restored. Finally the Sofitel Company, which now owned the hotel complex, closed the original between 2008 and 2011 for a complete update. Today, the Old is once again 'the New,' and the old "New' is the 'old new' and less expensive part.

When the sandstorm had hit Aswan, Sobhy had been working with a survey group from Germany, whose archaeologists had been involved in the Elephantine Island excavation for over half a century. They hadn't scrimped on accommodation and used the New Cataract. One morning the team awoke to the still air of a desert sandstorm that had arrived from Libya overnight. There was no crossing the Nile in that pea soup, nor would there be for nearly a week. All work was stopped, the only thing the group could do was paperwork, research and lab work. Although essential, and a great way to catch up on the minutiae of archaeology, all were anxious to get back in the field. But Sobhy had learned that patience was an integral part of archaeological work, and simply sat on the veranda, drank coffee and contemplated what little of the Nile he could see until it all passed.

*****

Sobhy calmed the Syrian down, and they waited out the storm. After it subsided a bit, they made plans to head into Palmyra and the insurgent camp adjacent to the archaeological site. They drove past the now abandoned Dediman Hotel and the Efqa Spring that had supplied the region with fresh water for centuries. To their left, about 500 m from the ancient site, lay the Bel Hammon Temple complex that had been destroyed in 2015 when ISIS occupied the city.

Another few minutes and they came to the checkpoint that Taybieh had visited the day before. The same guards were there and recognized the battered pickup and its driver. This time, they waved him to the barrier, rather than stopping several meters away. Once there, the guard reached in and shook his hand. Then asked for some identification from Sobhy, making it clear that since Taybieh vouched for him, it was a mere formality. However, Sobhy was still a bit nervous. The battered and creased driver's license pass muster, and it was handed back with a smile. Sobhy was welcomed to the camp, and the men drove toward the main building that served as Abu Bakr al Baghdadi's headquarters. To Taybieh, nothing had changed, and his main feeling was one of remorse.

The courtyard was basically the same, with the exception that all the stones had been polished, and the blood had thoroughly soaked into the sand with no trace remaining. It was if it was a nightmare that faded with the cleansing daylight. But Taybieh still had flashes of his treacherous behavior flicker behind his eyes. There was no way in hell that it would ever be erased from his consciousness. And for this he would suffer the rest of his life. However, his burden could be lessened a touch if he were to carry out this plan with Sobhy, to at least atone for some small portion of the sins that he had saddled himself with. Yes, it was all on him with regard to his former friend, el Moussa. And he accepted it. Now he could escape from it all with this one action. He could take his split of the money for the artifact, disappear into the Syrian Desert and reinvent himself. Maybe, just maybe, after the war was over, he could return to *As Suwayda* and start his old life over again. Then an image of Mohamed el Moussa and his family darkened the landscape. As a form of repentance, should he return to the village, he would make sure that some compensation be given to that family. At least that would allow him a bit of rest. But that was all theory. The reality was that he was having a hard time coping with the betrayal and he worried his fears might not allow him to do what he felt was right.

As he walked up to the door, all sorts of scenarios flashed through his mind. Of course, the most horrific was foremost- of being found out as a traitor and manipulator himself. This would carry the same sentence as his dead friend el Moussa. This thought was followed closely by other, almost equally devastating, alternatives. The guards, whom he knew, tightly smiled at him. They politely asked if he had any weapons that were not visible. Although he declared that he was unarmed, they cautiously frisked him anyway. However it was not with rough malice as it would be were he considered to be an enemy. With a great deal of trepidation, Taybieh knocked on the door and entered; following the directive issued from the other side. It was as if he was in a time warp. The room was the same, the figures all in the same place as well, with al Bagdadi seated at the center of the plank table, flanked by two of his subordinates. The second imam, the other one who was present at Mohamed el Moussa's 'trial,' was absent. That was the only difference. Ahmed approached the table and paused a couple of feet in front of it.

It took a few moments for the commander to look up from the papers that he was perusing. Whether that was a tactic to even further unsettle the young Syrian or was simply indicating that this matter was not as important as what was immediately in front of him made no difference. It was disconcerting and made him prepare for the worst. These fears would not come to fruition. Al Baghdadi stacked the papers in a neat pile and set them aside. He then stood up and smiled at his 'prodigal soldier' and reached out to shake his hand. Taybieh wasn't quite sure what to do. Should he approach or wait for an order? The commander saw his uncertainty and beckoned him with the other hand.

"Come, come, *y'allah habibi*!" He waved him forward. Taybieh took two steps toward the table and thrust out his hand as well. It was grasped by both hands of al Baghdadi and vigorously pumped. "You know, you ought to be shot for leaving us!" He sternly said, then broke out laughing with a deep from the chest roar. Ahmed's heart began to beat again, and he knew what it meant to 'be dead' for a moment. Although he did not join in the laughter, he smiled a bit.

"I was just playing you. After all, you are an integral part to our operation here, and your up and leaving left me shorthanded. Don't ever do it again," he whispered before releasing his grip. "The question is this, now that you are back, I do need to mete out some form of punishment for the sake of the others and discipline.

Publicly I will give you a couple of really shit patrols to lead for the benefit of the camp. But privately, know that you are merely on a 'parole' and nothing will come of it in terms of any real punishment. You are too valuable."

Taybieh didn't know what to say. But his relief was clearly evident. He mumbled a few words of thanks to the commander and saluted.

"I hear that you've brought a new recruit of sorts, from your hometown. Correct?" Nothing got past the commanding officer. Taybieh told him about Sobhy, his background, his connections back in Egypt and his black market contacts in the archaeological artifact world. He further explained about the vast resources out there for the purchase of illicit objects and how that could financially benefit the movement when other funds like oil revenues, were drying up as oil field territory was being lost to the advances made by the Syrian army.

"But I'm still a bit confused. Why on earth would anyone wish to buy illegal items when they know that UNESCO and other agencies would confiscate them immediately if they were discovered?" It was a perceptive question.

"I should let my friend explain to you," replied Taybieh before requesting permission to bring Sobhy in to meet the commander. With that, he turned and left to get Sobhy who was waiting out in the courtyard. Before he was allowed to bring him in, the guards took his papers into the office. They emerged a few minutes later, handed the packet of material back to Sobhy, and ushered them back in to the commanding officer.

It became clear that al Baghdadi was tremendously interested in obtaining more financial resources for his increasingly beleaguered fighters. Taybieh knew this, because, just as Sobhy was coming into the room, a coffee service was being delivered from the kitchen at the rear of the building. Only those visitors with extraordinary clout were treated to this protocol. In addition, the commander rose and walked *around* his table to greet him. This was something that was almost unprecedented. The guards within the room picked up on this, and immediately smartened themselves up, drawing themselves up straighter and flicking imaginary pieces of lint and other debris from their camo uniforms.

"*Ahlen ya* Sobhy!" al Baghdadi embraced the Egyptian and gave him the traditional kisses on each cheek. It was if he was greeting a long-lost relative. Sobhy was a bit taken aback but played along with similar enthusiasm. He needed to sell his story, and sell it well. "Can you explain to me, a poor, but pious, member of the Faithful why such a plan to sell blasphemous artifacts to Godless westerners will ultimately benefit our, um, excuse me, *Allah's* cause and raise us needed funds to continue our *Jihad* against infidels?" He certainly waxed eloquent when he needed to.

Sobhy nodded slightly, in deference to the leader, and explained in an equally precise and passionate way. "Can you imagine, Commander, sitting in a basement room," Sobhy's disarming sense of humor kicked in. "I mean, sir, if you had a basement room that was *anything* but a bomb shelter!" He laughed easily, and, after a moment, al Baghdadi thought about it and then joined in the mirth. This signaled everyone else in the room to join in, even though they hadn't a clue- including Taybieh. Sobhy then went on.

"In the west, a basement sometimes was called a 'man cave,' for relaxation and pleasure. So, envision a man wealthy beyond all imagination. A man who is accustomed to owning only the finest that rarest that money can buy. So fervently wanting to own something that he would do anything, *anything* to have it. In addition, he would even go to the extreme of not telling a soul, including his wife and family, that he had this object of desire. In this 'man cave' there would be a vault-like chamber, inaccessible except via a code to unlock the room, known only to him. The objects that he had, known only to him, would be treasures that the world would sorely miss. Yet the all-too-human urge to have, as the Koran states, in *Sura Al Baqqarah,* 2.35, the forbidden fruit, is universal."

Al Baghdadi smiled warmly. "You know our holy scripture well, *habibi!* I commend you. Yes, as I recall, we say *'O Adam, dwell, you and your wife, in Paradise and eat therefrom in [ease and] abundance from wherever you will. But do not approach this tree, lest you be among the wrongdoers.'"*

Another embrace, and then handshakes all around, and the blessings of the insurgent commanding officer sealed the deal. Now it was up to Sobhy, and to a certain degree, an unknowing Taybieh, to carry out the plan to rescue the Jewish artifact from Palmyra before it was wantonly destroyed by the unworldly troops of Syria's insurgency.

*****

Sobhy breathed a sigh of relief as he and Taybieh left the headquarters building. The other Syrian actually started laughing and slapped the Egyptian on the back, a celebration not so much of selling the plan, but of living through it all and enjoying more days to come. After all, he had deserted his post after el Moussa's execution at his behest. Taybieh and Sobhy went over to a smoldering fire pit, where a pot of coffee was still warm, and helped themselves- 'pulling up a couple of rocks' to seat themselves and figure the rest of the plan. The only two snags were that Abu Bakr insisted on sending one of his soldiers to the antiquity site with them, and he himself listening in on the conversation that Sobhy had with his contact, so that he knew it wasn't a ploy to get in touch with the Syrian Army to wipe them out. At this, Sobhy smiled inwardly. If the commander only knew that it was not the Syrian government he had to be afraid of, but the Israelis...

Once again, the caliber of education of the common insurgent fighter was third grade at best. The young Syrian peasant fighter sent by al Baghdadi had no idea what he was looking at or for. After a ten minute walk, the three of them came to the ruined perimeter wall of Palmyra. It was not an ancient ruin. The city walls had withstood dozens of attempted breaches over the thousands of years of history. The most recent rebuilding had been done at the behest of Diocletian, at the start of the 4th Century CE. It had been in one horrific year of occupation by ISIS, 2015, that the modern destruction of nearly 30% of the city had taken place. It was wanton stupidity, even tacitly admitted to in private by some of the Caliphate leaders. Although they agreed to the destruction of anything even remotely linked to the insult of Islam, the havoc wrought by the senseless blowing up of secular antiquities was felt to give further fuel to the fires of retribution by both the Syrian Army and rebel factions opposed to ISIS. At the time, they hadn't even thought of the notion of raised revenue from illicit antiquities sales.

While the fighter lounged just inside the destroyed city wall, Sobhy and Taybieh rummaged around the vicinity of the stone lintel where it was last seen, and hidden, by el Moussa. After pushing aside a few blocks, they found the one stone with the four line Aramaic inscription containing the prayer, the *Shema*. Once they uncovered it, Sobhy made sure that there were no more Jewish artifacts in the area. He was confident that his companion had no clue as to its origins, nor its intrinsic value. It was readily apparent that the rest of the distinct, and identifying, objects were destroyed when the ancient synagogue collapsed. All incised blocks or inscriptions were now gone as well after scores of stones had been ground up to make concrete for the insurgent camp accommodations adjacent to the site. Other architectural sculpture elements from surrounding buildings were gone as well.

Now that the inscribed stone was relocated and secured, the men brought it back to the camp. Al Baghdadi had long since left to inspect other positions, and there was no one other than one of his lesser lieutenants to look after them. With more pressing matters on his hands, Taybieh and Sobhy were pretty much left alone. However, there was always the chance of the commander returning, or calling in to find out what was going on. So Sobhy still had to be extremely cautious. He told Taybieh that he was going to call his contact in Cairo, with ties to the black market. He would use his battered Syrian cellphone.

Taybieh nodded in approval, though his body language telegraphed that he did quite follow the arguments completely. To Sobhy, it didn't matter. He pulled his battered phone from his pocket.

The protocol had already been set before he left Israel. He punched in the country code '20' for Egypt and proceeded to call his own private number in Cairo. But, thanks to Israeli technology, the phone was re-routed to Eitan's private cell in Israel with no trace possible. We chose this for a number of reasons- but foremost, his gravelly voice with a slightly western tinged Mideast accent would be unidentifiable by the average Syrian listener. The origin could be from anywhere in Europe, or the region for that matter. When Eitan took the call, he would then vouch for Sobhy, knowing that someone else would be listening in on the conversation. At that point, he would highly recommend a 'buyer' with exctremely deep pockets for the artifact. This would further entice the rebel leadership with the prospect of not only financial gain from this transaction, but the promise of more to come based on this success.

"Ahlen rais! Kif halek habibi!" Sobhy placed his hand over the microphone and then whispered to Taybieh, "It's my associate director friend in the Cairo Museum. He's also a 'good friend' when it comes to finding new homes for artifacts. And don't worry, his cut

will come out of my commission so none of you will be out any more money!" He smiled as warmly as he could under the circumstances.

"*Ahlen ya hamar!* Greetings you jackass!" Eitan's voice boomed loud but with a bit of static. That was just as planned. "It sounds like a bad connection from here," he said.

The pleasantries aside, they got down to the real discussion of things, with a very serious tone. Taybieh looked at Sobhy and was duly impressed. The name Dr. Badia Cattaoui came up in the discussion. The Cattaoui family were widespread throughout Lebanon, and wealthy Christians. What better cover for someone to purchase illicit antiquities, especially from a site that was of great importance to Judaism and Christianity- such as Palmyra. In reality, she was actually the professor working with UNESCO and Sobhy, Joanne Farchakh.

"I have a few names, and I randomly chose this one in Lebanon for a couple of reasons. First, the closeness. You only have to travel about 280 km to the vicinity of Baalbek, where this person said that they could meet us. Second, from what I could tell, this individual could possibly have both an emotional and spiritual connection to this place, Palmyra. This might easily boost the price that could be fetched," Eitan was doing a stellar job of 'selling.'

*****

"And how do you know her?" Taybieh asked. Apparently, he had been given a couple of instructions by al Baghdadi prior to his departure from the camp. This certainly was not something that the Syrian fighter would have come up with all on his own.

"Who's this?!?" Eitan/Egyptian archaeologist/ black marketeer demanded over the phone.

"My name is Ahmed Taybieh, a close friend of Sobhy, and one who wishes to see no harm come to him or this plan," he shot back, with more bravado than he really felt. But he knew that al Baghdadi was counting on him to ensure that the right things were done. And it wasn't just that the commander who was counting on him- Taybieh also felt that his own life hung in the balance as well. Because if everything blew up in their faces, he would be the second to suffer after Sobhy.

"*Tayib*, okay *habibi*. But you have to trust me as well. I've known our 'Syrian' companion a lot longer than you and hold him very dear to me as a friend and colleague. I too don't want anything to go wrong for all of our sakes. And if this works out well, we may be able to establish an ongoing arrangement; at least until your bloody war runs its course." Sobhy thought that he might have to put Eitan's name in the hopper for the Ophir Awards, also known as the Israeli Oscars.

Apparently, this did the trick, because everyone seemed to calm down and feel more comfortable with each other. Sobhy breathed a sigh of relief, Taybieh now sat back in his chair and seemed to be more relaxed. For his part, Eitan dialed back his strident tone a bit and took on an air of reconciliation. The final contact information was given out, Eitan told the two in Syria that he would inform 'Dr.

Badia' the good news that she would be getting a phone call about an object she would definitely be interested in, and then broke the connection.

Now it was Sobhy's turn to breathe a sigh of relief. Taybieh, simply looked at him with what could only be described as a 'shit-eating grin' of satisfaction. With all the pieces of the puzzle on the board, it was only a matter of a couple more days until the transaction, and transfer of money, would be complete. Apparently...

*****

The hardest part of anything is waiting. When there is nothing more to be done, the slowdown of time can be excruciating. This is what Sobhy and Taybieh were forced to endure. The 'Egyptian contact'- had closed the conversation with the final word being that the two in Syria would get a text message, cryptic of course, that merely stated that their 'cousin' in Lebanon would be ready to get their call at a certain time on a certain day. So they were waiting for that certain time and certain day. Not much was going on in the camp. Routine patrols were sent out at the bare minimum since al Baghdadi was not present. Apparently no one wanted to tempt the fates any more than necessary and risk getting shot, or worse. To Taybieh, it was similar to the heady days a couple of years earlier, after all their combat priorities had been met, and their camps were almost childlike in their overflowing glee as their easy victories early on. At that time, everyone sort of lounged around, comparing war stories, either real or made up, to regale their companions and boast of the new regional order descending on Syria. But those days were long gone and it was more often than not a fight for survival.

It was toward the end of the second day of anticipation that Sobhy's cell phone 'pinged.' The text message was clear as could be. The call to the 'Lebanese relative' was to take place the next morning at 9 sharp. Anything more than five minutes late and the deal would be off. That was it. No names, numbers or any other identifying words meant tight security. Anyone intercepting the text wouldn't have a clue other than the innocuous wording.

Taybieh laughed aloud and slapped Sobhy on the back. They were ready to rock n' roll as the Americans said.

Both men slept fitfully, wondering not what could go wrong, but *when* it would go wrong. Too many horrible situations in the Mideast had made pessimists out of almost everybody in the region. Sobhy couldn't help but think of a wildly funny, satirical movie made by the British Troupe Monty Python, in 1979. The *Life of Brian* was a wickedly funny parody of everything holy and sacred in the Holy Land. In the end, when 'Brian' (not Jesus) was crucified by the Romans along with other Judeans, they all began to sing- "Always look on the bright side of life. De-dum, de-dum de-dum-de-dum..." Sobhy first began to smile, then laugh, in his sleep. The racket he made woke the Syrian next to him, who came over and shook him violently out of his dream.

"What? What's going on?" He groggily asked of Taybieh.

"You were laughing out loud, almost screaming! It woke me up out of the dead of night! What is it?"

Sobhy recovered quickly and replied, "I was just dreaming about the money we are about to make, and the new lives we hope to start, away from all this. Now you go back to sleep too and dream the same things." He patted Taybieh on the shoulder and rolled over. Sleep now came quickly and solidly.

They rose with the sun the next morning. After their ritual ablutions, they recited the *Fajr*, the morning prayer.

"Allah-hu-akhbar. Subhaan-Allaah wal-hamdu Lillaah wa laa ilaaha ill-Allaah wa Allaah-hoo akbar wa laa hawla wa la quwwata illa Billaah"

God is great. Glory be to my Lord who is the very greatest, *Glory be to Allah, praise be to Allah, there is no god except Allah, Allah is Most great and there is no power and no strength except with Allah.*

Sobhy, although not a religious man at all, relied on past his memories and memories of his teachers, and silently added the following.

We have awoken, and all of creation has awoken, for Allah, Lord of all the Worlds. Allah, I ask You for the best the day has to offer, victory, support, light, blessings and guidance; and I seek refuge in You from the evil in it, and the evil to come after it.

The men then headed over to the tent that served as the mess hall, and got themselves some good, fresh, still warm *pita* and washed it down with extraordinarily bad, nearly cold coffee. Taybieh remarked at how someone could make such good bread while ruining the simple task of making a hot beverage. Sobhy raised his cup in a mock salute and nodded agreement. By this time the moment to make the phone call was near. Fortunately, neither man needed to rely on their watches and what might be 'iffy' time. Sobhy's cellphone clock was linked to the network and was accurate within the minute.

"*Ahlen*, ya doctor!" Sobhy placed the call. The Israelis working with the team were able to trace the call, and listen in as a three-way, for security purposes. In addition, they were able to degrade the signal a bit, making it 'staticky' enough to simulate a poor connection coming into Lebanon and out of Syria.

Since Taybieh asked to listen in on speakerphone, the UN affiliate professor would come across comfortably and give the proper impression. Was it infallible? Was anything these days? But it was as perfect a setup as possible- given an even greater probability of success due to the naiveté of the Syrian militants around Sobhy.

The phone call was placed precisely on time- and answered in as timely a fashion. We were able to verify each other via a couple of code words that were passed on to both of us. Once all that was established we got down to the matter at hand. Yes, she was very interested in antiquities, especially from Palmyra. She was doubly interested in them if they had a relationship to either or both Christianity and Judaism, as her family were Lebanese Christians.

Sobhy placed a hand over the microphone and whispered to Taybieh, "We should proceed with caution, play hard to get. That may in fact raise the ante for payment. The more for us, the better. Let's just see exactly *how* interested she is." The Syrian agreed.

As the phone call progressed, and the stipulations made, 'Dr. Cattaoui' indicated that she would like a photo texted over so she could get an idea of what was in play. Only then could the hard core negotiating take place. Both sides mutually agreed to talk after the image was sent out. They set a time later in the afternoon that same day.

Meanwhile, with her cell number embedded in the memory of his phone now, Sobhy took a snapshot of the inscribed lintel that they had removed from the synagogue debris and fired it off to the 'Lebanese' contact. The only thing then was to wait for the appointed callback. This time, it would be from Lebanon, rather than to.

*****

Late that afternoon Sobhy's phone announced that a text message had arrived. He barely heard it, since he had decided to take a nap in order to be fresh for whatever would be happening soon. He groggily reached for it, rubbing his eyes in the process. When he had woken up enough to read the text, he smiled. Everything was in order, the plans for the wire exchange needed to be arranged, as well as the transfer of the item. Now the hardest part would be put into play. He would need to arrange things carefully so that Taybieh and his commander would be none the wiser. Sobhy got up and went to find the Syrian.

He located him drinking coffee with a couple of his other friends. Sobhy muttered greetings to the other men, and gently pulled Taybieh away from them, explaining that he needed to go over some of the recruitment papers that he had been issued when he arrived in camp. An innocuous statement, greeted with indifference by the others, raised no alarms. The two walked a couple of dozen meters away and sat down on camp chairs near a secondary fire barrel. The text message was shown to Taybieh, and the two began an open discussion of what needed to be done now.

First and foremost, the price had to be set. What seemed reasonable, Taybieh asked. To Sobhy, from where he stood, given the state that the camp was in, he thought that any reasonable amount would fly well with the insurgents. He suggested a figure around 50,000 Euros. That way, he argued, it would pave the way for more artifacts to be sold. After all, they shouldn't get too greedy on the 'first dance' and later lose a contact. Taybieh agreed to this position, and said that he should call al Baghdadi to confirm it. There was no harm in it, Sobhy concurred, and the Syrian went off to make his call. Meanwhile, a text was fired off that reconfirmed that the transaction would go ahead, and that all plans should be made. This simple message would set the wheels in motion from Jerusalem's side, and the affair might be over within another day or so. Sobhy was starting to get just a tad nervous around these folks, seeing how unstable they really were.

After a few minutes, Taybieh returned with an all clear statement. The two were to proceed with as much speed as possible to get the transaction done- paving the way for future collaboration. Another text was sent out with the fee of 50,000 Euros for the piece.

The reply was instantaneous. Yes, it seemed a reasonable price. Could the meeting be set for the next day? The only caveat was that the wire transfer of funds would only be done when the object was seen in person and validated as authentic.

Taybeih balked at this. But Sobhy argued that it was the protocol for international business all over the world, and that there was nothing out of the ordinary. In fact, this was reverse psychology on Sobhy's part. If 'the good guys' could get not only the artifact rescued, but deplete the insurgents finances a bit, all the better. But this peasant Syrian fighter had no clue as to how the world operated outside of even a 500 km radius from his village, *As Suweida*. In fact, just beyond Palmyra was actually the farthest he had ever traveled, and it was only within the past year with his fighting unit. He had never used email or accessed the internet. His cell phone was his only interaction with modern technology- and only in calling and texting. Reluctantly he accepted Sobhy's explanation. But he had no authorization, nor the inclination, to deal with the banking stuff. As a result, he texted al Baghdadi for instructions.

Within moments, a text with the response came back. Details were given for the transfer to be in cash only. The commander didn't want any paper trail of this deal. Part of the reason was that any account, no matter how secure, could be compromised by the other side. But the main part of the reason was a simpler, more devious one. Cash could easily be skimmed, or made to disappear entirely. Even the naïve Taybieh saw through this. He came to the conclusion that al Baghdadi wished some of the funds for himself, personally. He smiled inwardly. This played right into his and Sobhy's hands.

After all, *they* were going to be ones who ripped off the insurgents, took the cash and then melt into the desert.

When Sobhy heard this, he too laughed aloud and clapped the Syrian on the back. Everything for them was falling into place easily. But the Syrian didn't realize what that was really going to mean. All that was left was for Sobhy to text with the new financial arrangements and pick the exact time and place for the next day's meeting and transfer.

An 'indignant' response came through, but in the end, the Lebanese 'buyer' acquiesced to their demand of cash. The slight change, however, meant that the meet would have to be delayed until late afternoon in order to get the cash funds. With that, no more communication would be made between the two, citing security, unless something dramatically changed the plans.

Sobhy deferred to Taybeih with regard to the route to be taken. He had no idea of the on-the-ground situation because of the civil war that raged. The route chosen was the best of options, although Sobhy was certain that the Egyptian Auto Association would have never routed them on a map this way for any tour. They were to head due west on a road that would take them past the small village of *Tyas*. Although the village was small, what was next to it wasn't. A major Syrian airbase had been constructed there following the 1967 war with Israel. Because much of the Golan was lost, the airfield still in Syrian control at the time was deemed too close to the new frontier, so *Tyas* was chosen. The base had been besieged by ISIS but never subdued in 2015. In spite of that, the road to *Furqlus,* and then on to Homs, remained somewhat safe. However, Taybieh was taking no chances. He assumed an air of authority, took charge, and enlisted the aid of a couple of his friends in the militia. He told them it was a direct request from their commander, al Baghdadi. The mere mention of his name put these fighters in a state of awe. He offered them 100 Syrian Pounds each, the equivalent of 2 months' pay, but only a few dollars in real money. They were sent to 'the shop,' a former cattle pen that was converted into an open air repair area, and got a vehicle to serve as an escort part of the way. They requisitioned a converted Toyota pickup with a 50 caliber machine gun welded onto the flatbed in the rear. It was topped off with gas, oil and tires checked, to ensure as best as possible that nothing would break. Given the already meager supplies available due to recent military losses, the chances of that happening, even with all precautions, were still at slightly over 50%. They would travel in convoy to the outskirts of *Furqlus* and then return to Palmyra. It was only about 90 km so they could be back quickly and not even be missed. This would take Sobhy and Taybieh into a safer zone on the way to Homs.

From Homs, they took the M5 south to *An Nabk*. There, they picked up a little used lane that ran due west to the border. A small coffee shop and rest house was still operating and the two decided to take a short break. Here, Taybieh found out that the checkpoint at the border had long been abandoned by both Syria and Lebanon; and that only barbed concertina wire closed the border, with no guards in the derelict huts on either side. This was the best news that there could be. They could slip across undetected, do their transaction with speed, and part ways by no later than around ten under the cover of darkness. Taybieh remarked that he would sleep extraordinarily well that night.

Just as described by the old men at the coffee house, the short drive to the boundary with Lebanon was uneventful. The border indeed was unoccupied on either side. It reminded Sobhy of one of the many small desert tracks that crossed the Western Sahara from Egypt to Libya, with no one in sight for kilometers. In those spots, there wasn't even concertina wire across the road. The assumption was that it would only impede the Bedouin. Any real military incursion wouldn't use those kinds of crossings.

None of this mattered to Taybieh. Suddenly he got cold feet. He'd never been out of Syria before, legally or illegally, and he was scared of being captured or killed. Sobhy understood his fears of the unknown, and it brought back memories of his first visit to Israel, when he was working on the recovery of a lost statue fragment that identified Moses as an Egyptian Pharaoh. It had been discovered at the excavations of Tell Lachish in Israel, when it had been under the British Mandate Authority in the 1930s. As the story turned out, a young Egyptian archaeologist had conspired to steal the fragment, killing the British excavator in the process, and spiriting it away to Cairo. There, he hid it in the Cairo Museum. Eventually, decades later, he became the director of the museum, thus ensuring that the piece would never be detected- until Sobhy, his American archaeologist friend and an Israeli team all worked together to recover it. But that had meant going to Israel, something that made him nervous even though it was decades after the peace accords.

*****

He recalled quite vividly where he was on the morning of 6 October, 1973. At the time he was a sergeant in the 2nd Army under the direction of Major General Saad Mamoun, as part of the 16th Infantry Division. They were assigned to cross the Suez Canal at 1400 hours, just north of *Deversoir* between the Great Bitter Lake and Lake *Timsah*. This was to be the moment that all Egyptians had been waiting for since the debacle of 1967. Once again, the pride of Egypt in all of her glory would be re-instated and the 'Israeli Zionist aggressor' would be pushed back from Egyptian territory. All were quite nervous, very antsy. The worst of anything is always the waiting immediately prior to the events. One of his dearest friends, Hasan Mohamed, actually puked all over his equipment, he was so, well, downright scared would be the word. After all, in spite of the exhortations by their fearless leader Anwar Sadat and the army's tape-recorded messages from Boutros Boutros Ghali to Brigadier Hafiz, leader of the 16th, as well as Sobhy's very own wise words to his platoon, *-no man wants to die, especially not in battle-*, faced with the possibility of a slow, painful and agonizing martyrdom. Regardless of what is seen on TV or read in the papers or hear from the *imams,* Paradise is not all that inviting to a 19-year-old with the best of this world yet to come. He was ready to meet God, *habibi*, but on somewhat different terms.

At precisely 1400 hours the barrage of both artillery and high-pressure water cannon began with a roar that threatened to burst-eardrums. Why was the Israeli army caught unawares? Because *it actually commenced on time!* The great sand wall of the *Bar-Lev* line, that impregnable 'fortification' of the Israelis, collapsed in a muddy, oozing heap. An enormous gap in the sand wall was created and, seeing it open almost magically before our eyes, they surged forward with the great cry --"*Allahuuuu, Akbar* !!!" "God is Great !"

Thirty-six hours after the crossing, the Egyptian High Command was congratulating itself on a stunning victory. At the same time, it set into motion an air of caution and, perhaps foolishly in retrospect, called for a slowdown of advance through the Sinai that likened itself to a snail's pace. This conservatism ultimately cost the Egyptians dearly.

The combat forces outran their supply lines- putting the lead troops in a precarious position. Without ample supplies, including ammunition, Sobhy was to take his platoon on a reconnoitering mission about 8-10 km. east of the Canal, not far from an agricultural station known as the 'Chinese Farm' by both Israelis and Egyptians. This patrol was to scout the area of *Beer Khebeita*, a small oasis about 2 km from the mountain ridge of *Jebel Khebeita*.

In an ensuing firefight, Sobhy took a bullet in the right wrist, shattering it. But God was with him that day. He would survive the battle, escape capture that was the fate of several thousand of his fellow soldiers when the Israelis crossed the Suez Canal to the west and surrounded the Third Army, and eventually return to civilian life and resume his archaeology career.

*****

Decades later, these ghosts would come back to haunt him *until* he actually went to Israel, saw the 'real' other side, and vowed never to let the stupidity of humankind's political leaders destroy the basic thread of 'sameness' that weaves all people together. And now, once again, he found himself working with those very same colleagues to preserve the legacy of the human experience from evil.

So yes, Sobhy fully understood the terror that Taybieh faced. The difference was that the young Syrian was truly caught between the proverbial rock and hard place. He had become so fully immersed in the insurgent philosophy that there was no political reasoning with him. Now his only desire was to survive the civil war and escape from fellow Syrians from two sides- Assad's army and ISIS' radical religious militants.

Sobhy needed to find a way around this because the entire plan was jeopardized if Taybieh pulled out. He grabbed the Syrian and sat him down. He knew to he couldn't explain that he understood exactly how Taybieh felt, as it could lead in the Sobhy's death as well. So, a revised plan had to be created- one that would not fuel Ahmed Taybieh's fears to the point of no return.

"*Tayib*, okay, how about this. Let me text this Lebanese doctor. I'll make up something, like the supposed quiet, unmanned border suddenly has military activity that wasn't there yesterday," Sobhy was improvising on the fly. He pulled out the well-creased road map that the two had been supplied with back at the camp. He scanned it and suddenly smiled, "I think that I have it. We'll tell this contact to meet us just here." He pointed at spot only a kilometer or so south. There was a small track that ended right at the border, at least according to the map. It was so small a path that, when Taybieh looked at it, he remarked that it appeared to be nothing more than a goat trail.

"Then that's perfect! We won't cross over anywhere with our truck, merely *schlep* the stone over..."

"*Na'am,* what did you say?" A look of confusion crossed the Syrian's face.

Sobhy paled, but quickly recovered. He had used a Yiddish word that he learned in Israel! *Oy favoy!* He thought. Then he realized just how close to his Israeli and American friends he had become. He was using their idioms.

"Sorry, I said that we'll *step* the stone a couple of dozen meters to the Lebanese buyer!"

"Ah, that's sounds really good to me." The Syrian clearly had no idea what Sobhy had really said... thankfully.

So they got back in the vehicle and drove the remaining short distance.

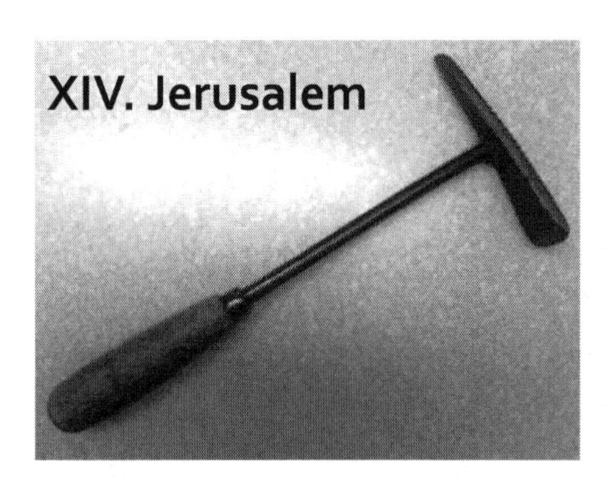

XIV. Jerusalem

Word was received. All would be set in motion now. The Israelis began to make their plans, setting up one of their operatives to act as Dr. Badia Cattoui, on behalf of Joanne Farchakh. Ben Dov's contacts in the Israeli Air Force started to orchestrate a drone attack on the Syrians once the transaction was completed. The Israelis had upwards of 60 drones in their air force repertoire.

The Hermes-900 *Kochav* was Elbit Systems' most recent long endurance unmanned aerial system. It is virtually undetectable with the eye from the ground, with a flight altitude of more than 9100 m and able to fly in all weather conditions. The Hermes-900 had a maximum payload weight of 300 kg. In fact, this drone had been purchased from countries and businesses all around the world. It was used during the 2014 World Cup in Brazil. The Hermes-900 was designated to be the 'strike force' that would complete the operation against the insurgents once Sobhy was safe and the artifact recovered.

But foremost in the minds of those waiting back in Israel was how to successfully extract Sobhy from Syria with no harm to him and the artifact. Another model in the Israeli Air Force (IAF) drone arsenal was to be used to rescue Sobhy. It was nicknamed the 'AirMule' from the aerospace company called UrbanAero. In fact, it could have flown right off the pages of a sci-fi comic book. This futuristic-designed helicopter style drone was like a FedEx delivery truck with wings and prop engines. It was built to take off and land vertically with up to 1,400 pounds of cargo and fly to its destination at over 160 kph. It was initially created as an air ambulance of sorts, set to transport injured soldiers from urban war zones where standard helicopters simply couldn't fly. Once the wounded had been stabilized by medics in the combat zone, the soldiers could load them onto this large-scale drone and whisk them back to safety and further medical assistance.

Before the mission launched, however, Ben Dov got a call from his office. He was to stop at the IAF drone training center at the Palmahim base, south of Rishon Le Zion just outside of Tel Aviv. Apparently there was a slight modification of plans, since it was still 24-36 hours until the final stages of the mission were undertaken.

It seemed that Israel would try to kill two birds with one stone. Command's reasoning was sound. If they were going to send a drone with surveillance and strike capability to Palmyra, to destroy the insurgent camp located there, why not first overfly the city of Aleppo. The purpose of that mission was to ascertain the status and condition of the last remnants of the Jewish community in Syria- the Jewish community of Aleppo.

The rich and diverse Syrian Jewish community had been dwindling rapidly during the 21st Century. As the only remaining group in Syria to have their identity cards and passports indicate their religion, they were oftentimes persecuted and singled out for special treatment by both the government and Syrian dissidents. Even the Palestinian refugee community would abuse them. While the government 'officially' protected its Jewish citizens, their situation was still precarious at best. Scores of Jews would flee the country if possible. In fact, many actually were able to make it to Israel. By the end of 2014, most agencies reported that there were fewer than 50 Jews in the country.

The largest remaining community was in Aleppo. With the ever increasing threat to Aleppo by ISIS in the fall, 2015, a major push was on to rescue the Jewish community there. A secret operation was carried out, and the Jews were transported overland to Istanbul, and from there on to Israel where they were relocated in Ashkelon. This action could only have been carried out with the aid of non-Jewish, pro-Western Syrians fighting against the government in the civil war. With those left behind in possible jeopardy, the names of the families were changed in order to protect them. That arduous process then left only about 18 Jews in Syria.

The Aleppo Jews were able to spirit away Torah scrolls and other religious items, but the synagogue and its Jewish architectural elements were left behind. It remained untouched and in relatively good condition, discretely watched over by the anti-government neighbors. However, in a major battle between insurgents and ISIS in the winter of 2016, the synagogue sustained damaged during several rounds of artillery fire from all sides. Although it was not totally destroyed, no one on the outside was able to assess the damage, or its current status.

This then, was the rationale behind the partial re-tasking of the drone mission. Check out the Aleppo Synagogue with flyovers to ascertain the situation. Then, if any further steps should be necessary, re-evaluate for the future. The 'eyes' on the *Kochav* drone were so sophisticated that they could transmit a visual inspection with great clarity. Since the interior had been cleared of ritual objects, the attention would be to the architectural detail and stained glass windows.

Ben Dov was pleased that the higher-ups could think even further outside the box on this one, and wholeheartedly agreed to get the drone reprogrammed for this flight. With this new protocol set in place, he found that he had to 'hit the road' again. This time, he would go directly to the heart and soul of the drone command, the Combat Intelligence Collection in the Negev. This was the core of drone operations in Israel, its exact location shrouded in secrecy, although nearly everyone knew about it. In Israel, secret facilities sometimes are secrets out in the open. Once, there, he was read in on all the emerging details of the overflight of Aleppo. It was to take place in just a few hours, timed almost to the minute with the extraction of Sobhy and the stone inscription at the Lebanese-Syrian border.

As he approached the Sayarim Training Base, he drove past the Nabatean archaeological site of Shivta. About 40 km south of Beersheva, it was designated a World Heritage Site by UNESCO in 2005; part of the Nabatean Spice Routes Trail that ran from Petra in Jordan to the Mediterranean Sea. It was known for its inventive use of dry farming methods and desert water storage. In addition, it was known in the ancient world for its wine production as attested to by the numerous wine presses excavated there. The production levels rival even today's wineries, with estimates as high at two million liters of wine produced. In fact, Israeli archaeologists and agronomists have collaborated quite successfully to re-create a working Nabatean farm. It has served as a model for modern kibbutz agricultural and vintner techniques as well. Ben Dov made a mental note to find a bottle of this 'new' old wine and toast it with the others once this mission was successfully completed.

Immediately after he pulled up to the main gate, an escort took him to the command center's tracking facility. He was welcomed in and explained where the mission was at that point. The briefing came from the commander himself, Col Ilan. He welcomed Ben Dov and ushered him into his office; a glass-walled room that looked over an enormous bullpen that housed a couple of dozen computer stations. On the far wall, facing his glass office wall, a four m high OLED monitor was divided up into quarter panels, each with its own display. Talk about a 'picture-in-picture' mode for the most rabid soccer fan...

Each monitor section showed real timing imaging from drones that were up and patrolling Israel. It would be here, Ilan said, that the two drones assigned this rescue and combat mission would transmit video of their particular tasks. On one hand, the *Kochav* surveillance/attack drone would get even closer than a bird's eye view of the remains of the Jewish Quarter and synagogue in Aleppo. From there, it would continue the 210 km flight southeast to Palmyra, take a spin around the insurgent camp from high altitude, acquisition it targets, and carry out the bombing raid. On the other hand, the AirMule would pick out a suitable landing spot and give Sobhy, the Israeli operative acting as the university professor, and the stone inscription a lift back to Jerusalem, a distance of just under 265 km.

*****

The Hermes 900 *Kochav* lifted off and sped toward Aleppo. As it passed into Syrian airspace, the ground crew back in the Negev took the drone down almost to the deck and artfully wove it in and out of the small wadis that dotted the landscape. It was, in essence, invisible to anyone trying to track it on radar. However, this close to the ground, although practically silent, it could be readily seen by anyone who happened to look up.

This concerned the base commander, who was monitoring the mission very closely. He was afraid that, should something occur to the drone, it might crash before the destruction signal could be given. And he certainly did not want Israeli technology falling into the wrong hands. He unconsciously twisted and turned his body with every 'dance move' that the drone made as a result of its officer's joystick commands. Ben Dov watched this with amusement. He was tempted to get out his cellphone and video the officer, with the intent of posting it online *after* the mission was successfully completed. But that was a fleeting fancy. He smiled and thought that it was a good dream, but that was all.

When the drone approached 50 km from Aleppo, the commanding officer whispered something in the ear of its controller. A quick nod, and the joystick flicked back. The nose camera suddenly noted nothing but blue sky for half a minute. Then all at once the Syrian countryside came back on the monitor. The Hermes 900 had risen a thousand meters in that time, and now was undetectable from the ground. Its small signature and stealth sheathing also ensured that it would not be visible on radar as well.

Ben Dov watched in awe. But he bent over the shoulder of the now seated base commander and quietly asked a question, "Were you or the drone operator controlling the flight plan and altitude so that our flight wouldn't be seen as it was on the deck, or was it something else?"

The other man turned and laughed, "*B'seder*! Okay, you sort of caught me out." At that, the controller, who also heard this, smiled as well. "Our stealth technology would have prevented the Syrian air force radar, antiquated as it is, from ever seeing our little bird at any altitude. We just wanted to see what it could do close to the surface in terms of maneuverability. After all, so far, our only training was with the video 'game' that Elbit supplied us. This is the first real deployment over enemy territory." He shrugged his shoulders and turned back to the screen.

"Were we ever at risk?" Ben Dov quietly asked.

"Never, we are so quiet with the electric motor we use down low, no one would really have had a clue. Especially since the angle of the sun at this time of day created a hazy horizon anyway."

The Israeli mission team member breathed a sigh of relief, because he was the only one in the room who knew that Israeli and Egyptian lives were at stake. The drone officers only were aware of the reconnaissance and Syrian military target aspects of the mission. The real goal was on a need-to-know basis, and the added responsibility certainly didn't need to be known.

The clarity of image from the Leica camera lens on the drone was astounding. The zoom capabilities made the view as if it was ten meters rather than a thousand. The headlines on the windblown newspapers along the road, and the labels on the discarded packages could be read without problem. The outskirts of Aleppo were now just ahead, and the controller began to readjust and aim toward the old city and the now abandoned Jewish Quarter. The goal was to examine the most famous synagogue in Syria, to ascertain its condition.

But problems started to arise. Due to heavy fighting that took place earlier in the day, a grey-brown haze blanketed the approach to the city. It seemed that artillery fire and the collapse of building had led to the creation of this smog-like atmosphere. The good news was that the smog was patchy in many places. There was still a chance at obtaining the visual that Ben Dov desired. Just as the coordinates for the Jewish Quarter appeared on the monitor as an overlay, the wisps of smoke dissipated. The once-magnificent Al Bandara Synagogue came into view.

Also known as Joab's Synagogue, it was a place of worship since the 5th century CE in Aleppo. When it was in its glory, it was considered to be the main synagogue of the Syrian Jewish community. Here the famous Aleppo codex was stored for over five hundred years until it was removed during the 1947 Aleppo pogrom; when the synagogue was burned and the community devastated. According biblical tradition, the original temple structure in Aleppo was constructed by King David's General, Joab ben Zeruiah, after the conquest of the city. The Book of 2 Samuel discussed this.

When the Arameans of Damascus came to help Hadadezer, king of Zobah, David killed 22,000 Arameans. Then David put garrisons among the Arameans of Damascus, and the Arameans became servants to David, bringing tribute. (2Sam 8.4-7)

The synagogue, and the Jewish Quarter, had survived countless governmental changes until finally, in 1400, it was destroyed during Tamerlane's subjugation of Aleppo. However, it would be rebuilt at some point in 1418. In August 1626, the Italian Jesuit, Pietro Della Valle, came to Aleppo and visited the great synagogue. He described it in detail:

> *'I went to see the synagogue of the Jews at Aleppo, famed for fairness and antiquity. Their street is entered into by a narrow gate, which is so much lower than the rest; that it is descended to by a considerable number of steps. After I had gone through many of their narrow lanes, which they contrive so, purposely to hide the goodness of the building from the Turks, I came at length to the synagogue; which is a good large square uncovered court, with covered walks*

or cloysters round about, upheld by double pillars disposed according to good architecture. On the right hand of the entrance, is a kind of great hall, which they make use of for their service in the winter when it is cold or rains; as they do of the court in summer and fair weather: In the middle of the court four pillasters support a cupoletta, under which in a high and decent place, like our altar; lies the volume of the Law, and there also their doctor and principal rabbi stands reading in a kind of musical tone, to whom all the people alternately answer: . . .'

The synagogue proper was divided into three main sections: a central courtyard that separated the western wing, an eastern section built at a later time during the 16th century which served as Beth Midrash, and finally an enclosed courtyard located along the eastern wing.

The clarity of the images transmitted by the *Kochav* 900 stunned Ben Dov. He knew of the great advances in aerial reconnaissance that the Israelis had made in recent years, but was unprepared for this. He gazed in awe at the crisp imagery and mentioned it to the techie who was guiding the drone. The soldier merely shrugged his shoulders and continued to focus on his job. Apparently this was 'just another day in the surveillance office' for this air force operative. No matter, Ben Dov was still 'wowed.'

The bottom line here was relief that the building still stood proudly, even though it was decommissioned as a religious structure due to Aleppo's occupation by ISIS. The only real damage seen on the outside was a desecrated *Magen David*, the six-pointed Star of

David symbol that originally was in raised relief above the main entry to the former sanctuary. Apparently this visual was too much a slap in the face of the ISIS contingent occupying the city. However, the stained- glass windows that were recreated in the 15th century when the synagogue was rebuilt were largely intact. The reason for this was that, following the rebuilding after Tamerlane's destruction, the synagogue elders chose to install windows that depicted floral and geometric patterns and not biblical scenes. They didn't want to run the risk of another iconoclastic controversy that might lead to their persecution. However, they very slyly did use depictions of the seven biblical fruits, the *shevat minim*, that all of Aleppo's Jews would recognize. These seven species on the windows were wheat, barley, grapes, figs, pomegranates, olives (oil), and dates (honey). Found in the book of Deuteronomy 8.8, their first fruits were the only acceptable offerings in the Temple that had stood in Jerusalem.

Once the flyover was complete, the drone was lifted back to a 3000 meter height and was programmed to head south and slightly east 210 km by air to Palmyra. With its maximum airspeed at 230 kph, it would reach the city in just under an hour. The staff were visibly relieved that none in Aleppo had noticed their flight. This gave the rest of the mission a greater success rate, since the military activity would be carried out at the higher altitude.

The drone had a 350 kg payload capability, but the ordnance officer chose the lighter AGM 114 Hellfire missiles for this sortie. There were two mounted under each wing. These air-to-ground missiles were reconfigured by the Israelis to fit the underwing pylons of the *Kochav*. The laser guided system was nearly faultless in execution in previous drone attacks. And although most of that success rate was due to mechanics, it was the unerring nerve of the drone commander who made it all possible. Added to the arsenal was a GAU-8/A 30mm cannon that could be guided to hit other ancillary targets.

The crystal clear image of the modern city of Palmyra could be seen peeking out from the wisps of clouds that dotted the landscape. Because of the relatively favorable weather conditions, the need for thermal imaging was not necessary and was turned off. The drone pilot began to isolate the areas adjacent to the ancient site that seemed to be at odds with the kind structures associated with an urban environment. This was somewhat difficult, given the degree of destruction that had been visited on the modern town during the ISIS occupation. However, just to the west of the antiquity site was a large, relatively clean clearing with what looked to be a couple of permanent buildings surrounded by scores of tents. In addition, there appeared to be a dozen of the ISIS-favored military vehicles, the ubiquitous pick-up truck with either 50- caliber machine guns or anti-tank guns welded onto the flatbeds. The pilot pointed these out to Colonel Ilan and Ben Dov. The higher ups in the chain of command had given the green light to the two in the Negev command center. It was up to their discretion on how to proceed with the strike.

Ilan requested another fly-around by the drone before issuing the final order to attack. This took on two purposes. He wanted to be certain that this was indeed the camp, and not a refugee center that was simply being protected with the vehicles. A sweep of the area would also reveal if there were any artifacts from the archaeological site that may have been moved into camp as part of the illicit sales activities that Sobhy had indicated in one of the rare calls he made while in Syria. If anything was seen, the nature of the strike would have to be modified or even called off for the time being.

He also asked for a thermal image to be brought up and displayed on a second screen. He wanted to know the disposition of fighters in and around the area. When the drone strike would be called in; he wanted as many of the enemy personnel eliminated as possible, not just the headquarters and vehicles. The overall fighting capability needed to be eradicated. Ilan knew that taking out this one unit would only be the proverbial drop in the bucket overall. However, it could ensure the security of Sobhy and company and perhaps allow this kind of operation to be run again if need be. The elimination of anyone vaguely familiar with Sobhy's short presence in that camp could buy safety.

The *Kochav* was gently, silently flown in a holding pattern that was about 2 km across. This gave an ample view of the area one more time. The real time images were scrutinized by operatives in the Sayarim Base. They also were seen in Tel Aviv and forwarded to the office of the Antiquities Authority director Jerusalem as well. But his was a vicarious involvement and he sat back; merely a spectator.

The drone operator swiveled around in his chair and looked expectantly at the base commander. With a silent nod, the go-ahead was given for the strike. While at the same altitude, the keyed-in command launched the four missiles at the building assumed to be the headquarters (the only permanent structure), a sandbagged enclosure that appeared to hold munitions, and the courtyard that was designated the vehicle maintenance area. Within moments, the entire base was lit up in fire and smoke. Secondary explosions rocked the Palmyra countryside as gas supplies and ammunition caches were touched off as well. Scores of individuals begun to run around helter-skelter in an attempt to isolate the source of the attack. Most thought that it was a ground-based incursion and hastily set up a perimeter and started firing blind into the surrounding area. It was a waste of ammunition.

After the missiles were loosed, the drone pilot resumed his 'race-track' fly-by. This served two purposes. The first was to let the smoke and dust settle a bit in order to assess the success of the missile strike. The second to plot the new targets that would be addressed by the cannon to finish the operation. At Sayarim Base, a round of subdued applause spread through the command center as the images were relayed back. The camp was decimated. It had been turned into a smoking ruin. Thermal imaging showed scores of fighters now trying to flee. The order was given, and the cannon took many of them out. After all was said and done, the main headquarters of al Baghdadi were now a thing of the past. The fighting capability of this base was eliminated. The threat to the antiquities of Palmyra was gone, at least for the moment. Everyone exhaled with a collective sigh of relief. The drone was on its way back to Israel; never detected by the enemy. They never knew what hit them. It was a 350 km flight to the Negev base. No one would relax for an hour and a half, until the drone was safely back in its hanger.

As Asa Ben Dov and Colonel Ilan headed to the canteen to get a well-earned cup of coffee and congratulations, an aide came rushing up. He had a neutral look on his face, the sign of a true professional who didn't let emotions get the best of him. He saluted Colonel Ilan, in a monotone congratulated him on the success of the mission, but attempted to draw him aside.

"*Segen* Alon, Lt. Alon, anything that you have to say can be said in front of the *Tat Aluf*, Commander Ben Dov. We are all in this together," stated Ilan.

"*B'seder Mefaked*, okay sir", said the young man as he snapped off a crisp salute. "We just intercepted a transmission from Syria, about 15 km from Palmyra. Apparently Abu Bakr el Baghdadi had just left the Palmyra Base on his way to *Deir el-Zour*. He was responding to a brief and incomplete radio broadcast about the chaos ensuing in the Palmyra camp just before the signal from there went dead. Immediately following was an open air broadcast transmission to *Deir el-Zour* telling them to beef up their defenses and expect him later in the day. *Ani Mitsta'ere*, I'm sorry to inform you sir."

Ilan and Ben Dov looked at each other and shrugged, "*Yom asal, yom basal!* One day's honey, another is onions, as our Arab cousins would say."

"It's just the luck of the draw I guess," was the stoic response. "But at least we still scored a major blow against the bastards!" And the two continued to the canteen for that drink... And maybe a *bourekas* or three.

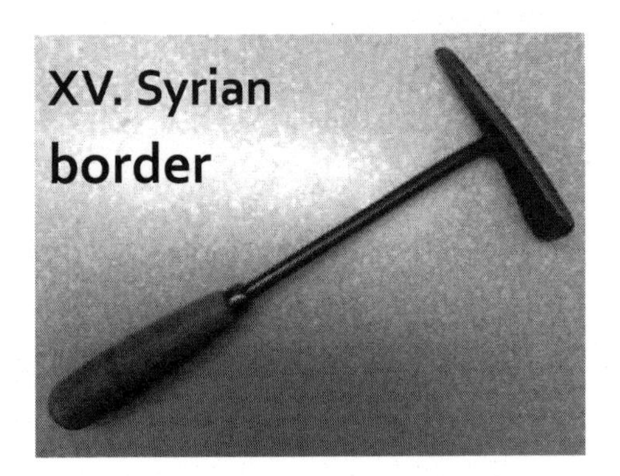

XV. Syrian border

Sobhy would need to find a way to get a bit of separation from Taybieh when the strike would occur. He also needed to try to separate Taybieh from his share of the 'sale' since the two had split up the money between them. Then they would attempt to make their separate 'escapes.'

They drove west toward Laboue, Lebanon, just opposite where 'Dr. Badia' was to meet them along the border. There would be two body guards with her, ostensibly due to the current political and military situation. Taybieh thought nothing of it, as it was not out of the ordinary, therefore it didn't raise any alarms with him. He remarked that he would have done the exact same thing- but made it four instead of just two. He then laughed uneasily. Sobhy could tell that his companion's nerves were getting frayed. He had absolutely no idea how the man must feel. After all, he felt betrayed by the radical movement that he had called 'his home' for months. He saw his best, closest friend murdered on what he considered to be unjust charges. He noted the mood changes and uncertainties in the orders placed by a man that he had revered, Abu Bakr al Baghdadi. And then witnessed the man's mercurial temper firsthand with some of his trusted lieutenants.

Sobhy's cell phone vibrated. He listened briefly, and when Taybieh moved over to hear a bit, he put up his index finger as a warning to back off.

"*Iwa*, yes, I get it. But it's very late for... *Na'am*, what did you say? You're breaking up, the signal is..." and suddenly the phone was receiving dead air. It reminded Sobhy of what the Israelis do now on *Yom Kippur*, the Day of Atonement. Following the near catastrophe of the 1973 *Yom Kippur* War, when Israel was attacked on its holiest day in a jointly coordinated battle plan carried out by Syria and Egypt, fingers were pointing at each other in the Knesset even before the enemy was successfully pushed back. So, following the war, the government declared that *Reshet Aleph*, Israel's Radio Station Number One, was to continue to broadcast even during the most holy of days. An uproar followed the announcement by the orthodox religious political parties, and they threatened to pull out of the governmental coalition. This would force the government to collapse and necessitate a new vote for leadership in the country. However, one member of the Labor Party, who was also a scientist, came up with a unique and government-saving solution. The radio station would broadcast 'in silence'- live and on air. Therefore, should an emergency arise, the station would instantly switch to a live broadcast to tell soldiers and reservists what to do and where to go. Sobhy would mimic that solution and keep the line open so that his phone's signal would be tracked. He quickly stuffed the phone in his pocket before Taybieh noticed that it was still an 'open' line.

"So what happened *habibi*? Who was that?" Taybieh had so many questions. Sobhy was ready for any contingency.

"It was the doctor that we are to meet. There are a few problems in the original meeting area. A couple of militias decided to engage in a turf war..."

"What? I don't get it," Taybieh clearly hadn't watched much American TV in the past couple of years.

"They are fighting over the land, and the area that they control, and our meeting point was right in the middle of it. So I agreed to a location just a couple of kilometers away, where it is quiet and safer for us all. I hope you don't mind," the sarcasm was dripping from his voice like a leaky faucet. Taybieh got it, and chastised, hurriedly agreed to the new plan.

Suddenly, off to the east, the roar of a poorly tuned, muffler-less pickup truck could be heard. Within moments, it came around the bend, the banner of al Baghdadi fluttering off the antenna. It came to a dusty, choking halt only a few dozen meters from where the two men were. The driver and one other *keffiyahed* fighter got out of the vehicle. Taybieh immediately recognized both of them as members of his unit. Although he was slightly alarmed at their sudden appearance, he had the presence of mind to greet them as if nothing was wrong. But to Sobhy, it clearly threw a monkey wrench into the machinery of the plan. He whispered to Taybieh while they were still out of earshot.

"What are they doing here?" He demanded of Taybieh. "How in the hell did they ever find us?"

"I was very nervous about this whole thing..." he began.

"I ALREADY KNEW THAT," Sobhy hissed. "But answer the damn question!"

"I thought that, if I called in, they wouldn't be suspicious of anything that we had planned. I didn't even think that they could track the GPS on my phone..."

"*Ya hamar*! You ass! If you don't take care of this we're done for!" Sobhy's outward appearance belied the inner turmoil.

"*Ahlen sadiqi aleaziz*! Greetings my dear friend!" Taybieh said to the driver. He quickly embraced him and kissed him on both cheeks. He then turned to the other man, who he knew only by sight. "*Marhaba, ahuya*, greetings brother." With that, he shook the other man's hand. Sobhy had hung back just a bit, giving the impression that Taybieh was running the show. He was beckoned forward and re-introduced to the driver and formally introduced for the first time to the other man.

The driver quickly apologized to Taybieh, still assuming that he was the point-man, and said that al Baghdadi had just survived a drone attack that was perpetrated by the Syrian Army. He made it clear, *Allah* be praised, that the leadership of the movement was still intact. However, the base that they had just left was not. The same attack obliterated much of the camp, scores of men were killed, and most of their supplies were gone. The surviving remnants of the fighter group were moving back to *Raqqa* where they could consolidate themselves with the main force. Al Baghdadi considered this mission to be of the utmost importance, the driver went on. In fact, he stated that it was crucial to the movement and needed to succeed. But apparently this low- level fighter had no real knowledge of the mission. All he said was that another man was sent by their leader to ensure that all went well; providing extra security. The driver would remain right where they were. Then, after the success, whatever it was, they were to return to him and be taken northeast to the new camp and be hailed as heroes.

"And what of our vehicle?" Sobhy enquired, clearly uneasy with the new arrangements.

"Don't worry about it. It's a piece of shit and probably wouldn't have gotten you back anyway, so I'll just wait while you meet whoever you're meeting. Then we'll go back together."

Sobhy suddenly felt a bit better. He remembered that he had left the phone on and was almost certain that the Israelis could hear the conversation and revise their plans.

Just south of the checkpoint they had initially located, a new location was identified. The contact also represented the NGO *'Biladi,'* 'My Homeland,' It was a Lebanese cultural organization. This lent even more credence to the 'official' transaction that was supposed to take place; the funds from it then going into al Baghdadi's coffers to further bankroll his terror.

Taybieh, now brimming with confidence with the arrival of his fellow militants, began to talk with an air of authority and dignity. He made sure that the additional soldiers were to hang back and come nowhere near the Lebanese border. They couldn't screw things up with the Lebanese contact. The entire episode was predicated on the notion that there would be future deals in the pipeline *provided* that everything went well. He intimated that, should the exchange 'go south' (apparently he *did* know a couple of American idioms after all) it would be on their heads and the authority granted to him by al Baghdadi would ensure their demise. The other fighters flinched at this pronouncement, and actually physically took a step or two back. Sobhy thought this was amusing and forced himself to keep from laughing out loud. A hint of a smile was all that he allowed himself. But the others saw it and paled. Apparently word had spread around the camp that the 'one recently returned from Egypt' had a particularly mean, sadistic streak to him- and wouldn't hesitate to employ techniques designed to strike fear and terror should it be required.

With a clear understanding of everyone's roles, Taybieh gestured to the others to return to their vehicle while he 'planned' the remainder of the operation. Near the pickup, they began to build a small fire to brew Turkish coffee and make a small meal.

"*Al Ahmaq*! You idiot!" Sobhy now got into the act. "Do you want the Syrian Army, the Lebanese Army, the Jihadists... to *all* come down on our heads? No one knows we're here, and what we plan on doing for our cause. What in the name of *Allah* would ever, EVER, give you the stupid idea of setting up a smoking fire? You can do without your precious *ahwa masbut*, your Turkish coffee. And a hot meal? You're in the field on a mission, for the sake of... oh, never mind! Ya Ahmed, when we get back we'll tell the commander about the *al humqa'a,* the fools that were sent to back us up on our crucial mission!" He glared at the others and turned and walked a few paces away.

Taybieh, gave a sneering smile to the men, reiterating without saying a word everything that Sobhy had said. They were on notice, and they suddenly knew it in great detail.

*****

In the Negev base, Ben Dov and Colonel Ilan had been patched through from the open line that Sobhy had created. The combat-hardened IDF soldiers had been through much worse in the past. They immediately began to slightly rework the plan that had been agreed upon. The two additional fighters were certainly not a problem. They could easily be dealt with. But now, a couple of IDF Israeli Arab soldiers would accompany the 'professor,' who herself was an IDF officer. As Lebanese military, with the proper fake IDs, they would dress in civilian clothing to complete the ruse. The same drone that had attacked the Palmyra base camp of al Baghdadi would be refueled and rearmed. Then it would be tasked to the Lebanese-Syrian border location that had been entered on Sobhy's phone's GPS. The camera on the *Kochav* drone would give a real time bird's eye view of the area and pick its targets carefully.

But Colonel Ilan had an additional idea. He would also send the other drone, the AirMule, to the area as well. Amir Ben Dov looked perplexed, until Ilan explained.

"We'll load the AirMule with all sorts of Syrian army equipment and weapons. In addition, I have found out that up north, at the Camp *Mahaneh Yarden*, in the Golan, there are a couple of Syrian Army bodies 'on ice.' They were part of a small patrol that decided that it would try to see our side of things up there, and cut through the barbed wire. The foray was repelled, the others in the squad fled back into the Syrian Golan, but four of their soldiers were killed. And there'll be no questioning about them, one even has terrible Russian dental work!" He laughed at this. "Complete with a steel tooth! So here's my idea. We fly them, along with the other Syrian stuff, to the exchange point. The *Kochav* will strafe the area and create a 'firefight' that will kill the Syrian militants of al Baghdadi. Once the firing stops, our three soldiers will stage the area on the ground, replacing Sobhy and the two henchmen of al Baghdadi with the dead Syrians. They then will set fire to the truck. One of our soldiers will engage the fellow traveling alongside Sobhy, knocking him out and then injecting him with a sedative. Once knocked out, our commando will cut his arm, looking like a wound. When he wakes up, he'll have a severe headache, a bruise and a slight wound. He'll see the burning truck and bodies inside, a badly burned body wearing Sobhy's clothing, and assume the worst. He'll even see a dead Syrian soldier from the other side. Meanwhile, Sobhy will take his share of the money and he'll assume it too was destroyed.

"But then, what about Sobhy and the rescue?" It was of utmost importance to Ben Dov to ensure his safe return.

"That's all part of the show. Sobhy and the Syrian will go through with the exchange, turn the artifact over to the 'Lebanese,' and then take the money and divvy it up. When they begin their return to the Syrian side, the fireworks will begin. Our officers will cross over, get Sobhy and all the money as well, and load him and the stone on the AirMule- and for all a short flight back to this base. *B'seder*? Okay?"

"As they say, 'sounds like a plan' to me!" Ben Dov smiled as he clapped the colonel on the back.

*****

After a bit of a heated exchange, Taybieh finally prevailed upon the two fighters to remain by the vehicles while they took the stone across into Lebanon. He stressed to them that al Baghdadi *himself* entrusted this important mission to him. There should be no interference at all since he was 'running the show.' Their deference whenever the leader's name was mentioned was obvious, and they certainly didn't want to run afoul of him upon their return to camp.

Unbeknownst to them, while this conversation was wrapping up, the Israeli 'offensive weapon' drone, the *Kochav*, had successfully completed its mission in Palmyra and was circling around to the coordinates where Sobhy and company had come to the border to exchange the object and ostensibly transfer the funds.

Sobhy glanced at his watch. He knew that the two of them had to cross into Lebanon and get the job done because of the impending strike. The good thing about the use of drones was the 'real-time' ability to use the camera to see exactly what was transpiring. It wasn't like the 'bad old days' when watches needed to be synchronized, and timing was exact because of the uncertainty of movements, etc. Back in the Negev drone command base, things could easily be tweaked according to the information seen on the ground. The only two glitches that could occur were the loss of the video feed or running out of fuel. Neither of these was foreseen as a possibility. That is of course, unless the entire timeframe was off by hours. Sobhy knew this, and would not let that happen in any way, shape or form. It could mean his death. He had already tempted the hooded sickle-bearer one too many times and didn't want to give him another shot at him.

Taybieh beckoned to the Egyptian, indicating that all was in order for the two of them to proceed through the tangled brush and poorly maintained border fence. It had taken them all of 15 minutes to get there. Most of the time was due to the heaviness of the stone artifact.

"Is it really worth all this money to the Lebanese?" Taybieh panted, the sweat dripping from his forehead down the bridge of his nose. "Can we stop just a moment to rest and take a drink?" He clearly was in distress. Being a fighter for the insurgents didn't come with a lot of physical training. It was more a 'point and shoot' philosophy of combat. No one expected anyone in the movement to retire of old age. The best that they could hope for was 'the death benefit' promised to the family if you were martyred in support of the cause. That was another reason for the dramatic turnabout and acceptance- he wanted to live and take the money and run. He was tired of war, especially with the cause's military downturn of events.

"*Alraja' alhudu,* be quiet!" Sobhy hissed. "Do you want to broadcast this on *Noor al Sham*?" He referenced one of the satellite stations sanctioned by the Syrian government. Taybieh took the hint and sullenly picked up his end of the stone inscription. But he smiled when he thought of the money that would soon come his way.

As they made their way down the overgrown path on the Lebanese side, they suddenly heard machine gun fire and a heavier sound that sounded like mortars. Taybeih dropped the stone, but fortunately, the tangled brush and soft ground pillowed the drop so nothing was broken. He dove into the shrubbery off to the side and curled up in a fetal position. Sobhy dove to the other side of the trail, but simply lay down flat, not moving. Part of the reason for his relative calm was that he knew exactly what was going on, and silently cheered.

Sobhy then crawled over to Taybieh, who was now visibly shaking. There was a soft rustling in the undergrowth from just a couple of meters away. A shrub was bent over, and the face of one of the 'Lebanese' escorts appeared. He looked scared to death- befitting an academic type. He crawled over to Sobhy and whispered a question. Taybieh asked what he said, since he was on the other side of Sobhy. He was told to 'shush,' lie down, and not move even an eyelash. Fortunately he did as was told.

The other man reached into his pack and withdrew a small syringe. Popping the cap off, he rolled over Sobhy and drove it into the Syrian's thigh. It contained Midazolam, a fast-acting but short-lived sedative. Within seconds, Taybieh's eyes fluttered and he was down for the count. Sobhy then punched him on the side of the head, raising a major welt with some swelling. It would also blacken his eye in a couple of hours. The Israeli next to him took out his knife, ripped Ahmed's shirt on his arm, and scored it. The wound wasn't deep but would bleed profusely for a few minutes before clotting. Sobhy then called out to the "Lebanese professor' and her other escort, who immediately emerged from the forested area. A quick nod of thanks, and the Israelis removed the stone artifact and carried it to the staging ground on the Syrian side.

The Israeli drone did a flyover first but was undetectable due to its elevation. When the operator identified the targets, the order was given to attack on the second pass. The guns of the *Kochav* 900 strafed the area of the two vehicles, and one of them burst into flames. It happened to be the one driven by the two fighters. They had made the bad choice of returning to sit in the cab and listen to a Syrian music radio station. The song playing was by one of Syria's top female pop stars, Asala. *Baeen Aedayek*, 'In Your Arms,' was the last thing they heard as the gas tank exploded, searing the entire area with diesel-fueled flames.

Within moments, the AirMule drone dropped down and landed a five and a half meters or so away. The sole IDF commando on that drone, a member of the famed Unit 101, quickly and efficiently rolled the three Syrian soldiers' bodies onto the ground. Two were still in their bloodied uniforms. The third was awaiting

Sobhy's return, and his clothing. In addition, the Syrian weapons and random bits and pieces of military equipment that they would have been carrying during a raid were strewn about the site. Not even a real estate agent could have staged the area better.

As the soldier stepped back to survey his work, he heard a thrashing in the brush coming from the Lebanese border. With Sobhy by their side, the group from Lebanon met up with the Israeli commando. Quickly, quietly, an order was given to Sobhy- "Take off your clothes!" He laughed aloud and said something about this being a weird place to be hit upon by a 'Lebanese female professor' and all the Israelis got a laugh out of that. He was handed an IDF uniform while his Syrian civilian clothing was placed on the third dead Syrian brought in by the drone. It was placed near the pickup truck that Sobhy and Taybieh had come in on. The area was sprinkled with gas and a soaked rag was stuff in the fuel filler pipe. A few Euros were scattered around as well. The final touch was the placement of stone fragments in the bed of the truck. The rag was lit, and within moments a second inferno engulfed the small clearing. The dead body of the Syrian fighter was badly burned as well. So now, it looked as if the stone never left the truck, the group was ambushed by the Syrians, the stone destroyed in the explosions along with the money.

The Israelis took one last look around, snapped a few photos on their phones for the record and loaded Sobhy, the money and the stone inscription onto the AirMule and radioed the drone commander with the simple phrase, '*HaBayita*, home!'

*****

About an hour later, Ahmed Taybieh woke up. His head hurt, his arm throbbed, and there was dried blood all over him. He tried to sit up, and the landscape about him threatened to spin him back into oblivion. He slowly lay back down and assessed his situation. The first thing outside of his physical condition was that he was alone. His friend Sobhy was nowhere in sight. The next thing that he noted were his wounds. He had a major bruise on his cheek and forehead. The swelling was substantial. There was a gash on his forearm. However, that didn't seem to be an immediate problem because the wound had clotted over and stopped bleeding. The problem was that his shirt, having been soaked in his blood, now adhered to the wound. If he tried to tear it away he ran the risk of opening it up and bleeding again. He had no way of stopping it or taking care of himself. He lay there a moment and took stock. He was alive, hurt but alive. He seemed to be alone. He instinctively knew that he should remain as motionless as possible to allow whatever head injuries he suffered to stabilize. So that's what he did for the next day. He shut his eyes and fell back into a deep sleep; a self-healing mechanism that seems inbred in humans.

He awoke in a confused state. First, he was in unfamiliar surroundings. He had crept under a bush at some time before he passed out again. The sky was extremely overcast and he had no idea what time it was. He had never owned a watch, and he remembered that Sobhy... WAIT! He now remembered a bit. He and that Syrian fellow who he befriended after the execution of his other friend... What was his name... oh yeah, Mohamed. Mohamed el Moussa. *So where am I and why do I hurt so much? Why is my arm covered with blood? Why does my head ache so?* The jumbled thoughts were no clearer than when he had woken up. *I really need to find out where I am, and to pee!*

Taybieh got to his knees, and slowly crawled from under the brush. He then grabbed a small tree trunk and gently pulled himself upright. He saw nothing but dense shrubbery on all sides. But in one small area it appeared that there was a faint, beaten trail. With no other plan, he approached it as quietly as possible. Hearing no other signs of any people, he continued down the path for a hundred meters or so, and came upon a scene of horror. In a small clearing, two pickup trucks continued to smolder. They were almost reduced to melted lumps of metal. However, he recognized that one of them had the trademark machine gun mount welded onto the floor of the bed. As he cautiously approached, the stench of burned flesh permeated the air. Even from a distance of a dozen or so meters he could see charred remains. Gagging, he came no further, there was no need. Not far away was the other vehicle. It was nothing more than a stock Toyota pickup. And he remembered. This was the vehicle that he and Sobhy had 'rented' for their 'adventure.'

And no everything came dramatically into focus for him. He remembered each and every detail of a scheme that, although risky, would have changed his life forever- provided that Abu Bakr al Baghdadi didn't catch him. But now all was different.

As the Syrian walked around the second truck, he saw a still smoking body. He recognized the scraps of clothing almost melted on the torso- it was his friend Sobhy's. Then, a few meters farther, the bodies of two bullet-riddled Syrian soldiers were partially still hidden in the surrounding shrubs. The evidence seemed clear to him. He remembered that Al Baghdadi sent a couple of soldiers as support for the mission that he and Sobhy were sent on. A mission designed to sell antiquities to a Lebanese and add money to the insurgent's coffers. But he remembered that he and Sobhy were going to 'take the money and run' on their own- and get out of the business of rebellion and war once and for all.

It was plain to see that *everyone's* plans were now spoiled by the sudden appearance of a Syrian army patrol. Taybieh slowly walked the perimeter, inspecting the mini-battlefield. When he was certain that there were no others alive, he formulated a plan. The up side was that he was alive, could continue living, go back to his old life and not be threatened by the rebel commander. The down side was that he had to go back to an old life that he didn't want to be a part of any longer.

His plan was simple. He would return to the insurgents. However, it would not be Palmyra, as the camp there was destroyed according to the two fighters that had come and almost ruined everything. *Allah be praised for intervening,* he thought. He would have to make his way to *Raqqa,* their supposed capital, where al Baghdadi had fled after the failed attempt on his life. But first, he needed to gather evidence. He walked around the edge of the area, and, thanks to *Allah*, used his cell phone, which still had a bit of juice, to take some pictures of the ambush. Immediately after that, it flickered once and died. He tried booting it up again, but the photo-taking had drained all remaining power. No matter, the evidence was stored. He could always find a phone to make a call if necessary. He wrapped a *keffieyh* around his nose and mouth to try to filter the stench of death- and picked up further evidence. He found Sobhy's bloodied driver's license in the back pocket of the one burned body near their truck. In addition, he discovered a few thousand Syrian Pounds in 200 and 500 Pound denominations. To him, it was a fortune. To the real world, where 500 Pounds equaled one USD, it was nothing. But it could get him a meal or two if needed. He plucked the ID cards of the two Syrian soldiers from their vests. Automatically, almost without thinking, he slid an AK-74 from under one of them and checked the banana clip. It was nearly empty, so he gathered two full spares from their vests as well. At least he was now armed for his trek back.

Taybieh quietly worked his way to the narrow road that led him and Sobhy to this spot. Once there, he picked up his pace a bit until he came to an abandoned hut. No one saw him as he slipped inside. As he thought, it was empty, and it offered shelter plus a bonus: There was a handpump over a sink in the small kitchen area. It was cold well water, but it slaked his thirst and allowed him to wash up a bit. He vigorously scrubbed his face and neck, and rubbed his hands somewhat clean. He wiped himself off with a rag of a towel that was still hanging on a hook. He then rinsed the cloth as clean as possible and very gently daubed at the scabbed over gash on his arm. He knew enough to soften the scab and then carefully wipe a bit at a time. He rummaged about in his backpack, and found a couple of gauze compresses that were with one of the Syrian soldiers' kit. He also found a small tube of antibiotic gel that he liberally applied before re-wrapping the wound. He figured that it would last until he could get regular medical treatment in Raqqa.

A wizened apple was all that he had to eat, but he was grateful for even this small bit of nourishment. After all this, he was exhausted. Taybieh lay down on the pallet at the front of the room and slept for a few hours.

When he woke up, dusk had found its way across the Syrian landscape. This was perfect, as he could travel along the road at night and not worry about running into anyone in the countryside. During this war that was raging, civilians tended to stay in when nightfall approached. It just wouldn't do to be caught out in the open by unsavory characters. He chuckled at this. He was one of those 'unsavory characters' himself at one time. Taybieh set off, and after a couple of stops to take a 'nature break,' and get off his feet for a bit, he figured that he had come about 35 km or so. He thought that he was very near Homs, and a main highway to Raqqa. But he still had a couple of hundred km to go. He found another hut, farther off the road and but with no well. Its position, however, seemed to guarantee isolation until the next evening.

The following morning he rose with the sun and, for the first time in weeks, decided to say his morning prayers. An old prayer rug lay on the floor. The words came easily and flowed with grace and comfort.

"*Allahu Akbar, Subhana rabbiyal adheem...*

God is great, Glory be to my Lord Almighty..."

He concluded with the one passage that set the morning apart from the other four times of prayer; "prayer is better than sleep."

During his recitation, he came to the conclusion that he would try to get a lift to *Raqqa*, because, at this rate, it would take until next week and he didn't have any time to lose. The longer there was no contact with the rebel headquarters, the more they would think that something was amiss and, should he be seen, he might get shot on sight and questioned later. So, after a deep breath, he strode over to the road and started walking northeast, all the while looking for traffic going his way. Only an hour after the morning haze had burned off, a battered pickup that was quite similar to the one he and Sobhy... ah, he missed his friend, had 'rented' in what seemed years ago, rounded a curve and approached him at the lightning speed of 40 kph. Taybieh stuck his arm out, and pointed his index finger at a 45 degree angle downward, and swung the AK-74 around his back. The driver slowed, then came to a halt about 40 meters further on. Apparently he wanted to take a good look before deciding to stop or not. And stop he did.

After a handshake, vague introductions, and the offer of a drink of water from an old Fanta Orange one liter bottle, the two settled down for a several hour ride. The driver, an old Syrian villager, spoke about a dozen words to Taybieh during the first portion of the trip. After about an hour and a half or so, he pulled off the main road at the small town of *Khirbat Isriyah.* He pointed to the gas gauge and simply said, "*Ghaz.*"

For Taybieh, this was the moment to make things good and seal the older man's loyalty. "*Urid yushtaraa benzene, rais*. I'll buy the gas." With that, he smiled and pulled out the wad of bills that he took off the dead men. And with that, the driver smiled toothlessly and muttered a heartfelt "*shukran*, thank you." He got out to pump the tank full, and Taybieh went into the small storefront opposite the pumps in order to pay. He also got a couple of bags of chips, and a real liter bottle of Fanta Orange.

When he came out with the snacks, the driver's toothless smile turned into a grin a hundred meters wide. He replaced the nozzle, clapped Taybieh on the back, and the two proceeded down the road to the northeast, and the Euphrates River. Raqqa lay just on the north side. After another hour, Taybieh was quietly begging for silence. The old man wouldn't shut up, now that he had the luxury of a full tank of gas, a new bottle of his favorite soft drink to wash down a bag of chips, and a traveling companion.

*****

Finally, after what seemed like a lifetime of travel, the Euphrates Valley could be seen in the hazy distance. Taybieh said a silent prayer of thanks to *Allah* for not only seeing him through the worst episode of his life, but also for bringing to an end a never-ending journey with the old Syrian villager. But he also knew that had it not been for the chance encounter along the road, the trip to Raqqa might have taken several more days. So, he thought, there was truly such a thing as a mixed blessing. As the men crossed one of the few remaining bridges to head into the town, the landscape was indicative of a country engaged in a several year-long civil war. Due to the constant ebb and flow of combat, nothing had been rebuilt, no one had resettled, and hopelessness hung upon the countryside like a smothering blanket. Taybieh prayed for the peace of Syria as the men approached a checkpoint.

The pickup slowed (even more than the snail's pace journey) to a crawl as it came near the sand-filled barrels and connecting bar that ran across the tarmac. A Daesh flag hung limply from an iron pipe that had been shoved into one of the barrels. A handful of guards with AK-47s at the ready eyed the pickup as if it were a homicide bomber's truck, laden with fertilizer/oil-style explosives. Dutifully, the driver stopped about 10 meters short of the barrier. The order was given to turn off the vehicle and stick their hands out the windows of the vehicle, with their ID cards dangled by two fingers. Once the two complied, two fighters approached warily, with their guns now raised. The hard glint in their eyes indicated years of a hard life, and personalities bent on exacting as much retribution on *anyone* not of their political and religious persuasion. The potential for disaster was 90% complete. It took the driver everything in his power to hold on to his license, he was shaking so badly. The rebel on the driver's side saw this and laughed; one of the ugliest sounds that Taybieh thought he had ever heard.

Within moments, in unison, the rebels snatched the ID cards from both men's hands and ordered them to keep the hands outside the windows while the papers were thoroughly examined. However, this was a problem. One of the fighters was illiterate. In order to save face, he declared that something seemed 'off,' and walked back to the checkpoint to 'confer' with one of the others. In reality, he asked his companion to tell him what Taybieh's ID card said. Once his companion saw it, he got on his cell phone and placed a call.

Raqqa came into view through a dust-filled haze. Suddenly Taybieh's nerves began to jangle. *Could he pull it off? Could he fool the commander*? He silently berated himself because any doubt in his mind would give everything away- and his life would be worth even less than the Syrian Pound. So he drew in a deep breath and steeled himself against the unknown.

Once at the outskirts of town, it took nearly another hour to navigate the triple layer of checkpoints and defenses of the only city left under the rule of Al Baghdadi. How quickly the movement had collapsed. It was clearly a last-gasp defense of this city- to the death. And if there was ever any remaining doubt in the Syrian's mind, it was erased by the abject desolation that he was now driven through on the way to the headquarters building.

Once there, after the mandatory frisking and unloading of his weapon, although allowed to keep it as a sign of respect given to him, Taybieh was escorted into the no-frills office outer room; but shown a modicum of deference. Apparently, word had filtered through the camp of his exploits that, although a failure, were noble for the sake of the cause and deserved to be praised for effort.

Once inside, the guard gestured him to be seated, and asked if he would like tea. Surprised, he smiled and nodded his thanks.

Apparently waiting a long time for al Baghdadi was the rule rather than exception because of the recent turn of events. After drinking his tea, weak but hot, it was another half an hour until the outer door re-opened. A young man with a Red Crescent emblazoned field bag came in and washed and dressed his wounds. He even did a sort of eye test to see if there was any evidence of a concussion. For this, Taybieh was grateful.

Another half hour, and the inner door opened and another guard beckoned him inside. Taybieh was surprised to find nearly the entire Council was present. He noted three empty chairs and assumed that they were indicative of the level of success that the drone attack had on the Palmyra camp. The commander quickly got up and walked around the table. He embraced the Syrian and kissed him on both cheeks- a sign that he might indeed make it out of here alive. Taybieh took a deep breath and returned the gesture. With his arm still around him, Al Baghdadi walked him over to the table, and each surviving Council member stood up and shook his hand solemnly and with respect. Then he was led to a seat facing them and asked to tell his story.

The young Syrian was feeling a bit more confident now. Why else would they patch him up unless he was going to be allowed to live. You don't give medical aid to someone that you're going to execute. He pulled out of his pocket all of the papers that he had salvaged from the battlefield site. These bloodied pieces of documentation clearly had an effect on the Council. In addition, he grabbed his cell phone and asked for a charger cable. Since it used a common cable, two members facing him quickly offered theirs- another sign that things were going well.

He continued his story of what had transpired, while the phone juiced up. He took his time, and 45 minutes later he wrapped up his blow-by-blow description. He had left nothing out, as far as he remembered. At this point, with his battered phone charged up, he opened the photo app for all to pass around the table. The images left no doubt at all. And looking at them once more, and the carnage that was captured, staggered the young Syrian. He wavered, feeling lightheaded. One of the guards quickly brought a chair and he nearly fell over as his legs gave way. He held his head in his hands and wept at the loss of his travel companion, and at the greater loss of his way out of the hell that was Syria.

However, this was misinterpreted by the Syrian insurgent council. They saw a man who mourned the fact that his mission wasn't successful for a cause that he fought for with all his heart and soul. They commiserated with him, nodding in support. The greatest cheerleader was none other than al Bagdadi. As a result, Taybieh was consoled, and welcomed back into the camp. After the medic looked him over once more and declared him ambulatory, a grim, but determined and triumphant commander wrapped his arm around his fighter and escorted him outside into the public courtyard. With many of his most loyal fighters waiting there, he proclaimed that Ahmed Taybieh was a hero for the cause. This gave rise to a great round of cheering, *Allahu Akhbar*, God is Great. And part of this celebratory expression was the firing off of AK-74s into the air, and some of the women ululating in the Bedouin tradition. While this was going on, Taybieh quietly slipped a few meters away, sat heavily on the ground, and poured ashes on his head.

The culture of spinning victories out of the crushing defeats turned his head upside down. It was clear to him that all the propaganda that was fed to the insurgents was just that- and nothing more. The loyalty that they all pledged to *Allah* was merely loyalty pledged to the Islamic State, and the personality cult of all Baghdadi. He knew now for certain that, even though he had no money from the failed transaction, and no friends left as well, he had to get out of this game. There was no spirituality here at all; something that he had not foreseen.

While the celebrations continued, Taybieh quietly whispered to his commander that the midday prayer was approaching, and that he'd like to slip away from the *hafla*, the celebration, and give thanks to God. As he was entirely caught up in the moment of 'victory' and the adulation bestowed upon him, al Baghdadi absently waved him away to go and do as he pleased. After all, it was no longer about the young Syrian, but the personality cult. With a word of thanks, Taybieh sought out his prayer rug and a peaceful spot on the edge of camp.

*****

Following the noon day prayers, Taybieh returned to the headquarters building with a clearer head. He asked to speak with the commander for just a moment of his precious time. He explained that he knew of the pressing matters of rebuilding that weighted heavily on their leader, but begged for only time to make a brief request. With the continued aura of celebrity still surrounding him, the guard allowed for this, and quickly went into the inner sanctum.

Within a couple of minutes he returned and said to make it quick, but al Baghdadi would see him.

Taybieh entered the office and found a distracted commander signing papers at his desk. He made it quick and hoped that the distraction would prevent al Baghdadi from focusing too clearly on the request. He stood silently until recognized.

"My esteemed lion, my fighter for *Allah*, what can I do for you?" He barely looked up from his work.

"Commander, given the difficulty of the operation, and the very slight wounds that I suffered..."

"They were not insignificant, *habibi*; your modesty and humility are appreciated but not necessary. You are a lion for the cause, and don't forget it." He still hadn't looked up.

"Thank you sir, but in light of all that, I humbly ask that I be granted an extended leave to go back to my village, *As Suweida* and family, in order to recover and reconnect."

"You know, that is a good idea. I will spread the word around the countryside of what a hero you are to the movement, and perhaps you can aid in recruiting more young men to our worthy goal once they see you as a paradigm of our fight on behalf of God. May Allah bless you and protect you and guide you in our cause. Heal quickly and perhaps when you return a promotion will be waiting. Take your time, simply check in every so often. Go with

God." With that, and a brief embrace as al Baghdadi came from around the desk, and Taybieh was dismissed.

So what now? He thought as he left the building. Maybe he would go back to the town and see who of his family remained. This would establish his presence. But then? Maybe he would head into desert. Maybe he would go to Egypt? Just maybe...

XVI. Jerusalem

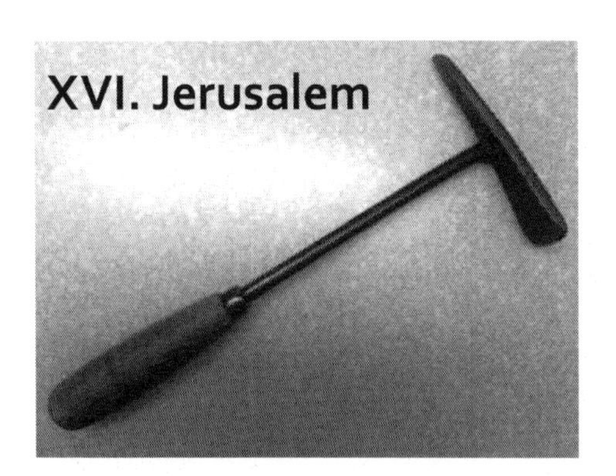

With Ben Dov on the way back to Jerusalem, and Sobhy en route via the AirMule drone, the others now 'got up' from the pins and needles that they had been 'sitting on' during the entire mission. What had made matters worse during the whole mission was the fact that they didn't have the necessary clearance to be 'read-in' on the moment-by-moment activity This made the 'what ifs' of the plan weigh even more heavily on all of them. It didn't help that every scenario they ran always, ALWAYS came out with a catastrophe. With everyone gathered in her apartment on *Bnei Batira Street*, Kati had told them time and again not to look at the darkest of outcomes, but the most realistic.

"You know, I am constantly reminded of one of your favorite movies," she said to me. You *know* the one, Bedouin man!" And she punched me on the upper arm. At that point she started to quietly sing the final song of the Monty Python movie, *The Life of Brian*. "Always look on the bright side of life- te-dum, te-dum, te-dum, te-dum, te-dum..." And she laughed, that lilting sound that sounded like cascading gold. Eitan joined in, as did Lior. Although she was tone deaf and hadn't a clue as to where or when the song came from. Soon everyone was laughing, and singing and shaking off the fear and apprehension that had taken hold for the past few days.

And just as the *Stock 84 Brandy* was being passed around for a second time, a knock on the door led Eitan to call out to be quiet, as Kati approached and peeked through the security peephole, a bit confused as it was a security building. But upon putting her eye up close, she laughed and threw open the front door. She wrapped her arms around the two men who came through the porta- Ben Dov and Sobhy. Suddenly, everybody was screaming and laughing and crying and laughing and screaming... and Sobhy, being Sobhy, simply said "*Yom Asal!* Today's honey!"

It seemed that another bottle was needed, and so it went. Ben Dov and Sobhy alternated telling their stories, and when knitted together, from both sides of the mission, it made for compelling listening. Ben Dov downplayed his role, as befitting an IDF officer. After all, they knew that it was the troops who made the success stories, not the officers. The closeness of the Israeli army units was well known throughout the world; as was the informality. Officers in smaller units were called by their first names most of the time, and they led the way rather than bring up the rear. This was one thing that Sobhy admired the most, for he had seen firsthand how the Egyptians were always led from behind- at least until after the 1973 War.

For his part, the Egyptian made the most of the intricate behind-the-scenes intelligence that went into the success of the foray into Palmyra, and the subsequent rescue of both him and the Aramaic stone inscription from the synagogue. He too ignored the praise that was given him by Ben Dov and the others. He was simply glad to be back 'home' safe and sound. Funny how he now thought of Israel as a second home.

After the celebrating had wound down a bit, I brought the group down to earth by mentioning that our next step was to address the significance of the inscription and how to deal with it publicly, if at all. We needed to bring in both archaeologists and governmental officials. After all, in spite of the nature of this 'rescue', the Israelis still had launched a mission into Syrian territory, a clear violation of international law. And, given the state of affairs in the UN and UNESCO regarding Israel, this could pose a major problem. We all debated this, and especially took into account Sobhy's take from an Arab world perspective. The final consensus was that we would let the government deal with the flak after turning the stone over to the Israel Museum and Antiquities Authority (IAA). Ben Dov would deal with the government. Kati and I would handle the archaeology end, with Sobhy as an unofficial consultant.

*****

The next morning, Kati was on the phone nonstop. First, she got in touch with her boss, Dror Amnon, the director of the IAA. He had been read-in on the scantiest of details of the operation a few weeks earlier, in part because at that time no one was even sure if the operation would be given the go ahead. He was delighted to hear that all went as planned, and was excited to see the piece, which was still in the IDF's possession at the Negev drone base. It was in the process of being sent north the very next day, with one of the regional archaeologists and heavily armed guard. It would be delivered to his main office, in the Rockefeller Museum just north of the Damascus Gate. After analysis and documentation there, it would be moved to the labs in the Archaeology Wing of the Israel Museum on the western side of the city. As a precaution, the convoy was told to take the road to Jerusalem 'the old way'- via *Tzomet Malachi* and *Kiryat Gat*. This would skirt the Occupied Territories around *Hevron* and *Bet Lehem.* No sense in tempting fate.

Her second call was to a Minister of the Knesset, Naphtali Bennett. It was a call that Kati was dreading, because he was not one of her favorite MKs. As part of the governmental coalition that leaned pretty far to the right without 'falling over', he was a member of the Jewish National Home Party, *HaBayit HaYehudi.* It was an Orthodox Jewish, religious Zionist party. Because of his support for the Prime Minister he was given the plum prize of Minister of Diaspora Affairs. Born of immigrant parents from the US, he earned his position by serving in the *Sayeret Matkal*, Unit 269, the Israeli Delta Force. He was chosen as government representative because of his portfolio. After all, Syria *was* in the Diaspora.

And finally, her third call was to her immediate boss, Eran Neuman, who had been Director of the Israel Museum since February 2017. His former life was as the Director of the David Azrieli School of Architecture at Tel Aviv University. All of the men contacted were thrilled to hear of the recovery of the stone inscription and were anxious to see it on the main campus of the museum.

Eitan was just as busy. As Director of the Masada Archaeological Park of the Israel Nature and Parks Authority of Israel, he had some 'juice' as well. He called his colleague, Benaim, at the Tel Sheva National Park. Benaim would arrange for a restoration crew who had been preserving some of the stone masonry that had been exposed since the 1970s to head down to the drone base. They would assist in the packing of the stone inscription, to spare it from jostling as much as possible. All of these precautions were an indication of how valuable this stone was felt to be by the Israeli government. A Jewish kingdom's legacy was on the verge of total destruction at the hands of madmen in east central Syria, yet a symbolic blow had been dealt to the insurgents by stealing this object out from under their noses. The entire world, not just the Jewish world, would take notice and take heart that the history of the human experience was worth fighting for- and worth saving as much as possible.

By mid-afternoon, a call came through to Ben Dov. The convoy had finally been packed up, and was about half an hour into its journey to Jerusalem. This set the team in motion as well. With just about an hour to hour and a half to go, the group began to make its way to the Rockefeller Museum close to the transition line from western to eastern Jerusalem. Today the city is physically seamless. The scars of the division from the 1949 Armistice to the reunification in June 1967 were healed and the neighborhoods flowed one to another. Even the relatively new light rail for the municipality made the transition flawlessly.

However, the emotional scars were another thing. As the focal point and nexus of the three great western religious traditions, the role of Jerusalem for Jews, Christians and Moslems was undeniable. It was just a matter of interpretation of degree of importance to each that was a point of contention. Regardless of one's spiritual inclinations, the words of the Babylonian Talmud continued to ring true nearly two millennia after they were written.

'10 measures of beauty were given to the world; Jerusalem took 9...
And 10 measures of sorrow were doled out; Jerusalem took 9...'
(Bab. Talmud, Tractate Kiddushin 49.2)

The Peugot Tender from the *Reshut 'Atiqot*, the Antiquities Authority, was able to hold all of them on the journey to the museum. But they would certainly need a second vehicle for the return trip with the added team members returned and present. They drove to the eastern side of the city via King David Street, past the King David Hotel and the western YMCA, to King Solomon Street. A right turn led them alongside the redeveloped Mamilla District to the northwest corner of the Old City and the intersection with the Jaffa Road. Here, a name change took effect. The road was now called *Rehov Tzanhanim*, or Paratroopers Road. Running along the northern wall of the Old City, and past the large open- air plaza outside of the Damascus Gate, the name would change once again-reverting back to the Arabic Sultan Suleiman Road that would front the museum, just on the north side.

A steep and narrow 1 ½ lane road led up to the parking area and main entry to the museum. Why 1 ½ lanes? Because when the museum was built, originally the Palestine Museum, by the British, dedicated in 1938, the asphalt road leading up to the entrance was wide enough for 2 lanes of 1930's-sized vehicles. Today, not so much.

I know what has been said of the British, that whatever the history of the region, 'blame it on the British' is a relatively true mantra. But in this instance, it is a good thing. In spite of the fact that the British Empire was a self-serving, imperialistic, and arrogant entity that did everything it could to exploit it's 'provinces', they *did* do something right- even for the wrong reasons. The colonial governments that were established all over the empire saw the 'God and Country' need to preserve and protect the heritages of the people that they subjected 'from themselves.' In other words, the Brits decided that the indigenous population was incapable of maintaining its own history, so it was up to the 'custodians of civilization' to do so. As a result, everywhere the British ruled a museum was erected and staff imported or trained. So yes, we could 'blame it on the British' with a bit of a smile here.

Both Eitan and I flashed our *Reshut* IDs and we were waved under the raised barrier just outside of the car park. From there, we all entered the octagonal tower that housed the main offices of the Antiquities Authority of Israel. Yes, the main labs and collection were all in the Bronfman Archaeology Wing of the main campus of the

Israel Museum. However, the original extensive research library had stayed in its reserved space in a side building. But, perhaps as a result of a bit of nostalgia, the main office of the Director, Dror

Amnon, remained here. After his appointment, he had installed an old roll-top style desk that might have felt right at home in the 80 year old building, and had hung up old photos of the construction and dedication that took place, finally in 1938. He had even located a set of the original blueprints and had them framed. All in all, it was a fitting tribute to the old museum.

Eitan, Kati and I felt at home in the director's office, but the others not so much. Archaeology was not their turf and both Ben Dov and Lior Rimon visibly fidgeted. The Director set them at ease by offering to serve them coffee. He smiled and they immediately warmed to the man. The ice broken, the room temperature was noticeably warmer.

As discussions went, the conversation was intense, but very cordial. Amnon was impressed with the precision of the plan, and the ability to roll with the punches when there needed to be tweaking due to changes on the ground. He praised his agency's people for being innovative. He lauded the IDF for its coordination of the effort. He profusely thanked the other people who had volunteered and aided their efforts. Lastly, he told everyone gathered that he had something special planned for Sobhy.

"*Yallah, rais*! Come over here my dear friend and colleague," Amnon beamed at the Egyptian with genuine warm and affection. "In spite of the fact that you beat the living hell out of me playing *Sheshbesh*, backgammon, I have something for you." He beckoned the man over. We all stood by in anticipation. None of us knew what was going to occur. "By the power and trust given to me by the Prime Minister and the *Knesset*, I have been authorized to present to you the

Jabotinsky Medal on behalf of the Government of Israel. You, as an Egyptian, may not be aware, but this medal is awarded to a civilian for outstanding achievements for the State of Israel. It is named after one of our heroes who helped to forge the modern state- but died of a heart attack eight years before its creation. Now bend over so I can place this damn thing around your neck!" The Director of the Antiquities Authority was laughing heartily as everyone cheered and applauded.

Magically, a couple of splits of champagne appeared on a sideboard and we all toasted our friend and the extraordinary success at recovering a lost artifact of Syrian Jewish history. But after a few moments of this, Amnon brought us back to the reality of things.

"We need to collectively make a decision about the status of this amazing piece of history and spirituality. And for that, I have colleagues waiting for us in the outer office." He buzzed his receptionist, and the young man ushered in two women. "*Hevrai*, friends, this is Dr. Orit Shaham Gover. Orit, these are the wonderful people of the international team that brought back home an extraordinary relic. Orit is the Chief Curator of the *Beit HaTefutsot*, the Museum of Diaspora Judaism, on the Tel Aviv University Campus. And this is Curator Amitai Achimon of the Synagogue Hall."

As the only one of us who had ever met Amitai Achimon before, Kati ran over and gave her counterpart a big hug and pecked both cheeks. Beaming, she was delighted and surprised to see her friend here in Amnon's office.

"I have to tell you all, that as the Chief Curator, Amitai was a delight to work with as she helped us create both the Masada and Herodion National Parks Visitors Centers." Kati was clearly overjoyed as she described her friend's *bona fides*.

Amnon went on, "Given the value of the piece and its setting, and the multiple ways that it reflects on our past, we have reached a conclusion that leaves us all very happy. We have decided that an exact copy of the stone should be on display in Beit HaTefutsot as well. It will be included in the Synagogue Hall, as part of the exhibit entitled ***Hallelujah! Assemble, Pray, Study –Synagogues Past and Present.*** It will be installed under the guidance of Amitai."

With that, we all applauded and shared another glass.

*****

Back in the Negev, in Sayarim Airbase, another *Kochav* 900 had been launched about an hour earlier. Programmed into its firing sequence was the GPS of Abu Bakr al Bagdadi's cell phone whose number had been embedded in Ahmed Taybieh's phone. Sobhy had jotted it down just before the fireworks had begun in what seemed like a month earlier. Flying at its maximum altitude of 3300 meters, and with its miniscule signature making it virtually undetectable, the drone slowly flew a race-track oval above the target. Once the operator was certain based on the imagery videocast back to Israel, the command went out. Two AGM 114 Hellfire missiles were loosed from their pylons and went streaking down to earth. The image from the drone showed the rapid descent toward an adobe building on the outskirts of Raqqa. A few seconds later, Colonel Ilan could have sworn that he heard two explosions as the building simply ceased to exist.

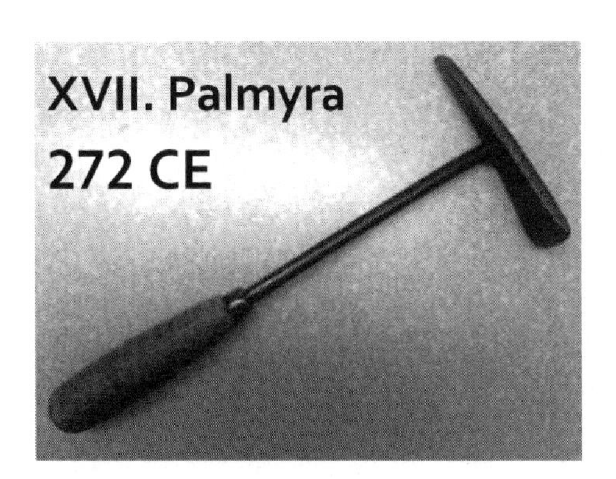

As hostages, Zenobia and her son were taken back to Rome. It seemed that a tragedy occurred on the road to the capital, and Vaballathus died before the end of the journey. Another year passed, before Zenobia finally would be presented to Rome as a 'trophy of war'. During the triumphal parade through the streets of Rome, Zenobia was witnessed as being led through the streets bound in golden chains. She bravely endured the taunts and insults that the gathered crowd hurled at her, along with other unmentionable things.

Apparently Lucius Domitius Aurelianus Augustus Aurelian, the Emperor, stunned by her beauty and dignity in the face of incarceration, granted her freedom. She would go on to live in luxury and became known for her evolving philosophy on life- something that she learned was a precious commodity in light of her impending death.

But she would languish in Rome, with the memory of the death of her son, Vaballathus, hanging heavy over her. She would ask, and be granted, leave to return to her homeland, to Palmyra. However, Aurelian had one major stipulation- that she would travel incognito back to Syria, lest the people see her as a model to rekindle the flames of independence and insurrection. She acquiesced to his wishes, and prepared for the journey.

Dressed simply and modestly, with a small escort of troops who also were dressed as commoners, plans were put into play to return to Syria. The difference was that these so-called peasants 'knew more about killing than any man should,' according to the chronicler, Roman Senator Marcellus Petrus Nutenus. Zenobia prepared for the voyage to Latakia, a distance of about 27,500 Stadia, or 2,500 km. It would take nearly 30 days. The overland trek was another 275 km to Palmyra which would add another 18 days. All in all, it was a grueling adventure, but the former queen felt that it would be worth it for peace of mind, and a certain degree of closure.

By the end of the 3rd century CE, the Roman navy had declined dramatically. Just a couple of years earlier, in 270, a barbarian fleet was defeated off the coast of Byzantium by the eastern general, Venerianus. It would be Rome's last naval gasp of glory. But the barbarians fled into the Aegean, ravaging many islands and coastal cities. Now, years later, the eastern Mediterranean and Aegean remained in turmoil. The trip was doubly perilous. Not only did the sailors need to be aware of the fickle weather that could turn the sea into a tumultuous cauldron, but the old standing fleets had all but vanished. The area was subject to a level of piracy not seen for centuries.

The travel party used a smaller oared vessel, such as the navis actuaria, with 15 oars on each flank; a ship primarily used for transport in coastal shipping, for which its shallow draught and flat keel were ideal. As a coastline 'hopper', no one paid much attention to it, but it took much longer to travel. Their ship was the 'Minerva', named after goddess of wisdom.

*****

The city that awaited Zenobia's return was a mere shell of its former self. It had sunk into its own depths of despair, with the loss of its independence. The trade routes had shifted as well, leaving Palmyra gasping for economic 'breath' as the Roman world bypassed her. She became a refuge for the refugees from the Empire. Even though diminished, Palmyra still offered a touch of stability to the unstable and nomadic province of Coele Syria. A legionary fortress was established in Palmyra as it nevertheless remained an important junction for Roman roads leading into and from the Syrian desert.

Perhaps had Zenobia been informed of the fate of her beloved city, and the fate of the Jewish community and synagogue, she might have had second thoughts regarding her return. The Archesynagogos and other community elders removed the sacred Torah scrolls, boxed up the fragments of texts from the Genizah, and reverently packed and removed the other ritual items. The Ner Tamid, the Eternal Flame, said to represent the 'spark of God's Creation', was gently boxed up in a ventilated iron cage, sort of like birdcage, then sent on a long trek to Jobar, near the metropolis of Damascus.

So where was this community? The Babylonian Talmud mentioned a town of name called Abi Gobar. The description states that there were ten villages surrounding the capital that had Jewish populations, and this was said to be one of them. It also talked about the work of a Rav, Rafram bar Papa, a fourth generation Amora, a sage who lived in the 4th Century. He prayed in Abi Gobar. We know that the sage was part of the Talmudic academy at Pumbedita, today called Fallujah, in Iraq. Perhaps they were one and the same.

Zenobia's overland trek was an arduous one. After disembarking from the small vessel, even the filthy, fishy-smelling port of Latakia was welcome relief. Zenobia and her escorts spent a couple of days there re-acquainting themselves with 'their land legs.' None had been seasick, but the non-moving land required an adjustment. During that time, arrangements were made to hire a cart and horses, as well as provisions, because it could be too risky to deal with merchants in the Syrian interior. One couldn't be too trusting in this day and age. While the guards made those arrangements, Zenobia sought out the elders of the Latakia Jewish community and inquired as to the fate of their brethren. She was informed of the flight from Palmyra and was directed to try to reach Jobar, near Damascus, should she desire to connect with the remnants. Being away from Aurelian, the escort granted her considerable leeway, on her promise not to disappear into the night. After the naval crossing, everyone in the group implicitly trusted each other. They had survived intact, only through working together on the passage.

However, this much leeway was not in the cards. Damascus and its surrounding villages was much too far out of the way for Zenobia to arrange a detour. She appreciated that decision and didn't press the issue, hoping, perhaps on the return trip it could be attempted.

After the restocking of supplies and procurement of transportation, following the directions given from the Gabbai, the sexton of the main synagogue, they made their way out of Latakia and headed into the an-Nusayriyah Mountains and the road to Palmyra. The mountains had an average width of 32 kilometers; there being no easy way around them. Directly to the east of Latakia was the highest peak, Nabi Yunis. With an elevation just over 1,200 meters. The group had absolutely no choice, unless they wished to add several days of travel in order to skirt the range. The guide that they contracted with to take them to Palmyra made it clear that the weather would not be a factor at this time of year, so the ascent was made. Although it was arduous, it was not an undue climb. Zenobia joked with one of her escorts that the descent would be much quicker, and easier. All laughed at that and carried on.

Once down the eastern slope, they entered a relatively flat desert plain that skirted to the south of Jabal Abu Rujmayn. Now the group really joked about Zenobia's previous comment, because there truly were no more mountains in their way. It would still be slow, however, due to the somewhat soft, sandy nature of the rest of the way. The footing was not treacherous- but it gave them a 'sinking' feeling, as the former queen would put it. Everyone was in a light-hearted mood as they spent a couple of days rounding the slopes. They passed the small village of Al Qaja and spent the night on the outskirts. Familiar with the Patriarchal and Matriarchal imperatives of her faith, Zenobia was aware of the tales of hospitality that were part and parcel of Abraham in the desert. However, it was a new age, and one that knew not of the ancient Hebrew faith. As part of the pagan Roman Empire, the residents of Al Qaja were not as kindly disposed to strangers in this day and age. The Roman escort felt the same way, and so a fire-less campsite would be the rule that evening. Cold lamb and flatbread would be washed down with water from the jug. From there, a stretch of uninhabited desert would lead to a greener, well-watered valley that approached Palmyra, a couple of days hence.

The group approached the city from the northwest. Zenobia saw the towers before anyone else. She gave a shout of joy, pointing toward the eastern horizon. Through the shimmering haze created by the Syrian sun, the others could soon pick out the details that she saw moments earlier. They all picked up the pace just a bit- as much as the animals could handle. The anticipation was palpable. But as they got closer, there seemed to be something wrong. The hustle and bustle of a thriving city wasn't there.

A thin layer of dust hung over the town like a pall. But it wasn't the same as a haze that hung over a city due to countless feet and oxcart wheels stirring up the road's dust. Rather, it reminded the soldiers of the aftermath of battle, when the dead outnumbered the living. It wasn't a good omen. An uneasiness descended on the small band as it drew nearer. And then, within a couple of kilometers, the smell hit them. It was the musty smell associated with dry decay and old death. Zenobia gagged on it, took her shawl and dipped it in the water jug and then wrapped it around her head.

As the group came within sight of Palmyra, the silence was all around. Not even nature chose to welcome the travelers. It was as if nothing was alive to greet them. Sadly, this wasn't far off the mark.

Where there should have been guards at the gate, no one challenged them and their business. The inner open-air court should have been bustling with the business of life- buying and selling, haggling and flirting, drinking and carousing. None of that existed any longer. They had entered what was primarily a ghost town of monumental proportion.

Since they had approached from the northwest, they missed the area of primary occupation to the west southwest. It was here that life had shifted in the years following the fall of Zenobia's kingdom. The main Roman camp, a Castra, was located here, straddling the east/west route that ran just south of the city. It was a 4 hectare enclosure, bordering on 10 acres. A squad of centurions patrolling off in the distance caught Zenobia's eye, and she shuddered as if a bone-chilling gale force wind had passed over her. The insignia on their uniforms were of the main legion situated here, the Legio I Illyricorum. This was the very legion created by the Emperor Aurelian in order to destroy Palmyra and capture its queen. The soldiers were from the Danube area. They remained in the East as a non-oriental element that had no local ties. As a result, they could be relied upon in this theatre of operations.

One of the soldiers took note of her discomfort and attempted to console her. She mournfully smiled and shook her head. A 'thank you' was offered to him, and Zenobia turned away to wipe a tear from her eye. Once she composed herself, she stepped through the gate and into the city proper. The guards, following their orders, immediately followed and sought to ensure her safety.

What Zenobia saw stunned and saddened her. Evidence of Aurelian's vengeance in light of her kingdom's opposition was a tragedy. Most of the city lay in ruins. The few occupants wandered around, picking through rubble and debris for anything salvageable. And this was a few years after the conquest and occupation! The once beautiful buildings that adorned the center-city had all of their architectural sculptures removed, to be utilized in other locations. It reminded the queen of the tales of the ancient city of Pompeii that she had been told as a child- a city destroyed so completely by a volcano that nothing remained. She mourned her city, and, even more so, more the loss of her citizens. While under house arrest in Rome, she was told of hundreds, thousands, sold into slavery by the Roman legion. The rationale was that her treasury was not ample enough of a reward to pay for the army's expedition. In other words, somebody had to pay the debt- and the selling of slaves was profitable. Secretly, Zenobia felt that it was nothing more than a reprisal against a proud city that had stood up to the might of Rome- serving as an embarrassment to Aurelian.

All she could think of as she slowly walked through the ruins was a quote that she had been taught in her schooling. The Roman poet, Livy, who lived a couple of centuries earlier, was already viewed as a legendary visionary. He said, 'Rome had grown since its humble beginnings that it is now overwhelmed by its own greatness.'

She felt that he meant that Rome had lost its way, and no longer knew what was right or good. The wanton destruction of her capital seemed to be evidence of this in her mind. Conquering an enemy she understood. Exploiting its resources she could grasp. Wanton destruction for the sake of vengeance... well... that was something she would never understand.

The small group endured the hard stares of the few residents left roaming about. One older woman glanced at Zenobia, and a flicker of recognition glinted in her eyes. Her gaze met the former queen of the city. Zenobia nodded ever so slightly, and a brief smile softened the lady's face a bit. But she knew not to tip her hand, as it could give cause for trouble. Zenobia walked over to her and embraced her. Her arms encircled what she felt was a skeletal wraith. Tears streamed down her face as she slipped her a small mesh bag of food that she had brought along from their encampment. The other woman began crying as well, and Zenobia wiped her tears away- that which partially washed off the grime of weeks without bathing. She then whispered that all of them needed to be strong and stepped back, continuing the trek to the interior of the formerly splendid city. She quoted Seneca, even though the old woman most likely had no idea who he was. 'Every new beginning comes from some other beginning's end.'

She rounded a corner that led to the synagogue plaza. What she saw stunned her. The once magnificent façade lay in a total shambles. The beautifully inscribed lintel was at her feet. Tears fell as she recited the prayer engraved on the blocks- 'Hear O Israel, the Lord is our God, the Lord is one...'

After several moments, one of the 'civilian' soldiers with her group gently grasped her shoulders and helped her up. She asked if they would mind remaining outside the ruined building to allow her to enter; alone with her thoughts. Seeing no one around who might do her harm, they acceded to her wish and remained vigilant outside.

As she entered, she thought back to the previous, vibrant glory that had radiated from this structure. She was reminded of the weddings, the Bar Mitzvot, and yes, of course, the funerals. Another lesson from her teachings came to mind- 'Great empires are not maintained by timidity." She remembered that it was Tacitus who said that. Clearly there was no timid approach to occupying Palmyra. But then again, Pliny said, 'Hope is the pillar that holds up the world. Hope is the dream of a waking man.' So she smiled at the thought of continued hope as she proceeded into the sanctuary.

She paused in front of the area that was the Bama, where the services had been conducted. In passing, she wondered what had become of the Torah scrolls, the menorot and other ritual items. But the loss of everything she held dear, including her son, overwhelmed her and pushed all other thoughts into the back of her mind.

She knelt down, caressing the stone step up to the platform, and mourned the loss of her son. She said Kaddish over him in the shell of the synagogue. And prayed for the future.

> *May the great Name of God be exalted and sanctified, throughout the world, which he has created according to his will. May his Kingship be established in your lifetime and in your days, and in the lifetime of the entire household of Israel, swiftly and in the near future; and say, Amen.*
>
> *May his great name be blessed, forever and ever.*
>
> *Blessed, praised, glorified, exalted, extolled, honored elevated and lauded be the Name of the holy one, Blessed*

is he- above and beyond any blessings and hymns, Praises and consolations which are uttered in the world; and say Amen. May there be abundant peace from Heaven, and life, upon us and upon all Israel; and say, Amen.

Yit'ga'dal v'yit'kadash sh'may ra'bbo, b'olmo dee'vro chir'utay v'yamlich malchu'tay, b'chayaychon uv'yomay'chon uv'chayay d'chol bet Yisroel, ba'agolo u'viz'man koriv; v'imru Amen.

Y'hay shmay rabbo m'vorach l'olam ul'olmay olmayo.

Yitborach v'yishtabach v'yitpoar v'yitromam v'yitmasay, v'yithador v'yit'aleh v'yitalal, shmay d'kudsho, brich hu, l'aylo min kl birchoto v'sheeroto, tush'bechoto v'nechemoto, da, ameeran b'olmo; vimru Amen.

Y'hay shlomo rabbo min sh'mayo, v'chayim alaynu v'al kol Yisroel; v'imru Amen. Oseh sholom bimromov, hu ya'aseh sholom olaynu, v'al kol yisroel; vimru Amen

---

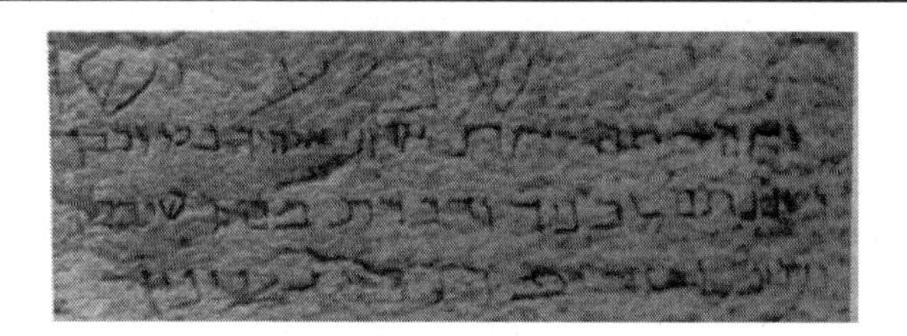